Giovanni Andreazzi

fairy tales and sea stories

by
giovanni andreazzi

Bloomington, IN Milton Keynes, UK

authorHOUSE

AuthorHouse™
1663 Liberty Drive, Suite 200
Bloomington, IN 47403
www.authorhouse.com
Phone: 1-800-839-8640

AuthorHouse™ UK Ltd.
500 Avebury Boulevard
Central Milton Keynes, MK9 2BE
www.authorhouse.co.uk
Phone: 08001974150

First published by AuthorHouse 11/27/2006

ISBN: 978-1-4259-5841-1 (sc)

Printed in the United States of America
Bloomington, Indiana

This book is printed on acid-free paper.

The front cover official photograph courtesy of the U.S. Navy, no. 327, released in 1966.

dedication

This book is dedicated to the more than 1200 men who lost their lives in the service of their country while serving aboard submarines. They are on eternal patrol having paid the ultimate price for our freedom.

thanks to:

Little Dickey – He has been a friend ever since my submarine days. We have stayed in contact over the years and I have watched as he and his wife, Mary, raised a beautiful family. He reviewed the book for me providing valuable comments, constructive criticism, and support. At his suggestion this book will be re-released with just the submarine stories to stimulate the memory of stories we sub sailors tucked away years ago when we closed that chapter of our lives.

Bear – His real name is Frank Rosenau and he is living in California playing the lead tuba for the Halleluah Brass, the Central Valley Brass Quintet, the Gottschaulk Music Concert Band, and the Modesto Junior College Concert band and Jazz Band. His grandson calls him "Oompaw." His rate was a First Class Missile Technician (SS) and he was the Missile Division leading petty officer during the missile launch I wrote about in this book. He qualified as Diving Officer of the Watch and edited the "Raven On," a newspaper we had on the sub. Being the curmudgeon he always was he prefers Mac to Windows!

This is not a sea story or a fairy tale. One month into writing this book, I received an e-mail asking me if I was the same fat missile technician as the one he had served with on the Sam Houston back in the sixties. I had not had any previous contact with Frank since leaving the Sam, so he must have been receiving vibes from all my brain-wave activity. In my first e-mail back to him I asked him if he was "Bear." "Yeah, my nickname was Bear, Big Bear, and Dancing Bear among others," was his response. After several reminiscing e-mails he also agreed to review my book. I value his input since he saw the boat from another perspective and made three more patrols on the Sam after I was discharged from the Navy.

Uncle Gill – He, like Little Dickey, has kept in contact with me over the years. He has been on extended "vacation" sailing the Pacific. Had he been in port I would have had him review the book too, but alas, he will have to wait until he gets back to land in the States to get a copy.

Jim – The author of the Jimisms, was never on the sub. He was a contracting officer I worked with in the eighties and nineties. I felt that interjecting his malapropisms and mixed-up metaphors added some humor to the stories. Our office collected over three hundred of his Jimisms before he retired.

My editor – Bobbi-Lou, one of the characters in "Moonbeam," agreed to be my editor for this book. She read the manuscripts as many times as I and provided valuable input along the way. I did not always do as she recommended, so if you see something that is not right, blame me.

forward

In writing this book, I tried to relate the stories from six years of one person's experience and present it as if one Navy man was telling another about his adventures. It's not a story about anyone, but a rambling of events which I tried to make interesting and funny. If I fell short, then forgive me, but I had a difficult time trying to remove the parts which may seem boring. Hopefully, if you hang in there, you might find something interesting in the second half.

I used characters with whom I was acquainted, but did not use full names unless permission was given. Different people may have performed the antics in the book, I simply could not remember who did what and to whom. I have taken liberties as an author to change some of the events and the characters' traits hoping to make the stories more entertaining.

Although I tried to get the events in this book in order as they happened, some may be out of sequence. However, it is not the order in which they happened, but the events themselves that are important. I tried to keep the technical aspects as basic as possible including just enough to help the reader understand. Since it's difficult to describe a submarine in words, I have included some schematics and drawings which may help. Even if the drawings are difficult to read because of the size, they will give the reader some idea of how complicated each system was. For those who have been a "Bubble Head," or "Sewer-pipe Sailor" I hope the descriptions and events resurrect memories and help recall stories which should be shared with others.

Historical stuff:

The frames for the Sam Houston, SSBN 609, the nation's seventh Polaris missile carrying submarine, were laid on December 28, 1959 by the Newport News Shipbuilding and Dry Dock Co., Newport News, Va.; launched on 2 February 1961; sponsored by Mrs. John B. Connally; and commissioned on 6 March 1962, commanded by Capt. W. P. Willis, Jr., (blue crew).

Following her first shakedown cruise, the Sam fired her first missile on April 25 off Cape Canaveral, Fla. The gold crew, commanded by Comdr. J. H. Hawkins, then took over, completed a missile firing on 11 May 1962, and then departed from Cape Canaveral for the gold crew shakedown training.

On her first patrol, the Sam, manned by the blue crew, operated continuously submerged for 48 days and 2 hours, then moored alongside the submarine tender Proteus (AS 19), in Holy Loch, Scotland. Following upkeep, the gold crew commenced its first patrol on Christmas Day, returning to Holy Loch in February 1963. The crews were again alternated, and the Sam departed on her third patrol in March. On this patrol, she was the first fleet ballistic missile submarine to enter the Mediterranean where she joined the NATO forces. She became the first Polaris submarine to make a port-of-call during a patrol with a short operational visit to Izmir, Turkey. With the two crews alternating every 90 days, Sam Houston completed her sixth successful Polaris patrol by the end of the year.

By the end of 1964, the Sam had completed 10 patrols. During 1965, she completed four additional deterrent patrols. During 1966, The Sam completed 3 more patrols, including her longest which lasted 71 days. On August 10, 1966, she returned to the United States for the first time since her deployment in 1962 and commenced a major overhaul at the Naval Shipyard at Portsmouth, N.H. On October 30, 1967, she got underway for sea trials, and, a month later, her blue crew began shakedown training. In January 1968, the gold crew conducted shakedown operations. Following further tests, she got under way for her eighteenth deterrent patrol and put into Holy Loch on May25. By the end of the year, she was on her twenty first patrol. During 1969, the Sam completed her twenty second through twenty fourth patrols. In 1970, she continued to operate with Submarine Squadron 14 until shifting to the Mediterranean on August 9 to join Submarine Squadron 16.

She operated out of her advanced base at Rota, Spain, until October of 1972. On November 27, she entered Charleston Naval Shipyard and began an extended in-port period, which included regular overhaul and the updating of her weapons and propulsion systems. On November 10, 1980, after 18 years of service, the Sam was re-designated as SSN 609 and, to comply with the SALT I treaty, concrete blocks were placed in the missile tubes to disable the missile launch capability. From September 1982 to September 1985, the Sam underwent conversion to an amphibious transport at the Puget Sound Naval Shipyard. This conversion allowed the Sam to carry Special Forces. Modifications included additional troop berthing and removal of some missile tubes. The Sam was finally deactivated on March 1, 1991, and entered the Navy's Nuclear Powered Ship and Submarine Recycling Program at the Puget Sound Naval Shipyard, Bremerton, Wash. The submarine was both decommissioned and stricken from the Navy list on September 6, 1991. Recycling of the Sam was finished on February 3, 1992.

introduction

The stories I have included in this book may make it appear to some that submarine duty was all fun and games. This can't be further from the truth in that living inside a metal tube for weeks at a time in itself is a test of endurance. Whenever I have told people that I was in submarines, almost all stated that they did not know how I could have done that. It wasn't easy giving up all but one-way communication with the outside world, or not being able to see unobstructed more than one-hundred feet at a time, or not seeing the sun until back in port. However, the duty had its rewards, two of which were the camaraderie developed with my peers and the time off between patrols.

We were in a war readiness status from the time we dove until we surfaced again at the end of the patrol. No one knew until that first communication with the fleet when we surfaced whether we had made it or not. Loved ones had to sweat out those two months until they knew we were on the surface and alive.

This, however, hardly compares to those bravest of all who served on the old diesel boats during World War II. Their lives must have been a pure hell when they were underwater being pursued by enemy surface ships looking for a "kill."

Their living conditions were much more cramped than ours and they had to endure extreme environmental changes. The food was not as good, and they couldn't take showers while at sea. Their patrols, although mostly on the surface, were longer and usually in enemy controlled waters.

Nonetheless, all sub sailors share the same pride when they wear the dolphins earned by qualifying on a submarine. All who have the dolphins are brothers regardless of all other factors.

episode one

"The house is haunted," the B&B hostess said, as she led me to my room. Her accent was typical for a long-time Maine resident. Her "r's" sounded like "ah's" and she had a sing-song lilt in her voice. When she said here, it came out like heah and year sounded like yeah. She also added r's where there were none.

This is no shit! I was staying at an old house in Boothbay Harbor that was listed as "quaint" in the Fodor's booklet about Maine. This was the first bed and breakfast I had ever stayed in and from what I had seen so far, would be the last. Quaint meant old rooms, no air conditioning, no television, no in-room telephone, and a shared bathroom down the hall. The bedroom didn't even have a sink or wash basin in it.

"What do you mean by haunted?" I asked, as I followed her up stairs that were walled in on the right and open to the hallway below on the left. They creaked with each step sounding like the un-oiled hinges on a rusty garden gate. At the top of the stairwell, was a corridor running parallel to the banister guarding the stairs we had just come up. On the walled-in side of the corridor and at its end were the rooms. There was another set of walled-in stairs going down opposite those we had come up. She led me to my room at the far end.

"Where do those stairs go?" I asked, pointing back toward the end of the hall.

"Down to the kitchen wheah breakfast is served," she responded. "Back in the early eighteen hundreds, this house was built and lived in by a sea captain. He and his wife lived heah for several yeahs. On one of his many trips abroad, he contracted a disease that left him bedridden for three months before he died in his wife's ahms. She was heartbroken and left the house to move back to Bahston. It sat vacant and unclaimed

1

'til almost the tuhn of the century when a school teacheah bought it. She claimed it was haunted and said she saw the cap'n from time to time walkin' the halls. She lived heah until she was in hah eighties and then was committed to the nut house in Bangah. I ain't nevah seen that sea cap'n."

I thought it crude of her to say "nut house," but this was Maine and she was an elderly lady herself not used to mincing words. She stood straight as a fence post and was thin, but not frail looking. I guessed that she was in her mid-seventies. Her hair was still dark, with streaks of gray. It was pulled back in a bun like Mamma in the Katzenjammer Kids, Sunday paper, cartoon page I used to enjoy reading as a kid. The hallway next to the open stairwell creaked like the stairs as we walked to the room near the front of the house overlooking the bay.

"You can put yeah bag in theah while I show you the kitchen," she said pointing toward the open room.

"How many other guests are there?" I asked.

"Yah the only one, and I expect no othahs. This is the off season and we don't get many guests now 'til summah. The bathroom is at the end of the hall. Yah towels ah in the dressah next to the bed. We got no television, but if ya wanna watch yah favorite show, the tavahn down the street is wheah ya have to go."

I plopped my overnight bag on the waist-high poster bed. It sank into the soft comforter a good eight to ten inches. I was thankful this was a one night stop on my way up the coast. I had another B&B to stay in tomorrow night and hoped it was better than this. She led me back down the corridor to another set of stairs on the other end of the second floor.

"Theah's the bathroom," she pointed out as we passed a room to the right of the top of the stairs.

I peaked in and found it to be quite spacious. The cast-iron enameled tub that sat on animal feet with a ball in each paw reminded me of the tub in my grandmother's home. At least this one had a curtain around it so I could take a shower. I hadn't used a tub since before joining the navy thirty years ago where there were only shower stalls in the heads.

"Are there rooms upstairs?" I asked, pointing to a door beside the rear stairwell.

"Nope, that theah's the way up to the attic. I keep the doah locked so's the captain stays put." I followed her down the stairs to a different part of the house.

"Heah on the left is the kitchen," she said, pointing to a door at the bottom of the stairs. "On the right heah is my portion of the house." She gestured to the right where the bottom half a Dutch door barred the way.

"I only serve light feyah for breakfast startin' at seven." If ya want sumthin' else, the tavahn down the street opens at eight."

I found out in the morning that "light fare" meant a heated frozen sweet roll and a thimble full of watered-down orange juice. There also was no brewed coffee, which didn't bother me since I drank only decaf. I wondered how the summer tourists "fared" with this "breakfast included" B&B. *The tavern down the street must do a hell of a business.*

"Any questions?" she asked. "If ya need anything, just hollah. I'll be in heah."

She opened the bottom half of the Dutch door and immediately a dog's head, the size of a football, appeared followed by the biggest dog I'd ever seen.

"This heah's Junyah," she said. "He don't take to stranjahs much, but he seems ta like ya. If he didn't, he'd be a bahkin at ya."

Junior's head remained above the bottom half of the door when she shut it. I reached out and gave the dog a pat after letting him sniff the back of my hand.

"I like all animals," I said, "and they seem to know it."

I headed back up the creaky stairs away from the dog that seemed to whine as if he had just met a long-lost friend and lost him at the same time. I was tired from my trek up the coast from Boston where I had landed following a long flight from Dallas. I was here to research a new book I wanted to write about my experiences in the Navy. On my way to the B&B, I had stopped at Portsmouth where I had spent a year in the shipyard as a missile technician aboard the submarine Sam Houston, one of the earliest missile carrying submarines. I had a late lunch in Portland, so was not interested in eating. I just wanted to make some notes before retiring to the big soft bed, read at least one chapter of a good book, and get some needed sleep.

At least this B&B offered a good view of the fishing boats in the harbor. Out on the wharf I could see an enticing looking lobster shack, but they were closing for the day. I liked lobster, especially fresh-on-the-wharf, right-from-the-lobster-boat type. That would have to wait another day since I would be leaving in the morning as soon as I had my "light feyah." I tried to look "down the street" to see if I could find the tavern, but it must have been down some other street. The day was waning and overcast. It was a typical early November evening on the coast of Maine.

After jotting down ten pages of notes I left my writing material on the desk by the window. I was ready to curl up with a good book and let the day ease out of my body so I could get a good night's sleep. I took my kit to the bathroom, brushed and flossed my teeth and took out my contacts. I was sure my hostess could "heah" my every move to and from the bathroom along the noisy hallway. The sound probably was painful to Junior's sensitive hearing. Before I undressed and crawled into bed, nude except for my briefs, I made sure the deadbolt on the oak door was in the locked position.

The creaking woke me up and I glanced at the luminescent dials on the travel alarm sitting on the table next to the bed. Without my contacts, I had to squint, but it was clearly triple ones. I knew she had said there were no other guests, so I wondered who could be heading in my direction.

Must be that damn dog, I thought, and buried my head in the pillow so it would cover my ears. I did keep my eyes locked on the bedroom door just in case. The noise stopped and I waited a couple of minutes before closing my eyes again. The next time I woke up my eyes were as open as they could be.

"Who the hell are you?" I asked. "What the fuck's going on here?" I looked at the clock and it was one thirty. A little more than fifteen minutes had gone by since I had heard the noise in the hallway. I propped myself up on my elbows to get a better look.

Sitting in the chair next to the bed was a man. I guessed him to be in his mid to late forties. He was lean looking, unshaven with a stubble of a beard, and salt and pepper hair combed back and tied in a pony tail. With only the glow from the lights along the wharf, I couldn't tell what color his clothes were, but they were dark. I could smell the ocean with a trace of seaweed that wasn't there before I went to bed. There was a meerschaum pipe carved like a mermaid in his left hand, but there was no smoke coming from it. In his lap was a charcoal grey cat which he was stroking with his right hand. The cat's eyes looked red to me, but I assumed that it was just an effect the light from the window made by reflecting off the inside of the eyeball.

"Cap'n Kane," he said. "Robert Kane to be exact, but you can call me Bob owah Cap'n, whicheveah you like. This heah's Dedra," he said, noticing that I was staring at the cat with the red eyes. "What be yah name?"

He didn't have as thick an accent as my hostess, but there was a touch of "old talk" in his response. His demeanor had a calming effect on me and I didn't have any fear of him.

"Giovanni," I said. "I used to be called Andy and Cap'n Gio when I was in the Navy." I was trying to make some connection to this man who obviously was a man of the sea.

"So, you be a saylah too?" he asked, then added, "an' cap'n to boot."

"Not a real captain," I said. "I just had the nickname when I was in submarines. It's a long story. I have many stories as a matter of fact, some of which I want to write about some day. That's why I'm here, to get in the mood and do some research."

Then I realized who this must be, the sea captain who had died here in his wife's arms more than a century ago. I didn't need to ask him if he really was the captain. There are some things better left unanswered. I was curious though if he was the one whose footsteps in the hallway had awakened me earlier.

While I was thinking this, the red-eyed cat named Dedra jumped down from the captain's lap, took one leap and ended up on the bed with me. The cat walked right up my chest and touched its nose directly to mine. It's what I used to call a "cat kiss" when my cat that died several years ago did that to me. The cat with the red eyes then walked down toward my feet, did a stretch, and curled up between my legs as if settling in for the night.

"You ain't seen my wife heah-abouts lately?" he asked ignoring the fact that his cat had just taken up residency on my bed.

"No, I haven't seen anyone but the lady downstairs. I hear your wife went back to Boston after you died."

"Ay yeah, that's what I was afraid of." His response confirmed my suspicions that he was the sea captain.

So here I am face to face with a real ghost. Is this real, or is this Memorex?

There was a moment of silence, so I pulled my legs out from under an unyielding Dedra. Feeling a chill in the room, I got up and put on a sweatshirt and the pair of running pants I had laid over the end of the bed for my morning jog. I then crawled back in bed slipped my legs back under the cat, put both pillows behind my back, and sat half upright in the bed. Captain Bob put his pipe in his mouth and took a long pull on it. Again, there was no smoke that I could see, but he seemed to enjoy the action anyway.

"What kinda ship is this submarines?" he said, coal-black eyes staring right at me.

"It's a ship, called a submarine or boat that goes under water and stays there for months at a time."

"Don't ya gotta come up for ayah once in awhile, like a whale does?"

"No. We made our own oxygen to breathe and took away the carbon dioxide with scrubbers." I could see he wasn't understanding any of what I was saying, or not believing it if he was. But here I was talking to a dead man, so I guessed we were on an even keel. "I've got some photos to show that might help you understand," I continued.

I got up again and went to the desk where I had the documentation I was using for my book. The captain and Dedra both watched me intently. I brought the folder back and climbed into the bed setting the folder down on the other side of Dedra who casually sniffed it, decided it was nothing of interest, and laid her head over her right paw.

"Here's a picture of the sub," I said handing him a photo. "I'm not positive if this is a picture of the Sam or not, because the bulbous nose is missing, which I'll explain later. The sonar nose may have been installed after this photo was taken, or this is after the shipyard overhaul when it was removed. It's also difficult to gauge how big she was, but I have a photo somewhere in my folder I can pull out later showing the relative size. If you look closely, there is a man standing on the fairwater

planes on the sail just below the periscopes. Those are the stick-like items pointing up from the sail. Three-fourths of the sub is below the water line."

I described the Sam while he looked at the picture.

"She was four-hundred-ten feet long, thirty-three feet at the beam, with a draft of twenty-nine feet, and displaced eight thousand tons of water submerged and seven thousand tons on the surface. She could move at fifteen knots on the surface and twenty knots or greater underwater. She was built in two years, commissioned in 1961 and scrapped in 1991."

"Tell me moah," he said. "Moah about this submarine and what you did with it."

I glanced at my alarm clock and noticed the time had not budged from one thirty. Either the clock had stopped or time was at a standstill. I guessed I could talk a little more and then just doze back to sleep as I had earlier, but I was wrong.

"The sub was called the Sam, short for Sam Houston. It was named after the man who was the first governor of Texas back in the early eighteen hundreds."

"Yep, I heard of him. Somethin' to do with Mexico I believe."

"Yes, he defeated Santa Anna at the battle of San Jacinto, liberating the territory of Texas. They named the town of Houston after him which is near where the battlefield was. He was named president of the Republic of Texas which was later made a state."

"Tell me moah about the submarine. You say you stayed undah-watah months at a time?"

"Yes. The typical patrol was eight to nine weeks." I realized I had better provide details for this sailor from the old days. Otherwise he might not understand what the modern terms meant. "A patrol is when we would go out to sea from our home port and not come back until we were supposed to. We were considered 'at war' the entire time and had no communication with anyone." I didn't tell him we could receive messages, but weren't allowed to send any. He might have a difficult time understanding what radios were, or I might have a difficult time explaining them.

"It would be much like you going on a fishing trip for a couple of months and no one knowing if you were coming back until you showed up one day."

"Woah, you say. Woah with what country?" he asked.

"The term used was the 'cold war,' where shots weren't fired, but we were ready in case the other side started a fight. The bad guys then were the Russians who also had submarines. Underwater, we were supposed to stay undetected so the enemy didn't know where we were. This was supposed to deter or keep the enemy at bay, since if they started a war, we would be able to launch our weapons from far away and out at sea. Ironically the policy was called 'MAD,' short for 'mutually assured destruction.'"

"Weapons, what kind of weapons?"

"We had bombs, one of which could destroy an entire city and make it uninhabitable for hundreds of years. It would be difficult to explain how they worked, but just believe me. We had sixteen of these bombs in each submarine mounted on missiles or rockets. The rockets were so powerful they could send a bomb a thousand miles or more toward a target. Rockets were used by the British in the war of 1812. That's where the term "rockets' red glare" in the "Star Spangled Banner" comes from. These were much bigger and faster. Since the enemy knew we had them and didn't know where, no one wanted to start a war."

"Didn't they have these rockets and bombs too?"

"Yes they did, but not on submarines when I was in the Navy. Later on, the enemy's government changed and we no longer needed the submarines with so much fire power. The subs are still there, but the enemies are different. We no longer live in fear of destroying each other's countries."

"How many men were on these submarines?"

"About twelve officers and one hundred sailors lived together those two months. We could stay longer since we had enough food for about six months and made our own water from the sea. We stood watches in three shifts of six hours each so two thirds of the crew were off resting for twelve hours at a time."

"You said you made your own oxygen?"

"We took oxygen directly from the sea. A little different from the way fish do, but there is plenty of it in the ocean." I left off the part about electrolysis, which would have raised a lot of other questions.

"We removed the bad air with chemicals and pumped it overboard." Again, I left off how it actually happened with soda lime (sodium hydroxide and calcium hydroxide) by passing the air through a bath of these chemicals and then pumping it overboard.

"The air was circulated through carbon filters to take out smells and impurities, much the same way charcoal was used in your days to absorb poison." He seemed to be satisfied with my short answers.

"How did you know wheah you weah if you were undahwatah the whole time?"

"Believe it or not, we used the same method you used. We looked at the stars and used charts to indicate our position. We had a tube with glass and mirrors on both ends, called a periscope that we could stick up above the water and look at the stars. We did this every so often, sometimes every six hours. We then plotted our position on a chart." I didn't tell him that subs now use global positioning satellites which are much more accurate and don't require the sub to raise a periscope. I also didn't mention the use of gyros to keep track of the sub's position between "star shots." Modern subs only need to occasionally check their position with a GPS.

I glanced at the clock again and noticed the time still had not changed. I could have been dreaming, or maybe we were instantly communicating through thoughts.

"I need to ask you a question," I said. "I heard a noise earlier as if someone was walking down the hall outside my room. Was that you?"

"Ay-yeah," he said.

"I assume you are an apparition and not real, but you must have weight to make the noise I heard."

"If ahppah-rition means ghost, that I am. But I can make noise sometimes just like I can talk when I want. I didn't want to scah ya if you wasn't awake when I came through the doah. I did knock fuhst, but when I came in you was fast asleep. So's, I just sat down and waited 'til you woke up."

I reached over and stroked Dedra for the first time. The cat felt cold to the touch like she had just come in from the outside on a December day. She didn't move, but started to purr the minute my hands moved across her.

"Was Dedra your cat?" I asked.

"Naw. I don't know wheah she come from. I just heahd her cryin' one day and theaya she was as if she just appeahed outta thin ayah. She smelled like the ocean like she just come off a boat. We just been tagetha evah since."

"Do you talk to guests often?"

"Naw, sometimes they justs gets scared and I disappeah so's not to cause no commotion. I didn't sense no feaya in you, so I just stayed. I guess I was right and Dedra also thought you was a good man. Ain't been no guests foah a long time that I could talk to. Most time, when a group does comes in, theah awe too many of 'em to select just one to talk to."

"What do you do while waiting for guests you can talk to?"

"Don't know. Time jus' seems to pass by. So, I feel this is impaht-ent that I talk 'cause I don't know when the next time will be. Tell me moah about the submarine and about how you got on theaya."

So, I decided to start someplace near the beginning...

"Captain Bob, this is no shit," I said.

Note to readers: From here on, except in a couple of places and to end the book, I am omitting the New England dialect, not only because it is hard to read, but it is even harder to write.

episode two

After boot camp, where I learned to "line up alphabetically according to height," I went to "A" School in Dam Neck, Virginia. I
can remember the night I arrived, September 25, 1962, because Floyd
Patterson fought Sonny Liston for the heavy-weight boxing title. My
dad used to let me stay up on Friday night to watch the fights with
him. From watching those Friday Night Fights from Madison Square
Garden, I had become a boxing fan. I was on schedule to get to the
barracks and listen to the fight on my portable radio; or, if I had been a
little late and could find a television, at least watch some of it. I checked
in to the master-at-arms just before the fight was scheduled to start.

From the noises I heard from the first floor, it seemed everyone had
a radio and I wouldn't miss any of the fight. I took my linens, sheets,
pillow case, and blanket, shouldered my seabag, and headed for my
bunk on the second floor. Climbing the steps, there was a sailor in
civilian clothes ahead of me and I had to stay behind him in the narrow stairwell.

I patiently followed the man who was moving, head down, very
slowly up the stairs. Barely audibly he was reciting a ditty over and
over again.

"I run through the jungle with my peter in my hand, I'm a mean
motherfucker, I'm a guided missile man."

I was going to ask him if he was all right, when I noticed the smell
of beer emanating from him. I then realized he was drunk, very drunk,
in fact stumbling-almost-falling-down drunk. I checked my watch
noticing it was time for the fight to start. *Oh well*, I thought. *I might
miss the first round or part of it.*

While following the drunk, I thought about the long train ride I had just taken from my home to Dam Neck, and how different the south was compared to Ohio. The first thing I had noticed at the first rest stop in a little town in Virginia had been the sign over the drinking fountain. It had read, "Whites only," which I had thought was unusual. My father hated blacks, but the ones I had encountered in high school and boot camp were just regular people, and I harbored no ill will. I had gotten a drink from the fountain and gone into the station to the lunch counter. There had been another sign which had stated "We reserve the right to refuse service to anyone." I found out later that they meant blacks. I had ordered a bag of peanuts, and left, getting back on the train.

Finally, the drunken sailor, still mumbling the ditty, got to the top of the stairs and through the door into a corridor where I could get around him. This floor had single bunk beds separated by a green, ceramic block, half wall. As on the first floor, I could hear the fight being broadcast from several radios over the partitions. As I plopped my seabag onto the bed, I heard the announcer say, "The fight is over. Patterson has KO'd Liston in two minutes and twenty-five seconds in the first round."

"Is that for real?" I asked the sailor in the cubical next to mine.

"Sounds like it," he said turning his radio down.

"I can't believe it," I said, as the drunken sailor, head still down, inched his way past my cubicle. I felt sorry for Floyd Patterson, who had been a great fighter, but even sorrier for the sailor who drank too much. I later had my bouts with the bottle too.

The first time I got really plowed was on three-two beer at a concert in Virginia Beach. Three-two beer was beer with an alcohol content of less than three point two percent and not as potent as six-percent beer. It was allowed in some states for consumption by eighteen to twenty-one year olds. I had started my training not long after I had seen the stumbling drunk. Roy Orbison was playing at the Peppermint Beach Club and three of my classmates and I decided to go. We took the "Gray Ghost" liberty bus into town, so called because it was all gray and ran into the early morning hours.

"Here's a picture of the four of us taken that night in one of those photo booths along the walkway by the beach," I told Captain Bob.

"Not very good shape, are it?" Captain Bob said

"No. The quality wasn't that good anyway, and after all these years, it has aged a bit."

The four of us got to the club early enough to get a table in the front row. We weren't old enough to drink regular beer or hard stuff, so we ordered pitchers of three-two beer. I was told that it was difficult to get drunk on the low-alcohol-content beer, but for me, all it took was a lot of it. I remember watching Roy Orbison not ten feet from me singing all the songs I liked and that I also went to the bathroom a lot. I don't remember how many pitchers of beer we drank at the table, but I had more than the others. The classmates I was with got up and danced a lot, but I didn't know how to dance, so I just sat there and drank. When the show was over, I was glad I had my buddies to help me to the bus station to wait for the last Gray Ghost of the night.

When we got to the bus stop, there were a lot of sailors waiting, more than the bus had seats for, and we were at the back of the line.

"Andy's not going to make it," one of the guys said.

"Yeah, and it looks like we'll have to stand on the bus all the way to the base too," another one said.

I remember the crowd looking at me while my classmates kept me in a vertical position.

"Let's get a cab," one of them said. They all agreed and I wasn't going to argue.

"Is he going to be all right?" the cab driver asked, as we piled into cab, three of us in the back and one in front. I'm sure he was worried that I'd "paint" the inside of his cab. Before the cabbie could object, my buddies put me on the passenger side back seat near the open window.

"He'll be okay," they said, and I was until we got back to the barracks. I spent half the night sitting on the toilet pissing and puking between my legs. Thank God for buddies that took care of their drunken shipmates.

But this story really starts in 1965, the year Muhammad Ali defeated Floyd Patterson, with a TKO in the twelfth round. I had finally been assigned to a submarine after three years in the Navy and was checking into the boat's barracks.

"You some relationship to that there movie star, you know, the one in Dr. No?" the Chief asked after looking at my name stenciled on my sea bag.

The chief petty officer, his bad English aside, did seem like an intelligent man. You don't get to be an E8 senior chief petty officer, eight grades up from boot camp, without knowing your way around the Navy. The five hash marks on his sleeve showed all that he had his twenty years in and was a career man. His name badge identified him as "COB Foster." I found out later what COB meant.

The roundness of his frame told the world he probably had spent more time in the chow line than most had spent in the Navy. He was about my height, just under six-feet, but he seemed a lot taller because of his rank of senior chief. I was still lean and muscular from lots of exercise at the Naval Academy, but that would change during my first patrol.

"No sir, she's not," I responded. He ignored my breach of etiquette when I called him sir, something not usually done among the enlisted ranks. The proper way to address him was "chief," or as I later found out, "COB."

"Then, do you know the difference between a fairy tale and a sea story?" He continued.

"No I don't," I said truthfully.

Even though I had been in the Navy three years, I was still green. All of my time after boot camp had been spent in school, a year of which was at the Naval Academy Prep School in Bainbridge Maryland. After that I did attend the academy for a short period, but quit of my own volition. Before the prep school, I had spent the first year and a half in missile technician school in Dam Neck Virginia and submarine school here at New London Connecticut. The last five months I awaited an opening on a sub.

"A fairy tale begins with 'once upon a time' and a sea story begins with 'this is no shit,'" he informed me. "Keep the two straight and you got no problem."

I surmised from his answer that there wasn't much difference between the two, but a sea story could be based on some truth. How I should have responded to his first question about the movie star was, "this is no shit, Chief, but she is my sister." This would have been an outright lie, but based on the truth that we had the same last name and could have been related.

My sea bag on my left shoulder, hand-carry bag in my right hand, and orders tucked under my right arm, I continued down the hall of the barracks following the sign indicating where the check-in master-at-arms (MAA) office was. I had just finished a long train ride from my home town to downtown New London on the other side of the Thames River. The sub base had taken its name from the town, but was located just to the north in Groton. I had taken a cab from the train station and, after a check of my orders and getting some directions at the main gate at the entrance to the base; I had walked almost a mile carrying my sea bag on my left shoulder and a small duffel bag in my right hand. It was time for dinner and I was hungry.

I passed the barracks watch, who was standing in the middle of the corridor. There was another man ahead of me at the MAA window, shorter than I, but with medium length, jet black hair, a lot different from my blond burr cut. He looked to be about my age, twenty, and, like me, had E-4 stripes, just three pay grades away from boot camp. Because of my stint at the prep school and Naval Academy, I had been kept from advancing in pay grade with the guys my age, who could be E-5's now. This guy must have joined at a later age to still be an E-4, petty officer third class. As I approached, he turned toward me like a very confident, friendly politician would do and introduced himself.

"Dick Schweinehun," he said as we shook hands. "I guess we're the new guys on the boat." He was wearing the missile technician symbol,

just like mine indicating we had gone through the same schooling at Dam Neck Virginia.

"Here's what that looked like," I said to Captain Bob.

"Looks like a phallic to me. This is how you knew he was a missile person?"

"Yes," I said. "All the individual ratings carried a different symbol. When I met someone, a quick look at the left arm of their uniform would reveal their job specialty and what pay grade they were."

"I guess we are the new guys," I responded, forgetting to mention my name.

He glanced down at my orders and saw who I was. "You related to that movie star, you know the James Bond babe?"

"This is no shit, but she is my sister," I said quickly. Then I retracted the attempt at a sea story with, "No not really, but I wish she were."

The master at arms appeared at the window and we handed him our orders almost simultaneously.

"You guys look too old to be third class," the MAA commented.

"It's a long story," I said. Dick said nothing; evidently he didn't want to acknowledge the snide comment.

"It looks like you two will be cube mates," the MAA said. "Cube number eight, second floor. Up the stairs, turn right, and down the hall on the right. Pick either open bunk; there are four per cube."

"Here are your linens," he added, handing us each a blanket, two sheets, and a pillow case. Pillows and what we called a horse blanket (a four-foot by eight-foot, gray wool sheet resembling the cushion thrown under a saddle) were usually on the bed. "Muster is at zero eight hundred hours in the lounge."

"Attention on deck!" shouted the barracks watch.

"At ease, gentlemen," said a lieutenant who had just walked in the door.

He had on a black armband with white capital letters OOD sewn on it. The arm band indicated he was the Officer of the Day, or Deck, or Duty, either one would fit depending on whom you talked to. He had a polished demeanor, which was necessary while standing his tour as duty officer because he would come in contact with the base commanding officer (CO) many times on his twenty-four-hour watch. Neatly trimmed black hair showed from under his hat. Normally all military would take their covers (hats) off while indoors, but being on duty mandated he remain covered. He was trim looking, with a square jaw and deep set eyes. I guessed his age to be twenty six or twenty seven. He had a name badge with "Mr. Inman" embossed on it.

"New men?" he asked us.

"Yes sir," I said showing him my orders.

Dick showed the lieutenant his orders too. Lt. Inman took both of our orders and glanced at them. He then looked at our left arms.

"You both are missile techs, huh?" he said. "I'm the weapons officer on the Sam. Welcome aboard. My last name is Lieutenant Jim Inman."

We had just heard the first "Jimism," as they became known, and were about to hear another. He looked at my orders again and said my last name out loud, followed by the second Jimism.

"Your name is familiar, but your face don't ring a bell," he said.

And then another.

"I'd like to keep a feel of the atmosphere we're in right now," he said.

So would I, sir. I like to be able to breathe. I almost said. Dick said nothing, probably still wondering why my face didn't ring a bell.

And yet another.

"You know," he continued, "keep it sort of informal, but not. We still need to have some astringent rules."

Seeing that we were dumbfounded (and unable to speak after an onslaught of Jimisms) he decided to let us go.

"Carry on, gentlemen," he said walking away toward the stairs.

As soon as he was out of hearing range, I looked at Dick and we both cracked up.

"What the hell was that?" Dick asked, not wanting an answer, but he got one anyway.

"That was the weapons officer, and you may be working for him some day," the MAA said. "But, we have a full billet of missile techs so you two will most likely be assigned to the seaman gang for at least your first patrol."

"That's where I was before I was sent to 'C' school," Dick said.

"You were on a sub before they sent you to 'C' school?" I asked.

He responded to my question with a little bit of pride in his voice.

"Yep, this one, the Sam Houston, but on the gold crew. I don't know many of the blue crew men except the ones I met during the turnover in Holy Loch."

"Good, then you can fill me in on what to expect," I said. We then headed to the second floor of the barracks.

The cubicles were all identical, twenty-foot square, gray tile floored spaces enclosed with six-foot high, green metal partitions. Four, eight-foot high by two-foot wide windows rose from a sill two feet off the floor and reached almost to the bare steel-joist ceiling. The windows were opposite the four-foot wide cubicle entrance giving us a lovely view of the other wing of the "H" shaped barracks. Cubicles on the side across the corridor from ours looked full. Those cubicles had a better view, overlooking the highway that ran along the east side of the base boundary line.

In each cubicle were four gray, tubular metal beds, two on either side. On each bed was the familiar six-inch thick blue and white mattress ticking. The mattress was folded in half, exposing the wire mesh spring system used in most military beds. On top of the mattress was a pillow of the same ticking material. Choosing the window bed, Dick tossed his sea bag and bedding on the open spring side of the bed and tossed his hand-carry bag into the adjacent six-foot high, two-foot wide, and eighteen-inch deep gun-metal gray locker that was situated at the foot of each bed. I did likewise, choosing the bed next to the corridor on the same side of the cubicle. The lockers were our armoires for our clothing and personal effects while we were living in the barracks. They had hasps on the doors and were secured with our own locks.

"I'm hungry," I said. "Wanna get sumpin' to eat?"

I was hoping he would say yes because I had a lot of questions about the sub and sub life. He would know, having already made one patrol.

"Sure," he said. "Let's go."

We hoofed it on down the hill to the chow hall talking all the way. On our right, in the distance, was the hundred-foot escape training tower standing tall against all the other buildings. We saluted several officers we passed along the way.

"Tell me about the Sam Houston," I said.

"The Sam is out at sea on patrol right now. In two months, we'll take a commercial flight from Providence, Rhode Island to Prestwick, Scotland then take a short bus ride to Holy Loch where we'll meet the gold crew for turnover."

"Turnover?" I asked.

"Yes. That's when the gold crew briefs the blue crew, maintenance on the sub is performed, and provisions are loaded for us to make our patrol. The gold crew will remain on the Sam for about four days while we're there. We take over when they leave, and then two weeks later we head out into the ocean, dive and come back up two months later."

"Do both crews stay on the sub during turnover?"

"No, the oncoming crew stays on the sub tender until the other crew leaves."

"Sub tender?"

"That's a support ship we tie up alongside that has all our provisions including missiles. There may be as many as six subs moored to the tender at any one time."

"Where are we when we're on patrol?"

"That's a secret until we dive and the captain opens the orders. We'll head to the North Atlantic, or the Mediterranean. I hope we go to the Med this time. We were in the North Atlantic last time and it was really rough. Do you get seasick?"

"I guess I'll find out," I said. "I like roller coasters and Ferris wheels and don't get sick on either one."

"That doesn't mean much when we're at periscope depth in a state-six sea with thirty-foot waves breaking over the sail. Like you said, you'll find out if you'll get sea sick. I saw some pretty big guys with cans around their necks most of the patrol."

"Cans around their necks?"

"Yeah. Number ten cans, a little bit bigger than a large coffee can. They tie the cans around their necks so they can puke on the go."

"Sounds like fun. You said "sail," what's that?"

"The sub has a structure forward of the missile compartment that sticks up about twenty feet. It houses the periscopes, antennas, and lookout platform. On it are the fairwater or sail planes that control the up and down motion of the sub like ailerons on an airplane. In the rear are the stern planes that control the up and down angle. Behind the rudder is the screw, or propeller, which is connected on the centerline aft of the stern planes."

"The MAA said we'll be in the seaman gang. What do they do?"

"During turnover and the two weeks before we go to sea, the seaman gang chips paint, repaints, does cleanup, and mess cooks. When we are on patrol, the seaman gang mess cooks and mans the diving station."

"Mess cooks?"

"That's the lowliest job on the sub. A mess cook gets up early, goes to bed late, and is treated poorly by the crew. You'll be glad to be done with mess cooking and get to stand a normal six hours of duty and have twelve off duty so you can get your dolphins."

"Is that what qualifying means?"

"Yeah. The earlier you qualify subs and get your dolphins, the better you'll be treated by the rest of the crew. Wearing a set of dolphins is a badge of honor. Dolphins are worn above all other decorations, even aviator wings. So get qualified as soon as possible. I started on my first patrol and since I'm back on the Sam, I can get qualified during my next patrol. Almost no one can qualify in one two-month patrol. There's just too much to learn."

"What do you have to know?"

"Everything about the sub. Every valve, tank, hydraulic system, mechanical system, electrical system, air system, everything, even the "lead pipes," which are the tricky items not in the books. After you have a qualified person sign off on a specific system, you're given a comprehensive written and oral test by a qualified officer. You flunk and your next assignment may be as a "surface puke" on the tender. The idea is that during an emergency you could take over any critical systems on the sub no matter what compartment you're in. You not only do you have to qualify submarines, you have to qualify in your discipline to stand a watch by yourself. In our case we have to qualify missile systems. Don't rely on what you learned in sub school. It's helpful, but they taught the pig boats."

I remembered that 'pig boat' was the term for the diesel boats. That's about all I remembered from the sub school I had attended a year and a half ago. Fresh water was at a premium on the sub because the distillery couldn't produce enough water for all to take a shower. Therefore, only the food handlers took showers. When the pig boat sailors came ashore, they stunk like pigs, hence, the name.

One of the worst jobs on the old diesel boats was distillery watch. Checking on the production of fresh water was a hot and noisy job, therefore, anyone found wasting fresh water was punished by assignment to distillery watch for a couple of days. Even on the nuclear boats, which had plenty of fresh water, we learned to wet down, soap up, and rinse off turning the water off between each step.

"Qualifying sounds like a rough program. I should have stayed at the Academy, which was easier."

"Academy?"

It was his turn to ask questions.

"Yeah," I said. There was no pride in my voice, since I was still deciding if I had made the right decision to quit the Academy or not. "I just came from the SubFlot, and before that it was 'C' school. Before that it was Anacostia Naval Station where I was assigned after spending some time at home when I quit the Academy."

"Where's Anacostia?" he said. He knew the rest of the places having been there too.

"It's across the river from DC. I spent a month at home and then three weeks there waiting for the Navy to decide what to do with me."

"Wha'd ya do there?" he asked.

"I worked in the mail room sorting incoming mail and putting it into slots," I said. "It was just busy work, but better than sweeping floors. On weekends I would visit the Capitol. My first trip into DC, I got lost and almost didn't find my way back. I bought a map and sat down and memorized it before heading there again. One of the guys from the station and I roamed around in the Capitol building. We followed some tourists for a while listening to the spiel from the tour guide, and then broke off on our own.

"Soon, we were all by ourselves and didn't know where the hell we were. We found a restroom since we both had to piss, and thought it was the nicest restroom we had ever seen. Marble everywhere and large stalls that closed in all around. When we got back in the corridor, we saw a guard with his back to us standing at the end of the hall and decided to ask for directions."

"'Sir, could you tell us where we are?' I asked. We obviously startled him.

"'How the hell did you get in here?' he said, looking concerned.

"'We just walked around.' We were in civilian clothes, so we got our IDs out and showed him we were in the military.

"'You still shouldn't have gotten in the part of the building,' he said. 'Stay with the tour guides and you won't get lost.'

"'Yes, sir,' we said and joined a group that had just entered the room where we were. I still don't know where we had been when we found the guard, but it must have been off limits to tourists."

"When you got home after leaving the Academy, I bet you made an impression in your officer's uniform," Dick said.

"I didn't have an officer's uniform yet. We reported to the Academy in our enlisted uniforms, which were shipped home after they gave us midshipmen jumpers, pants, and hats. I was measured for a uniform, but it hadn't been made yet. I was still a midshipman and technically an officer. Therefore, I couldn't wear my enlisted uniform to go home, but instead, was told I had to leave in a civilian suit. I called my parents to send one, but they were on vacation, so I called my grandparents. They dug up the only suit they could find in my old bedroom from my parents house. It was a suit I hadn't worn in years and was really out-dated, ill-fitting, and too hot for the summer.

"I had to wait for the suit before I left, so they put me up in a vacant part of Bancroft Hall with one other drop out. To keep from getting harassed by the upper classmen, we had to sneak into the chow hall to get food when no one else was there. The rest of the time we sat in our room. I got the suit in a couple of days and they gave me orders to go home. I rode a bus in July back to my home, in a suit I threw away as soon as I got there.

"While home those thirty days, I bought my first car, a green 1950 Dodge, for one hundred sixty five dollars. While I was home awaiting my orders, I met up with the brother of the man I joined the Navy with on the 'Buddy System.' The Navy allowed Frank and me to join together so we would have a 'buddy' to help each other in boot camp and, had we chosen the same paths, throughout our careers. We did make it as far as sub school together, but then he wanted to be a fire-control technician and I had my heart set on missiles. By then we were acclimated to the navy way of life and didn't need buddies anymore.

"Frank's brother Jim and I became friends and decided to go see Frank in Dam Neck where he was going to "C" school. Jim had a friend, Oswald, who had a car newer than mine, a 1957 Edsel, so we took that car instead of the Green Seaweed. The three of us stayed in a room on the beach for three days. After visiting with Frank, we spent time at the beach sunning ourselves. The three of us met two girls who were there with their mother on vacation and became instant friends. The problem was there were three guys and two gals, so the three of us had a discussion.

"When we couldn't reach a consensus as to who was going to bow out, Oswald said, 'It's every man for himself.' My luck with women so far had not been good, so I left them alone with the girls. I found out later that the one girl liked me and was disappointed that she had to settle for being with Oswald. The mother was with them the whole time so nothing untoward could have happened, but it was just the way my life had gone so far. I chalked it up to another lost opportunity.

"We got up early the next morning to leave the rooming house. I went to get a bottle of coke from the vending machine in the hall and noticed the door was unlatched. The three of us took several bottles each and drank them on the way back to Ohio, tossing the empties at the rock faces on the side of the highway as we drove."

"Still got that car?"

"No. That was a long time ago and I sold it after 'C' school to one of my classmates who was heading out to California. He paid me the same amount I had bought it for, one hundred sixty five dollars. We first drove the car to my parents' home for a couple of days, and then he took off for the west coast in that fifteen-year-old car. I wonder if he made it, 'cause it burned a quart of oil and had to be replenished every time I filled up the gas tank. I bought a '57 Plymouth after I sold the Dodge, which is what I have now."

"I've got a '59 Impala," he said. "So you've been in the Navy a couple of years too. I thought you looked older than someone fresh out of the missile training schools."

"I've been in a little over three years, actually. You're older too, where have you been?" I asked.

"I joined the Navy April 1963 in Long Beach, California," Dick said. "This was in response to the Cuban Missile crisis in the fall of 1962 and a cover story in Life magazine in March 1963 talking about boomer submarines like the Sam. You could say I felt a wave of patriotic duty. After 'A' school and sub school, I was sent to await a sub in the Submarine Commander Group 2, SubFlot you called it. There, I did a lot of menial tasks, none of which were enjoyable.

"Six months later I was assigned to the Sam's gold crew in the seaman gang. When we got back from patrol, I was sent to 'C' school and then here."

We finally had arrived at the chow hall where we got in line. Normally we would have had to present a chow card allowing us to eat here, but because we had just arrived on the base, our orders were sufficient. We each got a metal tray of food and sat down opposite each other. Dick said a little prayer and made the sign of the cross. So did I.

"So, we're both Catholic," I said. "Is there a priest on the sub?"

"No, there's no chapel either. One or two men usually take over and lead us in prayer each Sunday in the chow hall."

"What about shipboard terminology?" I asked.

"What you learned in boot camp is adequate. Just remember that a wall is a bulkhead, any opening without a door knob is a hatch and anything you go up and down on is a ladder, even if it looks like a staircase. A bed is a rack or a kip, where the officers eat and sleep is 'officer country,' and the chiefs eat and sleep in the chiefs' quarters, or 'goat locker.' When you're outside, below decks is in the sub. When you're inside, topside is outside. If you're in the sub, below is a lower level than the one you're on and the upper level is above the level you're on. A corridor is a passageway, a floor is a deck, and a ceiling is the overhead.

"The ranking chief is called the Chief of the Boat or COB, pronounced just like the inside of an ear of corn, and he is 'god.' Sometimes he tells the captain what to do and, sometimes he will call the captain 'sir.' Get your dolphins as quickly as possible. The rest you'll learn as time goes by."

"I think I met the COB on the first floor of the barracks," I said. "At least that's what his name badge said."

"Medium size black guy, kinda stocky?" he asked.

"Yeah, that's him."

"He's a hard-ass. I heard about him when I was on the gold crew. He doesn't like college boys. I guess that's because he never finished high school. Watch out for him. Just do what he says and stay out of his way.

"Don't dribble any coffee as you walk around with a cup in your hand. COB Foster has been known to follow coffee drops from the pot to the person who dripped the coffee. Then he makes the guilty party scrub the deck all the way back to the pot.

"The best part about the missile subs is the R&R between patrols."

"I heard about R&R, what is it?"

"Rest and relaxation. We get an entire month off when we come back. We can go wherever we want as long as we're within six hundred miles of the base when we call in twice a week to say we're still alive. That's why the barracks is so empty now. All except a couple of duty watches are gone on R&R."

"What about the other month we're not on patrol or R&R?"

"We go to training, but it's just lectures during the day. We're mostly done by noon and have the rest of the day to ourselves. The rest of the Navy is envious of our privileges, but you'll earn them on patrol."

We had finished eating and dropped off our empty trays on our way out. We talked some more on the way back.

"Are you from California?" I asked.

"No, I was staying with an aunt in Long Beach while going to school. I'm from a little town in Vermont called Winooski, just north of Burlington."

I had no idea which direction Vermont was from the base and no earthly idea where Burlington was.

"You?" he asked.

"A little town in Ohio about sixty miles south of Cleveland called Alliance, near Canton."

"That's where the Pro Football Hall of Fame is," he said.

"Yeah. It's about sixteen miles from my home."

"We'll have to go there sometime," he said, and we did. One of the R&R periods that I went home on, he went with me and we visited the Hall of Fame.

"Got any brothers or sisters?"

"I have three sisters, two older and one younger, no brothers," I said.

"I have one older sister."

"The name Schweinehun sounds German. Is it?"

"My dad is German, my mom Italian. Schweinehun is German for pig person. Save your breath, I've heard all the jokes. My nickname on the sub was Dickey Pig, because of my last name."

"My parents are both Italian," I said, wondering what else we had in common.

We made it back to the barracks and talked a little more, but we were both dead tired from traveling all day. We both "hit the kip," where I read a little from my James Bond novel before I fell asleep.

"Yeeeehaaa!"

The noise woke me up from a sound sleep. I heard someone in the cubicle across the hall mumble "goddamn rebels."

"Yeeeehaaa!"

It was a piercing sound. I had never heard the rebel yell before. There had been southerners in boot camp and in the navy schools I had gone to, but they didn't let out yells like that. I glanced at my glow-in-the-night wrist watch and saw it was oh two thirty, or two thirty in the morning.

"Shut the fuck up!" someone yelled at the screeching man.

It was the barracks watch who left his post at the middle of the barracks and walked down the hall in the direction of the screams.

"He's just a little drunk," said one of the men who had apparently come in with the screamer.

"Get him to his bunk, or I'll get the OOD to take care of his ass," the barracks watch said.

There were some more words said that I couldn't make out and the man did quiet down, or maybe passed out. I nodded back to sleep a few minutes later.

Such was my introduction to life in a submarine barracks.

The next morning, those of us who had to attend muster, slipped on our shower shoes and shuffled to the gang showers in the middle of the barracks by the MAA station.   I was in the shower when Dick came in. I couldn't help noticing he was hung like a donkey. I quickly turned away slightly embarrassed by my discovery.

episode three

"Captain Bob, you saw the picture of the submarine the size of the Sam, but to see it up close was something else. This is no shit, but..."

I couldn't believe how big it was the first time I saw the Sam, designation SSBN 609. The SSBN designation meant it was a submarine carrying ballistic missiles with a nuclear power propulsion plant. We arrived at Dunoon, Scotland by bus after a flight across the Atlantic in a chartered airliner.

The flight from Providence, Rhode Island was not my first airplane flight, but was the longest so far. It was non-stop to Prestwick, Scotland, but not uneventful. I witnessed my first exhibition of how sub sailors needle each other when we hit some especially violent turbulence somewhere over the Atlantic. Some sailors that had gotten on the plane drunk because they were afraid to fly were already sobering up. Being jostled about in the small one hundred-seat cabin had completed the process and their eyes were wide open. Their knuckles were white as they clutched the armrests in a death grip. Forget the fact that once we got out to sea, we would be in a "tin can" a hundred feet longer than a football field, thirty-three feet wide, and four hundred or more feet under the ocean. That didn't scare them, but flying in an airplane did.

"Eighty down in flames, Rat!" yelled Kozy, breaking the tense silence.

Everyone had nicknames and Kozy's was a shortening of his last name. Rat was another man's nickname, derived from the fact that he looked like a rat. Resembling whiskers on a rat, his scraggly mustache extended out from his nose and twitched when he was nervous. He was skinny and hunched over somewhat, like a rat slinking around in a sewer. He was buck-toothed (the navy took care of our dental needs, but not orthodontics) and his two top incisors protruded out from his narrow jaw under a long narrow nose. His hair was slicked back like he had just escaped from a can of lard, completing the look. Kozy was a sonar man and worked in the control center. Rat was an auxiliary man, and, suitable for his nickname, crawled around in the bilges and sanitary tanks.

"Fuck you!" Rat yelled back, which just incited Kozy that much more.

"Read all about it!" Kozy yelled back, even louder. "Eighty perish as plane plummets to earth in a fiery ball."

"Fuck you very much," came the retort from Rat. He had his head thrown back against the headrest, and his eyes tightly closed. There were little beads of sweat on his forehead. The sweat looked like that on Tetro's forehead (another shipmate) when he had to give a lesson in hydraulics during a training session and broke out in a nervous sweat.

The same Kozy had interrupted Tetro during his lecture with a "Hey Tet, is it rainin' in here or have you found a way to piss through your skin?" This made Tetro sweat all the more, and when the lecture was over, he had water pouring down his face. Kozy was merciless, but at least he spread his wrath around.

Before Kozy could mount another offensive, the turbulence stopped and the rest of the crew let out nervous laughs. We continued on without anymore outbursts, having left the states after dinner, and arriving in Scotland in time for breakfast. The entire flight was in the dark, so if I had had a window seat, I wouldn't have been able to see any of the ocean which we would be under in about four weeks. In the darkened cabin, most of us just slept. I was alert most of the time, just thrilled to be on my way to my first patrol, and a new adventure.

We landed in Prestwick around zero five hundred hours, five in the morning, and immediately boarded buses for the two-hour ride to Gourock, passing through Glasgow along the way. Since it was easier for me to sleep on a bus than on an airplane, I was in and out of consciousness during the drive.

"Now I heard of Glasgow," Captain Bob said, "but I don't know where the other town be."

"Here are some pictures I kept, that show the cities of Greenock, Gourock, and the Loch," I said, handing him the photos. "The two cities were adjacent to each other and Dunoon was across the Firth of Clyde. Here's a map of the area too."

Greenock

Gourock from Lyle Hill, Greenock

Holy Loch near Dunoon

"It looks like a pretty place," Captain Bob said.

"It was, but the pictures are deceiving. It rained most of the time and was overcast when it wasn't raining."

"Yuh got any pictures of the Sam in the water there?" Captain Bob asked.

"Yes I do, as a matter of fact." I said. Dedra stirred as I reached for the folder again, but she remained on the bed. The captain took another pull on his pipe.

"This is the one picture I am going to incorporate into the front cover of my book. It's a picture of the Sam approaching the tender in Holy Loch." I handed it to the captain as Dedra re-curled herself up against my leg as I stroked her still-cold fur. I continued with the story as he looked at the picture.

"She doesn't look any different than when I left her to go to "C" school last April," Dick said. He was smiling, his chest stuck out like a rooster's looking over his flock of hens. "After this patrol, I'll have my dolphins."

"What's that bulge on the bow?" I asked as we drew closer. On the front of the four hundred and ten-foot sub, was a huge bulge measuring fifteen feet across at its widest and shaped like a large teardrop. It looked a like a black version of W.C. Fields' nose compared to the rest of the relatively sleek body of the Sam.

"That's a sonar dome that listens 360 degrees, or nearly 360 degrees," Little Dickey answered. Without it, there's a blind spot behind the submarine in which someone could follow us."

"You mean the Russians?" I asked. I had attended "A" school at Dam Neck Virginia during the Cuban Missile Crisis in the fall of 1962 and "guarded" the Dismal Swamp from the possibility of invading Russians. Out of boredom, one of the other guards had shot a snake that had ventured onto a parking lot. After that, all of the guards had had to unload their weapons and carry our 45 caliber clips in an ammo belt.

The Russians also had a nuclear fleet of submarines, some missile carrying, purportedly less sophisticated then ours. There were stories of Soviet fast-attack subs following our missile-carrying subs around to plot their courses.

"Yeah," Little Dickey said, answering my question. "The 'Rooskies.'"

Our launch slowed as it pulled around to the other side of the sub tender, the U.S.S. Hunley. There weren't any subs tied up to that side, so we were able to dock alongside the lower level gangway, which was sometimes called a brow when it was shorter and connected two subs. The gangway led to the entrance of the tender. We left the launch, officers first, opposite the way we had boarded, and walked up the gangway to the guard at the top of the ladder. As per protocol, we saluted the flag at the stern and then the guard, requesting permission to come aboard.

I had a chance to look around at the beautiful panorama which was Holy Loch. Toward the northeast was the Firth of Clyde which led to the North Atlantic. Dunoon was off in the distance, the town shrouded in a mist which also clung to the tops of the emerald green hills surrounding the Loch. Sunshine was a rare commodity in this part of the world, but water was not. It rarely got below freezing, so vegetation grew year round.

A second launch, loaded with our sea bags, pulled in behind the first launch. The bags were hoisted onto the deck with a crane and we picked through them until we each had our own. I picked mine up, threw it over my shoulder, and followed the others to the transient crew's berthing on the tender. The bunk area was tucked up under the bow of the ship in a tightly contained row of beds and small lockers. We would be living out of our sea bags for the short time of turnover while the gold crew was still here. After getting settled in, we headed for the chow hall.

"How do you like it so far?" Dick asked.

"I'm not sure," I said. "I hope the sub sleeping area has more room than the tender."

"We'll be in the missile compartment which has individual three-man cubicles. It's a little more private than crew's berthing where all the other E6's and below stay. The missile compartment has its own head too with only one crapper, one shower and two sinks. It's cramped living conditions, but you'll get used to it."

"I can't wait to hit the skids tonight." I said. "I didn't get much sleep on the plane and I'm tired."

"Let's hope the guys who hit the beach don't come back and make a lot of noise late at night," he said.

"They couldn't be worse than that one who yelled our first night in the barracks," I said.

After the meal, I went up on deck and grabbed a smoke.

I had started smoking in sub school on a work detail. We were waxing and polishing a floor in the headquarters building when the petty officer in charge told everyone to take a smoke break. I was the only one who didn't smoke, but I went with them just the same.

"Get back to work," the petty officer said. "You don't smoke."

"I do now," I said, borrowing a cigarette from one of the smokers.

For a long time I never bought any cigarettes, always "borrowing." I only smoked when there was a need to, maybe four or five times a week. Cigarettes were cheap so bumming a cigarette and a light didn't hurt anyone financially. I heard a lot of sarcastic comments, like 'you want a kick in the ass to get you started' and 'you don't have the cigarettes, just the habit.'

One of my closest friends on the Sam was another third-class petty officer named Larry. I got acquainted with Larry in the superstructure chipping paint. He reported to the Sam later than Dick and I and kept to himself back in the States, so I never got to know him until we got to Holy Loch.

The round hull of the submarine is made flat from just before the sail to just aft of the reactor compartment by a built up deck called a superstructure. Saltwater and time blister or erode the paint which has to be chipped away and reapplied. Zinc strips are welded to the hull of the sub in various places under the superstructure to help prevent rust. I found out later they were "sacrificial anodes" in the lingo of cathodic protection engineering. It was not unusual to see the metal bars from the two ends of a zinc strip by themselves, the zinc completely gone having corroded away protecting bare spots on the sub where the paint was worn off.

"Here are some schematics showing parts of the superstructure outside the hull of the sub." I handed them to Captain Bob. "Not every part of the superstructure is accessible and there are hatches to get to the parts that need repainted."

Since there were too many missile technicians in the Navy by the time I finished all the necessary schooling to be assigned to a sub, I

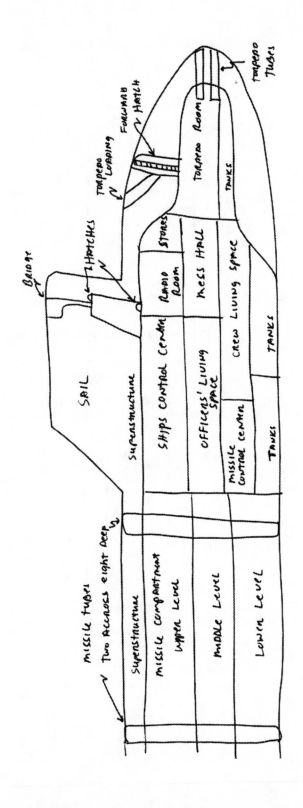

Missile Tubes
Two Accross eight Deep
Superstructure
Missile Compartment upper Level
Middle Level
Lower Level

Sail

Bridge
2 Hatches

Superstructure
Ships Control Center
Officers' Living Space
Missile Control Center
Radio Room
Stores
Mess Hall
Crew Living Space
Missile Control Center
Tanks
Tanks
Torpedo Loading
Forward Hatch
Torpedo Room
Tanks
Torpedo Tubes

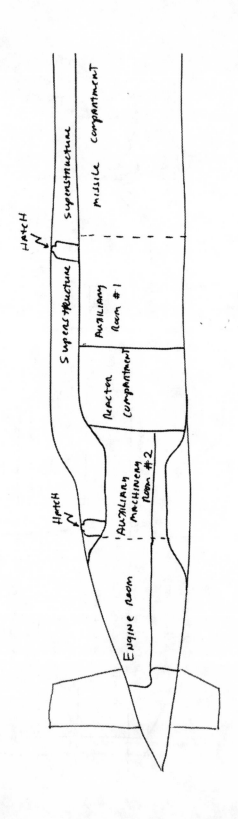

SUPERSTRUCTURE

HATCH

AUXILIARY ROOM #1

REACTOR COMPARTMENT

MISSILE COMPARTMENT

SUPERSTRUCTURE

HATCH

AUXILIARY MACHINERY ROOM #2

ENGINE ROOM

was placed in a seaman gang. Seaman gangs are usually populated with men just out of boot camp, enlisted ranks "E2" and "E3." Almost all of the seaman gang on the Sam were "E4" (petty officers, third class) and rated. That is to say we had a designation such as missile technician. I, Larry, Little Dickey, and a man named Felix were all E4 missile technicians. Another man, Bear, was also on the seaman gang, but he was an E5. He had been assigned to the George Washington (SSBN598) which was in the shipyard having an overhaul and swapped with another missile technician to be on the Sam Houston. He was also a musician and had been in a special company in boot camp. He was not as straight-laced as most military men were. It irked me to see lesser ranked "strikers" (those who wore a designation, but were not yet petty officers) not having to chip paint or mess cook.

"You chip while I nap," Larry said. "Then you can nap while I chip."

"Sure," I replied. "What if the COB catches us?"

"He has to come through the access cover, and we can see the light when it's opened. Wake me if you see him coming. He won't come looking as long as he can hear us chipping on the hull."

"Okay," I said. So, I chipped for about an hour and then napped an hour. It was boring work, so the breaks were worth it. Besides, this to me was "make work," something just to keep us busy until we went to sea. The chipping tool had chisels on each end. One end was curved like the neck on a goose and was used to chip and poke at the paint. The other end was straight and used to scrape away any paint loosened by the curved end. The scraping and banging made quite a racket which, under the superstructure, bounced around like balls in a pin-ball machine.

After a couple of days of chipping, we primed the bare areas with "red lead" paint. Then, the spraying gear was set up with long hoses which snaked down into the superstructure where the finish coat of black paint was liberally applied. The surfaces outside of the superstructure were maintained the same way. Left-over paint in five-gallon cans "fell" overboard with a big "oops" rather than being carried all the way back to the paint locker on the tender. The cans of lead-based paint were very heavy and sank immediately, even when half full. I imagine that, if it wasn't cleaned up by now, some of the toxic paint is leaching into the Loch contaminating or killing the fish population. That would be a shame, because I remember the Loch as being a beautiful, but raw, place.

The only break we got from the monotonous painting routine was when we stood deck watch. There were two men in uniform, white in the summer and blue in the winter, who "guarded" the Sam from unauthorized personnel. One was stationed in a guard shack at the foot of the brow to greet all visitors. It was his responsibility to keep a log book of events such as visiting officials, keel depth at hourly intervals, man overboard occurrences, fire drills, when various officers left or returned, etc. The other man was a roving patrol who read the keel depth from the gauges painted on the side of the sub and generally walked around making sure everything was shipshape.

The skipper, or submarine captain, was referred to by the name of his command and announced over the intercom called the 1MC. "Sam Houston arriving" (or leaving), was the call heard when the captain arrived or departed.

At night the two watches stayed in the guard shack most of the time talking to each other just to keep from getting bored or falling asleep. Nothing was off limits during those discussions. Some of the guys would talk freely about married life in general, and even their sex lives. I was a good listener, since being a virgin, my curiosity was overwhelming. The mid-watches were dogged. That is, instead of four hours from midnight to four in the morning, there were two watches of two hours each. The midnight to four was the worst because of the lack of sleep. It was difficult to go to bed at ten knowing a wake-up call was coming at eleven thirty. Then going back to bed at two thirty knowing reveille was at six made it difficult to get to sleep again.

It was great to get the first mid-watch in the spring when the time went forward, but a bitch to get it in the fall watch adding an hour to the monotony. There was no relief the next day after the standing a mid-watch either. The work day began at seven in the morning whether or not a watch was stood the night before.

The watches were armed, because there were protestors among the civilian population in the towns around the Loch. They didn't like the idea that U.S. warships carrying missiles with nuclear warheads were sitting out in the middle of their peaceful Loch. An attempt to board the subs didn't happen while I was there, but there were instances when it did happen. We were told not to shoot except as a last resort. If a boat got too close, an alarm would sound and the crew brought weights topside to toss at the boats. This supposedly would sink the small craft and then we would be forced to rescue them by pulling them aboard, which is what they wanted in the first place.

We were on port and starboard duty, which meant we had to stay on the submarine every other day for watches. Larry and I were on the same duty schedule, so he and I went to shore together whenever I did go, which wasn't too often. At that time I wasn't into frequenting the bars and was saving for college, so didn't have a lot of cash to spend.

Larry was a fisherman and wanted to try some fly fishing in some of the many streams around the Loch. We were able to get two sets of fishing gear from the special services office on the tender, and headed for the woods. I was amazed by how green the forests were, nothing like what I was used to in Ohio. The ground was like a sponge to walk on, not soggy, but soft. Every step felt as though I were bouncing on peat bog accumulated over thousands of years and probably was. Ferns and other dark-green forms of vegetation grew like a carpet between the tall trees. Only spotty sections of direct sunlight made it to the floor of the forest, but it was fairly bright all the same.

Before we went fishing in any of the streams, we were cautioned to first get permission from the closest farmhouse. Larry was bolder than I, so he always asked. The two houses we approached each gave us permission, so we waded into the icy streams with our hip boots, casting flies into the still pools of the streams. Larry had to show me how to fly fish. I had only used live bait and dough balls when I went fishing as a boy. After a few snags and tangles in the overhanging tree branches, I was able to do an acceptable job of casting, but caught nothing. Larry did get a few brown trout which he released so another fisherman could enjoy the sport. Because we lived on the sub, we wouldn't have had an opportunity or a place to enjoy our catch even if we did keep them.

That's how I spent my first turn-over period on the Sam, chipping paint, napping in the superstructure, throwing paint overboard, fishing, standing watches, and getting oriented to living on a sub.

episode four

"So, what did ya do on board when the submarine was underway?" Captain Bob asked.

"I have to start with my first patrol," I said. "That patrol was similar to my second one in that I had to mess cook for a little more than half the patrol."

"Mess cookin' is like what ya was told by that other fella, was it?"

"Yeah," I said. "Only it was no fun at all and this is no shit…"

My duties as mess cook included rising at four thirty, oh-dark-thirty as Little Dickey liked to call any time after midnight and before dawn. After getting cleaned up I proceeded to the chow hall to don my white full-length apron and prepare for the morning meal.

The chow hall consisted of five rows of two six- by four-foot tables. Each metal table was anchored to the deck with metal posts on the inside edge of each end. Benches with tilt-up padded seats on each side of the table sat six to eight sailors. In the benches were all types of canned and packaged food. At the end of each table was a swing up seat which latched into place so that ten men could be seated at a table at one time. The entire eighty-man enlisted crew was fed in two shifts, every six hours.

Unfortunately, during watch change was when the navigator wanted to shoot stars. We approached the surface, stuck up the navigational periscope, and got information from various stars to get a fix on our position. The North Atlantic almost always had rough seas, so it was an adventure to try to feed everyone while rocking and rolling back and forth. Sea legs were a necessity for navigating the rolling motion so that you maintained your balance while, what seemed like, walking up or down a moving hill with a plate of food in each hand.

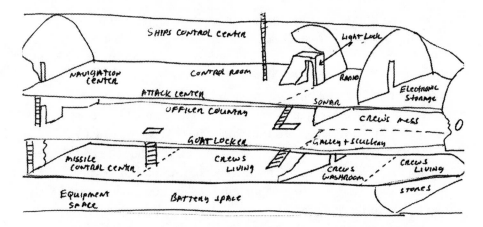

"Yeh, yeh, yeh," Captain Bob said, interrupting staccato like with the "yeh" I've only heard in the northeast. "I knows watcha mean about that North 'Lantic. It were a rough place, 'specially on the surface."

"One deck below the chow hall was crew's berthing where most of the enlisted slept," I continued. "The missile technicians, which included Little Dickey and me, slept in the missile compartment and had slightly better accommodations. The stairs on a ship are called ladders, even though they resemble stairs, albeit steep ones. On the aft end of the chow hall was the ladder leading down into crew's berthing.

"Here's an isometric of a portion of the front half of the sub."

At the top of the ladder was a ten-gallon coffee urn which always contained coffee or was in the process of brewing some. The coffee came in twenty-pound tins, each one lasting about five days. God have mercy on the mess cook who made a lousy pot of coffee! He would be placed in a torpedo tube and shot out to sea!

All the enlisted men queued up in crew's berthing at the bottom of the ladder waiting to be called up for the meal. A little piece of pre-printed paper called a chit was used for breakfast to indicate the number of eggs, the way they should be cooked, the number of pancakes, the number of portions of meat, and whether or not you wanted hash brown potatoes on your order.

When called up from below, the chit was turned in to the cook. You then grabbed a cup of coffee and a sticky bun and sat down to wait for one of the mess cooks to bring the food you ordered after it was dished up by the cook.

A sticky bun, is a cinnamon bun with frosting poured on top, usually plain, but sometimes maple flavored. Eating one was like grabbing a handful of melted sugar and trying to get it into your mouth before it got all over your face and hands. Most of it stuck to your fingers, hence the name "sticky bun." Sometimes the buns were pecan rolls, but almost any type of gooey bun was called a sticky bun. There were two pans of sticky buns left over on my first day of mess cooking.

At the other meals the side dishes and entrée were already sitting on the table before the call up from crew's berthing. If necessary, a chit was used to indicate how many portions of the entrée were wanted and how it was to be prepared. For instance, if steak was the entrée, the chit would indicate how many, and how well you wanted it cooked. Other types of entrées, such as pasta, were already on the table. When the community bowls of food were emptied and more was wanted, the guy who emptied the bowl held it above his head for the mess cook to retrieve, refill, and then return it to the table. Any delay in retrieving the empty bowl or returning it to the table resulted in name calling.

Forward of the chow hall, separated by a steel bulkhead and accessed through an elliptical four-foot hatch centered on the bulkhead, was the torpedo room. This was the forward most compartment on the sub and also the smallest.

"Tell me about these torpedoes," Captain Bob demanded.

"They are like little underwater missiles about sixteen feet long, two feet in diameter, and weigh more than two thousand pounds. We had ten of them on the Sam."

Captain Bob whistled, which I thought would wake the dog.

The torpedoes are loaded into a tube just like an artillery shell is loaded into a cannon. The rear hatch, called a breech door, is then closed and a hatch on the other end of the tube is opened to launch the fish. Torpedoes are called fish since they "swim" to their targets using a little propeller. They can go about thirty-six hundred yards to their target and then explode with the force of about five-hundred pounds of TNT." I didn't mention that some carried nuclear weapons, a term he would not understand.

My favorite place to sleep was in the torpedo room on top of a fish. I would lay with my arms and legs straddling the metal bomb just like

I was lying in a saddle. They were cold at first, but soon warmed up. The best part was that, in a mild sea, the torpedo room would move in a figure-eight fashion. Lying on a torpedo with that motion was like being rocked to sleep in a cradle. Some of the torpedomen also slept in the torpedo room on bunks that were chained to the bulkheads. The bunks could be triced up to make room for loading torpedoes in the tubes. One torpedoman used to sleep with a pair of his wife's underpants stretched over his head. No one asked if they had been laundered before he brought them on patrol.

We had never launched a torpedo except as a test when we were on sea trials. We were able to "shoot" the torpedoes out of the tubes with high pressure air or steam, just like a kid blows a pea out of a straw. We could also let them swim out on their own. Sometimes a torpedo would start to swim on its own without opening the outer hatch or launching it. That's called a "hot fish" and is considered very dangerous. We practiced what to do if we had a hot fish. We practiced (or what we called drilled) for problems like that all the time, but when we had real problems, they were nothing like what we had drilled for.

"What's a sea trial?"

"I'll get to that later," I said.

In the chow hall, to the left of the torpedo room access hatch, was a small, restaurant style juke box loaded with 45 rpm records. Selections were limited, but it was the only musical entertainment available. Individual record players were not feasible and because of the steel hull and at least fifty feet of water above us, radios were useless.

"Do you know what I'm talkin' about?" I asked not knowing how much he knew about modern day appliances.

"Sure do," he said. "I get ta nosin' around here a lot and have seen all the new fangled things people bring in here to use. I'll stop ya if I don't know what you're talkin' 'bout." That answered my question, so I went on.

On the starboard side of the chow hall just forward of the aft entrance, were the galley, or kitchen, and scullery, or dishwashing area, with pass-through accesses for moving food and dishes between the cooking and eating areas. In the aft corner of the scullery pass-through was the garbage disposal unit called the GDU, which is a ten-inch diameter steel tube extending from the scullery straight down to the keel. The GDU, which resembled a vertically mounted torpedo tube, had a breech door and a locking ring on the upper end. On the lower end was a large, hydraulically operated ball valve, like a cannonball with a hole through it. The ball valve assembly was welded to the outside of the bottom of the sub and when the ball was turned ninety degrees, there was a straight through hole to the ocean from inside the GDU. When we were submerged, all solid waste exited the sub through the GDU.

"Here's a diagram of the area."

On the same side and forward of the galley were a walk-in freezer and chill box or refrigerator. We called them walk-in refrigerators

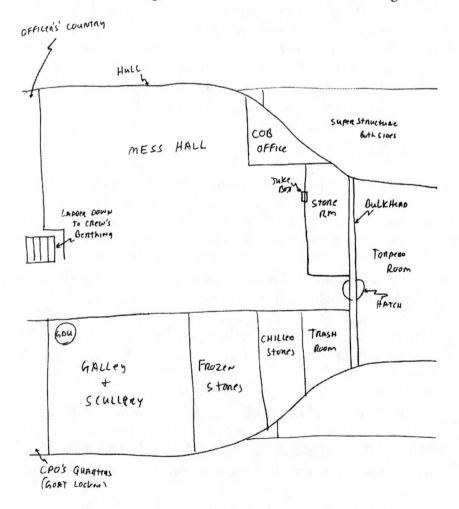

but they were only empty enough to walk into when they were being loaded at the beginning of the patrol and a couple of weeks before the end of the patrol when enough food was removed so a person could move about in them easily. Food was stacked to the overhead in both, requiring tunneling to find what was needed for each meal. Until the stores were diminished, mining one's way wearing arctic clothing to find a package of "horse cock," a four-inch diameter cylinder of lunchmeat about yard long, was a way of life for the cooks and mess cooks. Dry goods not stored in the benches under the seats in the chow hall, were stored throughout the sub in various nooks and crannies. The locations of dry goods and freezer contents were all meticulously mapped by the cooks.

The last room forward of the freezer was the trash and compactor room. Trash was stored there until it could be compacted and ejected through the GDU. The compactor was a split, cylindrical jacket with a plunger. Preformed and tabbed, perforated metal sheets were rolled into a cylinder four feet long and just under ten inches in diameter so they could fit inside the GDU. The tabs were crimped to hold the cylinder together and a bottom piece of metal was attached to form a tall can.

The can was set inside the split, metal jacket of the compactor and the sides were bolted together to form an outer cylinder. Weights were added to the bottom of the inner cylinder and then trash was set on top of that and compacted by a plunger forced down with fifteen hundred pounds of hydraulic fluid. When full, the cylinder was capped, and the jacket unbolted to remove

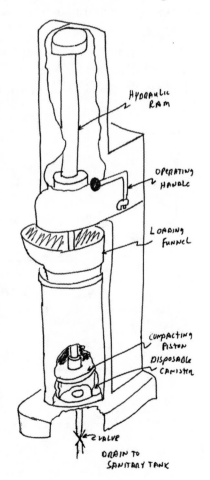

Hydraulic Ram

Operating Handle

Loading Funnel

Compacting Piston

Disposable Canister

Valve

Drain to Sanitary Tank

the inner trash filled cylinder. The entire package was then placed inside the GDU to be ejected with others.

"Here's a schematic of the trash compactor."

The officers ate in 'officer country' in the wardroom. The chief petty officers had the chiefs' quarters and their own mess area which we called the "goat locker." Stewards, who were usually black or Filipino, took care of the officers' and chiefs' needs. The Filipinos, who were earning their American citizenship by completing a tour of duty in the Navy, didn't have the security clearance to allow them to move freely about the ship as the rest of us could. As a consequence, we didn't see them very often. They also didn't have to be qualified on submarines.

"Here's a floor diagram of the officers' quarters and the goat locker."

While the cook prepared the meal, we set up the tables with all the condiments, including salt, pepper, ketchup, and Louisiana hot sauce. There were a few rebels, as we liked to call them, from the Southern states who insisted on hot sauce at every meal. If it wasn't on the table they would scream 'Where's the Louisiana hot sauce?' After getting yelled at a couple of times, I always made sure the hot sauce was at every table for every meal.

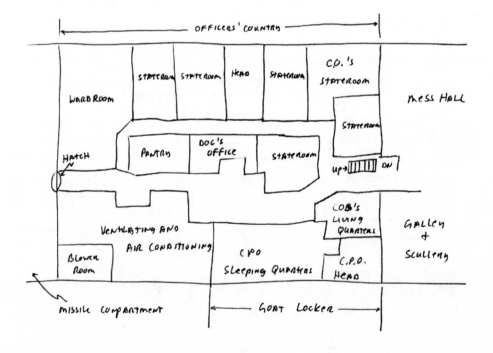

"You called them rebels," Captain Bob said. "What does that stand for?"

"Rebels were from the deep South, usually Mississippi, Georgia, and Alabama. They were really hard-core racists and were still fighting the civil war. My first encounter with them was in boot camp."

"I'm so horny." One of them said one day. "I sure could use some cock."

That was a shocker to me. I had always thought cock meant a penis, but apparently down South that means pussy. The northern guys just laughed at him. I never heard him say that again.

They also seemed to have trouble with spelling. I think it was because of the drawl they had that induced them to spell phonetically. I was relieving the topside watch, a man by the name of Delozer, during turnover one night when I noticed an entry in the logbook.

"What's this entry?" I said pointing to a line of writing made during his watch.

"They started the die-seal at twenty-one hundred hours," he said. He pronounced the word just like he spelled it, and then I realized what he meant.

"Oh," I said. "Diesel is spelled without the 'a'." I didn't make any other comments, but told the story to Larry and Little Dickey, who got a chuckle from it.

That wasn't the only misspelling I encountered. While in the transient barracks at Anacostia after quitting the academy, I saw a sailor making a sign to use for hitchhiking to his next duty station. On the sign was "Naval Air Station." To see what he'd do, I told him Naval was spelled n-a-v-e-l.

"It is?" he asked.

"Sure," I said.

"Thanks," he said and started a new sign. "Good thing you caught that or I'd look funny hitchhiking with the sign the way it was."

I never heard from him to see if he made it to the Bellybutton Air Station.

So, the hot sauce was set out for every meal. Except for breakfast, we set six place settings of plates, cups, and flatware on each table. We also set out pitchers of milk, when available, and "bug juice." Milk spoiled after a week or two, so there was not a lot of it in the chill box. Bug juice was a generic Kool-Aid of an undistinguishable flavor. One pack of the powder made a gallon of juice. Every once in awhile, meal worms or other vermin surfaced in the pitchers, giving the drink its nickname.

Mess cooks were the scum of the earth and were treated like slaves. It was always a mystery to me why one shipmate would treat another that way, but it was a form of initiation. Other 'non-quals' were treated with much the same disrespect, but not as much or as badly as mess cooks. If a sailor couldn't stand the harassment, he was not submariner material. I could tell who had had the misfortune of being a mess cook because they treated you more or less like a human. Mess cooking was the nastiest job on the submarine and being treated poorly just made the job worse.

I remember that back when I had first joined the Navy in boot camp, I had to spend my time mess cooking and on the serving line, just like everyone else. But that was for a couple of days and everyone had to take a turn. We tried to make it fun when we were cleaning up by sliding on the wet, vinyl-tile floors. When one of the men slipped and cracked his head open, we stopped the sliding.

Before breakfast one morning during my stint as a boot camp mess cook, four of us had to crack open enough eggs to scramble for the entire brigade, about fifteen hundred men. Six boxes of eggs were brought to us with four gross of eggs per box, or about two eggs per serving. I learned to hold two eggs in each hand cracking them four at a time. Any shells that fell into the five-gallon tubs were fished out with our bare hands.

We were lucky they had an electric potato peeler for that chore, but on the sub we had to do it the old fashioned way.

Since Little Dickey was the night mess cook, it was his job to peel the potatoes. I got to help occasionally, and learned how nasty a job it really was. The starch from the potatoes absorbed the moisture from our hands, leaving them wrinkled and raw. After over two hundred potatoes were peeled and ready for the cook, we applied what was called "bear grease" to get some moisture back into our hands. We were thankful that potatoes took up a lot of room to store and, therefore, fresh potatoes were not served very often.

Since the crew was on a six-hours-on and twelve-hours-off duty schedule, there really wasn't any night or day except for in the control room. The cooks and mess cooks worked sixteen-hour shifts with some overlap between the day and night shifts. The work was so grueling and tedious, a tour of mess cooking only lasted about three weeks. Then, a new group of mess cooks took over while you switched places and did their job for the remainder of the patrol. Since we were food handlers, we couldn't grow beards like the rest of the crew."

"Grow a beard?" he asked.

"Yeah," I said. "Most of the crew, even officers, quit shaving as soon as we left the Loch, and didn't shave until we were on our way back. After my mess cooking duties were over for the patrol, I started my beard, but the rest of the crew already had a two to three week start. Beards grew in all types and shapes. Some beards were scraggly, some looked nice, some were black, some were white, some were mixed black and white, some were wiry and kinky, and some were straight. Mine was red, curly, and grew rapidly. Even when I started my beard halfway through the patrol, it looked better than some that were started the minute we left Scotland."

"You braggin'?" Captain Bob asked.

"No brag, just fact," I said, and continued with the story.

"Mornin' Skinny," I said to the night cook. His nickname described his visage quite well and he was quite laconic.

"Yeah," was all he said. He had been up all night making bread and sticky buns and was ready to 'hit the kip,' sailor slang for go to bed. Even at his best, a long conversation with Skinny might involve three sentences.

Little Dickey was finishing his job as scullery rat washing the various pots and pans dirtied during the night. Because he had been on the Sam before, he had gotten the easier job of being the night mess cook. After he helped set up for the morning meal he was off to work on his quals.

There was a sailor, obviously from the control room, getting a tray full of coffee. He was wearing red goggles. There was always one helmsman who could go to the mess and get coffees for the bridge. After doing it a few times we all knew each others' tastes.

"Three black and nasty, two candy bars, one blond and bitter, one black and sweet," he mumbled to himself, while he pointed at the cups on the tray.

The first was a sailor's description for coffee without anything. Some liked to say 'put a cup around it' or 'black and nasty, just like my women,' which is the way I liked it, but I thought that might sound a little bit disrespectful of the COB, so never said it when he was around. A candy bar was two scoops each of cream and sugar; the other descriptions were easy to decipher.

There were also packets of instant cocoa which was pretty good for a change from all the coffee I drank. Wearing my goggles I would make the coffee run and add the cocoa for myself. While drinking it in the darkened control room, I found what I thought were un-dissolved bits of cocoa getting stuck between my cheeks and gums. It wasn't until I went into a space with more light that I ran my finger inside my mouth and pulled out a wad of larvae of some sort. Apparently we had gotten a batch of infected cocoa without knowing it. After that, I checked my cup before I drank from it, dumping the powder when bugs were present.

"You said he was wearin' goggles," Captain Bob asked. "What's that mean?"

"Night goggles were like glasses, tinted red and with solid side shields to keep any white light from reaching the eyes."

"What for?" he asked.

"The Sam's navigational equipment, helm, and operators were stationed in the control center directly above and a little aft of the mess hall. Here's a schematic and a profile of the area."

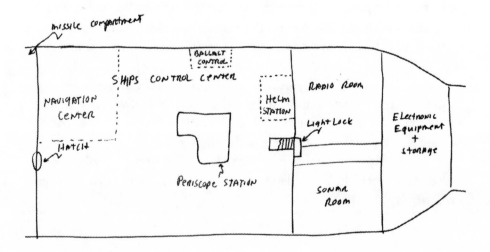

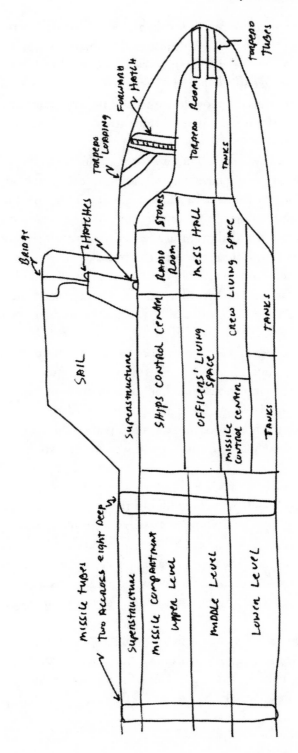

The ship's control center was kept "rigged for red" between sunset and sunrise with only red lighting to illuminate the space. Those in the control room needed to maintain their night vision in case an emergency surface was required. There was a "light lock" that kept any light from the spaces below from getting into the control room area. You can see it in the front, partial isometric I gave you earlier and these drawings.

The human eye takes about five to ten minutes to adjust to the dark; time a lookout doesn't have when heading to the bridge on the top of the sail to scan the horizon for ships or aircraft. Therefore, they wore red goggles when temporarily leaving the control room, reminding me that there was a real world above, but the sun was not yet shining on it.

"Mornin Larry," I said to the other mess cook who was on the day shift with me. Larry was a big guy from Colorado who looked like a Swedish ski instructor, and, like me, had gotten fat from eating too much. We shared the nickname of Fatso, except when I peaked out at two-hundred and forty pounds, he called me 'Fatsoer.'

I got so heavy that first patrol I couldn't eat without having to take a shit thirty minutes later. The pipeline from my stomach to my colon was so packed with food some had to leave to make room for more. If food was available, we were allowed to eat as much as we wanted. For example, if there were no pancakes, you couldn't order pancakes; however, if there were pancakes, there was no limit to the number you could get.

My eyes have always been bigger than my stomach; therefore, when I wasn't mess cooking, I would fill out the request chit by putting next to: servings of eggs – 6 over easy, servings of meat – 6, servings of potatoes – 6, and pancakes (if available) – 6. I like a nice round number, and, above all, consistency. It was also like that at lunch and dinner. When the meals weren't being prepared, there was an open kitchen. When the watch changed at midnight, it was "serve yourself," and I usually did.

Between one and two in the morning, the night baker would put out a couple of extra loaves of bread, hot from the oven. This was an invitation for me to cut the loaf in half lengthwise and spread butter on it for a "little" snack.

That's not all. For breakfast, after waiting in line and filling out the request chit, we were ushered into the mess hall. I placed my order on the counter, got a cup of coffee, and grabbed a plateful of coffee cake or sticky buns to eat while I waited on my six each of everything.

"Get rid of them," the cook said, that first day I mess cooked when there were two pans of sticky buns left over.

I was always taught that throwing food away was a sin and I couldn't just toss them into the chute that led to the sanitary tank. I had to try to eat what was left. After I started to get sick, I decided I couldn't save the remaining buns, and reluctantly tossed them away.

This availability of copious amounts of food was why I weighed so much after my first patrol. The old-timers told me they would have to pressurize the boat just to pop me out of the escape hatch.

"Got any pictures of ya when ya was fat?" Captain Bob asked.

"I only have this one taken when I weighed close to my maximum. It's a Polaroid, so it hasn't weathered well."

Larry and I mess cooked together for two straight patrols. Our friendship continued on and off patrol and later on I was even honored to be the best man at his wedding. I was on duty the night I thought he died.

I handed a picture of the floating dry dock to Captain Bob.

It was our first night back from my first patrol. Instead of pulling alongside the sub tender, we were guided into the USS Los Alamos, a floating dry dock. The tanks on either side were flooded so that it sank enough to pull the sub inside.

After we pulled into the partially submerged dry dock, wet-suited divers swam to the bottom of the sub and positioned large, wooden chocks to support the weight of the sub. Floating on the surface, the Sam doesn't weigh anything, but take away the buoyant force of the water, and she is almost 8,000 tons. Water was pumped out of the flotation tanks on the sides and bottom of the Los Alamos lifting it and the Sam above the water. It was the first time I had ever seen the screw, which was a massive, brass, seven bladed propeller.

That first night, I had drawn the eight-to-twelve duty watch and was stationed on the deck the same as if we were floating on the water, except we were fifty feet in the air. Liberty boats came alongside the dry dock and took boatloads of sailors to the Ardnadam pier for their first trip to land in two months. We didn't receive a paycheck at sea since there was nothing to purchase except from each other. The disbursing officer came aboard as soon as we docked and paid everyone in cash. I had almost all my pay going to savings, so out of the $400 owed me I netted about $50. Others pocketed their pay putting it in lockers with their belongings or spending it on a night on the town. There were also the ones who gave their entire pay to others to satisfy their gambling debts from the once-a-week casino nights. Larry was one of those headed for a night on the town.

I pulled out another picture, this one of the Sam in the dry dock shot from the bow end. The picture had been taken just before maintenance scaffolding was erected around the entire structure which was used to inspect and paint every square inch of the hull. The crew didn't

do the painting this time, it had been done by contractors. A picture of the stern was considered classified because of the design of the screw, so there were none taken for public display.

The large nose of the sonar dome was clearly visible.

The next time I saw Larry was at eleven o'clock that night. He was being dragged, feet first, from the liberty boat across the deck of the dry dock forty feet below. The dragger, the smallest guy on the sub, had been able to get Larry from the bar, to a cab, and on and off the liberty boat before Larry totally passed out.

"Corpsman topside," I requested over the 1MC.

This announcement brought a flurry of activity from below decks. The OOD, doc, and a couple of men on watch popped out from the sail hatch. They knew an announcement like that was not good news.

"Who's hurt?" Doc, the boat's corpsman, asked.

"Larry," I said. "He's down on the dry dock deck with Tiny. I think he's too drunk to climb the scaffolding."

The scaffolding, erected around the entire sub, had ladders interconnecting the platform levels which allowed us to get to the dry-dock deck below. This myriad of ladders and planks were difficult to navigate even in the best of conditions. The weather in Holy Loch was also misty a lot of the time making access even more treacherous. Doc and the others headed down the scaffolding.

"He's too drunk and big to carry up the ladder," one of the returning men said. "We're going to hoist him up on the body stretcher."

Two of the men went back into the sub and emerged through the forward torpedo room with a wire-mesh stretcher, molded like half a body split lengthwise, with straps in multiple places. They hurried down the ladder while I retrieved enough mooring line to reach down to the deck of the Alamos. With the rope lowered and attached securely to the stretcher, the strapped-in, stupefied sailor was ready to be hoisted to the top.

When he reached the top, I noticed he was unresponsive. I thought I had lost my friend until I got off watch at midnight and went to the missile compartment. There was Larry lying on a blanket on the deck. The doc was tending him to make sure he didn't aspirate his own puke should he upchuck.

"I'm still getting no response," Doc said as he poked Larry with a pin. "We'll have to take him to the hospital if he continues this way. Here is what we found in his pocket."

He handed me more than three hundred dollars which I took over to my locker for safe keeping. An hour later, Doc, getting a reaction to the pin pricks, breathed a sigh of relief.

"I'll stay up with him," I said.

"If he starts to puke, turn his head and keep it that way, and send someone for me," Doc said.

I was up the rest of the night, but my buddy was all right in the morning. He wasn't even hung over, but wanted to know the details. The next night Larry and I were both on liberty and went into town together.

Liberty from the Sam in Holy Loch was my first experience in a foreign country other than Canada. Before leaving the states, we were cautioned that, when outside the States, we were all ambassadors and were to present a favorable image of Americans.

Larry and I were walking on a street heading toward what was considered to be a pub frequented by submariners. The name was something like "The Cow and Pussy," but I don't remember exactly. I commented on how the cheeks of all the children looked so rosy. I didn't know at the time that it was caused by exposure to the cold and that there was no central heat in Scottish homes.

We were on one side of the street and an older lady was walking across the street in the opposite direction.

"Fookin' Yaankee basta'ds," she said flipping us the bird.

I had never heard a woman use that language before, and for her to give us the finger, unprovoked, was shocking to me.

"What the hell did we do?" I said to Larry.

"I don't know," he said. "She looks old enough to have been here during World War II. Maybe someone knocked her up and then went back to the states."

I let it go at that, but for us to be ambassadors and be treated like that in return bothered me for a long time. We continued on to the bar where we had been told sailors from the Sam were hanging out.

"Hey Larry and Andy," one of the guys called out.

"Howdy," we both said. After being around Larry I was picking up his colloquialisms.

Another sailor turned, saw new arrivals were in the bar, and yelled out, "Anybody who can't tap dance is queer!" This got an immediate response from everyone in the bar as they all jumped up and did a tap dance. No one wanted to be considered queer. Larry and I had heard this incantation before and tapped danced too. The din from a bunch of sailors banging their feet on the floor could probably be heard by the entire neighborhood. After five or six seconds it stopped.

The location of the only source of heat in a bar was where most of the sailors gathered. It was usually a stove or a fireplace. Larry and I went to the standing-only bar and ordered a beer. The bartender placed two mugs on the table and told us the price. It was a good thing this bar took U.S. dollars, because we didn't understand at first how to convert dollars to pounds. A pound, crown, thrupence, tuppence, or shilling meant nothing to us. For the dollars we presented for payment, we received "funny money" in change.

We found out later that there were two-hundred-forty pence to the pound or twenty shillings of twelve pence each. Add to that the exchange rate between the dollar and the pound, which changed every patrol, and we were easily confused. Even after we thought we had figured it out, all we did was lay our money on the table and let them take what they needed. Because we didn't know if we were being cheated out of the correct change or not, we spent most of the time in the American-run USO, where we paid in dollars, instead of in the local establishments which required "funny money."

At this bar tonight, there was a sailor drinking his dolphins, a rite of passage from a non-qual to submariner. A collection was taken up, not of money, but of booze. The collection vessel was a pitcher or other suitably large container, preferably one that was made of glass so that drinking progress could be measured. When the container was full, the earned set of dolphins was dropped in and sank to the bottom. The sailor had to stand on a chair or table and "drink his dolphins," without setting the vessel down. This produced the end result expected from drinking copious amounts of alcohol rather quickly.

"Drink! Drink! Drink!" was the chant that went up to the man standing on the chair. He tilted the pitcher back and swallowed as much as he could as the crowd chanted and clapped. What he couldn't swallow poured down his chest and onto the table and floor. When the dolphins slid down the container and he caught them in his teeth, the game was over. He would step down and have one of the men, usually his "sea daddy" pin them on his chest. In ten or twenty minutes, if he didn't throw up, he would be too stupefied to make it back to the boat on his own.

The owner of the bar went along with the ritual because these men were spending a lot of money catching up after three months of sobriety. After a couple of beers, I needed to piss so I headed for the restroom. The first thing I noticed was that it was damn cold away from the heated room. The second thing I noticed was that there were no urinals. A bare stone wall with a trough under it was where I relieved myself. It was a reminder that I was in a foreign country and not all countries living conditions were equal.

After a couple more beers Larry and I headed back toward Ardn-adam Pier, where the boat launch that ran every half hour picked us up and took us back to the Tender.

"Here's a picture of the pier," I said to the captain.

"I'm a little hungry," Larry said when we spied the little food stand at the head of the pier.

"I could eat something," I replied. It seemed like I could always eat something.

We looked into the little place and saw fish and chips, but I wasn't hungry for fried fish.

"I'll take a burger and chips," Larry said to the vender.

"Me too," I said.

"'At'll be two 'n twenty," the man said in a heavy sing-song Scottish accent.

We both just tossed some "funny money" on the counter that we had gotten in change at the pub. He culled through it and left us some coins of the realm. I had no idea how much the food had cost. We poured vinegar on our "big french fries" and headed down to the end of the pier to await the liberty boat.

I ate my burger, but the flavor was strange. I later found out it was not hamburger, but mutton. Oh well, what the hell! It was something different from sub chow.

By the time the boat got there at least ten other sailors were in line to go back. Some of them were really drunk, an indication to me of what was in store for me during my tour of duty as a sub sailor.

There was another incident while we were in dry dock that bears mentioning. It involved the torpedoman named Foster and a would-be, unknown champion of the crew. And this is no shit…

Hardhats were required when we were in the dry dock, so whenever we ventured outside the submarine, we grabbed one from the guard shack.

"I'm going down to look at the Sam from underneath," Foster told the watch as he put on his hard hat. He was one of the few who had their own hats with their names stenciled on them.

"See ya later, Dan," the guard said.

It was obvious the guard was on friendlier terms with P.O. Foster than most on the crew. He had felt comfortable addressing him by his first name which no one else I knew would, or for that matter, wanted to. That is why the guard was not suspected of dropping the wrench.

Foster was a back stabber. He was a petty officer, first-class, torpedoman who had been assigned to the Sam when it was being built at the Electric Boat Shipyard and, therefore, one of the plank owners. He always smiled while talking to me, but when I walked away, I checked between my shoulder blades for a knife. He was instrumental in my making up my mind to get out of the Navy and pursue a career in civilian life.

I had a pocket-sized log book I always carried with me. I jotted all types of notes in it, mostly tidbits I learned while qualifying, "lead pipes," they were called. "Lead pipes" were the answers to questions that could hit you on the head if you didn't know them. I also kept in my "little green book" reasons not to re-enlist. Among the entries were several that involved P.O. Foster. That's why I didn't thank God for saving his life.

The scaffolding was set up all around the Sam, but there were no workers or other witnesses that morning. They did work around the clock, except on Sunday. When Foster walked into the shack and grabbed his hard-hat, I had been on deck talking to the watch on duty, awaiting the boat to take me to the tender for Catholic mass. The tender had a chaplain assigned, so I was able to attend mass on Sundays when I was not standing a watch. It was when I returned that I heard the news. Because I had an excuse, I was ruled out as a suspect.

A pipe wrench and Foster's hard hat were on a table in the mess hall when I came back from mass. The hard hat was caved in on the top. Threads of fiberglass reached inward through a hole that had once been the protective cover. "Foster, TM1," was stenciled in black letters across the back.

"What happened?" I asked. Larry was the only one in the mess hall at the time.

"Someone dropped that wrench from the scaffolding and it hit Foster on the top of his helmet." Larry said, pointing to each item in turn. "Doc said it would have badly injured or killed him if he hadn't had his hardhat on. Foster said he had taken his hat off to adjust it and had put it back on just before the wrench hit him."

Now, I didn't like Foster, just like most of the crew, but I wouldn't have tried to kill him.

"Wasn't it just an accident?" I asked.

"It couldn't have been," Larry said. "There was no one working today. The only possibility is that the wrench was left by some worker last night and it happened to fall today."

"That doesn't sound right," I said. "Something would have had to knock it off, a vibration or bump. Did the watch see anyone?" Before Larry had a chance to respond, Foster came into the mess hall with the XO and Lt. Inman, who happened to be the Officer of the Day.

"Where were you a half hour ago?" Foster asked, accusingly.

"Over at the tender, in church," I said.

"Yeah," the sailor who was on duty in the guard shack said as he walked into the mess hall carrying an empty coffee cup, and headed to the urn. "I was in the guard shack when he left and came back. You walked right past him when you headed down to the scaffolding."

"I'm going to talk with my tongue in my cheek here," Lt. Inman said, pointing a finger at me. "We've got to bear with each other, and if you know anything, you better show some produce."

I bit my tongue to keep from laughing and noticed the XO doing the same. Larry just closed one eye Popeye style, and turned away from us. Foster squinted as if trying to figure out what had just been said. The off duty watch, who had just filled up his cup and taken a sip, choked and walked away coughing. Inman and Foster then turned and walked away, obviously satisfied that I was not the wrench bomber.

"That man does have a way of speakin'" Captain Bob said.

"I wrote all the Jimisms I heard in my little green book," I said. "I lost my train of thought. Where was I in the story?"

"You were tellin' me about mess cookin," Captain Bob reminded me.

"Oh yeah, beginning in the morning."

"Howdy," Larry said, in response to my greeting. He was putting on his full length apron. Even though I thought "howdy" was a silly thing to say, after being around Larry I said it too, but only when I was with him. Later, when I lived in Texas for almost thirty years, I said "howdy" as consistently as Larry did.

"Hi Felix," I said to the sailor who was taking over Little Dickey's night duties as scullery. Felix had the habit of getting seasick when we were in rough seas, which allowed him to leave his post to Larry and me while he ran to the head. One thing you didn't need in a chow hall was someone barfing during a meal.

"Mornin' Cooky," I said to Drummond, the day cook.

"Is it?" was his response. Cook Drummond was always in a good mood. "What the fuck you so cheerful about and get the eggs out."

"Will do, Cooky," I said. I only had a couple of more days to mess cook and was looking forward to doing something less demeaning. Cooky was an Army transplant who was used to slopping chow for ungrateful dogfaces. He had switched over to the Navy which sent him to culinary school before he was assigned to the Sam for duty.

I had been told a story that when another submarine had surfaced underneath a ship and damaged her sail, that Cooky baked a cake shaped like a submarine, only the sail was missing. It was sent to the skipper, compliments of the crew of the Sam. There was a saying at the Academy that "a collision at sea can ruin your whole day." Cooky was just trying to cheer them up.

According to psychiatrists who had studied the first nuclear submarine sailors on extended patrols, good food was a big morale booster. It took a sailor's mind off the fact that there would be no sun for two or three months at a stretch, on a ship where the farthest distance without looking at a bulkhead was 100 feet, in the missile compartment. The Navy, therefore, made sure its submarines were supplied with the best food and cooks in the fleet.

I opened the door to the chill box, a big refrigerator about half the size of the freezer. Inside were all the refrigerated items, including thousands of eggs in crates holding a gross of the white unborn chickens in each. Eggs remained edible for the entire two-month patrol, one of the few uncooked, unfrozen foods that did. Toward the end of the patrol, I watched Cooky crack eggs that had green yokes. When Doctor Seuss wrote "Green Eggs and Ham," he must have been on a submarine. We were usually near the surface during meal time, so the green and white globs would slide around on the three- by four-foot grill until the cook dispatched them with a flick of his metal flipper into the trough at the edge. From there they would slide on the bubbling grease toward a hole and slip sickeningly into a catch basin to be tossed into the sanitary tank at the end of the meal.

I pulled out a box of eggs that was on top and took them to Cooky. After I had done that, I went to the juke box to initiate my own form of harassment. There was a Roger Miller 45 record, which I particularly liked, but had heard some of the crew grumble about every time it came on. So, before they started marching in for breakfast, I punched "Chug-a-lug" about twenty times so it would play thirty minutes straight.

"Jesus H. Christ!" Larry said, as the speakers intoned 'Chug-a-lug chug-a-lug… makes ya wanna holler hi-dee-ho…' "Did you play that song again?"

"Yep, fuck 'em," I said. "They wanna treat us like shit, they're gonna get it back."

"You'll make a good sub sailor," Cooky said overhearing our conversation. He spent all his time in the galley where other noises drowned out the music. "Let 'em up."

"Okay," I said. I went over to the top of the ladder and motioned toward the hungry looking faces with a wave of my arm. There was a stampede up the ladder. Most already had their chits filled out and passed them through the window to the cook. With the same motion, they tore off sticky buns from the sheet tray and proceeded to a table or to the coffee pot to get a cup.

After a couple of sips of coffee and a bite of his sticky bun, Clark (nicknamed Snake), an electrician who was also the sub's barber, perked up his ears when the song played again and again. Snake was from the Boston area and didn't pronounce his r's in some words. When he said his own name, it came out Clawk. I asked him to pronounce his own name and "clock" together and they sounded identical. I gave him the same exercise pronouncing drawer and draw which he did also sounding the same. He said he could tell the difference even when talking to a fellow Bostonian. I realized then how special submarines were with the mix of race and cultures serving as brothers.

Snake had one fingernail he didn't cut. It was about a quarter of an inch beyond the tip of his index finger on his right hand and it was thick and flat on the end. I asked him why he had one fingernail like that.

"It's my portable screwdriver," he said. "I use it to "tweak" the electrical meters and gauges."

Everywhere Snake went, he always had a plastic bottle of gilly with him. Gilly, also known as torpedo juice, was pure grain alcohol used originally to fuel torpedoes. The torpedoes on the Sam didn't use gilly, but we had it for use as a cleaner. Snake dangled his bottle of gilly from his mouth by the curved tube protruding from its top. He said it was for cleaning electrical contacts so we must have had the cleanest contacts in the fleet since the bottle was always going empty.

As the only barber on the sub, he was in demand most of his off duty hours. He only charged a couple of bucks to trim hair and he even did the officers' coiffures. The navigator wore a toupee, but had hair on the sides and back of his head. One day he called Snake on the intercom from the control room to make an appointment for a hair cut. Snake, referring to the man's rug top, responded, "Send it down anytime," which was heard by all in the room, causing near hysterical laughter.

"That fuckin' song's playing again," Snake said as Roger blurted out '…burns your tummy don't ya know, chug-a-lug chug-a-lug.' "Son-of-a-bitch! I'm gonna break that fuckin' box."

I almost let out a laugh, but turned around to pick up the first order that Cooky had slammed down on the counter next to the sticky buns. Just as I delivered the plate of eggs, sausages, hash browns, and pancakes, I felt the sub angle up slightly. We were heading to the surface for a star shoot.

"A star shoot?" Captain Bob asked. "You're taken pot shots at the stars with them missiles?"

"Not quite, Cap'n," I answered. "A star shoot was when the Sam came up to within fifty feet of the surface and hovered. Like an underwater helicopter it attempted to remain motionless, at least as far as depth was concerned. The navigational officer then raised the type eleven periscope which was used to find stars. From the location and height of the stars above the horizon we could get a fix on our position. Because our underwater navigational systems weren't good enough to give us an accurate position, we had to check our coordinates a few times a week. Our position had to be calculated very accurately so that we could tell the missile where it was in relationship to its intended target. Here's a diagram of the sub's periscope and all the items that penetrated the sail."

"Go on." he said, studying the diagram.

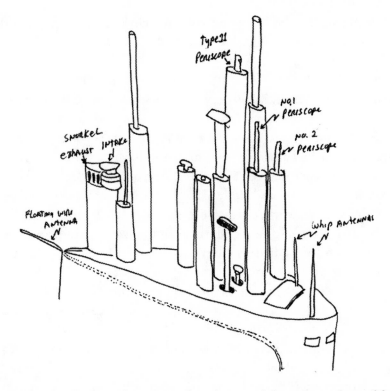

"Here we go again," Larry said, as he was delivering a plate of food to another sailor. "I wonder how rough the seas are this time?"

"It's rock and roll time," I responded as Roger sang '…juke box and sawdust floor, sumpin' like I ain't never seen ….' The ship started its slow rotation right and left as it rolled with the seas. I had learned early how to walk uphill from one side of the chow hall to the other and then wait for the deck to level out before turning around and walking uphill again. It was easier to walk on an upward slope than on a downward one and if I slipped, I could swing my hands forward to catch myself. This time the seas appeared to be a state five, with eight- to twelve-foot waves breaking over the sail.

The Sam had a huge gyro the size of a large car amidships in the lower level of the forward auxiliary room, where several pieces of mechanical/electrical equipment were installed. The gyro spun at high speeds and was supposed to stabilize the sub in rough seas, especially while it was hovering, but all the gyro did was bang loudly back and forth against its stops on each side. Since we were supposed to be undetected when out on patrol, it was used once during the first patrol and then it was turned off. In addition to being a noise maker, it didn't perform as designed. When we went to the shipyard it was cut up and taken out.

Just as I made the comment about rock and roll, Ski, a short stocky machinist's mate, who's real name was Jasinski, came wandering in from the engine room with a number ten can tied around his neck. He hailed from the coal mining area of Pennsylvania and was built like a fireplug. He had a bent nose rumored to have been broken in a bar fight and was unchallenged as the strongest man on the ship. He had a nasty scar running the length of his left arm as a result of a juggling act with a chain saw when he fell off a ladder while cutting a tree limb. He had no discernable neck and had arms the size of most people's legs. The two-inch hydraulic line running in the overhead above his bunk was bent downward from his grabbing on to it to lift himself into his bunk. He told us that at home he was the runt of the litter. This was confirmed after my second patrol when we arrived in New London after our flight from Scotland. His brother and sister, both bigger and taller, were there to greet him when he stepped off the bus from the airport. No enlisted men messed with Ski or even kidded around with him, except the COB that is.

His only outwardly displayed weakness was seasickness. Therefore, when he was out of his bunk at star-shooting time, he tied a number ten can (about the size of a large coffee tin) around his neck so he could upchuck into it instead of on the deck. The rule was, each person was responsible for cleaning up his own puke, even if you were sick as a dog and cleaning it up made you puke some more. It was unusual to see Ski around the chow hall in rough seas, so he must have been really hungry. He got a cup of coffee and sat (to the relief of all those eating breakfast) at an empty table.

"I gotta go to the head," Felix said as he tore out of the scullery and headed down the ladder toward crew's berthing, pushing aside those trying to make their way up the ladder. He didn't wear a number ten can because a can full of puke was not a good thing to have around a sink full of dishes, dirty or not.

"Fatso, get in here," Cooky said, obviously pissed off at Felix but taking it out on his other mess cooks. I never got seasick, no matter how hard I tried. There were few who could claim that. There was one fire-control technician, however, a skinny, tall black man named Robertson, who, like me, never got sick. Just to harass the others, during one particularly rough state-seven or state-eight sea, he and I sat together for one meal where tomato soup was being served. We both put slices of American cheese in our soup. Long strings of melting cheese draped in red soup oozed off our spoons as we slowly lifted them to our mouths. We both had full beards, and the cheesy soup clung to our whiskers in slimy strands. We cleared the tables with our performance, but, even though he was amused, Cooky forbade a second act for the next group coming off watch.

Damn it, I thought. *Mess cooking is bad enough, but scullery duty is the pits.* At least forty plates with the accompanying flatware, cups, serving plates, pots and pans had to be washed and dried. After the first eating shift, all the necessary eating items had to be cleaned, dried, and set out before the off-coming watch could eat.

Scullery rats, as they were called, wore long rubber gloves because the wash and rinse water was scalding. The water in the two sinks sloshed around in the rough sea, so that by the time I had washed half a dozen plates, I was soaking wet from the waist down and the deck was slippery with soapy water. And when I was done washing all the on-going shift's dirty dishes, I had to start all over again with the off-coming shift and the rest of the crew.

Clean plates and cups were stowed above the two sinks on metal shelves made to take the rolling motion of the sub without falling to the deck and breaking. Even so, care had to be taken placing the fragile-as-glass dishes in the racks. Too many broken plates meant there were no spare dishes for the next seating group and everything dirtied in the first shift had to be cleaned and ready for reuse by the second group of sailors.

No matter what care was taken, in a rough sea one or two dishes would hit the ceramic-tile deck of the scullery, shattering into a thousand shards which had to await cleanup until there was a break in the action. I was amazed when, more than once, a coffee cup would fall to the deck from six feet and just bounce two or three times coming to rest unbroken. Other times all it took was a slight bump to destroy the ceramic cups and dishes.

I had to make sure all the soap was off the dishes because if it wasn't rinsed off completely, the "non-ionic" soap used would give the entire crew the shits as if we all had mild dysentery. One drop of the soap could foam up enough to wash an entire load of plates, especially since the water from the distillery was very soft. I made the mistake once of trying to wipe up some spilled non-ionic soap with a wet cloth. It was impossible. The only way to clean the soap was with a dry cloth. Once, Felix (and I swear he did it on purpose) didn't properly rinse the plates, and the entire enlisted crew came down with the shits. It was so bad, empty buckets were used as toilets in the engine room where there was only one head and those on duty couldn't leave their posts long enough to come forward to the next closest toilet in the missile compartment.

So there I was, slipping and sliding while trying to get everything washed for the next group of eaters. Larry had to do double duty delivering the plates of food to those sitting down,

"Where's the other mess cook?" the booming voice of the COB asked.

"He's down in the crapper pukin'," said Cooky.

"Again?" said the COB. "Goddamn-son-of-a-bitch! I'm reassigning his sorry ass."

He did reassign him to the laundry, which was really a cushy job. He sat on his ass all day watching the washing machines and dryers spin. No one bothered him and we hardly knew he was there until he once failed to keep the lint traps clean starting a fire. After that he was booted off the Sam as unsuitable for duty in submarines. I got even, though, before that happened.

"How did ya do that?" Captain Bob asked.

The Sam was in Cocoa Beach Florida at Cape Canaveral (later renamed Cape Kennedy and then again Cape Canaveral) to shoot a missile. While tied up to the pier, we had port and starboard duty. I was a missile technician then and was so busy getting a telemetric bird (missile without a warhead) ready to launch, I only got ashore one night. Larry and I went to a topless bar and just stared at the tits all night and drank beer. I had never seen a real live woman's bare chest before and when one walked right up to our table and the big round nipples stared at me, I was hypnotized and almost starched my skivvies.

I believe Larry was as naive as I since he couldn't get his eyes back in his head either. I didn't know it then, but Cape Canaveral in the mid sixties was a wide-open town.

The next night around one thirty in the morning, I was on topside watch as part of my duty day when a cab pulled up to the dock by our gangway. Out poured a cab load of drunken sailors, one of whom was Felix, another was Kozy. After they stumbled around and collected enough money for the driver, they headed for the sub. Kozy was so drunk, he missed the brow by about three feet and slammed head first into the side of the hull and bounced into the water.

"Man overboard, starboard side!" I shouted to Larry, the watch by the guard shack, and to anyone else who was around. *Why do these fuckin' things always happen when I'm on duty?*

Larry grabbed the telephone which was connected to the officer of the watch below decks and relayed the information. He then headed for the side of the ship and jumped in feet first after Kozy. I was headed for the gangway about fifty feet away where the other drunken sailors were shouting "Swim, Kozy, swim!"

By the time I got to the side of the sub, the officer of the watch and another sailor armed with a Thompson sub-machine gun were on deck. The gun was for shooting hungry sharks that might be in the area homing in on Kozy flailing around in the water. Even though blood was gushing from his forehead he was doing a half decent job of treading water. I held onto a mooring line and reached down as far as I could to see if I could grab the flailing man. Larry had reached him by this time and had a good grip on him. I was able to grab Larry's free hand and hold onto him as he kept a tight grip on Kozy.

Now we had a daisy chain of sailors with Kozy on the end. Larry pulled him to where I could let go of Larry's hand and grab Kozy by the flap on the back of his sailor blouse. The others who had run on deck at the sound of the man overboard alarm grabbed me and hoisted both of us to safety. Larry was able to grab a safety doughnut attached to a lifeline tossed to him by one of the other rescuers. In seconds, all were safe aboard the sub as sirens sounded in the distance.

The ambulance pulled up along side the brow as two sober shipmates carried Kozy off the Sam using the same brow he had missed just minutes before. He was strapped to a gurney as the ambulance attendants applied a compress to his still bleeding head.

"Where're the nurses? Bring on the goddamn nurses!" came the sound from the ambulance as Kozy was loaded aboard realizing he was on his way to the hospital.

"Crazy son of bitch," I said.

The rest of the rescue party had gone below decks realizing the excitement was over. Larry went below decks too, since he was soaking wet. It was time to change the watch, so as soon as I finished the logbook entry I also went below. The entire crew knew already what had happened. When I got down to the missile compartment, I learned from one of the others who was with Kozy and Felix that they had been at a place called the Tiki Club. As the story was related to me, Kozy was already drunk when they arrived. At the entrance to the club were two large crossed bamboo poles as part of the decorations. Kozy took one of the poles, put it between his legs and walked into the club shouting, "God's cock!" Since that didn't get them kicked out, they proceeded to get even drunker.

Felix, who had a wife and two children, was drunk enough to get on a table and dance with a topless waitress, who did it for the tips. That was all the information I needed to get even with Felix.

The next morning, I was in the chow hall when a hung-over Felix entered to get a cup of coffee and some of the magic potions the doc set out for those "not feeling so well." Bennies (Benzedrine) and some other vitamins were all it took for the cure. As soon as he had filled his cup and sat down, I approached him and began my little get-even-with-Felix plot.

"Hey, Felix," I said with a big smile. "This is no shit. I saw your picture in the paper this morning."

"What?" he asked.

"Yeah, a reporter for the UP was in town to do a report on the night life in Cape Canaveral and was at the Tiki Club when you did your little table dance. Your full length picture and the back of the girl you were dancing with was front page news. I could tell it was you and that she was obviously topless."

"Bullshit," he said. I didn't think he was going to believe me until Yakovelli chimed in. Yako was another missile technician from the gold crew who had joined us for the missile shoot.

"Yeah," Yako said. "I saw it too. It had to be national and is probably on every paper in the States." Yako was not in on my scheme, but being a good sailor and a Paisan, he just decided to play along with whatever I said.

"Where's the paper?" Felix asked in a panic.

"I think it's back in the missile compartment," I answered.

Felix got up and left as Yako and I just grinned at each other.

I thought, *Well hell, I got him going. Running that paper down ought to keep him busy for awhile.* I hadn't told anyone else that I was going to play a joke on Felix, but it seemed that everyone went along and some even added to the story.

"What paper?" was the response when Felix got to the missile compartment and found the watch at the missile control panel.

"The paper with me dancing on a table with a bare-chested waitress," was Felix's answer.

"Oh, that paper," they said. "I think I saw it in the engine room."

So it went on most of the morning until Felix so believed the story that he called his wife and confessed lest she get a surprise seeing him in the news in all his drunken glory. I didn't know when he walked into the chow hall for dinner that he had called his wife. I had a guilty feeling so, I told him the story was made up.

"You bastard!" he screamed. "I called my wife and told her! Goddamn you! She bawled her eyes out. You son-of-a-bitch! Goddamn you, goddamn you, goddamn you!"

"What the fuck," I said turning to the rest of the crowd watching the scene unfold. "When I told him about the picture, I started out with 'this is no shit.' I guess I shoulda said 'once upon a time.'"

Felix left with the chow hall in an uproar of laughter from the others who by now knew about the joke. I really did feel vindicated, but somehow was ashamed for what I had done. I had no idea he would feel so guilty that he would confess to his wife before he actually found a newspaper and realized it wasn't true.

"That were a nasty trick, but can't say's why I don't blame ya." Captain Bob said. "You was talkin' about that star shoot."

"Oh yeah," I said, and continued with the story. "You need to look at the picture of the trash compactor I showed you earlier for part of this story."

The star shoot lasted a long time because of the rough seas, but by the time the off-going watch was almost done eating, we had leveled out at our cruising depth of 150 feet, plus or minus, depending on the thermal layer. When cruising, we always tried to get below a thermal layer to remain undetected. A thermal layer was a point in the water where two different temperatures met and cruising below that temperature change caused noise to reflect downward. The only way to hear a sub below a thermal layer was to drop a listening device that floated below the layer and sent information to the surface.

After cleaning up the chow hall, we had time to load a few trash cans and got permission to load the GDU. This was a chore I actually enjoyed. Putting all types of rubbish into the four-foot long by ten-inch diameter can and then crushing it gave me some satisfaction. I went to the trash room and loaded one of the preformed cans into the compactor metal jacket, closed it and latched it. Larry had gone to the con to ask permission to use the crusher, load the GDU, and jettison the canisters.

Five canisters fit in the GDU chamber and since four canisters had been compacted by Little Dickey last night, I only needed to make one more. I loaded the GDU weights into the bottom of the empty canister. A couple of seven-pound steel weights were needed to make sure the trash didn't surface, disclosing our location. I then loaded the first batch of cardboard, bottles, cans, and slats of wood from the cardboard boxes. I envisioned that the surface of the ocean would gradually rise over the years because the bottom was filling up with trash.

"Go ahead," Larry said, peeking into the trash room.

"Okay," I said with a nod. My right hand was already on the handle of the hydraulic valve which would shove the plunger down and crush whatever was in its path. I had heard stories about careless mess cooks getting their hands crushed by the machine, so I was careful to keep my left hand out of the way.

The noise was music to a trash man's ears. The loud popping and smashing went on for about ten seconds until the plunger could go no further. I raised the plunger and saw that the rubbish was one tenth the size of what it had been. I repeated the process, but saved some space at the top to place a little "present" for the sonarman.

The sonarman on duty had come on board the Sam the same time as us, was lower in rank, and three years younger. Because he had excellent hearing, he was selected to be a sonarman. There was a shortage of sonarmen so he bypassed a tour of mess cooking and sat in a comfortable chair for six hours listening to fish fuck. I was going to get even.

At the top of the canister, I loaded a ketchup bottle, making sure the lid was screwed on really tight. I chose a ketchup bottle because the glass was thicker and it could withstand more pressure than a thinner bottle. Then, without crushing it, I put the metal lid on top of the canister and bent the tabs over securing it to the can sides. Now I was ready to load all five canisters into the GDU.

"Hey Larry, get the GDU ready," I said peering out of the trash room.

I handed Captain Bob a diagram of the GDU

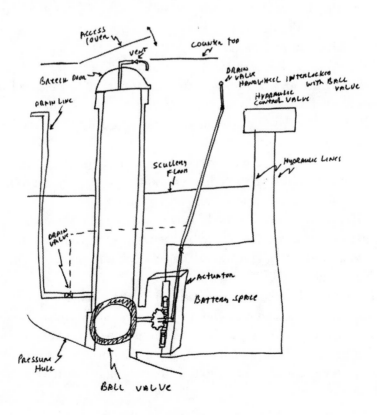

This was really a dangerous operation. If the ball valve was open or leaked when the breech door was opened the ocean would come pouring in. At one hundred and fifty feet, the water pressure is around seventy pounds per square inch, not a lot, but on a twelve-inch diameter surface the pressure exerted is almost four tons. If the hatch was opened, not even Ski could close it. Therefore, an officer had to be present during the operation to ensure the safety of the boat.

I approached the GDU with one of the canisters not containing the "present" for the sonarman. I was saving the ketchup-bottle canister to place on top so the weight of the other canisters wouldn't break the bottle. Larry was with the weapons officer, Lt. Inman, who also was the boat's safety officer.

"Let's do this right," Inman said. "I don't want to look bad in the captain's face."

I looked at Larry and he was smiling too. The weapons officer was again exhibiting his special talent for malapropisms and mixing metaphors.

"Yes, sir. You can't cry over spilt milk, but you can cry before it's spilt, right sir?" I responded, repeating one of his prior "Jimisms" as we liked to call his way of speaking.

"Right," he said, acting as if he understood perfectly what I had said. I thought Larry was going to injure himself holding back a laugh. "Verify the ball valve is closed."

"Ball valve closed," Larry said. I set down the canister I was carrying and went back for another.

"Vent the GDU," Inman said. Larry opened the small vent valve in the top of the GDU breach door. A loud hissing emanated from the valve releasing the air pressure trapped inside the tube.

"GDU vented and equalized," Larry said, when the hissing stopped. This meant the breach door could be opened safely. No water came out of the vent, indicating that the ball valve was not leaking.

"Open the GDU," Inman said.

Larry turned the locking ring and opened the hatch. If somehow the ball valve opened now, an emergency blow of all ballast tanks would be necessary to save the sub. Also, the compartment we were in would have to be isolated and pressurized to prevent further flooding. Even then, the water could come in so fast that we might not have a chance to get to the surface quickly enough. Water tends to seek its own level, so at one hundred fifty feet down, it wants to shoot up one hundred fifty feet. The force of the inrushing water would be so great those in the immediate proximity of the GDU most likely would die. The ball valve was mechanically locked with the locking ring, so, in theory, the two couldn't be opened at the same time. If the proper procedure was not followed, the old adage 'if anything can go wrong, it will' applied. There was no fucking around with the GDU and everybody knew it.

By then I had lined up all the canisters in front of the GDU. Larry grabbed the first one and slid it into the tube. Air rushed out around the canister as it eased its way down to the ball valve. The air already in the tube cushioned the falling canister so it didn't hit the ball valve with enough force to damage it. A splash was heard, indicating that the canister was at the bottom partially submerged in water left from the previous trash ejection. The rest of the canisters were loaded in succession. I loaded the last one with my "present" for the sonarman.

"Close the GDU," Inman said. Larry closed the GDU and rotated the locking ring.

"GDU closed and locked, sir," Larry said.

"Flood the GDU," Inman said. Larry turned a small valve which allowed seawater to flow into the GDU. The pressure in the GDU had to be equalized with sea pressure so that a water hammer didn't damage the top of the GDU.

"What's this here water hammer mean?" Captain Bob asked, while shifting the pipe in his mouth.

"It's the noise heard when a valve is opened or closed too quickly exposing liquid inside a pipe to high pressure. The longer the piece of pipe, the more the chance of a hammer occurring. It happens more with ball valves that are used on the submarine. They can fully open and close very quickly and there are a lot of long runs of high pressure piping on a sub. One of the jokes played on a new man is to ask him to get a water hammer. The unsuspecting person will scour the sub asking everyone where he can get one. As soon as the question is asked, he is sent on to someone else until he is told what it means.

"One such episode involved a new missile tech who was sent looking for a water hammer. In the engine room he was handed a relatively heavy shaft jacking tool, which he shouldered and headed forward to the missile compartment. In the tunnel above the reactor one of the reactor operators, who had witnessed the prank, tossed some distilled water on the deck and told him to stand still.

"'You're standing in radioactive water and are contaminated,' the man was told. 'Don't move.'

"The poor man stood there holding the jack on his shoulder while they did a simulated contamination drill. They even had him put on a contamination suit and booties and then took him to the missile compartment. There they had him strip and stand in a shower still holding the jack.

"I was told that a water hammer test had been done on the very first sub that had a GDU. The test was done after construction, during sea trials, at design depth which is the deepest the sub can go before bad things will happen. The ball valve on the GDU was cycled without equalization. That meant it was opened and closed as fast as the hydraulics could operate it. At fifteen hundred feet, the water pressure was six hundred sixty four pounds per square inch or thirty seven tons on the GDU breech door. During the test, the high-pressure sea water rushed in so fast it created a slug of water like a hammer (a very large hammer) hitting the top of the hatch on the inside. The top of the GDU jumped almost a foot from the massive force. The test was never repeated, as several officers and shipyard engineers had had to change their pants afterward."

"GDU flooded," Larry said as the sound of inrushing water stopped.

"Open the ball valve," Inman said. Larry turned the valve that opened the ball valve. There was no water hammer this time. The weight of the trash canisters took them out past the ball valve and toward the bottom of the ocean.

"Blow the GDU," Inman said. Larry opened yet another valve and high-pressure air forced out the water that had been let in during equalization. Not all of the water was to be forced out. If any air escaped the GDU, bubbles would be sent to the surface giving our position away. Hopefully all the canisters were on their way to Davy Jones' locker. If one got hung up in the ball valve as it exited, we would not be able to use the GDU the rest of the patrol. Then, trash canisters would be stored wherever room could be found until we threw them overboard when we surfaced at the end of the patrol.

When not quite all the water was out, a guess at best, Larry shut the valve.

"GDU blown clean," he said.

"Close the ball valve," Inman said. By now my "present" was approaching a depth where sea pressure would implode the bottle. I would have my revenge on the sensitive ears of the sonarman.

Pop! I barely heard the sound of the imploding bottle. The unmistakable sound was probably missed by all aboard unless they were expecting it. However, to the super sensitive ears of the sonarman with an amplified headset on, it sounded like a cannon going off right next to his head. *Score another one for the harasser*, I thought.

"Ball valve closed," Larry said.

"Secure the GDU," Inman said as he was leaving the mess hall.

That's when the sonarman came bounding down the ladder from the control room, mad as hell.

"Who loaded the GDU?" he asked.

At the same time, Larry and I both responded, "I did."

Seeing he was outnumbered and severely outweighed, he just flipped us the bird and stormed back up the ladder. He could have reported us, but that was not done on a sub. It was an unwritten code among the enlisted ranks, that you dished out and took harassment without squealing. Hopefully by the end of the patrol you broke even. If not, there was the next patrol and three months to plan revenge. Those that didn't put up with it didn't have anybody to talk to. That could make a two-month patrol a very long and unpleasant ordeal.

It turns out the skipper caused the ultimate harassment of the entire crew, and he did it more than once a patrol.

"How did he do that?" Captain Bob asked.

"With a procedure called a 'bailout', which was normally done during the pre-patrol shakedown cruise," I responded. "Here's how that went."

"Rig ship for small angles," came the sound over the 1MC.

"Oh shit!" I said. Larry and I had just set up the tables for the night meal. Tonight was meatloaf night, so bowls of mashed potatoes, gravy, plates of sliced meatloaf, and ketchup bottles were set, one for each table. Also all the place settings, flatware, dishes, and cups were ready, eight sets at each table.

"Call 'em up!" Cooky said. If the tables were full of hungry sailors, they would be able to grab and hold onto the plates of food and their own plates while the skipper, "Angles-n-Dangles" Brooks, went through his routine of thirty up and thirty down. Those are the angles he considered "small." I believed he picked chow time because of the watch change, the most vulnerable time, to test crew readiness.

The sailors were on their way up the ladder before I could wave them up. They knew if they didn't save the food on the tables, they might not get a hot meal before going on watch. In six hours they could have mid-rats, rations served at midnight, but that was catch-as-catch-can. I was relieved, as were Cooky and Larry, that almost all the places were filled and hands had already secured the loose items. Felix drained the wash and rinse sinks because angles as steep as thirty degrees would dump most of the water on the deck. Then it started.

"How'd he get that name, Angles-n-Dangles?" Captain Bob asked.

"Here is his picture," I said and handed Captain Bob a photograph of my dolphin ceremony during my second patrol. "We're standing in front of the entrances to the freezer and chill boxes. This was the middle of the patrol and, since I had been mess cooking previously, my beard is just getting started. I had also just finished a two-week hunger strike and lost about twelve pounds. I'll tell you more about the strike later."

Angles-n-Dangles Brooks had been a skipper of the older diesel fleet boats. He was my height and thin, with a receding hair line and rarely smiled. He was noted for his postulate that it always took at least two events to go wrong to produce a tragedy.

I was told that he was the skipper of the submarine shown at the beginning of the old "Silent Service" TV series.

One of the opening scenes of that series was a submarine broaching the surface almost half out of the water from one of his "thirty up and thirty down" exercises. The scene stopped as the submarine stalled like an airplane, dangling in mid air at a forty-eight degree up angle, water pouring from her bow buoyancy tank. The crew inside was probably clinging for dear life to anything that was attached securely to a bulkhead. What wasn't shown next was that the sub, after stalling, went back down stern first almost below her test depth.

That was when the skipper got the name Angles-n-Dangles, which no one dared call him to his face. We were told he had plans to try to get a submarine to do a complete loop and roll so that it would be headed back in the opposite direction at the same depth as when it started the maneuver. This would require the sub to be upside down until it rolled around and was upright again. The only reason he supposedly didn't attempt the maneuver was because the batteries would have spilled acid in the upside down position.

I remember being on duty in the control room one early morning when I had to report to the skipper all the sonar contact positions. This is normal, but it was two-thirty in the morning and the captain was asleep. I had five contacts to report and was a little apprehensive about waking the captain just to tell him what ships were in the area. I was briefed by the navigator and went over the bearings, size of the contacts, and range of each several times before I approached the wardroom and knocked three times on his door.

"Enter," he said.

My days at the Naval Academy had trained me to knock three times, enter when called, take three steps forward, stand at attention, stare straight ahead, and speak. I entered the darkened stateroom, took the three steps, and gave him my spiel. I wondered if he was awake or if he even gave a shit about the information I had just fed him.

"Tell the officer on deck to steer a course of zero niner zero and slow to three knots.

"Aye, Aye, sir," was my response.

Incredibly enough, he had taken in all the information and calculated a new course. No wonder all on board had a lot of respect for him. As I was taught, I took one step back, did an about face, and left the stateroom, closing the door behind me.

"So, what happened after this bail-out procedure started?" Captain Bob said.

Our first motion was down. Because we had practiced the maneuver in the simulator in New London, we knew the helmsman and planesman were strapping on their seat belts, which were primarily for usage in severely rough seas. A bubble indicator on the bulkhead over the entrance to the galley started to show a down angle. As it went past twenty degrees, the Sam started to groan. It was a deep, crunching noise much like the sound of an earthquake moments before the earth starts to shake.

When the bubble passed twenty-five degrees, the sound of unsecured items breaking loose could be heard. Next time those items, if not broken, would be strapped down or otherwise secured when the "rig ship for small angles" warning was given.

When we reached thirty degrees, it was almost impossible to remain standing without bracing a foot or holding onto a stationary object. Those sitting at the tables were holding onto the food bowls and other loose objects with both hands while their legs stretched out to brace their bodies. The ones sitting with their backs toward the bow were almost lying on the table. Those with their backs to the stern were leaning way back.

I heard thumping footsteps approaching the chow hall from the stern as if someone were running downhill. I looked over to see one of the new men trying to stop his forward progress as he headed across the deck of the chow hall. He was flailing in all directions trying to grab something to hold on to like a drowning man reaching in all directions for a floating object.

"Oh! Oh! Oh!" was all he could say as he gained speed across the vinyl deck. The last I saw of him was his butt and then his legs as his knees hit the bottom edge of the torpedo room hatch. He catapulted out of the chow hall and crashed into the closest torpedo, setting on its cradle. Immediately behind him was a fire extinguisher that had broken loose from its rack. It smashed into the bottom of the torpedo room hatch. Luckily for the new man, it didn't follow him through; otherwise he would really have been hurt.

Then the angle started to come off and we leveled out. I ran to the torpedo room hatch and grabbed the fire extinguisher, opened the door to the trash room, and tossed it inside so it wouldn't head back the other direction when the angle started back up. Luckily we had emptied the trash that morning which kept loose objects from making a mess in that room.

We hadn't stayed horizontal for longer than fifteen seconds when the nose of the sub started its ascent, giving us an up angle. Everything then reversed its movement. I heard the loose extinguisher crashing against the bulkhead in the trash room, but it wasn't going anywhere else. The up angle didn't seem as bad as the down angle, but we did get to thirty degrees. There was more creaking and groaning from the Sam, but she was holding together.

One more angle and then were through. I thought. Usually we went through one down, one up, and one down. Then we leveled out to our normal cruise depth and speed, but this time would be different. We started our down angle, but when we got close to the thirty degree mark, we heard the most dreaded announcement any submariner wants to hear next to "Flooding …"

"Bailout," came the screech over the 1MC. Bailout was a procedure used as a last resort to pull a sub out of an uncontrolled dive. In a real emergency, all ballast tanks were blown to make the sub as buoyant as possible. During a drill, as this was, the ballast tanks were not blown, which would allow air to escape the tanks and go to the surface giving our position away. At the same time, the screw was placed in "all back full" to stop and reverse the dive. The diving planes (flaps that make a sub go up and down) were set to the neutral position so as not to interfere with the backward ascent.

The sub began to shudder as the screw came to an all stop and then started to reverse. The screw started to cavitate as bubbles formed and collapsed making a clapping sound heard from stern to stem as the sea was forced forward.

Not only did we have a thirty-degree down angle, but we were decelerating. The forces were too strong for the seated diners to hold onto the food. Everything moveable headed for the forward bulkhead, leaving the tables nearly empty. Sailors ducked as items flew by in a colorful array of potatoes, gravy, meatloaf, and ketchup bottles. Crashing and smashing was the order of the day as all the food hit the bulkhead and smeared its way down to the deck like a banquet painted by Picasso.

The trajectory was low enough to miss the juke box, but one of the ketchup bottles hit the buttons on the front. Amongst all the noise, a distinct, familiar sound emanated from the two speakers "…Chug-a-lug, chug-a-lug, makes ya wanna holler hi-dee-ho…" I would have burst out laughing had it not been for the thought of the mess Larry and I would have to clean up when this was all over.

I could feel the force pulling us backward and upward as I held onto the table I had grabbed as soon as bailout was announced. The sub then did a slow up and down motion as it leveled out and rolled to the left and then right. I realized then that we had broached the surface and were riding on the waves. We had popped up like a cork.

"Surface, surface, surface," the 1MC blurted out. We were not supposed to be on the surface during patrol, but this was Captain Brooks' sub, and he did what he pleased. This was a drill (practice session) and not the real thing. The real thing was to come later.

"The drill is over. Restore conditions to normal," came the announcement.

"Restore conditions to normal!" Cooky blurted out. "We got a fucking mess down here and half the food is gone!"

"Need some help?" Little Dickey said emerging from aft. He was supposed to come on duty anyway so he had hurried forward after the bailout to see if he could help. He had been through a real bailout on his tour of duty on the gold crew. Ironically he had been mess cooking and the same scenario with the food happened. He remembered the date because it was Friday the thirteenth in November, 1964. That bailout had occurred because of a stern planes failure and there would be another.

"Sure as fuck can use some help," I said as we both headed for the bulkhead to pick up the big pieces. At least the mess was concentrated on the bulkhead and deck and not all over the place. Instead of serving a meal, we had smashed potatoes, mangled meatloaf, glopped up gravy, and crashed ketchup to clean.

"…sumpin' like I ain't never seen, and I'm just goin' on fifteen…," Roger continued his song. The sailor who had flipped into the torpedo room came through the hatch holding a bloody forehead and heading for the doc's office. He would remember what "rig ship for small angles" and "bailout" meant next time and grab the closest anchor instead of trying to stroll around like a thirty-degree down angle was a walk in the park.

Larry picked up the unbroken bowls so Cooky could reload them and feed the already-seated, on-coming watch with what was left in the galley intended for the next wave of diners. The off-going watch would get horse-cock sandwiches instead of meatloaf and mashed potatoes.

"What did ya do when ya wasn't mess cookin'?" Captain Bob asked.

"That's when I went through the sub, learning every system, pipe, and valve. I would do that until about one in the morning and then hit my bunk and get some badly needed sleep. About four hours into my sleep, Little Dickey, the night baker's helper, would wake me up."

When Little Dickey woke me in the morning, it was time for me to get ready for my fifteen-hour mess-cooking chores. The bunk beds on a submarine were long enough, but they were vertically and laterally the equivalent in size to the inside of a refrigerator. Potential submarine sailors could not be too tall or too short, but girth was not considered.

The bunks were stacked three high which meant the top bunk was at bad-breath level for someone standing next to it, the lower bunk was at bad foot-odor level, which left the middle bunk at bad-ass level. I had the bad-breath level which was hardest to get into unless I used the other bunks like a ladder by putting one foot on the bad-foot level and one in the bad-ass level.

Some upper bunks had exposed pipes in the overhead. If there was a pipe or two, they were great to grab hold of and use to swing up, over, and into the top bunk. As I mentioned earlier, Ski had one above his bunk which was permanently bent from they way he used it.

Now, this is no shit. Those in the middle and lower bunks, who were the same size as I, had to decide whether they wanted to lie on their backs or stomachs before climbing in. Once in, there was not enough room between the bunk and the one above to roll over without damaging a hip or shoulder. The upper bunks in the missile compartment had an open space above them so I had enough room in my bunk to roll over. There were curtains on tracks that ran the length of the bunk from foot to head which could be slid to provide privacy and block out any light from the passageway.

The mattress on the submarine was the thickness of the meatloaf at a cheap diner. Access to the mattress was through a zippered waterproof plastic, tarp-like covering which was hardly ever opened. I guess the intent was that if the sub went down and you were in the bed inside the tarp you could zip yourself in and would stay dry until rescued.

There were so many drills, like battle stations missile, battle stations torpedo, fire, nuclear spill, etc. that we always slept in our poopie suits. Even the old man slept in his poopie suit.

"What's a poopie suit," Captain Bob asked.

"It's a one-piece navy blue jump suit that, once underway, everyone wore, even the skipper. You can see both of us wearing them in the picture of me getting my dolphins. The suit had buttons from the crotch to the waist and Velcro closures up to the neck. They were so comfortable and stretched such that you could get fat and not even be aware of it. That's how I got to weigh two hundred and forty pounds my first patrol without feeling my clothes getting tighter. So, except when showering, we wore our poopie suits."

Only the very quick, the very stupid, or the very sick took off their poopie suits, unzipped the tarp bags, and slept between sheets. Sleeping with the poopie suit on, it was easy to just jump out of bed, put on your shoes, and go to your duty station, so most people slept on top of the mattress cover.

I learned my lesson not to turn my head to the side when sleeping. I did it once with my pillow still under the tarp-like covering. The pressure in the sub is constantly changing so when I tried to get out of bed, the air pressure was lower than when I had gone to sleep. The lower pressure caused my ear to attach to the plastic-covered pillow like a bowling ball to an Oreck vacuum cleaner. And this is no shit; I had to use a needle to poke through the plastic to equalize the pressure so I could release my ear. From that time on, I slept on my back with my pillow outside the bag.

In addition to emergencies and drills the 1MC was also used to announce all the events on the sub. It was used for such important events as, fire in the laundry, flooding in the engine room, explosion in forward torpedo room, as well as pizza and casino night. The speakers had the fidelity of those at a fast-food restaurant's drive-through window and were called squawk boxes for that reason. So that none of the crew would miss an announcement, the speakers for the 1MC were placed every six or seven feet and the volume was turned up to several decibels above the threshold of pain. Being at the bad-breath level, I had one of the speakers right next to my ear beside my bunk bed.

There was a light in each bunk just above the pillow. It was size and shape of the cardboard container for a dozen eggs. Covering the tiny fluorescent tubes was a cross-hatched metal grate that, when lying on my back was a mere two inches above my face. When I looked directly at it I got the impression that I was face to face with the grill from a '55 Chevy. It was nearly impossible to read using this light unless the occupant was near-sighted and had short arms, but we did it anyway.

At least I was easy to awaken. Some men became violent if they were touched while they slept. You were quick to learn who could and couldn't be roused with a light shake of the shoulder. For the others, their curtain was pulled back and their bunk light was turned on hoping that was enough. Sometimes it was necessary to return several times to make sure the man was awake and getting ready for his watch. It seemed like the violent ones and those difficult to wake were the ones who bitched most about missing a meal when they slept through a wake up call.

So, after I mess cooked from five a.m. to eight p.m. and qualified submarines until after midnight, Little Dickey, the night mess cook, came by a little after four, to get my sorry ass up to relieve him. Almost every time he woke me up he stood there, looking at me, laughing. Three weeks into the cruise, I would awake to some of the crew also laughing along with Little Dickey. It took me a while of staring at my sleepy face in the mirror while brushing my teeth and wondering what the hell those cross-hatched marks on my forehead were, to finally figure it out. After my shower, the marks disappeared, but one day I had a brain fart and put two and two together. So I confronted little Dickey with my guess at what was going on. After his tears of laughter subsided, he confirmed my conclusion.

Because of the lack of sleep, I slept so soundly that when he came to wake me, Little Dickey would pull back my curtain and turn on the light above my head. Startled by the sudden brightness, I would try to sit straight up from a lying position, and would crack my head straight into the "Chevy grill." I would hit it so hard, it would leave marks on my forehead and I would immediately go down for the count as if I were hit by Cassius Clay. He then would have to rouse me again until finally I awoke, a little less startled this time. Not remembering his first attempt to wake me, I would slide out of the bunk avoiding the grill the second time. Meanwhile he was laughing his ass off. It took me long enough to figure it out, in the meantime, he had most of the crew witness the event. I guess entertainment comes cheap on the sub and I was glad I provided some humor along the way. To this day, I cannot look a '55 Chevy in the grill without grabbing my forehead.

"So that was my first patrol," I said. "I mess cooked and stood planesman watches in the control room."

"What about this R&R period," Captain Bob asked.

"Because of our wasted time and talent when we were used as mess cooks instead of missile technicians, Little Dickey and I had gone on a radio show back in Winooski after our first patrol together."

During our first R&R, Little Dickey wanted to go to the west coast. I wanted to visit my family whom I hadn't seen in a year. First we went to see his parents in Vermont. His mother was an adorable, short, feisty, Italian who made gnocchi for us our first night there. The gnocchi were shaped with a fork making ridges along one side, not rolled into a rope and cut into small cubes like my Italian mother and Italian grandmothers made. However, it didn't matter what they looked like, they tasted great. The next day, we were listening to a talk show on the local Burlington radio station. The program was about waste in the federal government.

"I feel like calling that show and complaining about the wasted money the government has spent on us," I said.

"Whada ya mean?" Little Dickey said.

"We've been to three schools, counting sub school, and are supposed to be highly trained technicians. What do they do? They stick us with mess cooking and driving the sub instead of letting us use our skills," I said.

"Go ahead. Call 'em up."

I dialed the number mentioned during the broadcast and explained our situation to the man who answered the phone. He wasn't the man on the radio, but said they were interested in talking to us and invited us to be on the radio with the host tomorrow at noon.

"They want us to come to a restaurant in Burlington tomorrow at noon to talk to us live on the radio," I said to Little Dickey.

"You're shittin' me?" he said.

I was glad I was holding the palm of my hand over the phone's mouth piece, so the man I was talking too didn't hear the cuss word.

"No I'm not shittin' you. I think we ought ta go."

"Sure. Tell 'em yes."

The next day at eleven thirty, we put on our uniforms and drove to the address given to us. The restaurant was on the bottom floor of an old mill that had been converted into shops and restaurants. The talk show host was seated at an oversized table with a microphone in front of him. There was a transmitter off to the side operated by an assistant. Patrons were at tables around the host's table.

We introduced ourselves and he invited us to order from the menu, his treat. We each took a menu and my eyes lit up when I saw what the special of the day was.

"I'll have sweetbreads," I told the waiter when he came to the table.

"Where did you acquire a taste for sweetbreads?" the talk-show host asked.

"When I was a lot younger, my father used to bring them home from the butcher shops he inspected," I said. "We didn't get them very often, but I remember that they were delicious. I haven't had them in years."

"What is a sweetbread?" Little Dickey asked.

"There are two types, throat and stomach. Throat sweetbreads are thymus glands that are behind the sternum. Stomach sweetbreads are the pancreas glands. They can come from pork, lamb, or calves. The calves are the best because they are the most tender."

"I'll just have a hamburger," Little Dickey told the waiter.

At noon, the host started the show with his usual introduction and an ad for a local car dealer.

"I have two guests with me today who are stationed aboard a nuclear powered missile-carrying submarine," the talk show host said. "They have experienced government waste first hand and are here to tell us about it. What are your jobs in the Navy?"

"Right now, we mess cook, which is the same as KP duty," Little Dickey said. "We set up tables and serve food to the rest of the crew while out at sea."

"Is that what you're trained for?"

"No," I said. "We've both been trained to be missile technicians. We went to a year of schooling in what is called the Polaris Field Electronics. It's called Polaris because the North Star is used to pinpoint our location. Our submarine carries missiles with nuclear warheads capable of reaching any city in the world from out at sea. Our jobs now are serving food."

"That sounds like a waste," the interviewer said.

"We think so," Little Dickey replied. "We both have some college experience too. Keeping us from doing what we're trained for is making us think twice about re-enlisting when our tours of duty are over. Also, it's not just the two of us. There are other trained technicians on our boat in the same situation."

"I've just about made up my mind to get out in two years when my enlistment is up," I said. "I signed on for six years to get the training and to work on missiles. It's a shame the government spent all that money getting us trained and then wastes our talent on washing dishes. Now, they will have to train two more to take our places when we leave."

"Have you thought about contacting your congressman?" the interviewer asked.

"We could get in trouble just for coming on this show and complaining," Little Dickey said. "If we made noise higher up, we might receive disciplinary action or retaliation."

"Yeah," I said. We might have to wash dishes for the next two years. That's why we don't want to mention which sub we're on."

While Little Dickey and I were talking, a man, who was sitting at a table nearby listening to the interview, handed the waiter a note and said something to him which I couldn't hear. The waiter carried the note to the interviewer who read it and nodded his head.

"We have a question from the audience which we will answer when we return," the interviewer said. The waiter brought our lunch as soon as the radio station cut to the commercial. Little Dickey and I were curious about the question, but started our lunch while it was still warm.

"How are the sweetbreads?" the interviewer asked.

"Just as I remember them as a boy in Ohio," was my response. We continued to eat as the commercial played in the background.

"We're back," the interviewer said. "In case you are just tuning in, our guests today on this segment of waste and abuse in the Federal government are two sailors from aboard a nuclear powered submarine that carries nuclear warhead missiles. They just spent the last fifteen minutes discussing the waste of their talents that the Navy has demonstrated by taking highly trained technicians and using them to wash dishes. Just before the break, a member of the audience handed me a question which I will now pose to them. The question is, 'In the event of a confrontation between your sub and a destroyer, who would win?'" Little Dickey and I hesitated, but then Little Dickey, always the philosopher, spoke for us.

"I can't help but be a little prejudiced, but I believe the sub would come out on top, no pun intended. The modern-day submarine is designed to be very quiet and has detection techniques which would allow us to hear the surface craft long before they knew we were there."

"We also have weapons," I added, "that could destroy the enemy from a distance greater than the subs in World War II could. The torpedoes we carry are more sophisticated, run quieter, and carry larger warheads. However, our mission is to remain undetected. That's the value as a deterrent in the cold war."

"We can hide better than we can fight," Little Dickey intoned. "Our mission is to deliver nuclear warheads to the enemy thousands of miles away. There are other submarines in our Navy designed for fighting that are much faster, quieter, and more maneuverable than us. These subs, I have no doubt, would be able to destroy an enemy as the questioner posed. So, I stand by my answer."

"Very good answer," the interviewer said. The man at the table who posed the question nodded his head in agreement.

The rest of the discussion was centered on life aboard a submarine. A half hour later, the program was over and so was our lunch. The interviewer thanked us and we left.

"That was fun," I said, as we headed to the parking lot.

"Let's just hope the Navy doesn't find out what we did," Little Dickey said.

"Yeah, or we <u>will</u> be washing dishes for the rest of our naval career, maybe in the brig."

Little Dickey went off to California and I went to my parents home for a few days.

"When I got back from visiting my folks," I told Captain Bob, "I had some R&R time still remaining and didn't want to go to the bars like it seemed the rest of the crew was doing. I wanted to do something more relaxing."

"What were that?" Captain Bob asked.

"It was spring time and so three other crew members and I decided to go camping. One of the guys had a tent and camping supplies. He also had an old Plymouth station wagon and a motorcycle he parked in the off-base wooded area, outside the fence, across from the barracks. I don't know why he parked it there, but he must not have been able to register it to drive on the base for some reason. So, when we got back from Scotland, he picked up the cycle and car from his parent's house and drove them to the woods.

"The four of us borrowed a canoe from special services, put it in the station wagon, and took off into the backwoods of Connecticut near a lake where one of the guys had been camping previously. I drove the station wagon and followed the guy on his cycle. I can't tell you where the lake was, because, while there, I suffered a mild concussion and got lost."

"How'd ya do that?" Captain Bob asked.

I continued petting Dedra while I finished the story.

The first two days, we had enough supplies: beer, hot dogs, buns, potato chips, eggs, bacon, all the essentials. We swam in the cool water, paddled the canoe around, and hiked through the woods a little; but mainly just relaxed with nature. I loved to swim and had fins, a mask, and a snorkel I had borrowed from special services. I was able to see a good part of the lake on the surface from the canoe and under it using the snorkel.

I even found a rainbow trout, quite vigorously guarding a nest of roe behind a rock. She attacked me when I approached, even though I was nearly fifty times her size. I swam a distance away and observed her chasing off fish, protecting her un-hatched young. That is what the R&R period was meant to be. It was not supposed to be for drinking myself into a stupor every day as I did during the next R&R period.

By the third day of our camping trip, supplies were getting low. I volunteered to take the motorcycle to the store to pick up some beer and other minor items. The motorcycle had saddle bags, so I could put the provisions in them for the trip back to the campground.

"Can you drive a cycle?" the owner asked.

"Sure can," I lied. I was confident that I could drive one. I had driven a Vespa motor scooter during my high school years a couple of times. Before that, I had "motorized" my bike by hooking up a cart with a lawn mower engine to push it on the streets. That was when I was twelve or thirteen years old, so I rationalized that I could drive a 90cc Honda without any problems. Boy was I wrong!

I found the little store where I was told to go get the supplies. It was not far from the camp. I bought what we needed, loaded up the pouches on the Honda, and started out on the trip back to the camp. I was rounding a turn in the road and took it a little too fast. I went over the center line, which I could have recovered from had a car not been coming toward me from the other direction.

Afraid to lean any further, I panicked and turned the wheel. Gravel that had collected in the center of the road over the winter caused the wheels to slip and I went down on my side, my legs still straddling the motorcycle protected by a brush guard. Luckily, I slid off the road before the car passed me so I didn't get hit, but when I went down, I cracked my head on the pavement. Most bike riders didn't wear helmets in those days, so my head was unprotected. My head must have bounced and I didn't sustain any cuts. It happened in an instant, but it was like slow motion, the bike going down, my head hitting the pavement, the bike bouncing then sliding right off the road, the sound of screeching tires as the car went by me, my shoe flying off, and then silence.

When the man who was driving the car got to me, I was up and looking for my left shoe, a loafer that had slipped off and landed somewhere nearby.

"You all right?" the man asked.

"I can't find my shoe," was all I could say, but then I saw it lying nearby. "There it is."

"You seem okay," the man said, looking at me. I had a disheveled look and a two-day growth of beard. My patrol beard had been shaved off before I came back to the states, but I hadn't shaved since we'd been camping. I had worn the same clothes for the last two days and hadn't combed my hair that morning. The man was probably glad just to get away from me.

"I'm all right," I said. I pulled the bike up, got on it, and kick started it to life. The man was relieved and headed back to his car as I took off down the road. I drove about a quarter mile before I realized I didn't know where I was going. I drove back and forth on the same road looking for the entrance to the camp, but couldn't find it. In a panic, I saw a road sign and was relieved to recognize the name as the road that went to the entrance to the base, so I just kept going in the direction I was headed which I hoped would take me to the sub base.

I had driven about a half hour when the bike started to splutter. While going up the next hill, it just died on me. When it came to a stop, I unscrewed the gas cap and looked inside to see a little bit of gas on the bottom, but the bike still wouldn't start. I got off the bike and pushed it to the top of the hill and rode it down to the next hill. Three hills later, I saw the best sight I ever remember, the base chain-link fence on the right and my barracks on the other side of the fence.

On the opposite side of the road was the turn off where my buddy had parked his station wagon and the cycle. I pushed the Honda in behind the trees, took the keys and headed back to the road. I couldn't walk to the base entrance more than a mile away and enter that way because I looked a mess and might not be allowed in, even with my ID card. So, I crossed the highway and walked to a weak spot in the gate with a missing bottom rail where I could lift up the chain link and crawl under. I was lucky no one saw me for I would have been in a lot of trouble for entering the base that way. Once inside, I headed for my barracks, which was, thankfully, nearly deserted. I took a shower and lay down in my rack for a rest. My head was aching and so was the rest of my body from being banged around during the accident.

"What happened to you?" the motorcycle owner said, when I awoke. He was hovering over me along with my two other fellow campers.

"I had a wreck and couldn't find my way back to the camp site," I said in a groggy voice. "I slid off the road and hit my head. Then things got confusing."

"Yeah, I figured that out from the dents and scratches on the cycle."

"Sorry about that," I said. "I'll pay for it."

"Forget that," he said. "Are you all right?"

"I think so," I said. "The bike ran out of gas and I had to push it back some of the way."

"It's got a reserve tank," he said. "All you had to do was turn a valve on the bottom of the tank."

"Now you tell me," I said.

"You said you knew how to ride. You look like you need to go to sick bay."

I probably did, but didn't go until the next morning. The doctor said I was okay, but gave me hell for riding on a motorcycle and a lecture on how my body belonged to the government and damaging it was a court-martial offense.

To be less self destructive and more productive, when Little Dickey got back from his visit to the west coast, we got jobs working part time at a hamburger joint on the weekends.

I wanted to earn a little more money toward the college education I was saving for, and Little Dickey wanted something to keep him occupied. He was an active type and couldn't just sit still. There was a place that sold hamburgers for twenty five cents apiece in Norwich, Connecticut. We applied for part time help and got jobs where he waited on customers and I was a bun man helping the guy who cooked the burgers. There was no "have it your way" at this establishment, the burgers were all one way, grilled, put on a bun with a pickle and a glop of a mustard-mayonnaise mixture.

We went to work every Saturday and Sunday morning for almost two months. My job was to put the buns on one grill and turn them when they got toasty. To my left was the grill man who cooked the burgers. When the burgers bled through, he turned them and I turned the buns at the same time. By the time he got done turning the last burger, the first group of burgers were ready. He scooped up three at a time and plopped them on the bottoms of the buns. I put a pickle on each burger and then used a conical-shaped device with a trigger to shoot a measured amount of special sauce on it. I then placed a top on each burger and stuck them in the shoot above the two grills. Every once in awhile, a burger or bun would fall on the floor.

"It hit the paper," the grill man would say with a smile, and put it back on the grill. Everything was counted, even the cups. We could drink as much as we wanted as long as we used our own cups, but had to pay for any burgers we ate. There was a steamer to "rejuvenate" left over burgers from the previous day which I used to cook my burgers rather than fry them on the grill. I was still trying to lose my patrol fat.

They also served clam fritters which were globs of dough with little pieces of clams mixed into them. They were fried in the same deep fat fryer that cooked the french fries. We could eat as many clam fritters as we wanted and they were quite tasty.

I used to like to watch Little Dickey work the counter. He bullshitted with everyone who came in for an order of burgers and fries. He was like a politician running for office and he loved it. At the busiest time of the day, there were customers lined up around the corner to get the cheap food. One lady came to the counter and ordered forty eight hamburgers which only cost her twelve dollars. That set us back for the rest of the lunch hour. We could only cook twenty four at a time so two batches of burgers went to her.

We didn't "make money head over heels," as Lt. Inman once said, but enough for me to give my college fund a boost. One day we reported to the burger joint and knew something was wrong the minute we pulled into the parking lot. When we walked in the back door we

fairy tales and sea stories 95

saw soot clinging to all the surfaces. What had been shiny, white porcelain was now black and oily looking.

"One of the deep fat fryers caught on fire, so we won't be open for business this weekend," the manager said. "But you're welcome to stay and help clean up. I'll pay the same wages."

"No thanks," we said. It was almost time for us to head back to Scotland and my second patrol anyway, and we didn't want to be part of a fire cleanup crew. We did enough cleanup work while on the submarine to last us a lifetime.

"So ya was ta go on your second patrol, was ya?"

"Yes and this time I knew what to expect, although I didn't look forward to another dose of mess cooking. At least this time the weather wouldn't be so cold while we were scraping and painting the metal surfaces of the sub while tied to the tender."

episode five

"Man, this is no shit, I got a wink job last night," Rod declared as soon as he entered the chow hall. Rod was a big sandy-haired, farm-boy and had a very loud voice from working in the noisy engine room environment where shouting was necessary just to carry on a normal conversation. I, and everyone in the room, couldn't help but overhear all he said. Even if he talked softly, everyone would listen. Rod was known for being somewhat strange.

There still were no billets opened up for missile technicians, so I was mess cooking again to start my second patrol. The COB thought Larry and I worked together so well, he shared my fate. Larry, Little Dickey, and I had just spent the last two weeks of turn-over on the seaman gang painting the outside of the sub. The next week and a half before we got underway and for the first two or three weeks of the patrol we would be mess cooking. Little Dickey, again the night mess cook, had just gotten off duty, and headed to the missile compartment to get some rest. Larry and I were standing against the starboard bulkhead of the galley and could overhear almost every conversation in room. Rod turned in his chit, got a cup of coffee, sat down with Snake at the table just in front of us, and related his story of last night's liberty.

Rod was a "plank owner" on the Sam and had been a crew member ever since she was built. My first encounter with him other than to bring him food, was on my first patrol. I was in the mess hall taking a break from studying my qualification books and sat down across from him. His eyes had obviously "failed open," and he couldn't sleep anymore.

"What's that mean?" Captain Bob said, "Failed open."

"When a person is already qualified as a submariner, he has nothing else to do but stand his six-hour watch. If it's not time for a movie, most just eat and then go to bed to read for awhile before dozing off. So in every eighteen hour period they sleep about ten to twelve hours. After about a month of this routine, they can't sleep anymore.

"The term "failed open" comes from the position that some electrically or hydraulically operated valves automatically go to when they lose power. This is a safety factor for those valves which control a system critical to the operation of the sub. For example, if a bilge pump is removing water from inside the sub and the power fails, the pump will still be able to work, either manually or by emergency power if its valve remains open.

"This may also be called 'fails safe.' If a sub sailor doesn't know the answer to the question, "how's that work?" his favorite response is, "works fine and fails safe."

"Like I said, about the middle of the patrol, there are men walking around with glazed-over eyes. Most of them migrate to the mess hall to await the next meal or a movie. When their eyes fail open, they look like zombies wandering around, eyes wide open, just staring."

"I see," Captain Bob said.

"So, during my first encounter with Rod, I was sitting across from him. His head was bowed and he was playing with a four-foot-long sisal piece of string and talking to it. I didn't say anything, being content just to watch his antics."

"I rescued her from the GDU," Rod said, head still down and not directing his voice toward anyone in particular. For once he was talking softly, which was unusual for him. I did recognize the type of string he was playing with as the same we used to tie cardboard together while we were in port. We unboxed supplies that we had just brought aboard, flattened and stacked the cardboard, and tied it up with the coarse string so we could take it topside while we were moored to the tender. I had seen him dragging the string around the boat before, but didn't think anything of it. He must have kept it since we left the tender a few weeks previously.

"Isn't she a nice piece of string?" he asked. I felt obligated to respond.

"Yeah, she's a fine piece of string," I said

"Wanna fuck her?" he said raising his voice. He looked up at me with serious, zombie, failed-open eyes.

"Ahhhh, not really," was all I managed to get out. With that, he stood up as if I had offended him and his "girlfriend," grabbed one end of his string, and headed aft out of the chow hall dragging the rest of the string on the deck behind him. I looked around at the other faces, but they were ignoring the entire episode.

"That fellah's not right in the head, were he?" Captain Bob said, shaking his head.

"For a sub sailor, he was about normal," I responded. "So, there was Rod telling about what had happened to him the night before while he was on liberty in Dunoon."

"Okay," Snake said. "What's a wink job?"

"I met this Colleen over at the club," Rod said.

"I saw her," Little Dickey said. "She had excellent callipygian qualities."

"What the fuck does that mean, college boy?" Snake asked.

"She had a nice ass," I said. I knew Little Dickey wouldn't put it into crass terms that they could appreciate, so as a fellow "college boy," I spoke up for him.

"Yeah," Foster said. "I saw her too. She did have a nice ass, but was ugly and had funny eyes."

"One of them was fake," Rod said.

"Ya mean she had a glass eye?" Snake asked.

"Yep," Rod continued. "I was sittin' at the bar when she plopped down on the stool next to me. I asked her if she wanted a beer, and she said 'Why sure sailor.' 'Order what ya want,' I told her. She ordered a Carlsberg Special. You know, one a those strong beers."

"I never heard of that kinda beah," Captain Bob said.

"It is a very strong beah," I said. "I mean beer." I corrected myself. I knew that sooner or later I would start talking like him. I just couldn't help myself.

"On my first liberty in Scotland, I had a Carlsberg Special at one of the local pubs and one more was all I could handle. Someone told me they were like ready-made boiler makers. The alcohol content was the same as if someone had mixed the beer with whiskey. I found out later that Carlsberg Specials were made in Denmark, were nine percent alcohol, and served in pint glasses. Most American beers are around five percent and are in twelve-ounce bottles."

"After a few beers, I was gettin' kinda looped, but she was still sober," Rod continued. "Around eleven, she asked me if I wanted to take her home. I said 'sure.' I'm not one to turn down a potential piece."

"What was her name?" Foster asked.

"Hell, I don't remember," Rod said. "I think she told me once, but I was so shit-faced from the beer I don't remember. So when we got outside and the cabs were lined up, I asked her how far away she lived, thinking I should hail a cab. She said 'no.' She only lived a 'wee walk up the street.' So I said, 'Okay. We'll walk.' 'Cause you know how I hate to ride in those cabs."

I knew what he was talking about. My first cab ride in Scotland scared the crap out of me. They drive on the other side of the road and their passenger side was where I was used to sitting as a driver. The roads are narrow, so they drive down the middle of the street. When another vehicle approaches they move over to the left, but I'm thinking *he should go right*. It scared the hell out of me when it looked like he was going to hit the other car head on. They also have round-abouts and drive clockwise instead of counterclockwise, exiting the wrong way. After my first cab ride, I started walking most places just to keep my sanity.

"'Wee walk,' doesn't mean a short one," Snake said.

"Tell me about it," Rod said. I was almost sober by the time we got to her flat. Musta been two or more miles, 'up the street,' she said. When we got inside, she offered me another beer, but I was not in the mood for beer. I wanted somethin' else. Just to keep her talkin', I asked her what was wrong with her eye. I had noticed that it wasn't quite right when I first met her, but didn't say anything 'til then. She said it was fake, and then took it out to show me. Damn if it wasn't. It made a kinda suckin' sound when she plucked it out. Then she laid it right there on the kitchen table and the thing started rollin'. It had a bump on it where the pupil was and it rolled funny, with a plunk, plunk, plunk every time it hit the pupil. She said she got her eye poked out when she was a kid. Said someone threw a stick at her."

Larry and I were laughing along with the rest of the guys who were listening to his story, which included everyone in the chow hall by now.

"Order out!" yelled Cooky from behind me.

It was Rod's eggs and sausage, so I took the plate and handed it to him.

"Thanks," he said.

The crew was a lot nicer to me so far this patrol. I guess I had proven myself to be an okay guy on the last patrol. If you were an asshole, you had a hard time qualifying. A story circulated about one particularly unpleasant would-be sub sailor who went an entire patrol with no one to talk to. The story must have been true, because the person who told it to me started off with, 'this is no shit,' when he said the guy went nuts. He spent most of the patrol hunkered down in a corner of the crew's berthing, talking to himself. After the end of that patrol, he was "re-evaluated" and sent to the fleet to be a "surface puke."

"So, we sat on her couch for about ten minutes," Rod continued. Then she turns at me with only one eye in its socket and asked me if I wanted to stick my wee wee in it."

"Wee wee?" Snake said. "She called your dick a wee wee?"

"Yeah, a fuckin' wee wee. So I said, 'Hell, why not?' She grabbed my dick, excuse me, wee wee, through my pants right then and kissed me on the mouth. Used a lotta tongue too. I got me a hard on right then. Then she pulled it out and stuck it in that empty socket of hers."

"All of it?" Foster asked.

"No, just the tip. I ain't that small. It didn't feel all that good, until she started winkin', slow at first, and then real fast."

I was bent over with laughter. Cooky stopped cooking eggs and was hunched over with his head through the pass-through. He was smiling. This was the first time I had ever seen him with anything but a frown on his face.

"I almost got off in her eye socket, when she pushed me down and finished it, her on top. I'm goin' back tomorrow and get me another wink job," Rod said, and then concentrated on his breakfast.

Right after breakfast, it was "all hands on deck" for loading supplies. I had lifted weights at the base gym during part of the three months off in New London, so I had bulked up a bit. I hadn't lifted since "A" school, but my body responded to the training. Because of my strength, I was stationed in the auxiliary machinery room access hatch. I sat in the hatch just above the ladder so I could reach the man above me on the deck and the man below me in the sub.

"Here's a schematic of the aft portion of the sub showing the access hatch," I said, handing Captain Bob the drawing.

He took the picture and drew on his pipe, while Dedra turned over on her side, eyes still closed.

A crane from the tender loaded pallets of supplies onto the back of the sub. From there, the supplies were passed "daisy-chain" style to me, down to someone below me, and then on through the sub along the passageways to a designated storage space.

The worst items to load were the GDU weights and the large, five-gallon cans of coffee, flour, and sugar. The weights were packaged in cardboard boxes, ten to a box, and at seven pounds each, each box weighed seventy pounds. I never counted how many boxes of GDU weights we loaded, but there must have been over a hundred. The man below me had to have a lot of confidence in my ability to pass him the boxes without dropping one on him. Bear was usually the man below me because of his size.

The five-gallon cans were the next heaviest and most difficult items to load. Although not as heavy as the GDU weights, they were big and hard to handle while passing them through the hatch. Loading supplies took two days, with anyone not on duty or manning a station participating. Some supplies, especially refrigerated items, were daisy chained all the way from the storage rooms on the tender to their places on the Sam. After an hour of passing supplies through the hatch, I had to report for duty again in the chow hall. Thank God we only had two weeks before we headed out on patrol.

"Then ya went on another patrol?" Captain Bob asked.

"Yes, after the shakedown cruise where we tested all the systems and seaworthiness. This patrol was a long one in more ways than one. Two weeks into the patrol, after what was supposed to be my fourth and last week as a mess cook, I was to be rotated to the control room to be a planesman, but wasn't. I was told the bad news after what I thought was my last night wearing the apron."

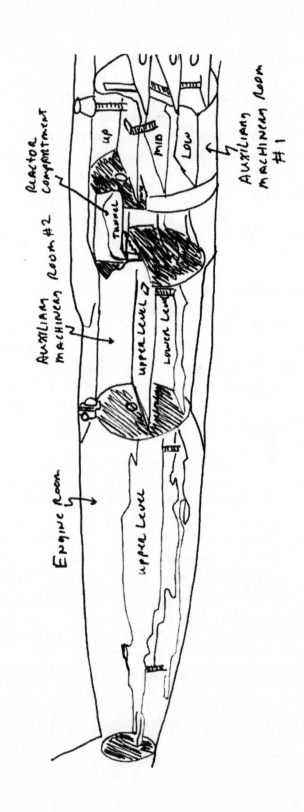

"You're on mess cook duties one more week," the COB said. He didn't have to offer an explanation, but did. "Your quals aren't up to date and the man who was to relieve you finished his quals early, so we're keeping him in control room."

This news depressed me. I couldn't understand how the COB justified keeping me as a mess cook just because I was behind in my quals. The reason I was behind was I was mess cooking with precious little time to attempt to get qualified. I was getting by on four hours sleep each night. *Of course my relief got his quals done. He was standing six-on and twelve-off watches and had three times the study time that I had.* I didn't say this to the COB. He was not a very understanding or sympathetic person and may have made me mess cook the entire patrol if I had made a sound of disappointment, so I started my hunger strike. I needed to lose weight anyway.

"I ain't hungry, Doc," I told Doc the next morning at breakfast. "I just don't have the appetite."

He shook his head and went about his business.

"What's wrong with you?" Cooky asked, when he noticed I wasn't eating.

"I ain't hungry," I said. "I don't know what's wrong."

"You better go see the doc. You ain't missed a meal so far this patrol and not many last, so you must be sick or sumpin."

"Doc already knows about it," I said.

After the second day, the entire crew knew I wasn't eating. I had their sympathy, but there was nothing they could do in the autocratic system. They did treat me with a little more dignity, knowing how rough mess cooking could be, especially for as long as I had had to put up with it. There were very few men with my time in service and rank who had to mess cook two patrols in a row just because no billets or positions were open in their discipline.

"So they continued to make ya a mess cook, huh?" Captain Bob said.

"Yep, they sure did, for another week, but I didn't eat anything the entire time."

Not many of the crew liked the COB for one reason or another. The fact that he was black raised the ire of the southerners who made up about a third of the crew. I was taught by my dad to hate the blacks, but didn't know why. I tried to change that attitude, but men like the COB made it difficult. Behind his back the crew called him the HMFIC, which meant "head-mother-fucker-in-charge." The alternative was the NOMFWIC, or "number one mother fucker what's in charge." The other chiefs were under the COB and were just titled MFIC." Two men on board had the last name Foster who had the same traits. I was starting to wonder if all men with that name were that nasty.

I had starved myself before, just to lose weight, once for ten days, once for five. So when the COB told me I had another week to go and I decided not to eat for the entire time, I knew how my body would react, physically and mentally. I would get weak and there would be dizzy spells, but otherwise I would be fine.

"You got to eat something," Little Dickey said. "You're only hurting yourself."

"I'll be all right," I reassured him. "You'll see."

It was difficult since I was around all that food almost all day long. The first two days, when I had hunger pains, were the roughest. After that, my body got used to not eating and started to metabolize my body fat and protein from my muscles. The first day I shit, but after that there was nothing for my system to process until I ate again, six days later. The only item I had that was not water was coffee. I didn't even have bug juice, which was loaded with sugar.

"You're destroying your liver," the Doc said one morning when he came through the chow hall.

"I can't help it, Doc. I just don't have an appetite. The sight of food makes me nauseous." I had to tell him that because I could face a court-martial for abusing my body. I had heard of instances where a sailor got a tattoo and it got infected. He was punished for damaging his body which belonged to the Navy. I don't know if that was a true story, but it kept me from getting a tattoo and made me complain about my appetite to the Doc, just in case. At least if something happened to me, I was covered.

I got no sympathy from the COB, but he saw I was doing my duties without any problems so didn't take me off mess cooking before the extra week was up. I was concerned that he would tack on another week or so, but was prepared to go to the end of the patrol without eating, if necessary. It wasn't. On the last day of my work as a scullery rat, he came and told me to report to the control room for duty the next day.

Just in case the COB changed his mind and put me back as a mess cook, I didn't eat until the night of my first duty day as a planesman,. That night, after I got off watch, was steak night and I ordered four raw steaks and a big plate of french fries. I ate everything on my plate. Later I was awakened by the worst cramps I can remember. I ran to the head in anticipation of shitting everything I had just consumed a few hours before. All that came out were two marble sized, and just as hard, turds that made a "plink plink" sound as they bounced off the sides of the metal john. It must have been the dregs of the coffee I had consumed over the last week. By the middle of the next day, I had returned to a normal digestive schedule.

"Ya said that was a long patrol" Captain Bob acknowledged. "Whereabouts in the ocean were ya?"

"Yes it was long as far as being tedious, but the third patrol was a lot longer as far as time is concerned," I said.

"The first patrol we were in the North Atlantic, but the second one we went to the Mediterranean. To get there we had to go through the Strait of Gibraltar.

"Cruise locations for the subs based in Scotland were the North Atlantic or the Mediterranean. Our enemy was, for the most part, the U.S.S.R. and the missiles could reach the western targets from either body of water. The subs made it through the Strait undetected and no one believed we were in the Mediterranean, so the Sam made a surprise visit to Turkey, the first missile carrying sub on patrol to ever do so.

"Here's the official photo of the Sam on the surface near Izmir in the Aegean sea," I said to Captain Bob, handing him the photo.

"I ain't never been to the Meda-tranium," Captain Bob said.

"I wasn't on board when they visited Turkey. It sure made a believer out of the Rooskies and our allies in Europe. The Med, I learned, was a much different place to patrol, lots of surface craft.

"We were heading through the Strait, and since I was the maneuvering planesman, the skipper gave me a reprieve from mess cooking so I could guide the sub. He wanted the best person to steer her, someone who could process and execute numerous and tricky commands, and I was the man; no brag, just fact."

The first indication we were headed into the Med, was the rise in water temperature. Normally it was at or below fifty degrees in the Atlantic, but the temperature went to sixty as we approached the Strait. Surface contacts started to become more numerous as ships traversed the Strait above us.

"Steady as she goes," the diving officer directed.

"Steady as she goes, aye, sir," I responded. "Steady at zero niner five." My response, using partial number phonetics, developed to eliminate hearing errors, told all we were heading a little bit south of due east. We used a three hundred sixty degree compass with north being zero degrees and east being ninety. This system was called a magnetic bearing. Relative bearing was the relationship of another vessel to ours relative to the bow, dead ahead being zero and port ninety degrees.

Just like being told to look for a "water hammer," new crew members were told to get some "relative bearing grease" from the engine room, with predictable results. A man would be sent on a wild goose chase until he was told what a relative bearing was. As soon as he was qualified, he was sure to be the first one to send the next new guy looking.

During this critical period of passing into and out of the Strait, the skipper was in the control room to supervise and take over if necessary.

"Tanker bearing, zero five zero," a voice from sonar called out. "Heading, one eight zero. Range, one thousand yards." These headings, given in relative bearings, told us the tanker was on a course which would take her very close to us. I recognized the voice of the sonarman who had been on duty last patrol when I had flushed the imploding ketchup bottle out of the GDU. Being able to work as a sonarman all last patrol and this one too, trained him to identify the size and direction of a target by the sounds it made. They also had a device to compare a ship's "profile" noise to a known library of ships' recorded noises so that they could tell the name of the ship.

A tanker passing directly overhead, could "suck" us up to the surface with the wake it made, especially with us at only one hundred feet. Therefore, it was time for some evasive maneuvers.

"Come right ten degrees," the diving officer said.

"Right ten degrees, aye, sir." I said.

"Make your depth two five zero feet," he said.

"Two five zero, aye, sir," I parroted back. I then called out the degrees in the turn and the depth as we passed through each five degree change in direction and ten degree change in depth. I was nudging the Sam down using the fairwater planes on the sail. They were employed to make gentle changes in depth and angle. Had he called for a down-bubble, or a drastically quick depth change, the stern planesman would take action. "Passing zero niner zero; passing one one zero feet; coming up on zero eight five; passing one hundred twenty feet; holding steady on zero eight five degrees."

"Belay the depth changes," the diving officer said.

Thank God, I thought. I hated calling out the changes, but that was part of the procedure. When I came up on two hundred fifty feet, I called it out, but was silent until then. The sonarman was calling out the position of the tanker as it closed, then passed to our right. The slight turn to our left gave the sonarman a chance to listen behind us for any ships that might be overtaking us. A ship approaching us from behind, without us knowing it, was a real possibility. The sonar array didn't work to our rear, partly because of noise from the screw. The "nose" on the bow was supposed to allow "aft-listening," but, like the big gyro in the forward auxiliary machine room, it was a good idea that didn't work. So, it was necessary to turn right or left periodically so we could listen aft, especially in a busy sea.

As we got deeper into the Strait, a strip of water thirteen kilometers wide (about eight miles), the temperature and saline content both started to go up. Our ballast tanks, which are used to maintain depth and trim (the up or down angle of the submarine) contained cold, less salty, Atlantic water. The more salt was dissolved in the water, the more buoyant we became. The warmer the water, the heavier we became. The diving officer had to watch our trim and depth closely as well as the contacts around us. Soon we had several ships all converging on the narrow Strait as we were trying to sneak through. Also there was a real possibility that another sub would be trying to come through too. Our Navy supposedly knew the approximate date we were going into the Strait, and what other subs our Navy had in the vicinity. Therefore, it was a slim chance we would hit one of our own, but other navies had subs too.

I was starting to use more down angle on the fairwater planes, just to keep us at depth. This indicated to the diving officer we were becoming more buoyant. To compensate, he started to add more of the heavier Mediterranean water to the ballast tanks.

"Flood auxiliary from sea one thousand pounds," he called out.

"Flooding auxiliary one thousand pounds, aye, sir," the auxiliary man, called out. The auxiliary man was at the control panel where the Christmas tree was located. It was so-called because of all the red and green lights indicating the positions of the numerous valves, red for open, green for closed. The panel was also where the emergency blow valves were located which blew water out of our buoyancy tanks. They were nicknamed "chicken valves" because they were used when the sub got in trouble and had to surface. When our approach angle started to increase, it was time to secure the flooding operation.

"Secure flooding," the diving officer said.

"Secure flooding, aye, sir," the auxiliary man said. Once the water in our tanks warmed up, we would have to add more water as we became buoyant, but that wouldn't be for another day or two.

"How many tanks are on a sub?" Captain Bob asked.

"A lot," I said. "Here is a diagram of the largest, the main ballast tanks, and the ballast control panel or Christmas tree. They wrap around the sub at three areas. There are at least a hundred other tanks of various sizes and shapes throughout the sub."

"That there's a lot of tanks," Captain Bob said.

"Yes, and most all had a vent valve, a flood valve, an indicator gauge, and piping in and out."

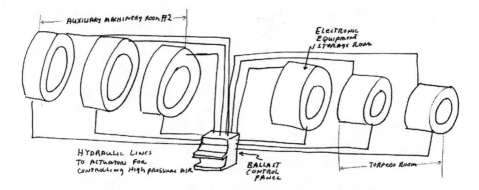

So there we were, in the middle of the Strait, trying to be undetected without surfacing or accidentally sinking. Like I said there were a lot of contacts around us, ships of all shapes and sizes, going at different speeds. There were so many that the navigator had a chart to plot them all. As one would get far enough away, another would move in. The sonarman was calling out contacts two or three a minute.

"There's another one," the sonarman shouted. Apparently a fast moving tanker had come undetected up from behind us and the sonarman had no time to call out direction, distance, speed, and type of ship. It was off our starboard and passed directly over the missile compartment at an angle. We had just changed depth to one hundred feet to be able to hear the contacts better. One hundred feet was keel depth, which meant the missile compartment had less than seventy feet above it, but the top of the sail was less than fifty feet under water. A ship drawing thirty feet of water could have come within twenty feet of hitting us.

Shoop! Shoop! Shoop! The sound of the tanker's propeller could be heard distinctly through the hull of the Sam. It was like the noise of slow-whirling helicopter blades, but slightly higher in pitch. In an instant, the wake of the passing ship sucked us up thirty feet, and almost broached the top of the sail. It happened so quickly, no one had time to react. I was angling us down to get back to depth when the sound faded over our port bow.

"Jesus Christ," someone said. "What the fuck was that?" He asked, but everyone knew the answer. We all breathed a sigh of relief when the navigator told us we were through the Strait. Our reward was a lot calmer seas than in the North Atlantic. Because of the much warmer water, the lithium-bromide air conditioning system worked a lot harder.

"So, there were no more problems on that patrol?" Captain Bob asked.

"If you don't call a fire a problem, I guess you could say that."

"A fire on a surface ship is bad 'nough, but I guess on a sub it's no fun atall?" Captain Bob said.

"Not much fun, and not at all like we practiced for," I said.

Like I said, we had drills, practice runs for all events, which included fire drills. At all hours of the day or night and usually once a day, we would conduct a drill. I already mentioned the "bailout" procedure. For a fire drill, everyone in the compartment affected donned masks. The masks had six-foot hoses which were plugged into connectors in the overhead. The connectors were part of a system of piping that ran the length of the submarine from stem to stern on both the port and starboard sides. Air was supplied to the lines from bottles filled with air independent of the sub's atmosphere. By plugging and unplugging the hoses, we could walk the entire length of the sub without breathing contaminated air.

The masks, once put on properly, were so tight that trying to breathe without the hose attached to an air supply would suck your eyes right out of their sockets. We trained in boot camp using filter masks in a building filled with smoke. Before we entered the building the instructor put his hands over each of the mask's filter. When the air supply was blocked off in this manner, the mask would be pulled tightly against the face with the eyes bugging out. This told the instructor the mask was being worn properly. Once all masks were checked out, we entered the building. Because we couldn't see in the dense, acrid smoke, we were taught to move through the building following the man in front of us. When we were all in the middle of the building, the instructor told us to take our masks off.

Within seconds, we were all coughing and choking, realizing how well the masks worked. After we put the masks back on we crawled the rest of the way out of the building. When we were all out in the fresh air we removed our masks revealing that we all had watery eyes and then we coughed until our lungs cleared. However, events happened differently on a submarine during a real fire.

During the second patrol, Felix, the puking mess cook, was assigned to the laundry instead of the mess hall. This pissed me off, but his puking ploy worked. I had never actually seen him upchuck anything, but the COB didn't want to take any chances of his upsetting the crew again. In his new job, all he did was put the laundry into the washing machines and dryers and then sort and deliver the cleaned, stenciled items back to the owners. While waiting for the machines to do the work, he was free to do whatever he wanted. However, he fucked this job up also. He did work in the laundry longer this patrol than I had to work as a mess cook, but the job was cushy and he could perform it longer.

Like all clothes dryers, lint would collect in the filters and had to be removed. While Felix cleaned the primary filter effectively, he neglected to clean the secondary filter as required by the standard operating procedure manual, which we called the SOP, pronouncing the initial letter of each word. SOP's were developed to be idiot proof, but Felix was a special type of idiot. When the secondary filter was clogged, the lint went into the main duct where it collected.

Air was circulated throughout the submarine using a series of ductwork, all interconnected. That's why we could smell unstoppable garlic fumes in all the compartments. The garlic aroma passed from the galley, through the ventilation and air conditioning room, and out to the rest of the sub. Here is a picture of the location of the room. The laundry was next to the head in crew's berthing, shown in the second picture.

No one knows what sparked the lint fire, but the best guess was static electricity. I was in the missile compartment working on my quals when the first indication I got was smoke billowing out of the ductwork. Within seconds, I couldn't see, even at deck level. The alarm was sounding as I grabbed the closest mask out of a locker. The mask lockers were scattered throughout the sub and their locations were one of the first thing learned while qualifying.

"Fire in crew's berthing!" blared the 1MC, followed by "Fire in the missile compartment!" Each compartment reported a fire as smoke traveled rapidly throughout the sub. Every hatch was closed as the emergency system shut down the fans, but not quickly enough. Every-

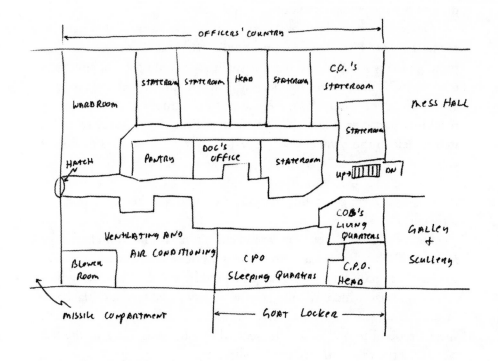

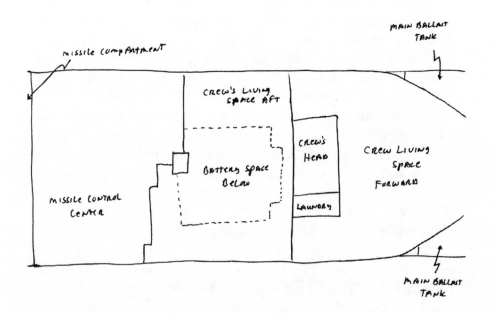

one was wearing the masks, which made investigation more difficult. I tried to move forward, but bumped into someone else moving aft. Soon we were competing for available places to plug in our air hoses. When I found one manifold occupied, I tried to move to the next one and found that occupied too. Some men shared manifolds with one man plugging in and then unplugging to allow the next man to plug in for a few breaths of air.

Because the fans were shut down, the fire was no longer being fed oxygen and it extinguished itself. There was no panic, just the realization that we were not really trained for this emergency and frustration that the source couldn't be found in a timely manner.

"Prepare to ventilate," came another announcement.

This started a process which we didn't use too often, but had drilled for. It required us to come up to within fifty five feet of the surface, raise the snorkel, and start the diesel engines. The engines drew combustion air from inside the sub while pulling in outside, make-up air. On a calm sea, this was a nice smooth process. In a rough sea, it was hard on the ear drums. The snorkel had a poppet valve that closed when waves broke over the top, preventing large amounts of water from entering the mast, but also shut off the access to outside air. The diesel didn't shut down when the valve closed, but started to pull a vacuum on the air inside the sub.

Every time the valve closed, our eardrums popped as if we were riding in a very fast elevator. We were taught in the pressure tank in sub school to equalize by pinching our noses and putting pressure on the inside of our ear drums with our lungs. This method didn't work during this emergency for two reasons.

One, we had masks on and couldn't reach our noses to pinch them. Two, this was a decrease in pressure, not an increase. Since my "incident" in sub-school training, I learned a trick that worked in both situations. I opened my jaw slightly and moved it side to side. This opened my eustachian tube and allowed equalization to occur. Those who weren't able to use my trick experienced a painful situation.

Another thing differed from the practice sessions in boot camp. Almost everyone had a beard which made the creation of a tight seal against the face almost impossible. I had just completed my tour as a mess cook and my beard was just starting, so I was able to get a tight seal. Luckily for those with beards, the fresh air was supplied by a hose and didn't come from outside the mask through a filter. The pressurized air forced the smoky air out of the mask, instead of the smoke getting into the lungs. We should have shaved our beards as a result of this emergency, but no one did.

Since we were in the Mediterranean when we snorkeled, the seas were calm, but this posed another dilemma. There was more shipping in the Mediterranean and the diesel smoke could be seen from a greater distance on a calm sea. But, this was an emergency and we had no choice.

I found my very own emergency air manifold and stood my ground, sharing the manifold with the occasional man heading forward or aft who was part of the damage control team. I felt the up angle as we headed closer to the surface and the unmistakable rumbling sound of the diesel as high pressure air was forced into its cylinders and it started. My ears started popping immediately and I equalized them. If make-up air didn't come in quickly enough, the diesel would shut down on low suction air. I felt my ears pop again as the snorkel broke the surface and outside air rushed in.

In less than five minutes, the air was clear, but the diesel continued to run for another fifteen minutes. When the diesel was shut down, we returned to our cruising depth, but it was another thirty minutes before the source of the fire was discovered. The findings which spread rapidly throughout the sub, made Felix the goat that he was.

Where will the COB put his sorry ass next, I thought. But nothing was done to him that I knew about. He just kept on doing laundry for another week, but cleaned all the filters according to the SOP. The only other emergency that was not a drill didn't occur until my third patrol while crossing the Atlantic en route back to the States for overhaul.

"So, the rest of yah second tour was uneventful?" asked Captain Bob.

"More or less. I did get qualified in submarines and as a missile compartment watch. You saw the picture of the skipper handing me my dolphins. Earning my dolphins and qualifying for the job I had been trained for meant no more mess cooking for my remaining two patrols."

episode six

"Okay, so ya had anotha R&R period when ya got through, did ya?"

"Yes, after turning over the boat to the gold crew, it's no shit that we had the next two months off," I said. "This time I spent almost my entire time at the local bar."

When our patrol was over and the turnover to the gold crew was complete, we flew back to New London for our rest and relaxation period. Some men, including Little Dickey, took leave and stayed in Scotland so they could see more of the world. I was saving my leave so I could get paid for it when I left the service.

For the first month of R&R, all that was required of us was that we call the sub base twice a week to verify our existence. Those who had leave to use and money to spend, like Little Dickey, took leave and traveled. We were supposed to be within 600 miles of the base and had to supply a telephone number where we could be reached, a rule that was not always adhered to. I had been saving for college ever since I quit the Naval Academy, vowing to earn a degree in electrical engineering. Therefore, I didn't have a lot of ready cash, but that didn't stop me from drinking up what I did have.

I had nothing else to do, so my routine consisted of getting up around ten and cleaning up (which we called the three "S's", shit, shower, and shave). I then headed to the base chow hall for lunch. Larry got married after our last patrol, so I palled up with a fire control tech named Dave. After lunch, we took the sub base version of the Gray Ghost, the same type of bus used in "A" school, the same navy gray color, to the town of New London across the Thames River. There was a bar there that both the blue and gold crews claimed as belonging to the crews of the Sam. I don't know how the bar made money for the one-week periods, twice a year when both crews were in Scotland, but when we were in the States, we filled the bar each night.

The bar opened at two in the afternoon and closed at two in the morning, so for twelve hours I sat on a bar stool and drank beer with my shipmates. For thirty days of R&R, I peeled the labels off the bottles as I drank and laid them out on the bar in front of me. At the end of the night, I had drunk enough beer to fill a case, more or less. To pay for some of the beers, I played the bowling machine, which I was quite good at. For food one of us would go to the sandwich shop across the street for take out.

Needless to say, my health was deteriorating and I had the DTs. When I got up in the morning, my hands shook uncontrollably until I got to the bar and downed that first beer. Then I steadied out. After the first month of R&R, there was a month of training and port and starboard duty which helped me sober up. I followed this drinking routine for only one patrol and part of the shipyard period. There were some sailors who did this for their full career of twenty years until their livers gave out. One such man was an E-6 boson mate whose name left my mind as soon as I quit the bar scene.

"Wanna see my twin screws?" he'd ask anyone who was new to the bar.

Without waiting for a response, he would turn around, drop trou', and bare his hairy ass where two propellers were tattooed, one on each cheek. Watching his performance night after night made me change my habits. The only good thing that came from this drinking binge was that when I went to college three years later, I didn't drink to excess. I guess I had matured a little bit and gotten it out of my system.

After three short months, it was time to go on my third patrol.

"So, for your third patrol, ya din't have ta mess cook atall?" Captain Bob said.

"No, I didn't, but, until we went to our dive point, I had to stand maneuvering and planesman's duties."

"Dive point?" he said

"Yes. That's where we commenced our patrol. We headed out into the North Atlantic to a specified location and then dove. The orders, telling us where we were to patrol, the North Atlantic or the Mediterranean, weren't opened until we were under water. First we had to make sure no Russian trawlers were near by."

"Ya mean them Rooskies?"

"Yeah. There is one story about a trawler that crossed our bow a little too closely. The skipper got pissed and headed right at them, nearly causing an international incident. We were supposed to dive undetected, so using binoculars we scanned the horizon for ships. We couldn't use radar, or they could have picked up the search signal. My past experiences got me the job as planesman and lookout ever since we had that one incident."

"What were that incident?"

"Here's a picture of the steering and diving station for the sub. You can look at that while I explain."

During my first patrol, after I got off mess cooking, I was assigned to the control room as a planesman. The job was like flying a plane on instruments, only underwater and a lot slower. There were two airplane like joysticks in front of two seats in the forward part of the control

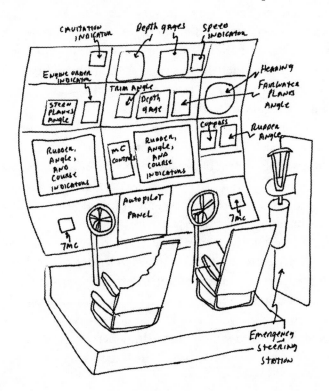

room, port side. In front of the joy sticks, were the gauges necessary to control all movements of the sub. There was a repeater station for speed in between the seats. The real controls were in the engine room which is in the aft-most compartment. The desired speed was dialed in and when the engine room received the request, they repeated it on the indicator. The rudder, stern planes, and fairwater planes were controlled from both or either one of the consoles. There was even an auto pilot that worked quite well, but was seldom used.

During sub school and during the time between patrols when we were not on R&R, we used a diving trainer in New London. Officers and enlisted both were subjected to simulated routine and emergency situations using the trainer. It was in a room with a platform in the middle so it could move in three dimensions like an airplane simulator. I discovered later that it didn't mimic the motions of the Sam that well, but it did get me familiar with the controls and instruments. At least if you had a simulated collision, you could walk away from it rather than wait to be rescued.

There was an experienced diving control officer, an enlisted man, usually a chief or first class, who sat behind and between the two planesmen. Moriarty, the first diving control officer I worked with, and I got along extremely well. He told a different sea story every watch, beginning with, "this is no shit". He taught me how to control the sub with gentle movements of the controls such that, after my first week, I felt I was an expert. I had a knack for handling the controls and all who observed me recognized it.

There was a feel to steering the sub in three dimensions and it was an exercise in finesse and anticipation rather than brute strength and forcing the controls. It was like comparing a ballet to a wrestling match. Although the Sam was built to move easily through the water and, while underwater, the sub did not have weight, it had mass; therefore, the sub didn't react instantly to a command.

So, when Foster took over as the new diving control officer, he wanted to direct every move the planesmen made, rather than allow us to do our job. We were in a particularly rough North Atlantic sea, at periscope depth, trying to shoot stars. It was something I had done on every watch for the last week and I was pretty good at it. The navigator was relieved when he saw me at the helm when he came to the control room to get a "fix" on our location. The largest scope, the type eleven, was the one used to shoot stars. It had to be fixed on one star long enough to get a bearing and elevation before being moved to the next star, and then the next. The longer the star shoot took, the longer we were near the surface and vulnerable to detection.

"Down angle," Petty Officer Foster said, leaning forward so that his face was just over my right shoulder.

Since I thought that was the wrong thing to do, I hesitated, but gave him what he wanted.

"Up angle," he said, right after the down angle command.

I looked at the other helmsman sitting to my right and he rolled his eyes. I did as I was told. The seas started to take hold and the Sam was popping around like a cork. The force of the ocean and how easily it could move an eight thousand ton vessel was amazing. When being moved by the waves, I felt the rhythm and made adjustments before the next wave pulled us up or pushed us down. Foster didn't have that anticipatory feel and his commands showed it.

"Down angle," he said, again at the wrong time.

"Up scope," the navigator said. I could hear the hissing as the hydraulics pushed the piston which drove the shaft up and out of the water.

"More down angle," Foster said, and I obliged.

Another hiss indicated the scope was up and air was being forced into the shaft to "float" the scope so that it could remain stationary.

"Up angle," Foster commanded, and I obeyed.

Now we were rocking and rolling in a state six or seven sea with at least twenty-foot waves breaking over the top of the sail.

"More up angle," Foster said. He was giving commands exactly opposite what I would have performed. As a result we started moving more violently with each wave.

"What the hell is going on?" the navigator said, as the type eleven banged against its stops, the air not able to keep it floating.

"I've got an inexperienced planesman," Foster said. I bit my tongue to keep from getting sent back to mess cooking. "He just doesn't execute my commands fast enough. Down angle!"

I obeyed, but the sub reacted violently as I thought it would. The navigator was thrown against the scope as he tried to keep his eye glued to the eye piece.

"Up angle," Foster said, louder and menacing, followed with a "Down angle."

"Let the planesman do his job," the navigator said, having had enough of the rough sea action.

"Hrummph," Foster let out, and leaned back in his chair and folded his arms across his chest.

I then took over and smoothed the sub out as much as could be done in that sea. The scope quit banging against the stops and the navigator called out, "Fix it," as he locked onto each star in succession.

"Good job, planesman," the navigator said, as he left the bridge.

Foster let out another, "Hrummph," and I was moved to the top of his shit list from then on for just doing my job. *Oh but for a dropped wrench*, I thought.

When we came back to Holy Loch after that first patrol, I was still a planesman; however, on the surface there was no need for someone to operate the stern and fairwater planes, so I was designated to be either a lookout or a helmsman. When coming into port, I was assigned as the maneuvering watch helmsman, an important job when navigating on the surface in tight situations.

There was an "outboard motor" on the Sam that was controlled from where I sat in the control room. The outboard was a small electric motor with a propeller that was housed under the sub directly below the auxiliary machinery room number two. It was lowered and used when there were no tugs to push us into position when mooring or as an emergency propulsion system if the main shaft was unusable. It rotated 360 degrees and I had a knack for visualizing where it was pointed and which way the sub would be pushed.

Commands were passed from the top of the conning tower using another communications system, the 7MC. The jack where I plugged in the headset is in the diagram. I couldn't see where we were, but had a feel for what was happening. We had to get close enough to the tender to have the mooring lines tossed to us so that we could be pulled alongside and tied off.

"Here is a picture of the docking operation about to happen," I said, handing Captain Bob the photo I was going to use as the cover for the book.

"Might purdy picture," Captain Bob said. "So's ya got ta do it again on your third patrol?"

"Just until we got to the open ocean, and then when we got near our diving point, I was called to the top of the sail to be a lookout."

"Front and center," the watch from the control room said. I was in the chow hall having a cup of coffee, already wearing my night goggles. On every patrol I had been on so far we dove at night and this was no exception. I poured out my unfinished coffee and set the cup in the window for the night mess cook to wash and return to the rack. It felt so good to be a missile technician for my third patrol that I didn't mind the maneuvering lookout job. In fact, I liked it.

"They want you up topside immediately," the COB said, when I entered the control room. I took off the goggles, put on my foul-weather gear, and grabbed the binoculars from the COB's outstretched arms.

Who are you going to harass this patrol, asshole? I thought. It was always a little cold and damp on the bridge especially when I stood on the platform behind and above all others. I put the binoculars around my neck and tucked them into the zipped up green jacket. I didn't want them to bang against the ladder on my way up.

"Permission to come up?" I shouted when I got to the inside of the sail. Asking permission was a necessity because there was precious little room on the bridge. Also, all hands had to be counted in case an emergency dive was necessary. It wouldn't be pleasant to be left on the outside of a submarine when it was about to dive in the middle of the North Atlantic.

"Here's a schematic of the inside of the sail showing the access ladders to the bridge," I said to Captain Bob, handing him the drawing. "It shows the platform near the top where I could wait if necessary until the lookout platform was clear. It's not like a crow's nest on your ship. It's just a step behind and above the others standing on the bridge deck."

"I see," Captain Bob said, when he looked at what I handed him.

"Any contacts?" I asked the man who was already serving as lookout.

"No," he said. "It's all clear."

I climbed up to replace him, strapped myself in and took a quick look around with my naked eyes. It was a clear and moonless night and with no interfering lights from the shore, stars shown brightly from

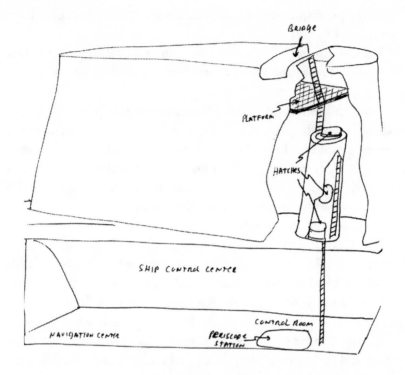

horizon to horizon in a three hundred and sixty degree arc. I was under a canopy of stars, a sight etched into my mind that will stay forever. Even in the dim light cast by the stars, we could see a school of dolphins swimming along either side the bow, occasionally jumping out of the water, landing just in front of the boat. They would disappear for a second and then repeat their playful behavior. I realized then why the pins we wore for qualifying submarines were called "dolphins."

"Did you report that light on the horizon off the starboard bow?" I said when I finished my sweep.

"What light?" he said. The officer of the watch turned around to look at me. He was wearing the headset with microphone allowing him to communicate to the control room.

"You're just seeing stars," he said. I put my binoculars to my eyes to verify what I caught with my naked eye.

"It's a moving white star with a red light on its port side," I said. "Looks more like a fishing boat to me. Its angle on the bow is three zero zero." That meant it was heading in a direction that would inter- sect with us. I could see the poles sticking off the stern which probably held a net. It was odd to see it so far away from shore away from the fishing beds. It could be a Russian trawler, but I wasn't going to make that call. I would let the officers identify the type of fishing boat it was. I couldn't see a flag from the angle it had on us.

"I believe you're right," the bridge officer said as he found the contact. The other watch left the bridge without saying another word.

"Captain to the bridge," the officer said into the 7MC communicating the request to the control room. "You saw that with your naked eyes?" he asked me.

"I just caught a movement, and there it was," I said.

"Damn good spot," he said. "Anything else?"

"No, sir," I said.

Just then the captain came up the ladder. He didn't stop to ask permission, since it was his boat.

I completed my first scan using the binoculars and let them rest inside my coat for a few minutes while I took in the breathtaking view. I had never been to the bridge as a lookout on such a clear night as this. In addition to the stars, there was iridescent plankton phosphorescing as it broke over the bow. The first time I was on the bridge as a lookout on the return trip from my second patrol, I had a full beard. The mist that hovered close to the ocean, collected on my beard and watch cap as we cut through the water on our way back to Holy Loch.

"Captain has the bridge," called out the officer. "The lookout spotted a trawler off the starboard bow, heading right across our path."

The captain took his binoculars and looked in the direction of the reported ship.

"I can't tell its origin," the skipper said. "Just to be safe, let's head toward our secondary dive point."

"Right twenty degrees, ahead one third," the officer called into the intercom. His commands were echoed back to him almost immediately by the helmsman, with an "aye, aye, sir," added on.

I could feel the boat start its turn to starboard. Up until then, the waves had been breaking over the stern. Now they would be coming at us from the side. My observation of the direction of the waves was correct, when the officer called out, "Wave!" and he didn't mean with our hands to the passing trawler.

Everyone on the bridge ducked below the clamshell that was used to seal off the bridge when we dove. Within seconds, the wave hit the sail and broke over the top. Had we not been alerted, as a minimum we would have been soaked. The worst that could have happened would have been a man being knocked overboard. That's why the lookouts were strapped in, since they were the most vulnerable, being higher than the rest of the bridge occupants. This time we were lucky the wave was spotted before it hit.

"Check on the trawler," the skipper said as soon as we had resumed our positions.

"Passing to port," I said. "Angle on the bow, one niner zero." This meant the boat had turned and was heading away from us and probably hadn't spotted us. The Sam's red port light, green starboard light, masthead light, and running light at the stern were all extinguished so we were running dark. The union jack was also taken in since it wouldn't be needed underwater.

"Very well," the skipper said. "Scan without the binoculars first."

"Aye, aye, Sir," I said. I had always had good night vision and being farsighted helped me see the horizon better than most. After a complete scan, without, and then with the binoculars, I made my report. "No contacts, sir, except the initial contact, bearing two seven zero. Angle on the bow zero niner zero and heading over the horizon."

"Very well," the skipper said. "Officer of the bridge, rig the bridge for dive and dive the ship."

"Aye, aye, Sir," the officer said. He moved the microphone close to his mouth and clicked it on. "I have the bridge. Clear the bridge. Control room, prepare to dive."

With the command to clear the bridge, I headed down the ladder just behind the skipper. The last man to leave the bridge was the officer, who closed the clamshell and followed me down the ladder. He was also responsible for securing all the hatches which led to the bridge. The last hatch into the sub was verified closed by the COB, who was waiting at the bottom of the ladder in the control room.

There was a green board on the ballast control panel Christmas tree indicating all systems were ready and the boat could submerge. The order to dive and the familiar "ooga, ooga" of the Klaxon told the control room and the rest of the sub we were starting our last patrol before heading for the shipyard.

episode seven

"So, ya started yah third one, huh?" Captain Bob said.

"Yes, and it was pretty much uneventful," I said. "I was qualified and stood missile watches. It was my second patrol during the Christmas holidays, so I was a little saddened and missed my parents and sisters, especially when I was the only one not receiving any Sam grams."

"Ya haf ta 'splain that one," Captain Bob said.

Sam grams were messages, up to four a patrol and limited to thirty words, which we received from family. Loved ones sent letters addressed to us on the blue crew, which the gold crew would receive in New London. The gold crew, seeing blue crew on the address then sent the message electronically and we picked it up on our low-frequency trailing antenna wire. But, before transmission, the letters were censored by the chaplain. It was the shrinks' idea to do the censoring since bad news while on patrol might affect our morale. So we all knew, if we didn't get any messages at all, it meant the worst had happened, which had the same effect as getting the bad news. It was sort of a "no news is bad news" situation.

On the first two patrols, I got my Sam grams regularly, but on this patrol I didn't get any. The entire crew knew I was not getting any news from back home and had sympathy for me. The doc watched me pretty closely for depression, especially at Christmas time. The rest of the crew hid their messages when I walked by and turned their heads. I thought the worst, that someone in my family had died. The mystery was solved when we pulled into Charleston and the gold crew met us. They had my letters and handed them to me when we tied up to off load missiles.

My parents had addressed them to the gold crew by mistake; and, since there was no one in the gold crew with my name, they just stuck them in a drawer. Finally, someone checked the blue crew list, realized the mistake, and brought them to the ship when we made port.

"How'd ya get them messages at sea?" Captain Bob said

"We trailed six hundred feet of wire behind the sub that picked up low frequency signals sent from surface ships or from communication stations here in the States. Most of the time we were only making about five or six knots. Any faster than that and we would have to haul in the wire or it would get cut by the screw."

Rue the officer who cut the cable by accident. It happened once or twice a patrol when the conning officer forgot to pull in the wire before he ordered a down angle or increased speed. The wire was stored next to the access ladder that went to the bridge. It trailed out from behind the sail and was designed to float near the surface so we could pick up signals.

The cable was extremely important because this is how we knew whether or not we were at war and when we were supposed to launch our missiles. It was also used to receive the Sam grams. There were other means of communication if we were in an emergency situation or had to send a message. We couldn't send a message with the low-frequency, floating antenna. It could only receive.

If the cable was cut, a radioman had to crawl up into the access tube and re-feed a new wire. First he had to pull what was left of the wire back into the sub and then feed it back through the water tight seals so that the length paid out could be determined. Apparently it was not a pleasant job because of the placement of the system and the cramped and cold operating position. I was on the planes one time when it was cut. The first indication was a call from the radio room stating that they had lost the signal, followed immediately by a lot of "aw shits." The next was an irate radioman stomping out of the communications room cursing his luck and the officer who had cut the cable.

It must have been tough work because the entire time he was up on the access ladder, there was a lot of cursing, which could be heard at the diving station where I was sitting.

"You were underwater for Christmas, was ya?" Captain Bob said.

"And New Year's Eve, which was an experience."

"Yeah, with nothin' ta drink."

"Not necessarily," I said.

My first New Year's Eve on the sub was uneventful. I slept through it all since I was mess cooking and qualifying. I missed any of the activities, if indeed there were any. But my second New Year's Eve I was up for the entire time. Some guys smuggled booze onto the sub. It was outlawed, but that was a hard rule to enforce. The officers had their own stash, but they knew how to behave when they drank alcohol. Most of the enlisted didn't. For those who didn't have any booze, there was gilly.

Someone had designed a component on the missiles that had a poro-prism mirror that could only be cleaned with pure grain alcohol. As I mentioned before, Snake used it to clean electrical contacts and always had his own bottle. Although there was not a lot of gilly, it was one hundred percent alcohol and went a long way when mixed with coffee or bug juice. It came in pint cans and I don't remember who had control of it, but it was distributed freely on December 31. I didn't drink anything alcoholic for fear of getting caught and sent back to mess cooking, but it seemed like the rest of the crew was feeling no pain. I also was on watch from midnight until six in the morning so had to remain alert.

One of the men got drunk and called an officer some names, or so I heard. Some of the crew were able to calm down the drunken enlisted man and all that happened was he received a verbal reprimand the next day. There must have been two or three gallons of gilly to clean sixteen mirrors and in my two patrols as a missile technician we only cleaned them twice. That meant a lot of gilly evaporated before we got back to port.

Since I was now qualified on submarines and standing watches in the missile compartment, I had a lot of time on my hands for some of the fun parts of the patrol. However, I first did what most others did until their eyes failed open; I slept. It took about three weeks and then one night after I got off watch I tried to sleep, but couldn't. After three weeks of sleeping twelve of every eighteen hours, I just couldn't keep my eyes closed anymore.

"Weren't ya a little bit buggy, not havin' nuthin' ta do for the rest of the patrol?" Captain Bob asked.

"We worked on the missiles occasionally, usually the guidance packages, which were the missiles' brains. They were about twice the size of basketballs and were mounted on the last stage of the missile, accessed through a hatch on the third level. Because it had the computer, gyros, and electronic controls in a metal case, it was very heavy. Spare guidance packages were stored on the third level too. There was an overhead-mounted rail system that went around the third level and was used to remove and install guidance packages. We weren't allowed to work on the packages, just change them when one went bad."

The operation could be done very quickly by two people, which was required anyway whenever a missile hatch was open. To access the guidance package, there were several screws on the surface of the missile that had to be removed and reinstalled in a patterned sequence. Just above the access cover was the arming switch that had to be turned with a special key only the weapons officer and skipper had access to. They each wore a key around their necks the entire patrol that opened a lock box where the arming keys were stored. It took both keys to open the lock box.

During a "battle stations, missile," drill we opened the hatches and simulated turning the key. All the steps were practiced and timed to determine how fast we could get all the missiles armed and ready to launch.

We also inspected the warhead by climbing inside the launch tube above the guidance package and working our way around the outside of the missile looking for any defects. We could actually touch the re-entry heat shield made of beryllium. We were told that if we got a piece of the metal in an open wound, it would have to be surgically removed or it wouldn't heal. Therefore, we were very careful while doing the inspections.

Most other items on the missiles didn't need any attention. If a missile had any major problems, the entire missile was replaced during turnover alongside the tender. The missile would then be sent back to the manufacturer for repairs. Once I did have to replace a hydraulic package on the bottom of the missile.

"We got a bad, first-stage hydraulic package on bird six," Little Dickey said. "We have permission to change it in an hour."

"Okay," I said. "We'd better read the manual."

"I've got it out on the workbench," he said.

I put my latest James Bond book in my back pocket and refreshed my cup of coffee. I had been sitting in the chow hall reading when I got the news.

Hydraulic packages don't go bad very often. They are on the nozzle end of the missiles and are accessed from the bottom level of the missile compartment.

"This is very simple, but it's more complicated than it sounds," Mr. Inman stated.

By now we were so used to his Jimisms, we either ignored them or came back with one of our own.

"You hit something right on the head, sir," I said.

"Yes sir, we need to make sure we don't cross the 'T' half way and dot every other 'I'." Little Dickey said using another Jimism we had heard from him before.

I believe he had no idea that we were mimicking him. If there was no one else around when he blurted one out, we were able to keep straight faces. Of course around other officers we were careful not to answer one of his quips with one we had heard previously. To do so could have been interpreted as insubordination.

After we both had gone over the procedure for removing and replacing a hydraulic package, we got Larry. His job was to squat outside the lower level access hatch of the missile tube to read the checklist to us and hand us tools.

"Well, you ready for this?" I asked.

"As ready as I'll ever be," Little Dickey said.

"Request permission to enter the missile tube," Larry said, over the headset connected to fire control and the torpedoman at the control panel. We always had to ask permission to enter a missile tube. That was a way of letting all know what we were doing and when. There were alarm indicators that would alert the fire control center and missile tube monitoring station when a hatch was opened. They also needed to monitor the down time for record keeping.

"We have permission," Larry said after a few seconds.

The tube was vented and then we turned the rotating ring to allow the hatch to be opened. The air that came out of the tube smelled strongly metallic.

"After you," Little Dickey said, gesturing for me to go in first.

There was a frame running right through the middle of the bottom of the tube, so I would lie on one side and Little Dickey would lie on the other while we worked on the missile. Once in the tube, I had about eight inches between me and the missile. I was looking up one of the four nozzles, at the solid propellant which could be ignited with a spark. It was for that reason that all of our tools used inside the missile tube were non-sparking, usually made of brass. If the missile ignited accidentally, I wouldn't even have time to say "aw shit." Of course the entire sub would be lost as the ignited fuel would melt a hole in the missile compartment the size of a cement truck. So, it was with a lot of consternation that I lay down on my back to work on the missile. Soon Little Dickey was on his back beside me, the frame our only separation.

"Comfy?" I asked.

"Sure," was his response.

"Unlock the patch connector," Larry said from outside the tube and the work began.

The bad hydraulic package was lowered onto my chest and passed out to Larry. He handed us the new one and we bolted it in place. The last item on the list was to double check the signal plug.

"Double check the Chicago connector," Larry said.

The connector which connected the two nozzles together got its name from the theory, that if it were installed wrong, everything would work backwards and the bird would fly west instead of east, hitting Chicago instead of Moscow. Moscow, however, was a lot farther north, but the idea was still there.

"The magafus is properly connected," Little Dickey said. He called a lot of objects a magafus and most tools were magafus tweakers.

I never got claustrophobia, mainly because I never thought about it much. Lying inside a missile tube with not enough room to turn on your side and having a huge missile on top of you would have made a few people a little nervous. To me it was just part of the job.

"Didn't everything in the missile get wet when that there missile was pushed out of the tube?" Captain Bob asked.

"No," I said. "The missiles were pushed out by high pressure air constantly expanding which formed bubbles around them. We weren't that deep when we launched, either. So the missile never got wet.

"There were other things to do besides work to divert our attention and to keep us from going nuts," I said to Captain Bob. "My first two patrols, I was so busy qualifying submarines and mess cooking, I had no time to think about where I was and what to do."

Morale on the submarine was a major concern of the brass and the doctors. Being cooped up in a metal can for two months or longer, never getting to see the sun and living in cramped conditions were a strain on mental well being. At least we were told that.

Psychiatrists roamed about the subs on the early patrols taking copious notes on how we reacted to various situations and stimuli.

"How would you feel if you were told to launch a nuclear weapon knowing that the sub was a deterrent to be used only if the U.S. had been attacked with nuclear weapons?" was one question they posed.

"I would be concerned that we couldn't reload fast enough," was the answer they got most of the time.

A psychiatrist once witnessed two sailors observing the two-man rule while working on a piece of electronic equipment. Sub sailors loved to distract each other and one way was to stick a wet finger in another's ear when he was trying to concentrate on one thing or another. It happened so often, that the one being stuck would just ignore the sticker and go about his business.

"Quit it! Goddamn it! Quit it!" one electronics technician said to another while the former had his hand in a sensitive piece of equipment.

The first electrician thought the man was sticking his finger in his ear, but the sticker actually had his dick out and was poking it in the man's ear. The first man just kept on working, never looking to see the man with his penis in his hand. He never saw the psychiatrist either as he walked around the corner, witnessed what was going on, wrote down copious notes in his book, shook his head, and left. From that incident, the powers that be determined that we needed a lot of great tasting food, steak twice a week, lobster on Friday, and pizza every Saturday during casino night.

I don't think the ingenuity of the sailors who volunteered for sub duty was considered in the equation calculating how we would react to extended stays underwater. The Polaris Field Electronics program attracted some of the more intelligent men from high school and college. We came aboard the Sam as missile technicians, fire control technicians, and electronic technicians. In addition, the nuclear power program attracted a special group of people. Even torpedoes became more complicated with nuclear warheads, guidance packages, and other electrical/mechanical improvements.

As a result, ninety percent of the officers and men on a submarine were highly trained and motivated individuals. There were also incentives to keep our morale high. Sub pay and "pro pay" (pay for being in a "professional" field) was added to a sailor's base pay to entice men into the submarines and to retain them. For those not getting pro pay, there was good food, casino night, R&R periods and movies.

The food was great except for fresh vegetables. The only ones that kept a long time were carrots. That was the good news. The bad news was we had a lot of carrots. There was also a lot of dehydrated cottage cheese which, when reconstituted, tasted like the white paste that we had had in grade school in the fifties. The cottage cheese was supposed to help us with our calcium and vitamin D deficiencies, a result of not seeing the sun for three months. We were served as much as we could eat anytime we wanted it, and the cooks went to culinary school to learn how to prepare great tasting food. However, some times they screwed up.

"What are these?" the COB asked, as he showed his plate to the cook on duty.

"Chicken croquettes," the new cook replied.

The new cook was on his first patrol, fresh from the culinary school. They had taught him how to spell and pronounce croquette, but obviously not how to make them taste good.

"They taste like shit," the COB said. "There's not enough ketchup on the sub to make me eat the rest of this."

With that, he tossed the conical shaped turd ball into the trash. The fact that the entire crew did the same didn't deter the cook from trying again, but with help.

"What are we having tonight?" the COB asked the next Friday.

"Lobster Newburgh," the new cook replied.

We had frozen lobster tails in the freezer, enough for eight Fridays. They weren't as good as fresh, but that's all we had. One of the crew, not a cook, worked at a four-star restaurant when we were in New London for R&R. A lot of us worked second jobs because the pay, even with pro and sub pay was too low. We also had three months with basically nothing to do. I worked to save for college and needed the extra money to meet my goal of getting through college with the least amount of financial pain.

The cooks were going to let the part-time chef prepare the meal with the cooks serving as helpers. No one knows what went wrong, but no one but the cooks were allowed to prepare meals after that experiment.

"This tastes pretty damn good," the COB said when he came back from the chief's quarters.

"Thanks," the beaming substitute cook said.

The meal did taste great; however, what couldn't be tasted was the bacteria that gave us all the shits three hours later.

"I gotta go," said Little Dickey.

"Me too," I said. Little Dickey headed for the missile compartment, while I headed to the forward head in crew's berthing. Luckily, I was off duty and there was still one stall vacant. However, I wasn't off duty for long and the stalls all filled up pretty quickly. Those on duty had to be relieved by those not experiencing diarrhea at the moment. The ones who didn't like or eat the lobster, and there were very few of those, didn't get sick. They also didn't get a break from standing watches while those needing to void themselves had to leave their stations. This went on for almost the full six-hour shift following the meal.

Doc didn't have anything strong enough or quick acting enough to stop the flow. The malady just had to run its course. The men in the engine room, the furthest from the toilets, were sitting on buckets while standing their watch. All who had eaten the lobster, from the skipper on down, were affected. Had the skipper been unscathed, I'm sure we would have had a bailout procedure, just to "test our readiness."

The doc determined that the lobster must have been kept at too warm a temperature on the tender before it was even loaded onboard. The eggs and cream were tested and found to be free from contamination, so the rest of the lobster tails were sent to the bottom of the ocean via the GDU. The poor part-time chef was never fully exonerated and had to endure the rest of the patrol as the "butt" of a lot of jokes.

Because we used a lot of toilet paper during this episode, I thought I'd have to use one of the tips my "sea daddy" had given me during my first patrol.

"Andy," Cooky said, "let me show ya how to wipe your ass with one sheet of shit paper." I didn't know if he was serious or not, but he was my sea daddy and had given me some good practical advice so far. I watched intently as he removed a square of toilet tissue from a roll he kept in the galley to use as kleenex.

"First, fold it in half twice, like this," he said. "Then take the corner which has the folds in it like so and tear off a small piece of it so's ya got a hole in the middle of the square. Set the piece ya tore off aside to use later." He tore off the corner, and set the small piece of tissue on the table. When he opened the remaining square of tissue there was a small hole in it the size of a quarter. The other men in the chow hall were now gathering around to see what this was all about.

"Now, put your pointin' finger through the hole and drape the rest of the paper over your fist and thumb to keep it from gettin' dirty." He placed the paper over the index finger of his right hand and smoothed the rest of the tissue out over his knuckles. "Now, you kin wipe your ass with your finger and then shake off the excess, like this." He then pretended to wipe his finger over his ass and then shook it like it had a booger on it. It was now that I knew my leg was being pulled.

"You're almost done. Take your clean hand and slide it up under the shit paper and remove it by twisting and wiping up, cleaning your finger at the same time." He took his left hand and slid it up under the tissue draped over his right-hand knuckles and slid the paper up pretending to wipe the right index finger on the way. "Toss the paper in the can and look for that little piece of corner you set aside."

"What's that other piece for?" I said, playing along with the joke.

"Well, ya take that piece and clean your fingernail with it." He never cracked a smile as he demonstrated the process, but those who had gathered around to witness the demonstration burst out laughing.

"One last piece of advice," he concluded. "Pick your nose with your other hand,"

There was another howl of laughter from the crowd, who must not have heard this joke either. Cooky just got up and walked back to the galley carrying his roll of paper.

"Other than fixin' and eatin' food, what was there to do?" Captain Bob said.

"Movies were a good way to break the monotony and they were shown almost every night." I said. "And that's no shit."

"I saw nipple!" Kozy shouted, jumping to his feet and pointing to the screen.

I was in the chow hall watching the nightly flick with most of the crew who were not on watch. Flicks were another one of the "morale boosters" which were supposed to keep sub sailors from going nuts. Enough movies were loaded for showing one a night, sixty in all, for the normal patrol.

The only media available to us was sixteen millimeter celluloid films shown from a projector set up in the chow hall on a pull-down screen. Because we had to wait for the movies to be put in the sixteen-millimeter format, we had only older movies to watch. When a movie, which was only three-years old, like *Viva Las Vegas* with Elvis Presley and Ann-Margret was on the schedule, every man wanted to see it. There were two showings of all movies so the men on watch could see the same movie when they were relieved.

I found out on my first patrol that watching movies was a privilege which could be revoked by the COB. After my mess cook duties were finished for the night and the movie was set up, I took a seat.

"What are you doing here?" the COB asked, scowling.

I didn't have an answer, other than the obvious one, which would have sounded like I was a smartass, so I just looked at him quizzically and waited for him to respond.

"Your quals aren't up to date," he said. "You can't watch a movie until they are."

I just got up and left, feeling angry. I had just spent more than twelve hours as a mess cook being treated like the scum of the earth, and I just wanted to relax a little. I had intended to work on my quals after the movie. I knew I couldn't stay, so I got up, went back and got my Navships Tabs, the eleven-and-a-half by four-and-a-quarter-inch illustrated booklets with all the submarine systems, and started hunting around the sub for valves. On the next patrol, when I was assigned as a mess cook again, I didn't even try to watch a movie. After I finished my tour of duty mess cooking and was qualified, I assumed I was allowed to watch movies.

Viva Las Vegas was shown on my third patrol. I was now qualified and standing watch as a missile technician. *By God I was going to watch every movie shown!* I never witnessed the COB telling another mess cook he couldn't watch a movie, so felt he had singled me out for punishment. Right or wrong, I felt I had been picked on because I had dropped out of the Naval Academy and the COB didn't like "college boys."

"What's showin' tonight?" I asked Snake, who always seemed to be the projectionist. It was the night before the nipple event.

"*The Bad Seed*," he said. "It's an oldie in black and white."

Indeed it was an oldie, from 1956 to be exact, and it not only had "bad" in its title, it was bad, at least by submariners' standard. Every once in a while, we got one of these "god-awful" movies that were on the shelf and taken because there were no others left to make up the required number for a two-month patrol. When this happened, we made a game of it.

"Here are the movie cards," Snake said when the show was over.

Only half of the men, who had watched the movie from the start, remained in the chow hall. *Goddamn it, I'm staying,* I said to myself when the movie got so bad people started to leave. *I have movie privileges this entire patrol and I'm watchin' every fuckin' one all the way through.*

"What's a movie card?" I asked.

"We haven't used one for two patrols, but this flick has earned us the right," Snake answered.

"Count me out," a couple of guys said.

"Not me," said a couple more.

"I'm in," some of the remaining guys said.

I still didn't know what was in store, so I took a card and looked at it. It was a wallet-sized card with squares marked off and a hole punched in one of the squares. It was much like the "give-a-shit" cards some of the crew carried around. When they were told something they didn't really care about, they would spout off, "Wanna punch my give-a-shit card?"

The cards Snake handed out were a little dog-eared as though he had carried them around in his pocket waiting for this opportunity. The guys who got movie cards stayed after the first showing, so I stayed too. I pulled out my James Bond book and started to read as though I knew what this was all about.

Twenty minutes later, the movie was all ready for the off-coming watch to view. When they started trickling in, they saw the others still sitting there. Little Dickey grabbed a cup of coffee and sat down next to me.

"I heard this is a punch-card movie," Little Dickey said. All news traveled rapidly throughout the submarine like water from a burst dam.

"Yeah, here's mine, but what does it mean?" I asked.

"When a movie is really bad, it's shown every day until the patrol is over. Those who stay through the entire movie get their cards punched. The person with the most holes is declared the "bad movie watcher" of the patrol. There was one movie like that on my first patrol, but because I was qualifying, I didn't participate."

"Give me a card," Little Dickey said to Snake, who handed him one similar to mine.

"Your card isn't punched," I said.

"It will be if I stay through the entire show. How bad was it?

"You'll see." I said.

Neither Little Dickey nor I won. The guy who was declared the winner watched all forty-two showings. I only made it through five.

"What?" most of us said.

"I saw nipple," Kozy repeated.

No one else had apparently seen it, but Kozy had a pornographic eye, and if he saw nipple, by God there must have been a nipple. All of the movies were censored by the chaplain back in New London, who had one of his aides go through the movies and remove clips of any scene that might remind us of sex.

On the last patrol, all of the clipped out scenes from the movie were in the black metal movie canister neatly curled around the outer edge of the reel. An aide must have thought the censorship policy was wrong and decided to give us something else to watch. The strips of celluloid were passed around the sub several times and rolled back around the reel for the next boat.

So when Kozy shouted that he had seen a nipple, some were in doubt, but, after all, this was Kozy who had made the discovery.

We all sat on the edge of our seats craning our necks in anticipation as Snake stopped the movie, unthreaded it, rewound it short way, and then rethreaded it.

Elvis and Ann were rolling around on the ground as the movie was restarted.

"Slow it down, slow it down!" Kozy shouted. "It's almost there."

The sight of a nipple after three weeks at sea must have been burned on his eyes. Snake did as he was commanded and stepped the movie forward in slow motion. Then, as Ann rolled slowly in jerk-step motion, a left nipple appeared on four frames. The eye is capable of seeing individual frames only if they go slower than twelve per second, so how Kozy saw those four frames when the projector was going at sixteen frames a second was amazing. The chaplain's aide had missed it too, but not Kozy.

Snake quickly rethreaded the machine and stepped through it again, this time stopping it when Ann Margaret's left nipple was in full bloom, only it was stopped a little too long. A bubble started in the center and quickly grew to engulf the entire scene. I knew from running projectors in high school, that Ann's tit was fried.

"Goddamn it!" Kozy shouted. "You burned her nipple."

"Sorry about that," Snake said matter-of-factly as he returned the projector to its normal speed.

Snake verified later that all four frames were damaged, so the nipple was gone forever, but not in our minds.

"What else were there?" Captain Bob said.

"There was pizza night," I said. I yawned as I stroked Dedra and glanced at the clock. It was only a minute later than the last time I had

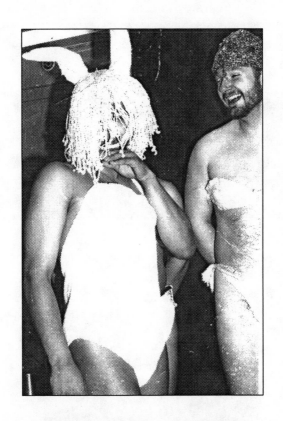

looked. I started to wonder if this was just a dream or if the clock had stopped.

Every Saturday night was pizza night and it was announced by the smell of garlic throughout the sub. Those whose eyes had not yet failed open and were asleep in their bunks, awoke at the first pungent whiff. The same rebel who did the yell my first night in the barracks and who always wanted the hot sauce, walked through the sub as soon as he caught a whiff of garlic. He had a dazed look in his eyes and muttered "pizza, pizza, pizza." The pizza was good and did remind us of the food we had left behind, so it was a meal not to be missed.

Every Saturday night was also casino night. Because the work day shifted by six hours every day, you only missed one out of every three Saturday nights. I never attended a casino night because I didn't get a thrill from gambling. My father taught me a valuable lesson when I was just a child. I wanted to play cards for money and wanted him to teach me. He did teach me the value of each card hand and at the same time the value of my money. Although we only played penny-ante poker, the pennies were all I had. He had no qualms about taking the pot and never gave it back to me at the end of the game when I ran out of pennies. From that day on, I didn't gamble my money away; however, some of the crew didn't learn at an early age and suffered as adults.

There were some big-stake poker games played on casino night. No one interfered, not even the captain. It was allowed and those who played were grown men and responsible for their own actions. There were also some small stake games, craps, and even a roulette table. Most of it was just for fun and only a few lost a lot. Those who lost big time, gave all the money they got paid at the end of the patrol to the winners. I felt sorry for them but it was their own doing.

Then there was the halfway party.

"What's the halfaway party?" Captain Bob said

"It was a celebration of making it halfway through the cruise. On this, my third cruise though, we would add on another six days crossing the Atlantic underwater. Here are some pictures of the two halfway parties I participated in. I'm almost embarrassed to show the one where we were supposed to be Playboy bunnies. It was when I was getting a bit heavy. In the first picture, I'm on the right and Joe is on the left."

"For the halfway party, some of the crew would get together and make up funny skits that the rest of the crew would watch, including the officers. It was one time we could make fun of the officers and some of the crew members and not get in trouble. We all could take a joke and if we couldn't, we didn't last long in the submarine Navy. The halfway party celebrated the end of the first month at sea and meant we were on the downhill side of another patrol.

"Some of the men had count-down calendars. The most inventive one was of a totally naked lady with her body sectioned off with the number of days in the patrol. Every day, the owner of the calendar would mark in a section, until she was completely covered. He saved the best parts for last. On my last patrol, I made a count-down calendar for the rest of the time I had left in the Navy. It was just the days listed in order which I drew a line through when completed. When I got to within thirty days of discharge, I got such a give-a-shit attitude, I even quit marking off the days."

"So yah crossed the 'Lantic completely underwater, did ya?"

"Yes. Other subs had done it before. One in particular was the George Washington, the first nuclear-warhead missile submarine. The underwater listening devices the Navy had were so sensitive, they could detect her passage and tell how fast she was going. When the George Washington came to periscope depth to fix her position and receive messages, the fleet headquarters, CINCLANTFLT, or Commander in Chief, US Atlantic Fleet, ordered her to slow down. We crossed at full speed without any problems."

"Then you got to the States?" Captain Bob said.

"Yes, we started preparing for overhaul. The first thing we did before pulling into port was to dump radioactive waste into the ocean. Divers went over the side with a pipe, shaped like a fin to reduce drag while we were moving through the water. It was attached to a valve on the side of the reactor compartment and then the divers came back on board. We sailed along leaving the toxic material in our wake. After the dump was over, the pipe was removed. I doubt that's done anymore, but who knows."

That was not the only experience I had with radioactive liquids. On my first patrol, I was following a piping system through the engine room and noticed water coming out of a pipe on the port side, front corner of the compartment. I was taught in sub school that water was not a good thing inside a sub, so I immediately reported the leak to the maneuvering room across the passageway on the starboard side.

"There's water coming out of a pipe on the port side," I said, shouting loud enough to be heard over the noise from all the machinery.

The lithium bromide air conditioning plant, two thousand gallon per day distillery, steam generating plant, propulsion system, hydraulic pumps, and almost all of the other major systems were in the engine room. The maneuvering room was where the reactor was controlled, including shut down, which was called scramming. The propulsion system was also controlled there.

"Where?" was the reaction I got, with one man immediately following me to the location.

As soon as the man saw the leak, he reached through the flowing water and shut a valve stopping the flow.

"Did you come in here?" he asked. I thought I was going to be accused of opening a valve, since I was unqualified. We were taught to test whether a valve position is normally open or shut, to turn it clockwise. If it turns, it is normally open. If it doesn't, it is normally shut. His intentions were not to blame me, but to determine whether or not I was contaminated. The valve was at the point where the secondary water from the reactor was tested and it could have been radioactive.

"No," I said. "I saw it from the passageway and came and got you."

"Go and get the engineer officer," he commanded.

I did, and there was a little excitement for awhile until they used a dosimeter to conclude that the water was not contaminated. Some still thought I was the one who opened the valve, until one of the enginemen confessed he "might have left it open" when taking samples. I went from being goat to being hero for having sounded the alert as quickly as I did.

We all wore film badges which were tested halfway through and at the end of the patrol to determine if we had been exposed to any radiation. A dosimeter, which was more of an instantaneous radiation indicator, was worn by those who had to enter the reactor room for repairs.

The closest I ever came to the reactor was in the passageway in the reactor room. The passageway was just bulkheads, deck, overhead and a hatch on each end and was referred to as the tunnel. There was a thick, metal-infused glass viewing panel from which the reactor and all the associated primary system piping could be viewed. The radiation we received on all of our patrols was less than a person living outside the sub receives during one summer at the beach. At least that was what we were told.

The next step after dumping the reactor water was to off-load our torpedoes in New London. We did it in four hours and then headed to the tongue of the ocean for sound trials.

"Tongue of the ocean, huh?"

"Yes," I said. "The tongue is near the Bahamas where the shallow water, thirty feet deep, forms an archipelago jutting out into the Atlantic like a tongue. Around the shallow water, shear cliffs drop down four thousand to six thousand feet. The Navy had sound buoys installed to record ships' noise patterns. Once there, we made passes at the buoys and a record was made of our sound patterns. After that, we headed back to Charleston, South Carolina, to off load missiles."

"You was on the sub for all this?"

"Yes. We were underwater for seventy one days on patrol and the transatlantic crossing. After the four-hour off load of torpedoes, we were underwater another thirty days. Except for those four hours, I didn't touch land, have contact with the outside, see farther than one hundred feet, nor see the sun for over one hundred days.

"After all missiles were off loaded, we took the Sam to the shipyard. Only then did I go home for R&R."

"Whad ya do there?" the captain asked.

"I visited with my folks, and rested up."

When I got back to the shipyard after thirty days away, I checked in to the barge and found my bunk. Instead of in a barracks, we lived on a barge that floated on the west side of the Portsmouth Naval Shipyard. The base was actually part of Kittery, Maine, across the Piscataqua River from Portsmouth, on Seavey Island. The locals pronounced Kittery as if there were no e in it and we quickly adopted that into our speech.

After I got settled in, I went to see the Sam. She looked kind of sad, sitting in a dry dock with no screw, a couple of big holes in her and the nose taken off. There were blue tarps over her fresh wounds, the biggest just aft of the missile compartment. The hole there was required to refuel the reactor and to take out the gyro from auxiliary machinery room one. Several other holes were cut to facilitate removal and replacement of upgraded machinery.

"What did ya do in the shipyard with no missiles to tend to?"

"We were on port and starboard duty again. There were no real military watches to stand, other than the watch on the barge, so they had us standing fire watches."

"Ya watched fires?"

"No, we had to sit by the welders with a fire extinguisher while they cut or welded steel. It was an extremely boring job and the welders felt sorry for us. The shipyard worked around the clock on the Sam so we would be awakened in the wee hours of the morning to go and stand a fire watch. The shipyard workers were sympathetic and usually told us to curl up in a corner. They would wake us when they were through. If we had gotten caught sleeping on watch, we could have been court-martialed. However, most of the welding jobs were inside tanks or under the superstructure with only one way in. That way we couldn't easily get caught. There was only one officer in charge at night and he was in bed, so there was little chance of getting in trouble

"It was difficult getting to sleep when I knew someone would wake me at midnight to stand a two-hour fire or security watch. Lights were out at ten and I was awakened at eleven-thirty to get ready to stand the watch. When I had to stay awake during a watch, I drank a lot of coffee which had been sitting in the pot since the evening meal.

"By the time I got off watch and made it back to my bunk it was two-thirty. I had a difficult time getting back to sleep with all the caffeine I had consumed knowing I had to get up at six to start the day. I drank so much coffee I developed sensitivity to caffeine later in life."

The day after my first fire watch I experienced flash burns. My eyes felt as if someone were sticking them with a hot, sharp poker. We had been warned about flash burns and told not to look directly at the bright arc of the welder. I was careful to turn my head, but there were welders everywhere and the flashes would catch the corner of your eye, or bounce off a puddle of water or some other reflective material. Almost every fire watch suffered from flash burns more than once. There was nothing that could be done about them except to let your eyes water and give the burns a couple of days to heal, just in time for the next watch.

Some of the welders would give us some smoked glass so we could watch them work. This took the edge off the boredom. Other welders took the time to teach us how to weld with rods and to cut steel with a carbon arc. That was a mistake, because one of the first things I did was tack weld a tool box to the exposed steel deck on the third level of the missile compartment. The worker was at lunch, so no one saw me do it. When the whistle blew ending the shift, I told one of the other fire watches what I had done, and we stood nearby the welded box to see what would happen.

He bent down on the fly to pick the box up, but nearly ripped his arm off when it didn't move. He saw us when we started to laugh and just shook his head. He grabbed an air chisel and quickly freed it, but I felt sorry for him since he was late leaving and never did that again.

Only once was there a fire where I had to use the fire extinguisher, and that was to put out a flaming welder. He was wearing a cotton sweatshirt which caught fire from the sparks of his carbon arc welder. Because he had a welders mask on, he couldn't see the flames. I had to tap him on the back, and then, when he raised his mask, he realized his dilemma. I used the fire extinguisher while he beat at the flames until the shirt quit burning. Because he had three layers of clothes on, he suffered no burns.

The shipyard was where I learned about "test depth tape," a precursor to duct tape for which the government paid all the development costs. It got its name when a shipyard worker used it to seal up a leak in a water line and then proceeded to test it to the depth a submarine was designed for. It supposedly held and was thereafter labeled test depth tape. To my knowledge it was never put to use during a real emergency on a submarine, but it was on board, just in case.

"Life on the barge was not all that bad. When we had some quiet time, we used to fish off the side away from the pier. Once I caught what I thought was the biggest fish in the river. When I hauled it in, it was only ten inches long, lean, and shaped like a little torpedo. I had no idea what type it was, but it put up a hell of a fight. Right before I tossed it back for someone else to enjoy, Larry told me it was a mackerel."

"Ay-yeah. They do fight on the hook," Captain Bob confirmed.

There were seagulls all around the barge, especially when we were fishing. They would land on the corner of the barge about ten feet away from us and wait for a treat. I had never seen one that close and noticed how large it was. I think they grew a little bigger in Maine.

For entertainment, we used to soak pieces of bread in Louisiana Hot Sauce and then toss them to the gulls. Some would catch the fiery morsel on the fly, but when the heat hit them they dipped low and headed for the water. They flew a few inches off the surface with their lower beaks acting like plows, scooping up water as they went. I was told we could get in trouble for doing that since the gulls are a protected species. I stopped as soon as I heard that. Besides, I felt guilty about doing it.

Once my shipmate. Gill, talked me into checking a canoe out of Special Services, the recreational office for the sailors in the shipyard. I agreed, and soon we had the thing in the water, life jackets on and paddles in hand, ready to go. We sat with our knees bent American Indian style which hurt a little until our legs went numb. We paddled up the Piscataqua River just as the tide was beginning to ebb. It seemed fairly easy and we got about two miles from the shipyard.

"Let's head across the river to that point over there," Gill said.

"Sure," I replied feeling good about the exercise.

We started out for the area Gill wanted to explore and about halfway across the river the tide started to turn. The shipyard was about two miles from the mouth of the river and the Atlantic Ocean was visible from where we started our trip. So, when the water started to flow toward the ocean, it moved rapidly.

"I'll just keep the nose pointed for the point," Gill said. I was in the front and he was in back with the steering responsibilities. I had never been in a canoe before so had zero experience. I just paddled as hard as I could, but the river was easily defeating us. About half way across, it became apparent we were not going to get to the place we were aiming for. We were now almost parallel to the shore line with the nose of the canoe pointing upstream and still heading out to sea.

"Paddle! Paddle!" I said. Both of us were breathing hard by now and we still had several yards to go before we could reach shore. Finally we made it, but the place we aimed for was not in sight. We looked across the river and found we were almost directly across from the Spe-

The Castle at Portsmouth Naval Shipyard

cial Services' boat dock. We had gone down stream trying to cross the river as far as we had gone up stream.

"Let's head back across," Gill said.

"Fuck you and the horse your rode in on," I said. "You see what's out that way, where we'll probably end up? The fuckin' ocean! And if we do make it across, we'll end up at the Castle."

The Castle was the Navy prison guarded by the meanest Marines on the planet. We were told that if a prisoner escaped on a Marine's duty watch, the Marine had to take the escapee's place. Therefore, there was no coddling in the Castle. One false story about the Castle was that Humphrey Bogart, while a Marine guard there during World War I, had his lip split by a prisoner which caused his lisp. This was not true, as he joined the Marines and served as a ship's gunner. While roughhousing on the vessel's wooden stairway, he tripped and fell; a splinter became lodged in his upper lip causing partial paralysis. The Castle was closed down in 1974.

I was not going to risk putting ashore within the restricted grounds of the Castle and end up as a prisoner myself. The other possibility was to end up at sea in the dark. It was nearing six o'clock. I think reality was also setting in with Gill.

"We don't have much choice then, but to portage the canoe up and over the bridge and back to the base," he said.

"How about we leave the canoe, walk to the base and then come back and get it in your car?" I countered. What we ended up actually doing was dragging the canoe upstream about a mile and by then the ebb tide had subsided enough to allow us fairly easy paddling back across the river, ending up where we began.

"Hey! Look at this brochure I picked up at Special Services when we got back," Gill said, as we sat, exhausted, in the chow hall eating cold food leftover from the evening meal. "It says 'at ebb tide, the Piscataqua River is one of the fastest flowing rivers in the world'." I would have strangled him if I could have moved my arms.

"Look at this," Rod said, holding out what looked like a ring.

"What's that?" I said.

"It's a ring made from a Monel nut."

"A what?"

"A nut, made from nickel, copper, iron, and manganese. The metal is called Monel. It's used all over the sub, because it doesn't rust and is better than stainless steel. Here, have a couple."

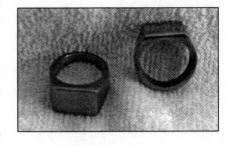

He handed me what looked like three ordinary nuts with a rather dull pewter-like finish to them. The holes in two of them were almost big enough for me to put my finger through. The other one nearly fit my pinky.

"How do you make them into rings?" I asked.

"While standing fire watch," he said, "use the air drill and a burr cutter to rough cut them. Change to a finer burr when you get close to the size you want the ring to be. Once it's just the way you like it, polish it."

I looked at the ring and thought it would be a worthwhile task, especially while doing nothing on fire watch. At least it would help pass the time. The next time I was on fire watch, I used the air drill and some burrs I got from the welder and started my first ring. In no time I had the ring rough cut. The next watch I was on I smoothed it out and was almost done. I made two more in the next couple of weeks. I obtained some jeweler's rouge and finished the job by polishing them.

"Ya got a picture of the rings, do ya?" Captain Bob asked.

"Sure do," I said, and handed him a picture. "I only made the three and gave the little one away to a friend."

"A lady friend, I assume."

"Yes, that's later in the story."

I did find a job that the COB found useful. I could get whatever he wanted from the shipyard. It started out when I fed the shipyard workers lobster left over from our Friday meals. Since we were on the barge, we received the same food allowance as if we were at sea. Sea rats it was called, short for sea rations. It was enough that we could get lobster, shrimp, and clams every Friday.

Crates of live Maine lobsters were brought in, fresh caught that morning from the channels around the base. I had never seen a live lobster before nor had I eaten a cooked one. When I saw the cook toss them in the boiling water of the steam kettle, I thought it was cruel, but was told that was the best way to cook them. They were green when they went in, but quickly turned a bright red. The first day we had them I didn't try one, but soon acquired the taste and would eat two or three every Friday.

Even after we had our fill, there were plenty left over. I started taking them to the shipyard workers who appreciated them very much.

"This is how ya eat a lobster," the welder told me. He then just broke it open and sucked on the green inside that I thought was lobster guts and shit. "Ya eat the green stuff first, and ya never get sick."

"Shit," I said. "I eat the green stuff and I get sick first off." He laughed and continued with his feast. I never ate the green stuff and never got sick either. I think he was just pulling my leg. After I had brought the workers lobster three weeks in a row, one had something for me.

"Here ya go young feller," he said. "We get these made up over at the sail shop."

He handed me a vinyl garment bag made from heavy duty material with a zipper that could hold up a truck. It was well made, but I had no use for it. All my uniforms were folded and we wore dungarees in the shipyard. I gave it to Chief Grayson, my weapons chief, who was a really nice guy to work for. He showed it around and soon I was asked if I could get some more made.

"Sure," I said, not knowing whether or not it was possible. "I just need to do a little trading."

The next Friday afternoon, I took the left over lobster directly to the sail shop, and soon I had several of the garment bags to hand to the chief. That started my procurement career in the shipyard.

There was a large storeroom below the water line in the barge that I set up as an office. The skipper wanted some Sam Houston plaques that he could hand out to visiting

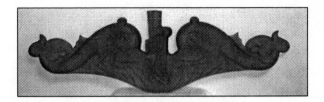

dignitaries. I found the shop that made molds and, after a few ten-gallon tins of coffee and sugar, I had what I needed. Some more trading and I had the resin materials to make the plaques. From one of the crew members who imbedded objects in plastic, I got a quick lesson in mixing and curing the resin. I commandeered some other crew members who were good at painting and I had the plaques being made, about five a day.

"Here is one of them that I saved for myself. Somewhere in the world are several others, probably in the hands of the men who went through the shipyard.

"I also made some large dolphins and was able to keep a couple of them myself. Here is a picture of one of them.

"I became the sub's 'cumshaw artist'."

"I've heard that term," Captain Bob said. "Some of the sailors that spent a fair amount of time in the Far East, used to talk about havin' to pay cumshaw to the Chinese in Canton. I guess that be where the word come from."

"I was the go-to man for anything the skipper wanted. Whatever I couldn't trade for I would just misappropriate. That was the Navy term for stealing something the government already paid for. Like in *Oliver Twist*, my gang of thieves and I would roam the shipyard looking for what we wanted and, if we couldn't trade for it, took it at an opportune time. It was on one of my foraging expeditions that I discovered two shipyard workers who had harelips."

Because they were from two completely different parts of the base, neither one of them knew the other. One ran a tool crib, where shipyard workers borrowed tools for the day. I fixed it so the other one had to go borrow a tool from him.

"Nyou haf a twelf-inth crethent wrenth?" the one asked when he got to the counter.

Several workers from the shipyard, who were in on the fun, were standing with me and a couple of my helpers.

"Wanth nyou thay?" the man in the crib asked.

"Nyou thun of a bith! Nyouth makin' fun of nth way I nalk! I'll kinkth nyour ath."

"Funth nyou, nyou bantherd. I'll kinkth nyour ath."

By then the audience was laughing so hard that the two guys figured out what was going on. They looked our way and, had they been armed, would have shot us all. With a flip of the bird in our direction, the one guy left and the other went to the back of the tool crib.

"So, ya lived on that there barge all the time ya was in the shipyard, did ya?" Captain Bob asked.

"We went into the shipyard in August, 1966 and not long after that, Little Dickey, Gill (the shipmate I went canoeing with), and I decided we wanted to live off base in Kittery. On the barge were bunk beds in a large room for sleeping, and gang showers used by all. We wanted a little privacy, so we found a place not far from the base, a little ways out in the country which we called a snake ranch. Where the term "snake ranch" came from, I don't know, but it was a place to live other than on the floating barge tied to the pier at the shipyard."

I had been in two other snake ranches before, one in Dam Neck and one in New London. The one in Dam Neck made me feel isolated and alone. I thought being in the barracks limited my privacy, but it did provide the camaraderie of being with other sailors. After going for a midnight walk in a drizzling rain, with my portable radio tuned to the song *Rhythm of the Rain* by the Cascades, I felt extremely lonely and moved back to the barracks.

The other snake ranch in New London was a disaster from the start. Again, four of us rented a place and spent the first night huddled on the couch under several blankets trying to keep warm. The oil tank was empty and we couldn't get it filled until the next day. We only spent a month there, and I felt bad because we trashed the house when we left. But after all, we were just sailors out for a good time.

This time I was a little more mature and secure when the three of us rented a one bedroom, one bath trailer with an add-on which included a living room and bedroom. It was located about five miles away from the base on Haley Road. There we had cramped quarters, three-to-a bedroom, and not much better privacy; but we could have a dog and parties on the premises. We had different duty days, so only one or two of us were at the trailer at a time. The front room of the main trailer had a bar in it, which suited us just fine. The tiles around the tub/shower were falling off, but with the help of Iacovelli, who had acquired construction skills from his father, we replaced the tile, making the shower useable. We actually left this place in better shape than we had found it.

It was here in the snake ranch where we got our nicknames. Little Dickey was named after we listened to a Smothers Brothers' comedy album and Tommy called his brother Little Dickey. It was ironic that Little Dickey was not a Little Dickey.

I got the Cap'n nickname from my attempt at being an officer in the naval academy. I don't know what or how Gill got the nickname Uncle, but that's what we called him from then on. We did hang out together a lot. Uncle Gill always had chutzpah and performed his Jonathan Winters routines for anyone who would listen, even if they didn't laugh. On amateur night at a local bar we went to, he sang a song and the regular singer thought he had a voice. She gave him voice lessons so that he could sing at the club occasionally, but a career as a singer was not for him.

"I just came from Kittery on my way up the coast and went by where

the trailer was." I told Captain Bob. "It was still there."

"You mentioned a dog," Captain Bob said.

"One day we decided we needed a dog. Here is a picture to look at while I tell the story. I had never owned a dog but thought the idea was a good one. We never considered what would happen to the dog when we returned to sea after the shipyard. That fate was decided for us."

Lamar Roy Jean was a black, part-everything dog about the size of a beagle. Named after a character from a Jonathan Winters album, he was a puppy when we got him and grew to adulthood, or almost, during the fall and winter months. When we were at the shipyard working, we let him roam around the outdoors, which was mostly rural. If it was too cold, he stayed in the sheltered entry way where he had a place to curl up and sleep. At night, he usually slept in my bed with me and woke me up with his snoring, bad breath, and stinky feet. I was usually very tired or half in the bag, so he didn't bother me that much. We used to give him beer until he walked sideways. Then he would curl up in the corner and sleep it off, waking up with his paws over his head as if he were hung over.

Lamar loved the neighborhood kids and followed them around when we weren't there. He was with them when they waited for the school bus at the stop across the street and greeted them when the bus left them off in the afternoon. That was his demise.

We arrived at the snake ranch one evening and Lamar wasn't around. It was a cold, New England day with a foot of snow on the ground from a nor'easter that had blown in the day before. We called and looked for him, but no Lamar.

"Have you seen our dog?" Uncle Gill asked a neighbor boy who was out playing in the snow. "He's black and about this big."

"He got run over by the school bus," the boy said matter-of-factly, pointing toward the school bus stop.

Gill and I went to the spot he pointed to and there was our beloved Lamar Roy Jean, lying in the ditch, frozen stiff. We picked him up without saying a word and carried him back, setting him on the back porch while we went in to tell Little Dickey.

"I'll dig a hole and we can bury him in the back yard," I said.

I grabbed a shovel and went to a spot in the back yard I thought would be appropriate. I cleared the snow and tried to dig a hole. The ground was hard as granite and I couldn't even scratch the surface. It was my first winter that far north and was much harsher than where I grew up in Ohio.

When it snowed, it snowed nearly a foot each time, and it didn't go away until late April. I remember Christmas Eve when the snow came down hard and left two feet on the ground by morning. I had to stand a watch on the sub until midnight and watched it accumulate. The next morning I walked to the parking lot to get my car to drive to the church outside the gate and almost didn't get out of the lot.

"We got to take him to the vet," Gill said. "They can cremate him."

"Okay," I said. "We ought to take his food bowl, food, and leash to donate to them too."

"Good idea," Little Dickey said. "I can't go with you. I have to go in and stand watch in an hour."

"We can make it before they close at six," Gill said. "I'll go warm up the car and you gather his stuff."

Ten minutes later we pulled up outside the vet's office. We approached the door carrying Lamar and his things when Gill stopped.

"The sign says all animals must be on a leash," he said.

"Well, here's his leash," I said.

By then we were over the shock of finding our little buddy dead and both of us being clowns, we hooked him up to the leash and dragged him into the office.

"What are you doing?" the elderly lady behind the desk asked.

"The sign outside said all animals must be on a leash," Uncle Gill said.

The woman behind the desk didn't think it was funny, but we did. We got 'Oh no's' and laughs every time we related the story to others. We picked Lamar up and carried him to a back room and laid him on a table.

"What happened?" the doc asked.

While we were telling the story, Lamar started to thaw out and his bladder let loose all over the table. The doc agreed to cremate him and dispose of his ashes.

After we paid at the front desk, we left, guffawing when the office door closed behind us, drawing dirty looks from the old lady. As far as we know, Lamar was laid to rest in the dumpster behind the office.

After Lamar died, the three of us spent a lot of weekends going back and forth to Vermont. Little Dickey was from Winooski, just north of Burlington. We had met three women in the town, hairdressers, and were dating them as often as we could get there, or when they could come to Kittery.

Because we had different duty days, sometimes we would drive our individual cars to and from Vermont. After my 1957 Plymouth blew a hole in a piston, I purchased a 1966 Dodge Dart. Again I was thinking of my future as a college student and wanted a car that would last through my student years. It was a demonstrator with six thousand miles on it and cost around two thousand. The payments were $68 a month and it would be paid for by the time I got my discharge in two years. I would then have a good, reliable, paid-for car to use the entire four years of college.

Because I left the Plymouth in the driveway of the snake ranch all winter, the block cracked when inadequate antifreeze froze in the harsh New England winter. In the spring I had to drive it to the junkyard with no water in the radiator. Since the plates were expired on the Plymouth, Little Dickey followed close behind so no one could see the expiration date. It was smoking by the time we pulled into the lot. The man took it even though the engine was shot.

Gill had a Volkswagen which we would drive on the sidewalk when we got drunk. Little Dickey had a '59 Chevy Impala. All three of us had to be back for muster on Monday morning so when we went to see the hairdressers, we would play follow the leader from Winooski to Kittery late Sunday evening into early Monday morning. It was all we could do to stay awake watching the tail lights of the lead car. We would stop every few miles to do jumping jacks and change leaders.

My date was only the second woman I had ever kissed, but she wanted more. I was too stupid and too Catholic to oblige her, so she dumped me. I was heartbroken and decided to move back to the barge. I went back to the drinking-when-off-duty routine that I thought I had left in New London. The Sam's bar this time was called "Karen's" and was just across the Piscataqua River on Daniel Street.

Before that, I tried my hand at skiing and one more woman. Little Dickey and Uncle Gill were both skiers. I had skied when I was a kid, but it was only down a small hill on a pair of skis with only a single leather strap on each ski to put over our boots. I didn't have any ski poles so it was just straight skiing with no turns unless I hit something. Uncle Gill and I borrowed ski equipment from Special Services on base and headed for the Sugarbush Ski Resort southeast of Burlington, Vermont.

"The best way to learn to ski is to start at the top," Uncle Gill said.

I didn't know any better, but noticed people on a small slope doing what was called snow plowing. They all were wearing nice looking ski pants, ski parkas, and knit ski caps. I had on my blue jeans, an old wool green coat I used to go sled riding in as a kid, and my navy knit watch cap. With my oversized body, I looked like a lumberjack, lost in the mountains.

"Shouldn't I start over there?" I said, pointing to the practice hill.

"No, that's for sissies," Uncle Gill said. "Just come with me. This is called a chair lift. All you do is sit down when it hits your butt and relax. Just do what I do."

We got into position when it was our turn and waited for the next chair to come around. I watched as Uncle Gill went first and was swept away on his chair. It looked easy enough, so I went next. I nearly fell off as I sat down when the chair hit my butt. I wasn't prepared for the drop when my weight shifted from my legs to the chair seat. I found out a few minutes later when I had to get off the chair that getting into the chair was the easy part.

"You okay?" Uncle Gill said. He had turned around to watch me get in.

"Yeah," I said. The next part was pure joy as the lift took us to the top offering a spectacular view of the mountain. *Mountain*, I thought. It was then that I realized this was not a little hill in my backyard in Ohio. It was steep and had trees on either side of the slope. I found out later Uncle Gill had taken me to the expert slope.

I watched as the other skiers ahead of me reached the end of the chair lift and skied effortlessly away on the ramp leading to the beginning of the slope. The beginning of the ramp was slanted toward the chairs and down the mountain. I didn't think anything of this until I got off the chair before I reached the top of the ramp. Instead of gliding away from the lift I started to slide backward toward the drop-off at the end of the ramp. As I fell, the ski-lift operator turned off the lift, ran from the shack, and grabbed me before I headed down the mountain.

"You know what you're doin'?" he asked.

"Sure," I said, but I was just trying to convince myself. I was able to make it down the ramp to where Uncle Gill was waiting. "I almost died!" I told him.

"You're okay," he said. I then looked at the steepness of the slope in front of me and started to panic.

"I can't ski down that!" I said. "I'll kill myself."

"Just ski to one side, fall down, and then ski to the other side and fall down," was his advice.

Then he took off down the slope. I looked to see if I could ride the lift back down the mountain, but it was only one way, and that was up. So I did as I was told. I skied across the slope and fell down. When I put my hand out to stop the fall, my arm went into the snow up to my shoulder and I never touched anything solid. I got myself upright and, seeing no other skiers headed in my direction, I skied to the other side repeating the procedure.

About a fourth of the way down, I took a rest and watched as kids nine and ten years old flew past me on their way down the mountain on skis half the size of mine. I cursed Uncle Gill with every breath, especially when he flew by me on his second run smiling all the way.

A little further along on my side-to-side skiing adventure, I saw a disturbing sight. As I was pushing myself up with my ski pole, which I found was the easiest way to right myself, the ski patrol went by. They weren't looking for anything; in fact they had already found what they had come there for.

Somebody had taken a little too close a look at the trees. There was a ski patrol man in front, and one in the back of a wire-mesh body sled. Except for the skis on the bottom, it was the same type we had hauled Larry up onto the sub from the dry dock with when he was dead drunk. The man in the sled was moving, so I guessed he hadn't killed himself. That's when I looked down and saw blood in the snow where I had just fallen.

I didn't suspect any injuries above the waist, since nothing could have penetrated the coat I had on, so I bent down to inspect my legs. During one of my falls, I must have crossed a ski in front of my right shin. I found a nice straight cut in my jeans that was oozing blood. I unhooked my boots and pulled back my pant leg. There was a cut about an inch long and to the shin bone. Because of the snow that had packed around my leg every time I fell, the bleeding had not been as bad as it could have been. The snow also numbed the area, which is why I hadn't felt any pain.

Another ski patrol came to a swishing halt next to me and looked at my leg.

"Are you all right?" he asked. Having visions of being taken down the slope on a body sled, I decided I was just fine.

"Just a scratch," I said, and packed snow around it. He continued on his way and I continued on mine, falling, skiing, falling. It took me the rest of the day to get down the mountain. Uncle Gill passed me at least four times. He was having a blast while I was vowing never to go skiing again. Every time I even think about skiing, I put a finger in the scar on my leg to bring me back to reality.

So, dismayed with skiing and coming off a romance with the woman I thought I would marry, I decided to try drinking again. Meanwhile, Little Dickey decided he knew what I needed and fixed me up with another girl his girlfriend knew.

Her name was Karen Pop-something-or-other-ski, not to be confused with the owner of Karen's Bar. Ironically her name ended in a sport that was not for me. She was my height and thin, bubbly and cute, and would have been okay with me had she been a little older. My first date with her was in a bar in Burlington with Little Dickey and his girl. It was a hang out for the students at the University of Vermont and had a large dance floor and band. After a couple of drinks Karen asked me if I wanted to dance.

I had only tried dancing once in my life and that had been slow dancing. The band was playing rock and roll, and I hadn't the slightest inkling of how to even start.

"I don't know how," I said hoping that would put an end to it.

"Come on, I'll teach you," she said, grabbing my hand and leading me out onto the dance floor.

"Just move with the music," she said.

I was scared to death of making an ass of myself, and did the only thing I knew how to do with my feet besides run and walk. I marched to the music, which would have been all right had they been playing John Phillips Sousa. So, I did make an ass of myself, but after a few more songs, I loosened up a bit, making myself less of an ass.

I had one more date with her to see the "cakewalk" at the University. It was an interesting show on ice which used to be done every winter at the ice skating rink. There was a king seated at one end of the ice and students in blackface "cakewalked" up to the king. It was entertaining but probably would be considered demeaning toward blacks today. That was the last time I saw Karen. We wrote to each other a few times, but the interest faded away. If I ever saw her again, I would thank her for "teaching" me to dance and paying a little attention to a down-in-the-dumps, lonely sailor.

So I was back to drinking again and hanging out in the bar the Sam sailors had designated their own. There were a lot of loose women in Karen's Bar, but I was uptight. One of the barmaids, who had big boobs and a loud voice, found out I was a virgin. She started calling me "Cherry" and shouted it every time I walked into the bar.

"Hey Cherry," she would say. "Wha-dya-wanna drink?"

I took a lot of ribbing, but mostly I just got drunk and had a good time. I almost got my cherry popped by a woman who was dating the yeoman on the Sam. She started flirting with me, but had to get rid of her boyfriend who was sitting at the table with us. She got him drunk, took him home and put him to bed. When she came back, another woman was sitting next to me and we were talking.

"What is this?" the returning woman asked. In order to get her yeoman boyfriend drunk, she had had to do a little drinking herself and was a couple of sheets to the wind. The two women got to trading verbal insults, so I snuck out during the fracas, my nickname still intact.

After four or five months of going to Karen's, I again realized that this was not the life for me. Shortly before the Sam's overhaul was completed, I quit the nightly drinking, started to diet, and exercised. One night of playing basketball with the guys was enough to convince me to quit smoking. I almost hacked my lungs out, realizing this habit wasn't good for my health either, and tossed away my cigarettes. I haven't had one since.

I even joined a touch-football team we put together from the Sam. We played the local marines and did a fairly good job against them. I had been a pretty good player on the neighborhood team before I joined the Navy, but had lost a lot of my edge. Also, because this was touch football, I wasn't fast enough to be used in the backfield or as a receiver. Therefore, I was designated as a guard.

During a game, I was playing at right guard and David was center. One of the marines was getting to Joe, our quarterback, by running directly over Dave and in the process was beating him up pretty badly. This was supposed to be "friendly" game, but our pride was on the line, so the coach decided to let me try the center position. At the first snap of the ball the marine and I went sprawling, but he didn't penetrate the backfield. I had earned his respect and he backed off for the rest of the game.

"It's party time!" Little Dickey announced.

It was summer in Maine and Little Dickey wanted to try having a luau at the snake ranch. Uncle Gill and I were living back on the barge. Little Dickey was getting serious with his girlfriend and had taken over the trailer. He replaced Lamar Roy Jean with a larger, part-collie dog named Twelve.

Little Dickey made all the arrangements for the luau and bought the pig and most of the food. It was BYOB and B with an open invitation to the entire crew. I showed up with a bottle of vodka and a bottle of Rose's Lime Juice so I could make my favorite drink at the time, a vodka gimlet.

The party was a success by submarine standards. Everyone got drunk, no one got hurt (almost), no one upchucked (almost), and no fights were started. Rod walked around with the eyes from the roast pig, optic nerve still attached, bobbing around in his drink, which disgusted no one. Another missile technician from one of the southern states busted open the pig's skull to get to the brains, which he called "a delicacy in the South" and promptly devoured them.

"Woody drove his "Vette" into a ditch," Rod said, as he stormed in to the snake ranch. I had been sitting under a tree in the back yard with Woody's wife, who, I think, was trying to seduce me. That put an end to her attempts, thus keeping my reputation intact again.

Haley road had a ninety-degree curve about a quarter of a mile up from the ranch. The turn was difficult to negotiate even when sober and driving slowly. In this incident, neither was the case. Almost everyone who hadn't left already headed out the door, piled into a car, and went to see if they could help. I was too wasted to join them.

"He's okay," was the report that came back fifteen minutes later. "His car is a mess but it's drivable and we were able to pull it out."

"That's good news," Little Dickey said.

"Great," I interjected, downing the last of the vodka gimlet I was nursing.

Noticing my bottle of vodka was empty but the Rose's Lime juice was not, I looked around for something else to mix it with.

"Here," Little Dickey said, handing me a bottle of gin.

I didn't really care for the flavor of gin, but it was there, so I emptied the last of the lime juice into my glass and topped it off with the gin. The party was essentially over at two in the morning but I was too plastered to drive back to the base. I decided to sleep it off on the front seat of my car. Not too long after I lay down with my head on the passenger's side, the mosquitoes started to bite. I kept checking the window to make sure it was rolled up tight and it was. Not only were the mosquitoes eating me alive, but I started to get nauseous. I spent the rest of the morning until seven o'clock swatting biting insects and opening the door to puke gin. The smell of regurgitated pine was incredible and I forever lost my ability to get past the smell of gin. When I sat up to drive back to the base, I saw that the driver's side window was open, the source of entry for the mosquitoes.

I would have stayed longer to discuss the night's events with Little Dickey, but that weekend my parents were coming to see me. They had driven to the East Coast to see New England and were going to stop in and visit their sailor boy before returning. It was noon when I met them at a Chinese restaurant.

"Hi," I said with a pounding head.

"Hi," my little sister, six years my junior and still in high school, said back and we all hugged until I thought my head was going to split wide open.

"Hungry?" my dad asked.

My mom's eyes were welled up with tears and spoke as soon as she was able.

"You look good," she said.

But I felt like shit. I was severely hung over, I had mosquito bites over ninety percent of my body, and was bleeding to death through my eyes. I had lost a lot of weight since the last time they had seen me when I weighed two hundred and forty pounds. I was exercising now and eating less. I had also quit smoking. The last thing I wanted, though, was to eat, but I had to for my parents' sake. We went into the restaurant and got seated.

"I'm going to have a shot and a beer," my dad said. "You want one?"

At the thought of another drink, my stomach did a double back flip reminding me of the Chug-a-lug song.

"No, I have to go on duty tonight," I lied.

I don't know how I got through the meal with the strong odors coming from the Chinese food, but I did.

"You're hardly eating," my mom, always the Italian who believed food was love, observed.

After we said our goodbyes, I went back to the barge and crashed until the next morning.

The loud-mouthed barmaid with the big boobs at Karen's had gotten me started on vodka gimlets. Before that, I had been drinking vodka Collins, a habit I picked up when I was in "C" school shortly after I had quit the Academy. I had tried one at the enlisted club at Fort Story at the end of Ocean Front Avenue, north of Virginia Beach, Virginia. The drinking age at that time was eighteen for beer and twenty-one for hard liquor, but once in the club on the base I was able to order the hard stuff.

My first trip to the Fort Story enlisted club had a little excitement to it. I was driving my first car, a 1950 green Dodge Meadowbrook four-door sedan.

Its failure to start after a near miss by a hurricane was the only trouble I had with the car. After I sponged water out of the spark plug well on the top of the flathead six engine, it started just fine; however, I did have to put a quart of oil in it with every tank of gas. Almost every weekend I drove the car back and forth between Ohio and Virginia. It ran great on those long trips except that when I let up on the accelerator on a downhill slope, smoke poured out of the exhaust.

The Dodge was our party car when I was in "C" school in Dam Neck. We dubbed it "The Green Seaweed" although it had more oxidized orange color than the original dark green from the factory. The transmission was an automatic stick shift that could be banged through the gears or left in third without touching the clutch. Acceleration in automatic was slow at best, which was ideal when I was incapacitated with vodka.

The fifteen-year-old car outweighed and outsized the newer cars like a sixth-grade bully to a first-grade wimp. So when I was rear ended on a rain-slick road it was no wonder the 1965 Ford was totaled and I drove away with only a dent in the bumper. I installed seat belts as soon as I got the car and have used seat belts ever since. When the cop investigated the accident scene he had to look twice to believe my old Dodge had seatbelts. Seat belts weren't mandatory then, having been standard equipment for only a few years, but his accident form asked if seat belts were in use. He got one yes, from the driver of the fifteen-year-old Dodge.

He cited me and the other driver which I couldn't believe. I had stopped because the car in front of me had stopped first to make an illegal left turn off the highway. Of course he was gone after I got hit, so I had no way to verify my story. The Ford that hit me couldn't stop and slammed into my rear bumper. Green Seaweed hardly budged and avoided rear ending the car making the illegal turn.

"I can't determine who was at fault" the cop said. "That's up to the judge."

The driver of the Ford was cited for failure to stop and I was cited for stopping on a highway.

"But I would have hit the car in front of me," I pleaded.

"Tell it to the judge," he said as he handed me the ticket.

I got the ticket dismissed, but I had to go to court to do it.

About two years, five-hundred quarts of cheap oil, and thirty-thousand miles later, I sold it for one-hundred fifty dollars, fifteen dollars less than what I paid for it.

In the summer, four of us would take The Green Seaweed to the Friday-night showing at the drive-in after first stopping to get some libations. I looked old enough to buy the hard stuff, so I always was elected to procure the liquor.

"Wa'd ya get?" Caulkey, one of my classmates and drinking buddies, asked.

Caulkey and I once had an argument about whether or not the brain itself was sensitive to pain. I called my hangovers "brain pains," and he informed me that the brain cannot feel pain. He was right of course, since there are no pain receptors in the brain. I still felt I had the right to call it what I wanted, because brain pain resonated off the tongue better than hangover. Every time I called it that he felt he had to correct me, so I quit speaking to him. I would piss him off by asking someone else to tell him what I wanted to say to him. He would get so aggravated he would shout at me, "Speak to me, goddamn it!" I would of course ignore him, which aggravated him further. Why we remained good friends after that little tiff ended was amazing. When he asked me what kind of booze I got, we were speaking again.

"Orange juice and this," I said holding up a quart of "Old Mister Boston" vodka.

"I never heard of it," quipped one of the guys in the back seat.

"It was cheap," I said. "All you guys gave me was two dollars apiece. I ain't gonna foot the bill for the more expensive stuff."

We then headed for the drive-in where, for some reason, I drank a lot more than the other three and got more than a little drunk. It could have been because I had skipped dinner to work out in the gym with a health-nut classmate. The only thing I ate at the drive-in was popcorn, and a lot of it. When the movie was over, Caulkey and I were wasted so one of the others offered to drive. I let him drive while I took the front seat passenger's side. I rolled down the window and stuck my head out allowing the fresh air to alleviate my feeling of nausea. I would have made it all the way to Dam Neck too, had we not stopped to pick up a hitchhiker.

"Hey!" Caulkey said from the back seat. "There's one of the guys from our class hitchin' by the gate."

"I see him," the driver said. "I'll stop and pick 'im up."

The main gate to Oceana Naval Air Station was between the drive-in theater and Dam Neck. They had an enlisted club, but checked ID's and only let us drink beer. Since Oceana was so close, men stationed at Dam Neck would hitch a ride between the bases.

We pulled over to the side of the road just past the hitchhiker. As soon as the cool night air stopped blowing, my stomach started churning. As the hitchhiker walked toward the car, I let go. Old Mr. Boston and popcorn quietly erupted in a volcanic flow cascading down the front door of The Green Seaweed.

"Is it okay to ride with you guys?" asked the hitchhiker as he approached the passenger's side of the car and saw the slimy-white lava flow.

None of the others heard the near-silent protein spill, and didn't know why he was asking the question.

"Sure," Caulkey said opening the door and scooting over to take the middle seat. "The driver isn't drunk."

The man got in keeping a wary eye on me. Had it been earlier in the night he might have waited for a more sober-looking group to pick him up. Not until we got up enough speed to whip the frothy mess up onto the window on the rear door next to the hitchhiker did the others realize the true intent of the question.

"Jesus Christ," Caulkey said. "Andy puked!"

I turned around and silently faced them with a shit-eatin' grin from a bubbly white mouth.

Everyone started gagging and, once upon a time, the whole car erupted with puking sailors. The driver covered the dash board and inside of the windshield, while the backseat passengers unloaded on each other and themselves.

No, that didn't happen but I did know one sailor who did paint his dashboard while driving. The witness said he turned his head to say something to the passenger and at the start of the turn, he started spewing. He didn't finish until he was facing the passenger, who felt a little queasy himself. The only way we could awaken the puker for classes the next day was to put a cold, wet, dirty sock in his face.

We got through the main gate at Dam Neck. By then, the mess had spread itself along the entire right side of The Green Seaweed from the front door, along the back of the rear window and up over the top of the trunk. The gate guard waved us through, but shook his head as he got a glimpse of the side of the car.

The next morning I got up to check out the mess on my car, and there was Caulkey hosing it off in the barracks parking lot. Now that's a buddy.

Getting back to the Fort Story tale, neither I nor Caulkey knew exactly where the enlisted club was as we headed down the main drag inside the base. We tried to follow the instructions given to us by the gate guard, but the "dog faces'" instructions were not clear. We made a left down an unmarked road and almost as soon as we turned, a tank pulled out from behind a bunker. It turned muzzle first toward us in the middle of the road, big tank against my little tank. I decided to turn around and find a safer direction to the club. My rearview mirror revealed we had made the right choice when the tank retreated back behind the bunker awaiting another unwary prey.

"That was ya social life, then?" Captain Bob said, "Partyin' all the time?

"I guess you could say that. I got most of the urge to be wild out of my system while I was in the Navy, before I headed to college."

"I did attend church every Sunday I could when I was in the shipyard. Had there been a chapel on the base, I could have been excused from duty to go to mass. However, the closest church was outside the shipyard gates, so I went there when not on duty. One morning I put on my civilian clothes, stepped off the barge, and was heading for the church. The parking lot where my car was parked was so far from the barge that it was just as quick to walk to the church as it was to get my car, and it was a nice morning for a walk. I had gotten to the end of the barge when the Corvette owner who ran off the road after the luau pulled up beside the barge."

"Park my car for me, will ya Andy?" Woody said. "I'll be late for duty if I run it up to the lot and I can't leave it here next to the barge."

"Mind if I take it to church first," I said.

"No, not at all," he said, tossing me his keys.

I got in the Vette and noticed it was stick shift on the floor. I hadn't driven a stick in a few years and had never used a floor shifter. On top of that, it was so close to the ground it was like sitting directly on the pavement. I started it up and put it in gear. It took off, but was a little sluggish. It wasn't until I left the parking lot after church that I found out I was putting it in third gear instead of first. It sure wasn't sluggish after that.

When I got to church I saw Little Dickey entering in his uniform.

"Let's sit together," I said.

"No." he said. Since I'm in uniform I'd rather just stand in the back I don't want to be conspicuous."

I took a seat in a pew on the far right of the church and Little Dickey stood in the back on the left side. When it came time for the sermon, which is called a homily now, the priest was in a pacifist mood. The gist of his sermon was how wrong all the wars in the world were, specifically the Vietnam War, which was going pretty strongly at the end of 1967. Larry and I had volunteered to be helicopter pilots in Vietnam the year before we went to the shipyard, but they wouldn't take us because of our top secret clearance for nuclear warheads.

The priest's sermon was reaching a crescendo and he got to the part where he mentioned the shipyard. Specifically, he mentioned the submarines the shipyard was overhauling with all the death and destruction they held on board in the form of nuclear weapons. I was cringing in my seat for fear I would be recognized as one of the sailors aboard the nuclear weapons-carrying subs when he practically pointed an accusing finger toward Little Dickey standing in the back of the church.

"...and those who serve on them," he said.

Some of the faithful turned around to see a red-faced Little Dickey, trying to get as small as possible without drawing any more attention toward himself. I'll never forget the look of dismay and guilt on his face. The next time I saw him I mentioned the event, but he seemed not to be affected by the sermon.

"The sermon didn't bother you?" Captain Bob asked.

"No. Like Little Dickey, I also didn't feel guilty about having a hand in the nuclear arms race, nor in providing the support that kept our country safe during that period. I just did my job and finished out the overhaul period."

"And ya never got yourself laid, huh?"

"No, and I don't know how I avoided it. There were 'almost' periods, especially at Karen's bar, but something always spoiled it. I believe some of the women in the bar wanted my cherry, and some didn't want an un-experienced man. I'll never know. Hell, I couldn't even buy a piece."

episode eight

"When did ya leave the shipyard?" Captain Bob asked.

"The overhaul period was completed the end of October, 1967 and we went on sea trials and a shakedown cruise until December. Afterwards we picked up some midshipmen at my alma mater, the Naval Academy, for some training."

"Sea trials and shakedown cruise?" Captain Bob said.

"Yes. After a ship is built, or in our case, after the completion of an overhaul, the ship is put through maneuvers to prove her seaworthiness. Some shipyard workers went with us for sea trials. When the Thresher, a nuclear fast attack boat went down, there were shipyard workers aboard. She was on sea trials at the time. Every weld done in the shipyard was x-rayed to detect slag and voids. If any were suspected, the area was cleaned out and re-welded. A good welder would have no voids or slag in his welds, but just in case, there was the fear that one of the welds they did would end up causing the sub to go down. Going on the sea trials with us was an incentive for them to do a good job."

Sea trials was a cruise out in the ocean to make sure all the systems worked as designed. We took her down to her design depth, where she is supposed to operate normally. Strain gauges were placed at various locations to check expansion and contraction of the hull and internal components. We had our own strain gauge in the missile compartment. While on the surface we tied a string tightly from one side to the other side in the middle of the third level of the missile compartment. When we submerged, sea pressure compressed the hull and the string bowed in the middle. The deeper we went the more the bow.

At design depth the sub was checked for leaks. All the valves on every pipeline were opened and closed. All systems were operated at maximum power to test them and went through every checklist and operating manual we had. If anything was found not to be operating properly, it was corrected on the spot, if possible. When we got back from sea trials, we dropped off the shipyard workers and took on provisions for the shakedown cruise.

A month later, we were ready for the shakedown cruise. The crews were split into Blue and Gold again and we had a new Skipper, Commander Alford. I stayed with the blue crew who took her out first. We went back down to the tongue of the ocean for some more sound trials to get a before and after profile of the sounds the Sam makes. While we were on the way south, Rod got appendicitis and had to be transported to the hospital in Bermuda.

Had we been on patrol, the doc could have done emergency surgery, but since we were only on sea trials, the man was transported to a shore hospital. I don't know what other types of surgery the doc could have done, but apparently he was trained for a lot of emergencies. We were given thorough medical exams before each patrol to preclude any unexpected illnesses. One "this is no shit" story that circulated was of a man who died on patrol. There was nothing else to do but put him in the freezer until the sub returned.

"The COB wants you," the watch said. I was in the mess hall talking with Little Dickey. He had put in, and was accepted for a program called NESEP, where he would be sent to college to get a commission as an officer upon graduation. He was trying to talk me into doing the same thing.

"I already had this talk with Chief Grayson," I said. "When I quit the Academy I was told I would be ineligible for any other officer incentive programs. As far as I know, there is an entry in my service jacket stating such."

"It's worth checking into," he said.

"When I quit the Academy, I decided not to make a career of the military. I had my chance and gave it up."

"You've already got six years in. Go another fourteen and you can retire."

"I know all the pluses and minuses, but I've made my decision, right or wrong," I said. "Well, I gotta go. Duty calls."

I left Little Dickey and followed the watch up to the control room.

"We need a lookout on the bridge," the COB said. "There's a helicopter on the way here to pick up Rod and you've been selected for lookout duty."

"On my way," I said, and headed up the ladder, stopping at the top to request the usual permission. I took the binoculars from one of the lookouts and relieved him of his duty, taking my position standing next to the other lookout on the platform behind the officer of the bridge.

"The helicopter should be coming from off the starboard bow," the officer said pointing in that direction. "That's where the base is."

"Aye, aye, sir," I said and started my scan, alternating between bare and aided eyes. *They don't need me up here*, I thought. *They got the radar mast on and scanning. I guess they just want a visual when the radar picks up the 'copter.* I had noticed the radar detector spinning as soon as I had come up on the bridge. We only used it when we didn't care about being "seen" by other radar detectors. This was one of those times.

With my bare eyes I noticed movement on the horizon and then raised the binoculars to verify what I thought I saw. There was an aircraft very low on the horizon. I took a chance that it was what we were looking for and told the officer.

"Helicopter bearing zero four five," I said. "It's heading toward us and just off the horizon."

"Can't be," the officer said, raising his own binoculars. "Point to it. I don't see it."

I pointed in the direction and he looked again.

"Oh there it is. It's just a speck. You sure it's coming this way."

"Yes, sir," I said. The helicopter had moved toward us now to where I could make out its blades. I wondered why radar hadn't said anything and so did the officer.

"Bridge to radar," he said over the intercom. "The lookout has the helicopter in sight. Can we get a confirmation?" While he waited, he took another look.

"No sir, we don't have verification," the response came back.

"Why not?" he asked, a little pissed off. "How can the lookout spot it before radar?" He didn't wait for an answer. "Radio room, can you make radio contact with the aircraft?" about thirty seconds passed before the response came back.

"Sir, we do have radio contact with the helicopter."

"Captain to the bridge. We have the helicopter in sight and confirmed by radio," the officer said into the microphone.

The skipper was on the bridge in seconds, sporting his binoculars. He looked at me and nodded as if in understanding.

"Radar still hasn't verified, sir," the officer said.

"Very well," he said. "I thought our lookout would spot it first." He looked at me again. "Good job, son."

"Thank you, sir," I responded. I wanted to add *just doin' my job*, but thought I'd better not.

"Launch party to the after deck," the skipper said into the microphone.

Five minutes later, the crew was coming out of the hatch leading out of the auxiliary machinery room number one. Rod was strapped to a full body, wire-mesh stretcher. There were a number of other men with him. One looked like Kozy in his dress whites and he had a seabag with him. The helicopter was about two miles away when radar reported a contact.

"We have an aircraft on the scope, twenty-five hundred yards and closing,"

"A little late," the officer said to the skipper.

"The radar can't detect an aircraft coming in at that low an altitude," the captain said. "My guess is they were playing a little unauthorized war game, but didn't count on us having a lookout with eagle eyes." Again he looked in my direction and smiled. "We beat them at their own game."

My reward was not being allowed to watch the transfer operation. I was sent off the bridge when the helicopter started to hover above the crew on the after deck. I found out later that, to provide Rod with assistance, Kozy was transported with him to the hospital. A little R&R in Bermuda was all he would need to fuck himself to death.

The skipper took advantage of the unscheduled surface run to expend some of the expired forty-five-caliber ammo we had stored aboard and get rid of some trash at the same time. Since I was on the bridge, I got to do some shooting.

Because a BB gun was my constant summer companion while growing up in Ohio, I was a very good shot with a rifle and pistol. I scored expert at the rifle range with both the M-1 rifle and forty-five-caliber service revolver. I scored better than the weapons officer and most of the southern boys who had grown up with rifles. No brag, just fact. However, I didn't know how to handle a Thompson automatic rifle, but after a couple of demonstrations by the armament expert, I was allowed to try one out.

Trash was tossed from the bow of the sub, and we shot at it standing on the sail planes. I had heard stories of how difficult it was to hold a Thompson on a target because the recoil causes it to travel up and to your right, no matter how steady your aim. I found that out to be a myth and was able to hit the floating trash several times in one burst. After we finished shooting the trash, we headed back out toward the tongue of the ocean to continue the sea trials.

What did ya do on sea trials?" Captain Bob asked.

"We took the Sam through all types of maneuvers, yes, including a bail out. There were a lot of drills, missile, torpedo, fire, flooding, collision, every exercise imaginable. One in particular was going backwards at a depth of four hundred feet. Again, I was chosen as the helmsman for this maneuver."

"Make your depth four hundred" the diving officer said.

"Four hundred, aye, sir," Little Dickey responded. He was in the chair to my right and I was at the helm, responsible for everything aft of the control room, which included the stern planes, rudder, and speed. Little Dickey was the fairwater planesman with the job of taking us to and keeping us at proper depth. If a down bubble was called for, then I would use the stern planes. I don't know why they picked four hundred feet to do the all back maneuvers, but I guessed it wasn't arbitrary.

"All stop," the diving officer said, as soon as we achieved the desired depth.

"All stop, aye, sir," I responded. It was time for me to go into action. As soon as the repeater indicated all stop, I announced, "Indicating stop."

"All back one third," the diving officer said.

"All back one third, aye, sir?" I said, "Indicating all back one third."

"Maintain your heading."

"Aye, aye, sir. Heading zero niner zero." A few minutes later he called out a different speed.

"All back two thirds," he commanded.

"All back two thirds, aye, sir. Indicating all back two thirds. Passing zero eight five." I called out a different heading because we had drifted more than five degrees off course. I was having trouble maintaining heading. Then I thought maybe I needed to reverse the steering because we were going backwards. If the water was flowing over the rudder in the opposite direction, it would have the opposite effect. I tried my theory and it seemed to work. "Steady on zero niner zero."

"Very well," the officer said. "All back full."

Again I echoed the command and the indication when it had been received.

"Passing zero eight five," I said. Now, nothing I seemed to do would control the heading. So as not to make it worse, I put the rudder amidships and left it there.

"Passing zero eight zero," I said. I tried a little rudder in both directions with no effect.

"Helmsman, can you control your heading?" the officer asked.

"No sir, I can't. Neither right nor left rudder controls the heading. Right now I have it amidships." All eyes were on me now. I felt as if I were failing the entire crew.

"Leave your rudder amidships. Give her her head. That's what the book said, that there is no control backing down. You did good to control her past one third. All back full."

"All back full, aye, sir." I felt a little relieved now. It seemed like the entire control room relaxed. Then I did something on the spur of the moment that cracked everyone up. I kept my left hand on the steering wheel, turned in my chair to my right, put my right arm over the back rest, and looked straight astern.

"What are you doing?" the COB asked. He was in the diving chair behind me as the enlisted diving control officer.

"Were going backwards and I'm just looking to see where we're going, so we don't hit somethin', that's all." The control room erupted in laughter, even the skipper smiled. I thought Little Dickey was going to fall out of his chair, and might have had he not been wearing his seat belt.

After the maneuver was over, we returned to a forward moving direction at cruising depth. Little Dickey and I were relieved of our duties and went down below for a well earned rest. When I first came in the Navy, there were old salts that used to say to me "I've got more time waitin' in line at the chow hall than you've got in the Navy." Now, I could respond with "I've got more time backin' down at four hundred feet than you have waitin' in line." Yeseree, now I was an old-salt sub sailor.

"Where did ya go after that?" Captain Bob asked.

"Our shakedown cruise ended December eighteenth. It was then the gold crew's turn to take her out for a month. We returned to New London where we had a month off over Christmas. I went home to visit my family for a week over the holidays. When I got back to the base I continued my weight loss program with exercise at the base gymnasium. I stayed away from the bars. Instead I researched tuition at the colleges I wanted to apply for in the fall after I got out. I only had six more months to go before being discharged. The middle of January, we were flown to Cape Canaveral where we would relieve the gold crew."

Our flights to the Cape were on C-130's, military transport planes. The officers, chiefs, and higher ranking petty officers went on one plane and the rest of us, about eighty, went on another ill-fated plane. Our seabags were piled high in the middle of the back cargo bay. There were open webbing chairs that were too uncomfortable to sit in, so some men just stood and others lay down on the stacked bags. We loaded from the rear bay door that closed after we got on board. The noise was horrendous with no insulation with the turbo prop engines ahead of us on each wing. There were two porthole type windows in the side doors with no place else to see outside.

Instead of a head, there was a curtain behind which was a funnel with a tube going outside the aircraft. It was difficult to stand still while aiming at the hissing funnel, sucking with ferocity everything that fell into it. I was afraid of leaning too close and getting my wiener sucked right outside the plane while I stood hopelessly inside. I hadn't even used my dick for its other intended purpose, so I just decided to wait until we landed, which happened unexpectedly. I don't know what we would have done if we had had to take a shit. I guess we were supposed to open the bay doors and stick our asses out yonder in the soon-to-turn-brown wild blue.

The first thing to go wrong was that the rear antenna outside the fuselage broke loose. Because it was still attached to the lead-in wire, it banged around against the skin of the plane adding to the noise level from the engines and wind. It finally broke loose before the next thing started to fail.

I watched as the flight technician carried a can from the front of the plane to the port side near where I was sitting. He poured fluid from the can into a reservoir, empting the can. Fifteen minutes later he returned with another can and repeated the procedure. *You think they would put a bigger reservoir on whatever system that is instead of refilling it all the time*, I thought. *Oh well, it's the Air Force.*

I could almost set my watch by the return trips the airman was making. Then I found out what was happening.

"This is the co-pilot. We are making an unscheduled stop in Cherry Point," he said. "We have a hydraulic leak in the control surfaces of the port wing. Return to your seats and buckle up in preparation for a landing. That is all."

"Shit, that's enough." I said, only no one could hear me above the noise. I thought it wasn't right that they were filling that reservoir so many times and now I knew why.

The last problem was that there was a hell of a crosswind when we landed requiring the pilot to come in sideways. When the plane hit the pavement, it jerked badly to the right to align with the runway giving us a jolt while we were seated in our lawn chairs. This flying experience made submarine duty seem mild and safe.

We were supposed to be at the Cape having lunch by the time buses arrived to take us to a marine chow hall, which was not expecting us. We were dumped off in front of the old barracks-converted-to-a-chow-hall structure. It was a one-story wood-frame, built-on-pilings–pounded-into-the-sand building and reminded me of the World War II barracks at boot camp. We didn't know what else to do but file into the chow hall, only they were not expecting us. They had already cleaned up and put all the food away, and, no doubt, were getting ready for the next meal to be served in about four hours.

The layout of the dining part of the hall was such that a continuous line of lean and mean, fighting machine men and women filed in, walked briskly through serving lines, and proceeded just as quickly out to the seating area. Most dining facilities in the military were designed to get the military man or woman in and out in seven to ten minutes. There was no room where eighty, mostly over-weight sub sailors could congregate and wait for food to be prepared and served.

When we first filed in, we headed for the tables to sit, but were told by an angry tech sergeant to wait in the area just inside the door. He was pissed that he had to serve a bunch of "gobs," slang for Navy pukes, and that it was past the normal feeding time.

"Just wait here, goddamn it!" he said, and stormed back into the kitchen.

There were too many of us to fit comfortably in the area where he told us to wait, an open area about thirty feet square. We did finally fit in by shuffling around in a tight group, but the weight was too much for the old pilings. There was a loud "Wump!" and the group of sailors in the middle sank about a foot. The wood flooring was forgiving enough not to cave in completely and when everyone moved away from the center there was a large depression in the middle of the room. The noise and commotion brought the sergeant on the run to see what had happened.

"You broke my fucking chow hall!" he screamed. "You broke my fucking chow hall!" I swear there were tears welling up in his eyes. He stormed out when we gave him the Sea-Bee salute, by turning our palms forward, shrugging our shoulders, and a twisting our heads to one side.

We ended up eating horse cock sandwiches, but that was enough to hold us over until the plane was repaired and we headed to McCoy AFB, near Orlando, which I don't believe is there anymore. We got there in late afternoon, but in time for a normal dinner. Somehow the story of how we "broke the fucking chow hall" at Cherry Point preceded us and they were quite prepared to feed an extra eighty men without waiting.

We were taken to the in-transit Air Force "dormitory," where the sergeant in charge apologized for having to put three of us in a room.

"Normally, you would have individual rooms, but we have an overflow group and you have to triple up," he said.

We couldn't believe the accommodations. We were used to four men to a cubicle, not three to a room. And they apologized! We had our own telephone, air conditioning, and private bathroom. It was similar to the accommodations at the Academy. Right then I decided I had enlisted in the wrong branch of the service.

I was assigned to a room with Larry and the rebel named Delozer who had misspelled diesel. Larry never smoked and I had quit smoking in the shipyard, but Delozer had the habit in a big way. It was the first time I had ever seen someone reach for a pack of cigarettes when the morning alarm went off, and then smoke three cigarettes in a row while still lying in the rack. I was sure glad I never got that bad. In the time it took him to smoke the three cigarettes, Larry and I had enough time to do the three S's and get ready for the day ahead.

Before we took over the Sam, we got to tour the Apollo space program facilities and launch sites. There was a Saturn V rocket in the assembly building at the time. The building was so large and tall, it had its own weather pattern. When we were there we saw vapor clouds near the ceiling, and were told that sometimes it rained inside. We also saw the large transporter that moved the rocket to the launch pad at a snail's pace, one foot per hour. This tour was a treat for those interested in the space program and for us missile technicians in particular.

After one more night under the "pathetic living conditions" of the Air Force dormitories, we were taken to the Sam for a short turnover. It was there that Kozy almost bought it and I got even with the slacker, Felix.

'Then ya went on the last patrol?" Captain Bob asked

"First we test fired a missile, went to Puerto Rico, loaded missiles, and did some PR work."

"PR work?"

"Public relations," I explained. "We took some people on trips on the sub."

When we took over from the gold crew after they got back from their shakedown cruise, we found out they were supposed to fire a telemetry missile, but failed. It became our responsibility to "get the job done," which quickly became an issue of pride.

"The gold crew couldn't do it, but we can," chief Grayson told us, and we believed it.

I had never been witness to a live shoot before. The closest I had come was when a water slug was "fired" at the Guided Missile School in Dam Neck, Virginia. There was a mock-up of a submarine missile tube behind one of the school buildings at Dam Neck. It was used to impress dignitaries by showing how the missile was pushed out of the tube with high pressure air. It also gave an idea of what air pressure can do. Aimed toward Dismal Swamp, it was filled with colored water to make the demonstration more impressive, and it was impressive, but as the saying goes, if something can go wrong it will.

The story I heard was that a group of dignitaries, both military and civilian, came from Washington to view how the taxpayer's dollars were being spent. They would have been impressed had the wind been blowing the other way; instead, they got wet. The base commander had gathered them around the base of the launch tube which was tilted toward the swamp. It was aimed for an area just above some dense underbrush and small trees. Above the vegetation, the wind was blowing toward the spectators and couldn't be felt or observed from ground level.

The tube was filled with pale green water and the count sequence began. The tube top hatch was opened and locked back with a loud clank.

"...five, four, three, two, one. Launch!" said the controller.

The tube responded with a prolonged "whooosh" as the high-pressure air entered the bottom of the chamber, expanded rapidly, and forced the water out of the top in a seven-thousand-gallon slug of green. As the water lifted toward the sky, the wind pushed it back toward the awing crowd. The "awes" turned to "aw shits" as the green mass plummeted down on the well-dressed group of observers, scattering men and women like stampeding cattle.

The officials who staged the demonstration were more than embarrassed by the incident and in successive shots the wind direction was checked first. Also, because it used a tremendous amount of fresh water, demonstrations were limited.

The missile, or bird as we called it, was loaded with telemetry equipment instead of a warhead. Data could be recovered that would

help determine the accuracy of the payload. The blue crew was successful in
launching the bird, which flew to within
one-hundred feet of the intended target.
From inside the sub, the only way we
were aware that a launch had taken place
was a slight jolt and the noise of water
rushing into the missile tube to take the
place of the missile.

"That was our missile shot." I said. "Not very exciting from inside
the sub, but here is a picture of the missile as it left the surface of the
water. The sub's antenna and periscope are visible to the right of where
the missile came out of the water. Our successful launch was a source
of pride, especially since the gold crew had been unsuccessful.

"What happens if the missile don't go where ya want it?"

"On that telemetry test flight, there was a range officer on the observation vessel from which the picture was taken. If the bird started to
fly erratically, or headed in the wrong direction, then he would destroy
it. For a real launch, when we are at war, we have no control once it
leaves the sub.

"However, there are arming sequences for the warhead, so if it
doesn't follow the intended pattern, there won't be a chain reaction
explosion. But, when it hits the ground on reentry, the high explosives
used in the sequence to detonate the nuclear weapon most likely will
explode. Then, radioactive material will be scattered all around the
impact site."

"Then you went to Puerto Rico?" Captain Bob asked. "Ain't never
been there neither." I hear it's a beautiful place, that there Kara-be-
an."

"Yes, it was, but before we left the Cape, our captain almost 'missed
movement,' which is military language for missing the boat, a serious
offense."

It was time to cast off and head out for the missile shoot, but the
captain had not reported aboard yet. It was critical that we leave the
dock on time because everything was in motion for us to launch at a

specific time. Just as the number one mooring line was to be cast off leaving the skipper behind, a cab pulled up and out stepped the old man. He hurried over the brow and asked a relieved XO if the sub was ready for sea.

"Yes, sir, it is," the executive officer responded.

"Then let's get this fucker underway," the skipper replied.

The scuttlebutt was that the captain had been "entertained" by a woman who was a fan of submarine captains and that she had kept him later than he wanted to stay.

When we pulled into Rosy Roads (short for Roosevelt Roads) it was the first time I could see the bottom hull of the Sam in thirty feet of water. The water was so clear, visibility was good to one hundred feet. The water was a beautiful greenish-blue and contrasted with the white sand and the deep blue tropical sky."

"That place named for Teddy Roosevelt?" Captain Bob asked.

"No. It was named for Franklin D. before he became president in the thirties. We were only docked in Rosy Roads five days and I never made it off the base."

"How come?"

"We were on port and starboard duty on the sub, and were on standby duty for the base in case they needed us. The first day I had to stay on board for duty. On the second day a group of us wanted to just relax on the beach, so we got some beer from recreational services and went to the beach on the base. We swam and lay on blankets in the sun drinking beer almost all day. I hadn't been able to sunbathe in several years and was white as a ghost. Sorry about that ghost comment."

"I ain't no ghost, I'm, how'd ya put it, aba-rishun?" Captain Bob said.

"That's right, an apparition. You don't exist. At the end of the day I thought I'd be burnt, but wasn't. I never did understand that. Because it was so inviting, warm and soothing, I did go into the water a lot, so maybe the dried salt protected my skin. Some of the guys decided to swim to a tiny island about a quarter mile away, but I wasn't drunk enough to try it. They made it, but when they came back they had cuts on their feet from the coral they had had to walk on. The salt water kept the cuts from getting infected, but they limped for a couple days.

"The next day I had duty again and couldn't leave the sub. The guys that had gone to San Juan, about fifty miles away, on the previous two days, said there were lots of women there. I planned to lose my nickname of "Cherry" the next day, but fate got in the way again.

"The base needed some men for Shore Patrol, SP duty for short (like MP in the Army) and my name was drawn from the list. So, I spent most of the day with another SP stationed at Rosy Roads in my ill-fitting, dress-white uniform. I was still overweight and my gut stuck out in the middle, which gave me additional incentive to lose some more fat. Anyway, all we did was drive around the base picking up drunken sailors and taking them back to their barracks. The next day was my regular duty day on the sub and the morning after that we left Puerto Rico. My nickname was still intact.

"We then headed to Charleston to load missiles where I almost got in trouble."

When we got to Charleston, the old man wanted to load all the missiles in one day. He was proud of the record we had for the shortest overhaul period and wanted to add another feather to his cap. This was a new skipper and he was not concerned about the stress it would put on his crew. The missile loaders on shore worked in shifts, so they could load all day and night without getting fatigued.

Loading one missile took almost two hours, so loading sixteen took more than a day. Checklist after checklist had to be followed because an accident in loading a missile with a nuclear weapon could be disastrous

for a lot of people. Once they were loaded, we had to test them out, one by one.

I handed Captain Bob a picture of a missile loading operation being done from the tender. Loading from the pier in Charleston followed the same procedures using similar equipment.

We loaded and tested all sixteen in twenty four hours, again breaking a record. I was up the entire time starting at six o'clock in the morning. Torpedomen were required to open the hatches, but once they did that, they were through until we had the missiles in the tubes and checked out for operation. The torpedomen then put the covers over the missiles at the top of the tubes and closed the hatches. The covers were Mylar membranes used to keep water out before launching. They were stretched across a ring and bolted to the top of the tubes. The missile launching would penetrate the membrane as it lifted off on its way out of the tube, but to make sure the Mylar didn't interfere, prima cord, imbedded in the membrane, was exploded at the moment of launch to rip it open.

It was two in the morning when we finished loading the missiles, but testing was still required. I told the rest of the missile techs I could finish the job of testing and they could hit the rack. Being dead tired, no one argued with me. I finished all the testing at six in the morning when Lieutenant Inman came on board to see how much we had gotten done during the night. He came down the hatch in the auxiliary machinery room one, just aft of the missile compartment and made his way forward to where I was wrapping up the testing. When I saw him he was agitated.

"You're cutting your own throat and not realizing it," he said, starting his day with a Jimism.

"Sir?" I said, really confused. I had been up twenty-four hours doing some intensive work. My mind was about as clear as my eyes must have looked.

"Problems is not a word, it's a real fact," he added, confusing me even more. He then stormed out of the missile compartment without telling me anything.

I shook my head and went back to testing the last bird. Five minutes later, Chief Grayson came up the ladder from the second level.

"Inman is all in a stir," he said.

"I know, but he didn't tell me what was wrong."

"He said you have the upper tube hatches open exposing sixteen nuclear warheads with only one person to guard them. If a saboteur comes on board, he could cause a lot of problems."

"Guard them? I don't even have a weapon! What does he want me to do, throw instruction manuals at them?"

"He said that at least two men are required in the upper level when nuclear weapons are exposed. Where is everyone else?"

"In the rack," I said. "They were up until two and I told them get some rest and I could finish the testing."

"Go wake them up and get some men up here now," he said. I headed down the ladder to wake the men.

"And you got in trouble for that?" Captain Bob asked.

"Almost," I said. "Lieutenant Inman wanted to fry my ass, but the old man didn't want a court-martial to ruin the fact that the missiles had been loaded and tested in record time. He countermanded Inman's report and instead gave us a commendation. We all knew that if the skipper hadn't been pushing us, we would have done the missile loads in two days, resting a night in between. Then there would have been two men on the upper level at all times."

I was able to go into Charleston the next night and visited a few bars with some of the guys, one of whom was Kozy. I intended to get laid, but didn't know the first thing about picking up a woman. I thought being with Kozy, I could observe and later use some of his successful methods. I was wrong.

The second bar we went into, a group of us sat down at the bar. I sat on the end, two stools down from a woman who wasn't all that bad looking, especially to a sailor who had already had two drinks. I heard Kozy proposition a woman for money. He started out by asking if she would go to bed with him, and she said no.

"Would ya go to bed with me for a thousand dollars?" he asked.

"Maybe, but you don't look like you have a thousand," she said back.

"Maybe I don't, but at least we established what you are and now we can haggle over the price," he said back to her, smiling. She got up and left, obviously pissed off. I decided to try my own ploy, so I looked at the woman two stools away until she looked back.

"Can I kiss your pussy for a buck?" I asked, with my best Kozy smile. In the mirror, I could see Kozy and a couple of the other guys looking in my direction.

"Honey," she said, with a coquettish smile, "you can't even smell it for a buck."

I turned away, obviously put down and not knowing what to say next. Kozy came to my rescue.

"Hell, we can all smell it from here for nothin'," he said.

"Who are you?" she shot back, "Needle dick the bug fucker?"

"It may not be very big around, but it sure is short," Kozy said.

She got up and walked away to the laughter of my shipmates.

As she left, Kozy said, "She reminded me of a pygmy whore."

"What's a pygmy whore?" I asked.

Kozy held his hand about four feet from the floor and said, "A little fucker about this high."

This brought another round of laughter.

We left that bar after another beer and headed to another one next door. They had a live band and a singer, so we pulled up a table and sat down. We had a couple of more drinks and started to have a drunken good time. The singer was actually enjoying our rabble-rousing and when he found out we were sub sailors, proposed a toast.

"To the men who go down in ships on purpose," he said, and hoisted his drink. Some of the audience laughed, but Kozy didn't find it funny.

"Let me propose one back," Kozy said.

I thought, *oh shit, we're gonna get kicked outa here, or they're gonna call the SPs. I'll be in trouble this time for sure. The chief won't be able to get me out of this.*

"Sure." the singer said. "Come on up to the mike." He gestured to Kozy, who got up and walked up to the stage.

"Ahem," Kozy cleared his throat. He hoisted his glass toward the singer and started, a toast I have never forgotten.

"May the bleeding piles distress you, and corns adorn your feet.

And crabs as big as roaches crawl across your balls and eat.

And when you're old and feeble and a syphilitic wreck,

May your backbone fall through your asshole and break your fucking neck."

He then took a drink. I would have done the same, but was laughing my ass off and trying to remember the lines.

"I think you boys'd better leave," the bartender said to us when he approached our table after the toast. We obliged him and I headed back to the sub, not wanting to be with this group any more in case they got in real trouble.

"So ya didn't get laid again, did ya?"

"No, sure didn't, but I heard stories from the others about how they found a whorehouse on that strip of bars and they all got laid. I did get a piercing on the way back to the sub."

"A lot of sailors get the eaahs pissed." I had to think a moment on that response. I finally figured out right that he meant "ears pierced."

"No, it wasn't my ears that I got pierced."

"What were it then?"

I was a little hesitant to tell him the truth, but thought, *what the hell, he's not real. I can tell him whatever I want.*

I was headed back to the sub by myself and passed a tattoo parlor along the way. They seemed to abound along any strip sailors frequented.

"Come on in, sailor," the female barker said. "Get a tattoo. We have specials discounts for sub sailors."

Yeah, I bet you do, I thought.

"Can't do it," I said. If it gets infected I'll get court-martialed." This was something told to us in boot camp, although I never heard of it happening.

"We use clean needles," she said. "You won't get infected, guaranteed. If you don't want to mark your body up with a tattoo, get a piercing."

"Can ya pierce my dick?" I said, hoping that would shut her up.

"Sure can," she said, matter-of-factly. "You got one, we can pierce it." I thought a minute, and thought *what the hell, that would be something to talk about.* I was just drunk enough and carrying a zero float, so decided to go ahead.

"What's a zero float?" Captain Bob asked.

"It means drunk, but not stupefied," I responded, but thought I'd better explain a little more. "On a submarine there are batteries that provide emergency power and, in the case of the "pig boats," also provide propulsion, when running below snorkel depth. Pig boats, you'll recall, is another term referring to the fact that the men on the old diesel boats didn't have enough water to shower, so when they got back from a patrol, well, they were a bit stinky and unkempt.

"When charging the batteries, the electrolyte is tested and, if the ball in the tester floats at zero, the batteries are fully charged. Above or below zero, it's a positive or negative number indicating either an over or under charge. At zero float, a small amount of electricity, called a "trickle" current, is used to maintain the charge.

"So, when a sub sailor gets to the level of inebriation that he set out to achieve, he just drinks a little more at a time, like a trickle charge, to "maintain a zero float," or stay drunk at that level."

"Yeah, sure," I said to the tattoo lady. "Does it hurt?"

"No, we numb it," she said.

"How do ya numb it?"

"Same as we do an ear, we put an ice cube on it. The cold also keeps you from having any exciting accidents," she said, with a wink. "I'll hold it if ya want."

"Who does the piercing?" I asked. "I don't want any accidents." I winked back at her.

"That man in there," she said, pointing through the open door to a rather skinny looking person behind a counter inside.

"How much?" I asked.

"Just a minute, I'll see," she said and stuck her head in the door. "How much to get a dick pierced?"

"Small or large?" he asked. "I don't mean dick either," he added, and then just blurted it out. "Small skin-to-skin is fifteen, all the way through is fifty. That's 'cause the stud is bigger."

They both laughed at the dual meanings of what he said. I thought about how much an all-the-way through would hurt and how the hell would I piss with a pin in my dick.

"I'll get a skin-ta-skin," I said and walked in. "I'll pay after, just to make sure I leave with what I came in for."

"You'll pay now," he countered. "I don't know if you'll be able to reach in your pants afterwards." Again they both laughed.

"Can I hold it?" she asked again.

"No," I said, reaching in my wallet for the money. "I think I know where it is and am quite able to get a grip on it."

After giving me change for my twenty, the man led me to a room to my left with the door missing from the frame. As I entered, I saw the woman barker with a disappointed look on her face head back to the street.

The man wrapped an ice cube in a wash cloth while I undid the thirteen buttons on my pants.

"Ya want it top, bottom, or side?" he asked.

"Uh, bottom" I said.

"Get it out and turn it so's ya kin put this cube on it, unless ya wanna do it without freezin' it," he said, pointing toward a chair for me to sit in.

I did as he instructed while he got an instrument from the table behind him and a silver-looking stud with a ball on each end. The instrument looked like a grommet-hole maker with a pin of some kind in it.

After about five minutes I felt numb and he had finished bathing all the implements with alcohol.

"Ready?" he asked.

"Sure," I said, a little nervously.

"Wipe it with this," he said handing me a cotton ball saturated with alcohol.

After I wiped the area to be pierced, I held the skin of my penis out for him to put on the punch tool and snap, it was over. I felt a little pain, more like a sting than a cut. When he was done, I was left with a pin in my penis where the hole was. There was a little blood, but not much. He handed me a rag.

"Stick this in your pants in case it bleeds a little. Keep it clean with alcohol and don't try pounded your pud 'til it's healed." He laughed and handed me the silver stud. "When it's healed up in a couple of days, take out the stud that's in it now, and put this stud in it to keep the hole from closin' up."

"Thanks" I said.

"Don't mention it," he said.

I didn't. Not to my shipmates or anyone else. The girl gave me another wink as I passed her while she was trying to talk another sailor into a tattoo or piercing. The wound healed nicely without infection and I still wear a stud, occasionally.

"Next was your PR?" trip?" Captain Bob asked.

"Yes, the first PR stop was at Annapolis to pick up some midshipmen."

I was at the helm during the cruise up the Chesapeake Bay to pick up the middies. I would have liked to have seen the Academy from the water side, but was needed to steer the sub. My only views of the Academy would remain the ones I already knew, that of the base from the land side. There were sailing boats for training middies out in the bay, but I never stayed a midshipman long enough to use them.

The middies were brought to the boat using a skiff. There were only six of them and I watched as they came down the ladder into the control room. It was possible that some of them could have been my classmates from the NAPS, short for Naval Academy Prep School. The Napsters, as we had called ourselves, were now in the middle of their senior year and these middies were seniors. I waxed a little nostalgic thinking I could have been one of them and I would be graduating next spring.

Since they were officers, we were not allowed to chat with them except when they asked us questions. They took over the bunks in the missile compartment and those of us displaced moved to the upper level of the missile compartment to the "overflow" bunks. They shared the head in the missile compartment with us.

We then went to New London to load torpedoes. We spent the night tied to the pier and I had duty so stayed on board. I was standing the deck watch when the middies returned from shore leave in civilian clothes. They must have gone to the officers' club for a few drinks because they were obviously drunk. I saluted them as they stumbled on board and headed for the after-hatch going down to the auxiliary room. I think one of them fell part way down the ladder from the concerned reaction of the others. I just laughed a little at their antics.

It was probably their first time drinking in uniform on a base. I knew from when I was at the Academy, that midshipmen were not supposed to drink until after they left the Academy. These guys must have just turned twenty one recently and this probably was their first time on liberty from a ship. When I got off the deck watch, Chief Grayson, who was the officer on duty that night, cornered me.

"Someone puked in the scuttlebutt in the missile compartment," he said. "Clean it up before you hit the rack."

"Scuttlebutt was what we kept water in on the ship," Captain Bob said.

"The word came from that, but it was our drinking fountain," I said. "Also, when sailors gathered around the scuttlebutt they would pass along the latest gossip, so any rumor became known as scuttlebutt. We were always asking, 'What's the scuttlebutt?' to find out the latest information. We also said 'What's the skinny?' It was the same question, but I don't know where the name skinny came from."

"It was those middies," I said to the chief, only it didn't matter. They were officers and weren't expected to clean up their own mess, even it was from drinking too much.

I was lucky in that most of the puke was watery and washed down easily. I wanted to take the chunks and put them in their shoes so that they would get a nice squishy feeling first thing in the morning, but decided against it. I only had one-hundred days and a wake up before I was out and didn't want to add to it with brig time.

The next day, some dignitaries, among them some Catholic nuns, and crew's dependents came on board. It was the first time I had seen women on the ship. The second would be once upon a time on my third patrol. We headed out to sea for a short cruise to let the visitors experience life on a submarine, at least the diving and surfacing part. When we got out to sea, I was relieved of the diving duties and went to the mess hall to get a cup of coffee. I was sitting down talking with Larry when the announcement to prepare to dive came over the 1MC. I wasn't ready for what followed.

"Dive! Dive!" blasted the speaker, followed by the familiar "Ooga! Ooga!" This was not unusual, but what was strange, was that the voice was high pitched and shrill.

"What the fuck was that?" Larry said.

"I think it was one of the nuns," I said. "When I left the control room, they were on the diving stand talking with the skipper. I guess he let one of them make the announcement."

Later on when we surfaced, we heard a similar, shrill voice, only it was, "Surface! Surface! Surface!" that was screeched.

At the end of the day, we returned our visitors to the dock. The next day we loaded supplies for my last patrol and the middies left us for more training at the sub school.

One of the auxiliarymen got lye in his eyes, but through fast action by the Doc, he didn't have any permanent damage.

"Lye?" asked the captain.

"Yes. It's used to scrub the carbon dioxide out of the air when we're underwater for two months. It's a complicated system and there are many other systems on the sub that are just as complicated. That's why it takes two patrols and additional training to learn them all."

The man with the lye in his eyes was also the sailor who had almost lost a finger when his wedding ring got caught on a ladder as he slid down into the sub. That and one other incident prompted me to never wear a ring again aboard the sub, a habit I then carried throughout my adult life.

That other ring incident happened to a radioman who had an unusual scar on his elbow. It looked like he was growing another finger since it jutted out about a half inch from his skin.

"What happened to your elbow?" I asked.

"You mean this?" he said, touching the outcropping of skin.

"Yeah, what is it?" He showed me his ring finger which had a similar sized scar, only this one was inward.

"I was working on a live radar cabinet when the ring on my finger presented a good source for the high voltage to connect to. I was lucky my elbow was touching the back of the cabinet or I would have gotten fried. It hurt like hell for a long time."

Since I worked on electrical cabinets a lot and slid down the ladders entering the sub, I decided not to wear any jewelry, not even a watch.

"Our overhaul period, sea trials, shake down cruise, missile shoot, and PR trips were behind us. We had all our missiles, torpedoes and supplies loaded. There was nothing left to do but head out on patrol. I would get to cross the Atlantic underwater again and I was not going to be a mess cook unless I messed up big time. I had seventy-five days and a wakeup left before being discharged. My last patrol turned out to be the most exciting."

"I'm all ears," Captain Bob said.

episode nine

"Here," I said to Captain Bob. "You'll need to see this as I begin the unbelievable story about my last patrol." I handed him my perpetual calendar so he could see what I was talking about.

"What is this and where'd ya get it?" Captain Bob said.

"When I was twelve, my family visited Washington D.C. and stayed at the Manger Hayes Hotel. The hotel provided a calendar souvenir which is good for the years 1955 through 1982. I kept it with me and used it regularly. I used to set the thumb wheel year on the appropriate month and the calendar days appeared at the top. I found out on the last patrol that with a conversion chart it can be used for any date." I then started the story of my last patrol.

My last patrol started on April Fools Day. Three days later we received a message stating that Dr. Martin Luther King had been killed by an assassin. I was standing in the passageway outside officer's country talking to a second class petty officer named Goode. When the an-

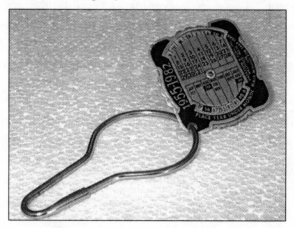

nouncement was made I was speechless, but Petty Officer Goode, who was from Alabama, had something to say.

"About time somebody shot that son of a bitch."

He had said it a little too loudly and with way too much hate in his voice. He was overheard by a couple of officers and the black steward. He stood a captain's mast, was reprimanded and reduced in grade for two months, a period which lasted the rest of the patrol.

A couple of days later the adventure of a lifetime began.

Once upon a time...

"Andy, get up," Little Dickey said. "We've got a problem with a missile tube power supply."

On this, my last patrol, my primary job was to take care of the power supply cabinets affixed to each missile tube. The cabinet was the interface between fire control, navigation, all of the ships systems and the guidance portion of the missile's computer. When there was a malfunction with the cabinets, I was the primary person called to investigate.

"Aw, man, is this a drill?" I asked with disappointment, looking at my wrist watch. "I just got off duty an hour ago." I rolled onto my side and slipped out of the bunk, still wearing my poopie suit. I still slept clothed and in my stocking feet on the top of the vinyl bunk cover in case there was a "drill."

"No, this is the real thing," Little Dickey answered. "Fire control can't figure it out, so they need our expertise."

"Let me guess. Is it tube sixteen?" I inquired, trying to clear the fog in my brain.

"Bingo! How did ya guess," Little Dickey asked.

"That power supply cabinet has been giving me trouble every time we boot up," I said, pulling on my shoes. "I watch the start-up current and have to tweak it to coax it through the test. I think I know what's wrong, but was hoping it would last through the patrol. You know what a pain it is to fill out a repair report. Get the storekeeper so I can get any parts I might need. If I gotta get up, I'll make sure someone else is bothered too."

"Aye, aye, Cap'n," Little Dickey said with a smirk. He turned left in the passageway and went forward to check on the storekeeper while I went right and headed for number sixteen missile tube.

The storekeeper was one of the few black guys on the sub who was not a steward or a cook. I didn't see him as black, just as another crew member. As demonstrated by petty officer Goode, the men from the Southern states carried the most prejudice and were openly hateful toward any black crew members. The storekeeper was also from a southern state, Mississippi, making the hatred even worse. One man from the South even had a ceramic monkey with the storekeeper's name printed on it. He kept it in a restricted area where the storekeeper couldn't go, but most of the crew knew it was there. So when I wanted Little Dickey to get the storekeeper, it wasn't with malice; it was so we wouldn't have to track him down if I needed a part. Missile downtime was frowned upon.

When I got to the number sixteen missile tube and around to the inside where the power supply cabinet was, I pulled out the TL-29 electrician's knife almost everyone on board kept in a pocket in their poopie suits. I had three of the cabinet front's four retaining screws hanging by their keepers when Mr. Inman came up from the starboard side.

"Without getting too many of my fingers in the fire, tell me what's wrong," Mr. Inman said. He was smoking a cigar, a habit he had picked up in the shipyard.

I shook off the Jimism and looked up, trying not to laugh in his face.

"It looks like it might be a diode, sir," I responded out of respect. "I think I can get it repaired in about 15 minutes or so."

"Make sure you dot your P's and Q's in the report, because this is going as downtime on the records." The Jimisms became more numerous when he was under pressure.

"Yes sir, I sure will," I said. Just then Little Dickey came around the missile tube with the storekeeper in tow. Mr. Inman turned on his heels, cigar jutting from his pursed lips, and headed forward. I went back to removing the last screw from the cabinet front cover.

"What can I get you, Andy?" the storekeeper asked.

"Let me get to the circuit board and see if I guessed correctly," I said as I pulled off the front cover to the cabinet and set it aside.

"Don't you have to kill power to the cabinet?" Little Dickey said.

"Yeah I do," I said. "Follow me over to the power distribution panel and be my backup. The two-man rule is in effect since the panel has live power to it and can't be shut down."

All three of us went to the starboard side of the missile room toward the distribution panel that was in the overhead between tubes thirteen and fifteen about six and a half feet up. I dropped the panel with the two knurled knobs that secured it on one side. The panel swung to the side, held in place by a piano hinge on the outboard side.

Above me were the panel and relays that controlled power to all the missile tubes. I knew it was dangerous to reach over the top of the panel and blindly unscrew the terminals by hand and remove them from the power relay for number sixteen missile. Turning off power to this panel was not an option, since that would mean all sixteen missiles would be in the dreaded downtime status.

I had done this before and was trained to use one hand while I kept the other away from any grounded source. My shoes provided protection from the metal deck which was also vinyl-covered providing more insulation. So as I touched the live 440-volt terminal, there wouldn't be any path for electricity through my body and, therefore, I should not get shocked. Little Dickey and the storekeeper watched as I reached up with my right hand, bent my wrist around the relay, and felt for the wing nut that held the wire in place.

I found the nut and was starting to unscrew it. It was a long nut and required about sixteen, one-half turns to completely remove it. About two or three turns from the end, fatigue was starting to set in. After all, I had been robbed of my sleep period. To give my straining muscles some relief, I unconsciously reached over with my left hand to brace myself on the metal table at the side of the passageway.

I heard Little Dickey say, "Andy don't!" but it was too late. I provided a path for the electricity from the live electrical connection, through my right arm, across my chest and down my left arm to the table, which was grounded to the submarine.

And this is no shit, the shock of four-hundred-forty volts coursing through my body knocked me free of the panel. It felt as though a horse had kicked me in the chest as every muscle in my body contracted at once. I flew through the air, hitting my back against the wrapped foam insulation of the number eleven missile tube and bounced to the deck, butt first. Little Dickey immediately came over and grabbed me by the shoulder. The storekeeper just stood there, wide-eyed and said "Lawdy, lawdy."

"Man, you okay?" Little Dickey asked.

"Shit, yeah," I responded, shaking my head. "Did you get the license number of the truck that just hit me?"

"I'm gonna get the doc," he responded and headed toward the forward bulkhead, going right through the restricted missile-tube-control panel. Foster, who had just witnessed the whole shocking event, quit plucking his beard long enough to get out of the way. Normally the area where Foster was standing his watch was off limits to all but the watch and some officers, which necessitated going to the other side of the compartment or the upper level to travel forward. This time PO Foster said nothing as he gawked at me sitting on the deck.

With Foster still staring at me, I braced myself with both hands, and rose up to a squat. The perpetual calendar, hooked to a loop in my poopie suit, sent sparks to my forearm. My right arm twitched a bit from the spark, but it didn't buckle while I pushed myself to a standing position.

By the time Little Dickey had returned with Doc, I was back up and reaching for the loose wing nut, this time keeping my left hand behind my back.

"I got it," I said proudly as I showed them the wing nut. I reached back up and disconnected the live wire disabling the power supply interface cabinet.

"You fool!" Doc said. "You didn't observe the two-man rule."

"I sure did, Doc," I responded with a grin. "Little Dickey was right here beside me when I got bit, weren't you Dick?"

"Not before!" Doc yelled, "Just now I saw you by yourself with your hand in a live panel. Sit down and let me check you out."

"Naw," I said. "The storekeeper is right over there." I pointed to the place I had last seen him.

"He went to the head to throw up," said PO Foster. The puking sound was reaching all but me, since my ears had been ringing ever since I had gotten shocked.

"Well, PO Foster was right behind me," I said trying to justify my action. "Besides, I'm all right," I said, pulling the stool out from under the bench and sitting down. "Just a sore back from when I hit the tube." My calendar sparked against my right arm again, but I was the only one who noticed it.

Doc felt my pulse and then placed his hands on my neck to check the tension of the muscles. He had me cross my legs and tapped the knee joint with the little hammer he always seemed to have in his pocket. As he listened to my heart with his stethoscope, Lt. Inman, came around number one tube and passed through the restricted area with a concerned look on his face. He was holding the half chewed cigar in his right hand.

"Okay, what happened?" he asked, in a take-charge voice. "If we've got egg on our face, we're just going to have to eat it."

"Andy got hit with four-forty volts," Little Dickey responded holding back a snicker.

"What about the power supply cabinet?" Inman inquired. He apparently had no concern for his men, only the fucking downtime.

"I'll fix the cabinet in fifteen minutes, sir," I said trying not to sound sarcastic, but I know I did.

"Fire control to missile. We've lost power to number sixteen missile tube," crackled a voice from the intercom near PO Foster.

"Good," I said. "Now I can do my job." I walked back toward the power supply cabinet just as the storekeeper came out of the head wiping his mouth with a sheet of toilet paper.

"Lawd," he said. "I thought you was dead." The doc snickered as he left us to our devices, obviously convinced I would live.

"I'm fine," I said, trying to reassure him. I felt another spark going from the calendar to my left arm. "I just got 'bit' a little." We used the term "bit" to refer to an electrical shock, whether or not it knocked you on your ass.

I reached into the dead cabinet and pulled the circuit board I suspected of causing the problem. I turned the board over in my hands as the doc, Little Dickey, the storekeeper, and Mr. Inman all looked on with concern, much like doctors witnessing a delicate operation.

"Here it is," I said holding up the board for all to see. "A corroded circuit board around these four power supply diodes."

They all had looks on their faces as if I had just pulled a baby from the birth canal and slapped it on the ass.

"Storekeep," I said. "Get me four of these diodes. I'll get them soldered in and have this missile back up and running in no time." He took off with the board and headed for his office to find the location of replacement diodes. He had limited stores of electronics, but the diodes were a common item so I knew we had some replacements somewhere on the ship. If I had to, I could take some out of a non-essential piece of equipment.

"You'll need to fill out a report on that item," Mr. Inman said unnecessarily, pointing with the lit end of his cigar. "Maybe there are others like that in the fleet that might cause unnecessary downtime. Once we report it, the monkey's in their court." He stuck the cigar back in his mouth, looking like a tall Edward G. Robinson.

I wanted to say, *you and your fucking downtime*, but because of his Jimism, I bit my tongue. I also wanted to jam that *fucking cigar* back into his face and smash it against his nose. I didn't have much respect for the man, but feared a Captain's mast, which would punish me, probably putting me back as a mess cook for the rest of the patrol, even if it was my last.

"Yes sir," I said, more as a wisecrack than anything else.

Within ten minutes the storekeeper came back waving the diodes. I replaced the faulty components and put the board back in the cabinet. As Little Dickey replaced the wire and wing nut in the distribution panel with the storekeeper watching him, I put the cover back on the missile tube cabinet.

"Power restored to number sixteen missile," crackled the 1MC speaker. "Going through testing procedures now."

"Wake me if there are any other problems," I said to Little Dickey as I headed for my bunk.

When I crawled back into bed, I rubbed the calendar which was still crackling. I noticed it had moved off the date I had previously set, but was too tired to reset it. I pulled my latest book out from under my pillow. I wasn't reading a James Bond novel, but had found a World War II book on the Pacific Theater which I thought might be an interesting read. I set the book down by my side and quickly dozed off. Tossing and turning in my sleep, my pocket pen came out and worked its way down my bunk toward my waist and touched the calendar. I rolled over as the sub shuddered as though it were bumped by a giant fish.

"What were that bump?" Captain Bob asked.

"I didn't find out until much later."

"Trim party," someone said. I had been awake about fifteen minutes and was reading my World War II book. Hearing the words "trim party" from the passageway outside my cubicle, I got quickly out of bed. There was a new officer on board and he must be the diving officer on his first watch alone.

We always maintained a little bit of positive buoyancy, just in case we needed to come to the surface in an emergency. The opposite, negative buoyancy, meant the sub sank if we lost propulsion. To keep the sub at depth, we kept a slight down angle of three to six degrees. That way, the water we were moving forward through pushed down on the upper surfaces of the sub, counteracting the buoyancy force of the seawater pushing us up. Archimedes' principle was being put to practice on the sub whenever we were at sea.

To maintain a constant down angle either the fairwater planes were kept at a down angle acting like the flaps on an airplane, or the sub could be made heavier in the bow and light in the stern. This teeter-totter effect was called trim and there were trim tanks forward and aft connected by piping and a pump. Whenever we flushed tanks, or had some other changes to buoyancy such as a temperature change in the water around us, the sub had to be trimmed. A large down or up angle on the fairwater planes or a change in the down angle were indicators the trim had to be re-done.

Apparently a re-trimming had been ordered and someone in the control room had passed the word. We were about to play with the mind of the new diving officer. I headed in the direction of the mess hall where most trim parties originated. I got to the forward end of the missile compartment as a group of men were heading aft.

"Trim party aft," Bear said, and pointed the way.

I joined the group, now numbering about fifteen. When we got to the very back of the engine room we all stopped and listened. Some were giggling like school kids. Then we heard the sound of the pumps taking water out of the aft trim tank. Our combined weight was pushing the nose of the sub up so the diving officer was pumping water from the aft trim tank to the bow trim tank to offset the imbalance. When the pumping stopped, it was time to head forward. We moved quietly so as not to sound like a "turd of hertles," moving through the boat.

As we passed the engine room the guys manning the reactor and steam turbine control panel looked and smiled.

When we got to the torpedo room, we waited again. We had picked up a few more of the crew and now numbered about twenty. Within seconds, the trim pump sounded and water was being pumped from fore to aft. When it stopped, we repeated the process. On our way back toward the torpedo room we were stopped by the COB.

"Knock it off," he said. "We're on to your little game, but we have a real problem. The water is really getting warm around us and we can't figure out why."

The group dispersed, but the many hours I had spent as a helmsman/planesman the last three years made me want to be closer to the action, so I went to the control center to find out what was going on. The skipper was at the con along with the navigator and the new diving officer we had held the trim party for. The COB was also there, but he and I still didn't get along, so I asked Little Dickey who was also curious and standing off to the side, what was going on.

"You missed a trim party," I said.

"It was obvious what you were doing," he said. "Obvious to all but the new diving officer, that is. He's been having trouble with the trim ever since we hit the warm water. Then, you guys really messed him up."

"We're in the North Atlantic," I said. "How warm can the water get?"

"It's normally in the fifties at patrol depth, but it's in the seventies right now."

"Can't be," I said. "We must have drifted south, into the Med."

"The navigator decided we need a star shoot," Little Dickey said. "That's where we're headed now."

"All non-essential personnel clear the control room," the skipper said. That was our clue to leave. I went back to the missile compartment to get ready for my watch. Chow would be going down in a half hour and I wanted a shower first. I was growing my beard, so I didn't have to do the three S's.

After I was cleaned up and fed and before I went on watch, I wanted to check the number of days I had left in the Navy and update my countdown calendar. I looked at my perpetual calendar and noticed again that the date was off. *Must have happened when I got slammed into the missile tube*, I thought. I went to pull my pen out of my pocket to cross out days, but couldn't find it. I was about to go to where I had been knocked on my ass to see if it had fallen out there, when I glanced on my bunk and found it in the middle of the green canvas. I picked it up and when I brought it near the perpetual calendar, sparks crackled from both and I jumped back. I looked closely at the perpetual calendar and saw 62, the year I had joined the Navy, was set on August. I put my pen away and with the thumbwheel, moved the 68 back under April, where I had had it the last time I had checked. I then left to stand my watch.

"Something's going down," Little Dickey said about halfway through my six-hour watch. I had been up on a ladder in the upper level of the missile compartment cleaning the dirt from between the frames on the sub's hull. There was a coating of residue (which I found out later contained asbestos) left from the overhaul period that had collected on the curved "I" beams, or frames, and all other horizontal surfaces. We were tasked with removing it when there was no other work to do during our watch. I added this absurd make-work endeavor to my list of reasons "why I want to get out of the Navy." It was the old boot camp philosophy that if you didn't have anything to do, then run in place. I had a rag in one hand and a bucket of water in the other when he found me.

"What do you mean?" I said.

"We're not only way off course; we're on the wrong side of the world, in the wrong ocean!"

"What?" I said. "How can that be?"

"That's what the skipper wants to know. He has the radio room monitoring signals right now to see if something's happened with the world."

"What? World War III started and blew us into a different ocean?"

"It gets even weirder," he said. "What I heard is that we are at the end of the Second World War."

I almost dropped the bucket and rag and had Little Dickey not grabbed the ladder and steadied it, I would have fallen.

"That makes no sense. Did I miss something after I got my dick knocked stiff?"

"Not anything more than the rest of us."

"All hands not on watch report to the mess hall in five minutes," the 1MC blared, jolting me upright and nearly knocking me off the ladder again.

"Take notes," I said. "I wanna know everything."

"Will do," Little Dickey said over his shoulder, as he headed forward.

I got off the ladder and decided to suspend my cleaning chores until later. I headed back to the second level to ponder what I had just been told and to wait for the results of the meeting. I didn't have to wait long.

"This is no shit, but it's more like 'once upon a time'," Little Dickey said. It was as if he had the biggest bit of gossip to tell and he was the only one who knew it. "We are at the end of the big one, World War II." My mouth fell open and I just stared as if I were in a weird dream. "And, we're in the Pacific Ocean somewhere near Japan. That's why the water is so warm. It's the first week in August, 1945 according to the radio signals we picked up. They're trying to confirm the exact date now."

I remembered that I was born on a Thursday in 1944 and that my birthday was on a Thursday in 1961. I remembered that fact because of Mad Magazine.

I had been an avid reader of Mad since it first came out in 1952. The 1961 March issue, which happened to be their sixty-first issue, observed that 1961 was the first upside-down year since 1881 and the last until 6009. I checked my birthdays in 1881 and1961, and found them to be on a Wednesday and Thursday. The dates stuck in my mind after that.

Tingles went up my spine recalling the year 62 was under August on my perpetual calendar. *If 1944 and 1961 had the same calendar dates, could it be that the next years 1945 and 1962 had the same calendar dates?* I would have to check.

"This is a joke," I said. We started our patrol on April Fools Day, so this might be a belated joke concocted by the captain.

"Not according to the skipper. You should have seen the long faces on the officers. Some of the crew questioned the sanity of it, and the skipper reassured us he was dead serious. The skipper said that if it is the first week in August, we should be able to see the atomic bomb exploding over Hiroshima. The navigator has plotted a course to get us there before it goes off."

"How can they tell from radio broadcasts?"

"Juan, the steward is Filipino and he speaks Japanese. He has been in the radio room for the last four hours translating what we can pick up."

"I ain't believin' this shit," I said, shaking my head. Just then, the COB walked around the number fifteen missile tube, saw us, and headed in our direction.

"I saw you reading a book on World War II the other day," he said. "Still got it?"

"Yeah, it's on my bunk," I said. In the recent excitement, I had almost forgotten I had the book.

"I need to borrow it to verify some dates and times for the skipper," he said.

"Sure, go ahead and take it. It's kinda boring anyway."

"When you get off watch, report to the chow hall after the meal," he said looking directly at me. I didn't ask what for. The COB didn't like me and the feeling was mutual. I just nodded yes and he left the same way he came.

"What's that about?" I asked, although I suspected Little Dickey didn't know anything more than I did about what the COB wanted.

Little Dickey with a shrug of his shoulders gave me the sea-bee salute and walked away. I spent the rest of my watch wondering what kind of trouble I was in. When I got to the mess hall, I found that I had worried for nothing.

The XO was there along with some of the guys from the seaman gang who stood the planesman and helmsman watches for this patrol. They were new guys, not yet qualified and were also my replacements as mess cook. I had talked to a couple of them when they had come to get signed off on various systems in the missile compartment. Other than that, I didn't see much of them.

"Gentlemen, I'll get right to the point," the XO said. "We're going to try to sneak into the bay where Hiroshima, Japan is situated. We're going to maneuver to within five miles of the shore so we can observe one of the atomic bomb blasts that was instrumental in ending World War II. If there is an explosion, then we will confirm what we're already pretty sure of, that we have, somehow, traveled back in time.

"You, gentlemen, are going to steer us through the very narrow channel, so get a good night's rest and we'll see you tomorrow at zero nine hundred hours. Any questions?"

"We're going through a narrow channel in the daytime?" I asked.

"Good question," he said. "There are a lot of ships going in and out at that time and we figure on sneaking in under one of them. There may be submarine nets that are pulled back as the ships pass by and if we can stay under one of the ships we should be okay. If someone comes after us all we have to do is fire one of our torpedoes and knock them out first. They don't realize our capabilities and that is to our advantage. Any other questions?" There were none. "I've had the COB change your schedules around so you are all available for as long as it takes. See you tomorrow morning." He then walked out.

I took his advice and headed for my kip and a good night's rest. Little Dickey was not around for me to tell him why I had been wanted. The cook had taken in the entire talk from his galley pass through, so the rumor mill would keep the entire crew informed.

The crew was passing along information as fast as it was given. No announcements or all-hands meetings were necessary and when I awoke, it was zero five hundred. I remembered that I was going to compare the calendar dates for 1945 and 1962.

As I lay in my bunk before getting up, I reasoned that the day of the week moves ahead one day each year except for leap year when it jumps two. I remembered JFK was elected in 1960 so I listed the leap years back from that date. They were 60, 56, 52, 48, and 46. Therefore, 1950, with two leap years in between, would be the same as 1945. The same for 1956, itself being a leap year; and then, yes, with one leap year in between, 1962 would share the same days of the week as 1945. I was able to verify this with 1956 on my perpetual calendar, so now I was sure.

When I got to the mess hall, someone had posted a computer-generated calendar on the bulkhead. August fifth was circled with the word today written above it.

"Who did that?" I asked.

"One of the fire control techs," Cooky said. "I think it was your Uncle Gill."

"Okay," I said. Most everyone knew the nicknames we had for each other. Some of them used the nicknames also, except for mine because it would smack of impersonating an officer. I was still referred to as Cherry, or Andy. *Maybe he can generate more calendars for me if I need them.* I thought.

"What da ya wanna eat?" Cooky asked. He liked me since we had gotten along great when I was mess cooking. The rest of the crew knew he was my "sea daddy" and didn't object when I didn't have to wait in line in crew's berthing and fill out a breakfast chit like the others. Most of the older sailors each adopted a newer member of the crew to help him through his quals and to adapt to life in a metal can. There were never any hints of sexual relationships; in fact, we all had been screened for those tendencies prior to reporting on board. If a sea daddy took a liking to you, qualifying was a lot easier.

I used to help him clean up the grill and his pots and pans when my chores were done. I didn't have to, but I did. He taught me some tricks he had learned cooking in quantity for the crew. One of which was, when he put too much salt in a macaroni salad that I helped him "build," he dumped some sugar in to counteract the salt. We always asked "Whatcha buildin'?" It was never "what are you making" or "what are you cooking?"

"A couple over easy, some hash browns, and an order of meat, please."

"What the fuck?" he said. "You on a diet or sumpin'?"

"Yeah, I'm gettin' out in a couple of months and wanna look purdy." I said.

"Assuming we can get back to where we were," he replied.

I had never thought about that until now. I grabbed some utensils and sat down near the jukebox. I looked to see if Snake had put "Chug-a-lug" back on. He hadn't.

I finished my breakfast and stayed around shootin' the shit with Cooky until zero eight hundred hours when I headed to the restroom to void my bladder. I didn't want to have to take a piss while steering a course in enemy waters.

We snuck through the small strait without incident and sailed into the bay where the city of Hiroshima was situated. We rigged for silent running and used the electric propulsion motor which was wrapped around the drive shaft. The sonarman was the same one as when we passed into the Mediterranean Sea, but he was a whole lot calmer. The order was given to take the sub down so we could sit on the floor of the bay until the next day.

To maintain silence, we ate horse cock sandwiches and didn't take showers. Movement was restricted around the sub to stocking feet only. Then, the next morning we went to periscope depth to witness the bomb drop. We were about five miles from the city, but because we didn't want to stick the scope too far above the water, we couldn't see any buildings. We listened carefully for any boats in the water, but all the contacts were distant. It was easy to hover in the calm waters of the bay, and at zero eight hundred the order was given to raise the scope. From history, we knew the bomb had gone off sometime around zero eight fifteen, only now there was no explosion. There was no "A" bomb to confirm the date. At zero nine hundred hours we retraced the path that had gotten us into the bay and headed back out to sea.

Scuttlebutt started flying about why there was no bomb blast. Had the translations of the date been misinterpreted? No, not according to the intercepted signals and the translations our Filipino steward provided. Were we in the wrong place?

"No," the navigator said, "Not unless the stars had all moved in the past twenty three years." We also had visual sightings of Japanese ships before and after we passed through the channel. Did we have the wrong time or date of the blast? No, not according to my World War II book that the COB had taken from my bunk.

The radiomen put the antenna up and received some additional messages. The intercepted messages all mentioned a bomb that had hit the city of Hiroshima and exploded on impact, but with little damage. We were at the right place at the right time and the bomb was dropped but didn't work as it was supposed to.

episode ten

Once upon a time…

The captain called an all-hands meeting in the mess hall to discuss what had happened during our last surface run. The Sam was manned with a minimum crew which allowed fifty of us to cram into the thirty-man dining room. Some of us grabbed a cup of coffee and the cook put out a fresh pan of sticky buns. There was a din of excitement when the COB called "attention on deck" and we all stood up while the XO and captain walked in.

"Sit," the captain said. Those of us who had a seat, did.

"What happened, as far as we can tell," the captain started, "was that we went back in time to the end of World War II. What we saw from the con was the bombing of Hiroshima, only the atomic bomb they used didn't work. There was a small explosion, a dirty bomb that spread radioactive material over part of the city, but did not have the devastating effect that helped to end the war. The dropping of the Hiroshima bomb was on Monday the sixth of August, 1945. In three days another bomb will be dropped on Nagasaki and I have asked the navigator to plot a course full steam ahead so we can be in position to witness that bombing. If that weapon fails, we will have to decide what to do, since the end of the war was a result of the bombings. The wardroom has discussed the "what ifs" in this situation and what we have come up with is the following:

"We will arm one of our missiles and re-program its guidance package to hit Nagasaki in case that bomb also malfunctions. If we can figure out how we traveled back in time, we may also be able to go back and hit Hiroshima the same way. We will then steam for Pearl Harbor to see if we can get back to the U.S. If we can figure out how the time travel happens, then we will plan accordingly. I will now turn this meeting over to the XO for questions and answers."

"Attention on deck," the COB said, and all hands got to their feet. As soon as the captain turned the corner heading toward the wardroom, we relaxed and the COB told us to take our seats.

"Questions," the XO said.

"What if we can't get back to the future?" Kozy asked.

"We don't know," said the XO. "We'll have to decide whether we want to surface and make ourselves known, or sail around until we figure it out. We can operate almost indefinitely on the reactors. The only limiting factor is food. We can pull into a port and get supplies if needed, but that would expose us to many questions about our sub and about us."

"What about women?" Kozy interrupted. "I can't go long without getting my pipes cleaned out." This brought a muffled laugh from the rest of the crew.

"I'm sure Doc has some shots to fix that," the XO continued, getting more laughs. "And from what I heard of your last R&R, you dipped your pen in infected ink anyway. It might be best for the world and for you if you remain abstinent before you go impotent." This brought even more laughs. "More questions?"

"Sir," I said. "Our warheads are set for ground blasts. Weren't the bombs on Hiroshima and Nagasaki aerial? Also what about the discrepancy in size of the payload? Our nuclear weapons are ten times the size of the ones used on Japan."

"Good point," the XO acknowledged. "If we can't re-program the blast height, we'll just have to use what we have. There's nothing that can be done about the size of the weapon, and we have fusion warheads instead of fission, but I don't think the type of weapon will make much difference. Fire control and missile techs will have to work on a solution to change the blast height while resetting the trajectory."

"Sir, with all due respect," Little Dickey said, "our missiles are fifteen-hundred-mile missiles. How can we observe Nagasaki, get the proper distance away and fire a missile to hit close to the time as the failed attack?"

"If we can't reprogram the missiles, then we'll have to figure that out. Since history has indicated that the blast happened, then we must have succeeded. Something must have allowed us to achieve the objective of Nagasaki and, somehow, Hiroshima too. My guess is we figured out how to adjust the dates of our time travel and got into position at the right time and place. If we hadn't, history would have changed and we might not even be here.

"Effective immediately, we need to ration our stores of food, so I'm asking each of you to eat less and the cooks to prepare an inventory of food and report our consumption daily."

"No more six eggs over easy, Andy," shouted Kozy, causing everyone to laugh.

"Fuck you, Dickhead," I responded. "We'll have to ration your supply of penicillin, puss piss."

"We all need to cut back," the XO said. "Therefore, pizza night will be limited to once a month until we sort this out."

Groans were the response to this announcement. Pizza night was every Friday and no one missed it unless he was on watch.

The risk of ridicule kept me from mentioning in front of the entire crew my discovery of the settings on the perpetual calendar and the changes in time we experienced. If it was necessary, I would address that separately with the XO through the chain of command, bypassing the COB if possible. First I would try to change the time on my own as a verification of my discovery.

After the meeting, I decided to see if I could change where we were in time by moving the wheel on my perpetual calendar. I pulled it out and checked the date. The "M" was over the days 6, 13, 20 and 27. That meant the day was the same as what the skipper described for the Hiroshima bombing. I looked at the year under "Aug" and it was 79. Not surprisingly, the gadget didn't go back as far as 45, but what if 1979 and 1945 shared the same dates as I discovered about my birthdays? I went looking for Uncle Gill. I found him in the forward torpedo room shootin' the shit with a goofy electrician nicknamed Sparky.

"Hey, Cap'n Gio," Uncle Gill said, when he saw me come through the hatch. Sparky went forward to talk to the torpedoman on watch. Uncle Gill didn't care about disrespect, so he was the only one on the sub who referred to me as Cap'n. Once on liberty, after a few too many, Lt Inman told him to straighten his cover, military for hat. Uncle Gill looked right at him and said 'with all due respect sir, fuck you.' I thought I'd never see him again except on the other side of the wall of the Castle, the Portsmouth prison. All he got was a Jimism in return.

"You're walking that line with a thin chalk, Mister." Lt Inman said.

"Hey Uncle Gill." I said. "I got a favor to ask. Can the general purpose computer in fire control create a calendar for any year, just like you did for 1945?" The fire control technicians liked to refer to the MCC (missile control center) as the fire control room, because they were the ones actually using the room. Since there were no missile technicians in the room on a routine basis, we referred to it as fire control also.

"Whada ya mean?" he said.

"If I give you any year, say 1962, can you verify August 6 was on a Monday and print out the rest of the calendar for the year?"

"Yeah. The calendar generator punch cards I used to print 1945 can do that. We normally use it to go forward to get information needed by the guidance packages for the missiles. When do ya need it?"

"Now if ya got the time," I said.

"Let's go on down to the fire control room and see what we can do," he said putting a hand on my shoulder and guiding me back to the hatch.

When we got to MCC, which was, on the same level and aft of crew's berthing, he used his key to get in. This was where all the target coordinates were calculated and fed over cables to the computer in the missile. Three rows of consoles were in the center of the brightly lit, white, sterile-looking room. Banks of file cabinets lined all the outside bulkheads. In the cabinets were row upon row of punch cards. All data which told the missile computer where the targets were was stored on the cards. One other piece of information needed by the missile guidance package was our location, which was constantly updated by the duty navigator. Data for weather and earth's rotation, etc. were also fed to the computer to allow for in-flight corrections.

I knew some of the guys in the room, but most of them kept in a clique of their own. Because they worked with and programmed computers, fire control technicians thought they were a cut above the rest of the crew. They worked in a secure room where no one was allowed in without an escort. They slept right outside the room in crew's berthing and ate together. Once they got qualified they didn't associate with anyone else on the crew. Uncle Gill was the exception. He went to one of the file cabinets and pulled out a stack of cards.

"Okay, he said what years do you want calendars for?"

"The war years, 1941 through 1945." I said.

"Easy enough," he said. He took the stack of cards over to a card punch reader and fed them in. At the monitor at one of the consoles, he punched in the dates and some other keys. I couldn't see what he was doing from where I was standing and no one else in the room gave him a second glance. Over in the corner, a wide-carriage impact printer started making its braaaack, braaaack noise as the print head went back and forth across the sheets of continuous paper being fed in from a box on the tray beneath the printer.

"Let's go see what we got," he said, with matter-of-fact confidence. He tore off a few sheets of paper when the printer quit and folded the page up. The top sheet had the heading 1941 and under the year in tabular form were the months with each day under that. He handed them to me.

"Thanks," I said. I put the sheets under my arm and headed back toward the door to the room.

"Ain't ya gonna check them?" he said smiling.

"Naw," I said. "I know they're correct if you did 'em. Thanks again."

I took the printouts back to my cubicle and noticed the COB must have returned my WWII book, because it was on top of my bunk. I shoved the book aside and laid the printouts under the light on my top bunk. I turned to the page dated 1941, took my perpetual calendar out, and compared the two. It was as I thought.

The days of the week matched when I rotated the wheel to each month. Just to be positive, I went to February to make sure it wasn't a leap year. It wasn't. I then checked each year and made a note of which war-time year matched the dates I had on my perpetual calendar. It took awhile, but I made a little chart in my notebook:

War years	41	42	43	44	45
Same as	58	59	65	72	62
	69	70	71		73
	75	81	82		79

I put the notebook and pen back in my pocket and shoved the computer-generated calendars under my mattress. I then put the '58 date on December on the perpetual calendar to match the chart date of '41. *How can I get the sub to go back to that date now?*

While making the chart I had noticed that whenever my pen was near the perpetual calendar, I could feel a tingling in my hand. Also sparks jumped back and forth between the two when they were near each other. This gave me an idea.

I held the perpetual calendar against the World War II book to steady it and took the pen back out of my pocket bringing it next to the 58. I felt the tingling, this time in both hands. As I slowly brought the pen closer, small sparks jumped between the two as if they were sending electronic signals back and forth.

Just to test it out, I touched the pen to DEC above the 58 and then to the upper date, Monday, the first. A little crackle could be heard both times when the pen touched the perpetual calendar. I quickly removed the pen when a rumble came from deep in the sub. There was a shudder in the heavy steel deck and bulkheads of the cubicle.

That happened sometimes when we went through a horizontal thermal layer, but we were going straight with no up or down motion. If this was how we had gone back in time before, I would know soon enough. I returned the perpetual calendar to my belt loop and took out my notebook. I wrote down the date I had touched, December 1, 1958. I was curious to find out if the sub was still in 1945, or had I pushed it back to 1941 as I had wanted to do. What if it went to the future, 1969 or 1975?

I had the duty for the next shift, so I went to crew's berthing to wait in line for dinner. They were blowing the crappers. I always wondered why they picked dinner time to empty the sanitary tanks.

There were five sanitary tanks on the Sam. Two tanks were directly under crew's berthing, one was under the officers' head, another was back in the missile compartment, and the last one was in the engineering spaces, aft of the reactor compartment. Gauges indicated how much waste was in each tank, but sometimes the indicators would get hung up on a rag or other object and give a false reading. Rather than take a chance that the indicators were off, the tanks were emptied once every twenty-four hours.

Rags could also hang up on the discharge valve preventing the tanks from being emptied. When this occurred, an auxiliary man would have to put on self-contained breathing apparatus and go into the tank and remove the obstacle. They would come back out of the tank with horror stories about what they found. We were told there were turds the size of footballs, swollen from exposure to salt water. No one ever challenged this observation, though many doubted it.

Except for the seats and lids, the toilets were made of stainless steel and had two valves, one for filling and one for flushing. A ball valve was used instead of a "P" trap to separate the holding tank contents from the toilet bowl. After using the toilet, the ball valve was eased open using a four-foot lever on the right side of the bowl requiring the user to stand directly over the bowl. A second valve was then opened to flush out the contents with sea water from a supply tank inside the sub. The ball valve was then closed and, after the bowl was partially filled with sea water for the next user, the water valve was closed.

Sometimes residual pressure was left in the tanks from the empting process or from pressure changes from inside the sub. Opening the ball valve with pressure in the tank would adorn the flusher with whatever was in the bowl. Even a small pressure difference would cause a blowback with tremendous consequences. I was told that this usually only happens once to an individual. From then on they knew better.

An auxiliaryman put up warning signs and then started the process of empting the tanks. All valves were closed leading into the tanks. Then high pressure air was let in to equalize the pressure between the inside of the tank and the sea water outside the hull. When the gauges indicated the pressure inside the tank was the same as sea pressure, a hydraulically actuated ball valve in the holding tank was opened and the waste material pushed out. In order not to make bubbles that would give away our position, the tanks were blown to a small bubble. As with the GDU, as little air as possible was permitted to go out to sea.

When the tank gauge indicated empty, the fun part began. All of the air in the tank was at the same pressure as the sea and couldn't be vented overboard. It therefore, had to be vented into the sub spaces, crews, berthing to be exact. Although there were charcoal filters to absorb the odor, they weren't effective, so sewer gas permeated the spaces like the plague of Egypt. Groans could be heard throughout the sleeping area. Standing in line waiting to eat was a test of endurance.

Worse than that was that the officers holding tank also vented into crew's berthing. There were a lot of officers who thought their shit didn't stink, but I had news for them. Needless to say, the auxiliary-men were not the favorite people on the sub. After I ate, I went back to the missile compartment for my six hours of duty and then hit the rack for some sleep.

"All-hands meeting in the mess hall in ten minutes," the 1MC blared out. I had been awake for about an hour reading my latest James Bond book, *Goldfinger*. I had set aside the WWII book for something a little more entertaining. A friend of mine, also nicknamed Bear, hooked me on the Ian Fleming series in sub school before I went to the Academy.

That Bear's nickname came from his appearance and demeanor. He had a matting of thick black hair over every surface of his body. It was even growing on the tops of his feet. He was tall and full shouldered like a bear. He had to shave his neck down below his shirt, but the remaining tuft stuck out anyway. My bunk was above his, so I couldn't help noticing the "hair carpet" he left on the sheets when he got up. He also snored like a bear. It didn't take long for him to get the nickname.

He had had two years of college before he enlisted and was saving money to go back. Like me, he was in for six years in the Polaris Field Electronics program whereby we were given two years of schooling as either a missile, fire control, or electronic technician. In exchange, we obligated ourselves for six years of active duty. When Bear found out that six years away from college meant he would have to start all over as a freshman, he decided to shorten his tour of duty.

He had told me he had a plan to get out, but little did I know that it was by suicide, or an attempt at it. One night he put a note on his pillow where the roving barracks watch could find it and then went into the head and took a few aspirin, flushing the rest down the toilet. When they found him, he was supposedly unconscious. As they took him out on the gurney, he opened his eyes just a little and gave me a wink when no one could see. I knew then that his attempted suicide was a fake. Being one of his friends, I was asked questions at the inquiry, but of course, knew nothing. I don't know what happened to him after that, but the scuttlebutt was he got a medical discharge as being unsuitable for military duty.

His lasting legacy with me was the time we went to see *Dr. No* at a theater in New London. I started reading the Ian Fleming Bond books and kept at it until I entered the Academy. Once I was a plebe, there was no time for relaxation reading. After I quit the Academy, I started reading the series again.

At the all-hands meeting it was announced that we were not going to Nagasaki as planned. Something had happened to our "time table," as the captain put it. We were headed to Guam to see if we could contact the naval forces. As far as he could tell from radio intercepts it was early December, 1941.

My eyes got big when he said that. My little gadget had worked and, therefore, I must hold the key to the time travel the sub was experiencing. For the next two days, we headed for Guam and another adventure.

"Andy," Little Dickey said waking me from a deep sleep. "Get up. Mr. Inman wants to see us, right now, in the wardroom."

"What the fuck?" I said. I was dazed and almost cracked my head on the reading light directly overhead like I did my first patrol. "What is it?"

"I don't know, but something's come up on Guam. Scuttlebutt has it that the place is overrun by Japs."

"No fucking surprise. It's 1941," I said remembering the time change.

I hopped out of my bunk and grabbed my shoes from the end of the mattress and put them on. I was already in my poopie suit, so I only needed to tighten my belt. Little Dickey was already heading forward toward the next compartment.

"What's going on, Andy?" came a sound from Felix in the bottom bunk.

"I don't know," I said. "I'm just followin' orders." I was hot-footing after Little Dickey as I finished the sentence.

"The reason I have you three men here is very simple, but it's more complicated than it sounds". Mr. Inman said.

Oh boy, here we go again. Please, God, give me strength not to laugh out loud. In the room were me, Little Dickey, and Ski. I had no idea what this was about.

"We intercepted some radio communications and it sounded like Japanese, or oriental, or something like that, he continued. We also heard communications in English from nurses who indicated that they were trapped on a corner of the island and needed to get out before they were captured. As near as we can tell, it's December 7, 1941. If I remember history, Guam was overrun by the Japs on December 10. So, we have three days to get to shore, find the nurses and bring them back."

"Why us, sir?" Ski asked.

I cringed at his having interrupted an officer. My question was "why me?" There were trained divers on board who might be better suited to the task. They also had their own wet suits and could swim ashore if necessary. Then I remembered that this was the South Pacific and there would be sharks about.

I also wanted to ask why we're doing it in the first place, but apparently the decision was made. I could just change the date again, but that would mean the nurses would be stranded and maybe killed by the Japs.

"I'll be in charge," he said. "You, Ski, are the strongest man on board. Little Dickey is, probably the smartest enlisted man."

"You left someone out, sir," I said, a little miffed that he hadn't even looked at me.

"Oh, yeah," Mr. Inman said. "You are the best shot on the sub and can see like a hawk at night."

"Sir," Ski interrupted again. "Hawks don't fly at night."

There was no response to this observation. The fact that I knew little about guns except how to load, aim, and shoot left me a little perplexed as to why one of the machinist mates wasn't selected. The reason was probably that there were plenty of missile technicians in the subs. I was, therefore, expendable.

There was some truth to the 'seeing at night' comment. It was no shit that I was the lookout of choice when we were on the surface, day or night. I was farsighted and had worn glasses since the third grade until I entered the Navy. During my routine eye test in boot camp, the Navy discovered I could see fine without them. I was told if I got caught wearing glasses I would be "out of uniform" and would face a court-martial.

Lt. Inman then continued with the plan to surface at night, row ashore in one of the inflatable rafts used for escape and rescue, pick up the nurses, and bring them back. He said the radiomen were trying to communicate with the nurses on shore now. If they were unsuccessful, the plan would be scrapped.

"Let me run this over you again," he said and explained the whole plan one more time. "Any last requests?"

"Sir, I hope you mean questions." I said. Hearing no response from him, I continued. "Where will the sub be while we're ashore?"

"The sub will submerge as soon as we're clear of the boat enough for them to dive safely without sucking us under," he said. "The whip antenna will be up so we can radio the sub when we're headed back."

The whip antenna was like a car antenna and could extend above the surface of the water while the Sam was submerged. It was hinged at its base and rotated to the up position when needed. It was from this antenna that all the radio traffic was picked up giving us clues as to what day it was. The star shoots determined where we were.

"That's all," Mr. Inman said. "The navigator is preparing some maps. To make sure we cross all your P's and Q's, there will be a final briefing about an hour before we leave. We will dismember in the raft tonight at twenty-two hundred hours. Get some rest."

I hope he meant disembark, but get some fucking rest? I couldn't sleep now if my life depended on it. Shit, my life does depend on it. Before we leave, I'll see the doc to ask him for some bennies for tonight, and maybe enough for a day or two. I wanted to be on my toes for the whole ordeal in case we had to be up all night.

Little Dickey and I headed back to the missile compartment.

"They didn't even ask for volunteers," I said.

"Would you have volunteered?" he asked. "I wouldn't miss this opportunity for the world."

Little Dickey was adventurous and would head out on any assignment given him. I, on the other hand, was more cautious but, at the same time, a little excited about the unknown aspects of this rescue mission. I would make sure my little bauble and pen were along for the ride. If it got too dicey, I could flip us back to the future. I wondered how close to the perpetual calendar everyone would have to be to travel back with me. I also wondered whether it would work outside the Sam.

"I was just thinking," Little Dickey said. "What if the Sam goes further back or forward in time while we're ashore. How will we get back?"

"Don't worry about it," I said. "I've got it under control."

He didn't ask me what I meant. I wasn't ready to tell him my little secret. Not yet anyway.

Twenty-one hundred hours came soon enough. As I had thought, I couldn't sleep another wink. I tried reading some more of my book, but couldn't do that either. I didn't find Doc, but that turned out not to be necessary. He was at our briefing and had some pills for all four of us.

"Sorry I don't have any suicide pills for you to take in case the Japs get ahold of ya," Doc said.

"Thanks a fucking lot, Doc," I said. "That's all I needed to hear. How many bennies does it take to put you to sleep?"

"You don't have enough," he said.

"Who was this Doc?" Captain Bob asked. "You mentioned him before."

Doc Jenkins was a corpsman with special training. He was like a paramedic and as I said previously, could even perform some emergency surgeries, like an appendectomy, if necessary. He always placed pill cups in the mess hall which were full of bennies and vitamins for the mornings of the first few days in port after a patrol. Sailors got drunk and were hung over the morning after that first night off the boat when they had gone two months without any alcohol.

Doc was stocky and short with the nicest disposition of anyone on the sub. He was a Chief Petty Officer, but unlike the other chiefs, didn't try to throw his weight or privilege around. Every week at field day, he cleaned his own spaces rather than sit back and let some lowly steward do it for him.

He was also a good sport. One of the electronic technicians and I once devised a plan to pipe high frequency noise into his cubicle. The theory was that he couldn't hear it, but his subconscious could. We had read that it would drive him nuts. He just laughed when he found the speakers and correctly surmised it was us. I didn't know if the noise affected him or not, because while we were piping it in, he didn't act any differently.

"What's a field day?" Captain Bob said.

"Once a week, usually on Friday, all hands "turned to" for a thorough cleaning of the sub. John Philip Sousa marching music was piped throughout the sub on the 1MC. It started with the announcement, 'Now here this! Commence cleanup fore and aft.' I say 'all hands,' but those E6 and above were usually excluded. Someone else got to clean up their mess. Doc was the exception."

"You cleaned only once a week?"

"Except for the mess hall, it was once a week. There were occasions when someone had made a mess and was caught. Like I mentioned before, the COB had been known to follow drops of coffee from the mess hall all the way back to the engine room to find out who created the trail. When he found that person, regardless of who they were, they had to clean the decks all the way back to the coffee urn. I got very good at carrying a full cup without spilling a drop, even in a rough sea.

"As mess cooks, we had field day everyday and a thorough cleanup on the Friday field day. On one such occasion, I smashed my thumb in the latch of a collapsible side seat on one of the mess hall benches. I ran to the doc with a throbbing, bleeding, swollen thumb. It hurt like hell, but if it got me off mess cooking it was worth the pain. He was cleaning his spaces and stopped long enough to look at and wrap my thumb, give me two aspirins, and send me back to work. Later, he drilled a small hole in the thumb nail to let the blood out, but it was too late to keep the nail from falling off a week later.

"We discovered that the bug juice we drank when we ran out of milk, was great for cleaning the metal commodes. When mixed with seawater, it would dissolve any residue that had collected since the last cleaning, leaving the metal shiny and new looking.

"At the prep school, field day had two meanings, the one I just described and another meaning I'll tell you about later."

Another story about Doc was the time when Kozy got the clap for the umpteenth time and Doc told him he would become impotent from scar tissue if he kept abusing his penis. Kozy just laughed and made fun of the word "impotent." Along with the penicillin to cure the clap, Doc got even by giving him some pills that made his piss blue. Kozy came screaming up out of crew's berthing yelling that he was dying after seeing his azure piss. That was good for a laugh. The infection from his dose of the clap also made him drip, which left blue streaks down the pant leg of his dress whites when he was on liberty. He didn't get laid for a long time after that. The dye washed out easily enough, but the Scottish barmaids and Colleens, as we called the Scottish girls who frequented the bars, remembered the Yank who could piss a blue streak.

We donned our dungarees and blue chambray shirts the darkest ones we could find. Each of us was handed the familiar red goggles to wear so our eyes would become accustomed to the darkness when we went topside. We wore deck shoes that were stained black. Our faces and hands were smeared with grease to better hide us in the night. We carried flippers for swimming, flashlights, compasses, and 45 caliber pistols. I had my perpetual calendar and pen tucked inside my front pant's pocket wrapped in food wrap to keep them dry.

"It's overcast tonight, so there will be no moon or stars to guide by," the XO said. "When we surface we'll be within sight of the shore. There are two small islands on either side of our position and one behind. It's high tide right now, but in six hours it will be ebb tide which will help you on the return trip. The nurses will be waiting due north of our position. Just keep the one island behind you and the two other islands on either side. Any questions?"

We all shook our heads, but said nothing.

"Godspeed," the captain said.

He was seated at the table with the XO, but didn't say anything else. It looked as though he wanted to go with us, but knew he couldn't. The three of us followed Lt. Inman out of the wardroom without any more instructions and went to the control room to wait for the Sam to surface.

I wonder what the hell Godspeed means. They say it in all the war movies, but I have no idea where it came from. I found out later in life that it came from god spede, Middle English meaning God prosper you.

"Sonar, report any contacts," the OOD said through the speaker to sonar. The officer of the day was the navigator. We took off our goggles now that we were in the darkness of the control center.

"No contacts," the speaker announced back.

"Captain in the con," someone behind us announced.

"Carry on, gentlemen," the captain said.

Usually when the captain was in the con he took control, but not tonight.

"Request permission to surface, Captain," the OOD said.

"Permission granted," he replied.

"Surface, surface, surface," the OOD said over the intercom.

When the command was given, valves turned at the push of a button letting air into the buoyancy tanks, that when submerged, were filled with water. Everything was done by a checklist since we didn't do this procedure very often. Hopefully, submerging and surfacing would be done in equal numbers.

When we broached the surface, the OOD went up through the conning tower to crack the hatch. When this was done and the hatch was fully opened, he and two lookouts went to the bridge to scan the horizon. When the "all clear" was sent back down, the captain joined them. As always, a careful count of the number of personnel on the bridge was kept in case an emergency dive was necessary. This time they would dive four short of a full boat.

The seaman gang went up the ladder and out a side door in the sail pulling the inflatable life raft with them. Next, it was our turn. I followed Ski, who followed Mr. Inman. Little Dickey was close behind me. The smell of the sea hit me and the warm tropical night air filled my lungs. The air actually smelled bad to me after breathing the purified air of the sub.

We exited through the side hatch in the sail. The night was overcast, still, and quiet. I scanned the horizon and got my bearings from the three outcroppings of hills that were the islands to the east, west, and south of us. We were still above the equator, but not by much. To the north was a lower outcropping of land which was the southern coast of Guam. According to the map, Aga point was where we were headed. The sub was able to get quite close to the shoreline as we were in some of the deepest waters on earth, to the west of the Marianas Trench which, at the deepest, was thirty-six thousand feet.

We walked along the port side of the sub to the section that tapered off into the water, called the turtleback. The seaman gang had already launched the raft and were holding it by a lanyard. As we climbed in for the ride to shore, we were each given a life vest that had been painted black. I noticed extra vests already in the raft for the nurses. The raft was a large, eight-man, inflatable raft. It was not one of the survivor rafts, which were international orange, but black, for clandestine use. I didn't even know we had one on board. The transmissions had indicated four nurses in all, so the ride back would be a cozy one.

Once all four of us were in the raft, Ski and Little Dickey took the oars and when the man holding the line tossed it our way, they started to paddle. Being out in the raft reminded me of the time I had fallen off the sub in Holy Loch during my second patrol.

"You fell in the lake?" Captain Bob asked.

"Not a lake, loch, which I think is Scottish for, well… lake, and this is no shit" I said, deciding to tell him about my unscheduled swimming adventure.

As described before, the superstructure stopped at the end of the missile compartment as did the stanchions holding up the guard ropes. The hull of the sub began at the end of the superstructure and tapered off to the water line to the port, starboard, and aft. It resembled the back of a partially submerged turtle, hence, the name, turtleback. Some twenty feet further aft, the rudder jutted up to a height of ten feet or more, depending on how far the Sam sat out of the water.

To maintain the sides of the sub between the waterline and the top of the superstructure, a platform was lowered with two men on it. A dinghy, a small row boat, was used to reach the rudder and other places close to the waterline. Sometimes we just hung over the side holding onto the stanchions that were placed in holes along the top of the superstructure. Chains were strung between the stanchions to keep us from accidentally falling over the side as we worked topside. We were required to wear life jackets when outside the chains.

For sailors to fall into the water was not uncommon; however, a man overboard was always taken seriously. In the winter, the loch was snowy, windy, and cold and the water was always cold, winter or summer. An unplanned dip became an emergency as the sailor could numb very quickly and drown. Those in a dinghy always wore life jackets in addition to heavy, dark-brown, navy-issue winter work coats. Our dungarees were the only other protection from the elements.

Little Dickey took a plunge before I did. He was leaning over the missile superstructure a little too far. He went head first into the water with a loud splash. There were a lot of men on deck, so the "man overboard" alarm was sounded in a hurry. A life preserver with a line attached to it was tossed to the flailing man who grabbed hold and was pulled to safety before any further action was necessary. The shivering Little Dickey was escorted below decks and was given a glass of rum by the doc. A half hour later he was back up on deck in a fresh set of dry clothes chipping away at some more rusty spots.

My swimming session was a little different. I was assigned to the rudder painting detail. It was my turn to hold the line attached to the dinghy while Bear and Felix donned their life jackets and manned the little boat with their supply of paint and rollers. I was their safety line standing on the turtleback while they floated to the rudder. I was supposed to pull them back when they were done. All went well until they moved to the other side of the rudder and asked for more slack in the line I was holding.

There was little slack to give from where I was standing next to the stanchion, holding onto the guard chain. To provide more slack, I ducked under the chain, walked outside the safety area, and moved closer to the water line. There I stepped in the algae slime that always grew on the wet parts of the sub in the Loch. I turned inward as I did a slow-motion slide into the water. The cold instantly hit me and I kicked so hard I stayed dry from the shoulders up. Bear and Felix were yelling "man overboard," but because we were away from the rest of the men on deck and the noise from the tender was so loud, no one heard them. Noticing I was still hanging onto the rope, Bear pulled me to safety on the dinghy just as the alarm was sounded by someone who had seen me flailing. Sam sailors ran to the turtleback as we tried to toss them the too-short line. Finally, Bear was able to reach one of the men with the line just as a speed boat loaded with men in wet suits arrived around the back side of the tender. All three of us were pulled to the turtleback and I got out of the boat, wet and shivering.

"Get below," the OOD said as the rescue party was secured.

Oh boy! I thought. I'm going to get rum.

I didn't. I got my ass chewed by the COB instead for being in the dinghy without a life jacket. I tried to explain that I didn't start out in the dinghy, but was pulled there by Bear. Not good enough. The fact was, I had violated a rule, and that was that. No rum, only dry clothes and back to duty.

"We always had plenty of rum at sea," Captain Bob said.

"I think the officers on the sub did too," I said. "Now then, once upon a time…"

Lt. Inman and I sat in the raft while Little Dickey and Ski paddled. None of us had said a word since we left the Sam. My heart was racing a mile a minute. Once we started to move toward shore, I moved to the bow of the raft, and scanned the horizon.

"Can you see anything?" Little Dickey whispered to me.

"Nothing yet," I whispered back.

Ski and Little Dickey were doing a good job of rowing with knees bent and sitting back on their heels taking deep bites with the paddles. They kept in sync with each other without any cadence. The raft lurched forward with each stroke. I turned around to look for the southern island so I could judge our direction. The Sam was gone, slipped under the waves to await our return.

I could see the tree line when we were about halfway to the shore. The clouds were starting to break up, but there was no moon. Overhead the stars were starting to twinkle. It reminded me of my patrols in the North Atlantic before we dove. With no city lights to spoil the view (actually there were no artificial lights at all) the stars provided a canopy of endless sparkle and twinkle. It was a blanket of light from horizon to horizon, a 360 degree light show. Moonless nights were the best. Effervescent algae broke over the bow in a cascade like fireworks on the Fourth of July.

My dream was broken by something that caught my eye.

"I see some movement," I whispered peering onto the darkened beach. "Hold your oars for a second to let me get a better bearing."

"Damn, Andy," Little Dickey said. "I don't see anything."

"Me neither," Mr. Inman said.

We were all whispering, trying to be as quiet as possible.

"Don't look straight ahead," I instructed. "Look off to the side a little to get the field of view off your optic nerve." Ski had no idea what I was talking about and Mr. Inman was probably wondering too.

"There it is again." I whispered. "Steer about fifteen degrees to starboard. It's at least three people and they're hiding behind a group of coconut trees."

I held my right hand out, finger tips extended, palm inward, indicating the way. The two oarsmen dipped their oars into the water and rowed as silently as possible following my direction.

"I see them too," Little Dickey said. "What if they're Jap soldiers?"

"Then they're queer, 'cause they're wearing skirts and got tits," I said relaying the information my eyes were feeding to my brain.

We were very close to shore now. I waited until I felt the raft scrape sand before I put one leg over the side and eased myself into the water. The water was warm and felt inviting. The oarsmen pulled their oars into the boat and Ski joined me in the water. We both pulled the raft up onto the shore.

"Ski, stay here with the raft," Mr. Inman commanded. The rest of us took off our life jackets and laid them on the beach.

"They don't see us yet," I said. "Let's move in behind the row of trees on the left and work our way toward them."

We did a crouch walk for about fifty feet to the tree line and then stood up. We walked another quarter mile to where the women were. I had my pistol drawn just in case it was a trap, although I was pretty sure of what I had seen.

"There they are," I whispered holding up my hand for Little Dickey and Lt. Inman to stop. "Let me go by myself from here."

I counted four women on the ground and one standing looking out toward the sea. I holstered my gun and felt for my perpetual calendar and pen. The bulge assured me that they were still safely nestled in my pocket.

"Pssst," I said as softly as I could. "Hey, Americans."

The one woman standing turned her head quickly in my direction and squinted in the darkness. I was standing next to a tree ready to shield myself should this be a trap.

"Someone there?" came a reply soft and high pitched, and then. "Hello?"

Only an American would talk that way.

"Yes, over here, only move slowly toward your right," I instructed.

The other women were on their feet now and looking in my direction. I saw no other movement.

I could think of nothing else to ask to determine for sure if they were not the enemy, so I blurted out, "who was at the Alamo?"

"What?" she said in disbelief. Then she realized the question was a test. "Davy Crockett and Sam Houston and Santa Anna and a bunch of guys from Tennessee."

She started to run in my direction with the other nurses close behind.

"Slow down," I whispered and moved my hands up and down to indicate this request. "Slow down."

They did slow down a little, but were almost out of breath by the time they reached me.

"Are there any enemy soldiers nearby?" I asked.

"No," said the nurse who had reached me first. "I'm Lieutenant Mary Grimes, and these are lieutenants Jenny, Linda, Lucy, and Bonnie."

"No time for introductions," I said. "I'm from the Sam Houston and we're here to take you off the island. We were told there were four. Are there anymore than five of you?"

"No," Mary said. "This is it. Lucy joined us after our last transmission asking for help. We've been hiding from the Japanese soldiers for a week. Thank God you're here."

They were all smiling broadly and the two she introduced as Jenny and Lucy had their hands folded as if in prayer with tears starting to well up.

"Follow me," I said.

I headed back to where Little Dickey and Lt. Inman were hunkered down.

"Oh!" one of the nurses said when Little Dickey and Lt. Inman emerged from behind a rock.

"This is Lt. Inman and Little Dickey, I mean Dick." I said. There is one more man watching the raft. Follow me." I wondered why Lt. Inman wasn't chiming in. Maybe he was a little out of his element. At least one Jimism might have been comforting. We headed down the line of trees toward the raft, while I searched out over the water for the Sam.

"Shit!" I said, when I saw the small craft.

episode eleven

"What do ya mean, small craft?" Captain Bob said

"Small craft is a Navy term for small boats, like a torpedo boat or a pleasure boat. It was near the beginning of World War II, and there were Japanese all over the South Pacific. That's what I spotted... enemy patrol boats."

"Shit!" I said again.

"What?" Lt. Inman asked.

"There's a boat out by the farthest island, closing fast on where we were dropped off by the Sam."

"Let's head back to where Ski is," Lt. Inman said. "I don't want to get caught with something on our face."

Sir, this is not the time for Jimisms, I thought. "Depends on what that "something" is, sir," I said instead.

If it hadn't been for the situation we were in, I think Little Dickey would have laughed. The nurses just didn't get it. We walked back toward the south, staying in the shadows of the palm trees. At least the southeast side of the island had some foliage above six feet high. Typhoons kept any trees other than pine and palm knocked down on most of the island.

"Let's hide the boat with some palm branches," Lt. Inman said, when we got to where Ski was guarding the raft. That done, we moved back to the tree line and sat, watched, and waited.

"Sir, there is a small craft in the water," sonar said over the head-set.

"Bearing and distance?" requested the OOD.

"Bearing zero four fiver starboard, range a thousand yards, and closing. Angle on the bow zero one zero degrees starboard."

"Chief, send someone to bring the captain to the con," the OOD said. Normally he would have said 'captain to the con' over the 1MC, but the ship was rigged for silent running. "Right full rudder. Ahead one third. Maintain depth."

"Right full rudder, ahead one third at zero seven zero feet aye sir," the helmsman said. He dialed in the speed which was mirrored on the engine room speed indicator.

There were three helmsmen/planesmen on watch at any one time. One was on the helm/sail planes, one on the stern planes, and the third was relief. The chief of the watch sent the one not sitting at a control station to get the captain.

"Sir, I have another small craft bearing one four five and five hundred yards, also closing, angle on the bow zero one zero degrees port," sonar said, this time giving all the information without being asked.

"Passing zero niner zero," the helmsman called out.

"Steady as she goes," the OOD said.

"Steady as she goes aye sir," the helmsman said. "Steady at zero niner five."

"Captain has the con," the OOD said, as the skipper rounded the corner and hopped up onto the platform.

"Situation?" the skipper asked.

"Sir, we have two small craft in the water heading in our direction and closing. They could just be heading toward each other or they may have spotted us before we dove."

"Let's get a look at what type of small craft we have," the skipper said. "All stop, come to periscope depth."

"All stop, aye sir,"

"Passing zero seven five feet sir," the planesman called out.

"Hold at zero seven zero feet," the captain said.

"Aye sir,"

Hovering at periscope depth without moving required pumping to and from the trim tanks, and blowing and flooding ballast tanks. Orders were given for pumping as needed, depending on the change of angle and depth.

"Sonar, report on targets," the skipper said. The skipper meant contacts, but he was from the old pig boats in World War II. He was unconsciously recalling the battles he had been in.

"Contact one bearing dead ahead at five hundred yards and closing. Contact two directly overhead."

"We can't raise the periscope now," the skipper said. "Let's make a run for the trench. All ahead flank. Make your depth five zero zero feet."

"All ahead flank, aye, sir," the helmsman said, dialing in the speed.

The skipper was heading out to deeper water in the Marianas Trench, a slit in the ocean floor to the east of the Marianas Archipelago. Guam was the last major island in the archipelago. The trench floor was thirty-six thousand feet deep and exerted a force of more than seven tons per square inch, more than enough to crush a submarine like the Sam to half her size, or less.

"We're supposed to pick up the landing party and whomever they find in an hour," the OOD said.

"We can't while there are small craft in the water, probably Japanese patrol boats," the skipper said. "They don't have sonar or would have used it by now. We'll just head out to sea and come back in awhile to see if they're gone. The men on shore will have to make do until we come back."

"Aye, aye, sir," the OOD said.

Japanese patrol boats ran all night out in the area where we were supposed to be picked up. The boat had either headed out for deeper water, or was lying on the bottom rigged for silent running. The Japanese were not used to a sub that could stay under indefinitely, so they must have been waiting for it to surface or try to make a run for it. Also the Sam could make better than twenty knots underwater, faster than she could go on the surface, so she would make a run for it submerged. Ski and I had been up all night, acting as lookouts while the others slept. I was too excited to sleep and didn't need the bennies in my pocket. Ski did get tired and I let him fall asleep around two AM. There was no sense in both of us being up all night.

The rising sun was beautiful and we had an unobstructed view to the east. The boats from the night before were gone and so was the

Sam. I heard the others stirring and I stood up and stretched. I had been sitting under a coconut tree and was trying to figure out how to get some of the fruit down to cut it open so I could get a drink. I was getting thirsty. Hunger I could fend off, having been on starvation diets before, but going without liquid was new to me. I sat back down, leaning up against the tree. It was a good thing it was humid so that we didn't dehydrate as quickly as we would have in a drier climate.

"Mornin' sir," I said to Lt. Inman. My voice was dry and cracked.

"Up all night?" he asked.

"Yes sir. Ski and I traded turns at watch," I lied. Ski was out lying down in the grass next to the same tree. I didn't bother to get up when Mr. Inman spoke. I was too tired. Sleep deprivation was starting to take hold.

"We need to find some water and food," Mr. Inman said. "The nurses must know of some provisions near here.

Just then, I saw a flash of light out of the corner of my eye. I looked at the hill to the right of us and saw it again.

"Binoculars," I said.

"What?" Mr. Inman asked.

"Up on that hill," I said, pointing. "Someone is up there and they must have binoculars. I'll bet that's an observation point for this end of the island. Maybe they saw the Sam last night and called in the patrol boats."

"We'd better get under cover then," Mr. Inman said. "Before they spot us."

"What's happening?" Little Dickey asked.

He had just come out from the underbrush and noticed us pointing and looking toward the hill. We motioned for him to move back in the direction of the trees and we followed. Ski was still sleeping near the tree.

"I think there's a spotter up on the hill to our south," I said. "I saw a glint from what must have been binoculars. I think I'll head down the beach and see if I can determine if it's a spotter for sure."

"Be careful," Mr. Inman said. "Let's get Ski up, go back and get the others, and find a place to stay under cover. Then one of us will come back here and wait for Andy."

That was the first time I had heard an officer use my nickname. The circumstances of being on Guam at the beginning of World War II must have removed the officer-to-enlisted barrier that existed on board the Sam.

I walked on the beach toward the south taking care to be just inside the sheltered camouflage of the tree line. When I thought I was close enough to the hill to be able to see to the top, I went further in from the beach instead of risking exposure on the open sand. I was rewarded by finding a rise which must have been the foot of the hill used by the suspected spotter. A little further in from the beach I came upon a one-lane road paved with crushed seashells. It provided enough of a clearing so that I could see the top of the hill. Staying on the beach side of the road beside a pine tree, which was more like a bush than a tree, I scanned the hillside. I soon saw the reflection I had seen from the beach.

Holding the binoculars was a man in a khaki uniform. The binoculars were aimed directly out to sea, catching the rising sun and bouncing it back toward me. During the five minutes I watched him, he kept the glasses pointed out to sea. As I was about to give up my scouting and head back toward the others, he put the glasses down and picked up a large box. He took a microphone out of the back of the box and put it to his mouth. While he was talking, I crossed the road and decided to explore it on my way back to the others. The road was almost straight and looked like it followed the coastline north with dense underbrush on both sides obscuring any view of the beach. So that I could return to the place where I saw the lookout, over to one side I made a little pile of broken shells taken from the road.

When I had gone north for what I estimated was the same distance I had gone south on the beach, I crossed the road and looked back toward the hill. A slight bend in the road gave me cover so I couldn't be seen by the spotter as I crossed. I made my way through the tangled growth in the direction of the beach. As sand started to replace craggy rock, I saw Little Dickey about one hundred feet south of me looking in the direction I was supposed to be coming back from. I didn't want to risk shouting to him and I didn't want to startle him into making a noise, so I headed back in his direction.

When I was close enough I kicked a palm frond with my foot to make a soft noise. He turned around and I put my finger to my mouth to indicate not to say anything. He walked over to where I was standing.

"How'd ya get past me?" he whispered.

"There's a road about fifty feet from the beach that I used," I whispered in response. "There's a spotter up on that hill and we'll have to deal with him if the Sam is going to have a chance of coming back to get us."

I glanced out toward where the Sam had left us and saw another patrol boat approaching.

"I think the spotter may have seen something and called in another boat," I said.

Little Dickey snapped his head around toward the ocean to see what I was talking about.

"We'd better keep under cover of these trees then," he said. "The others are not too far up the beach. The nurses said they know of a hut we can stay in until it gets dark tonight."

About a quarter mile away, we came upon the others sitting in a circle on some rocks.

"Wha'd ya find out?" Mr. Inman asked when we were close enough to talk.

I filled them in on my findings and we discussed what to do.

"We've got to take him out," Ski said about the lookout without hesitating. "Otherwise, the Sam can't surface and pick us up."

"You mean kill them?" the nurse named Mary asked.

"Yes," Ski said. "There ain't no other way."

"What if he has to call in every once in awhile?" Little Dickey said.

"That's a chance we'll have to take," Lt. Inman said. "The real question is, who's going to do it?"

"I'll do it," Ski said. "I had some Seal training when I first joined up. I almost made it through hell week before I decided it wasn't for me."

"Andy, can you go too?" Lt. Inman asked.

"I can, but I've gotta get some sleep or I'll be as useless as tits on a boar hog," I said, using an expression I heard the southern boys use.

We all turned toward the beach as the sound of an approaching boat wafted in on the breeze. The boat I had spotted earlier was headed toward the beach where we had landed. It was about a mile out, but definitely headed toward shore.

"Is the raft hidden?" I asked.

"Yes," Little Dickey said. "We moved it further in from the shore and covered it with palm fronds while you were gone."

"How far away is the hut?" Lt. Inman asked the nurse named Mary.

"Two or three klicks up the road," she said.

"Klicks? Little Dickey asked.

"Kilometers," she clarified. "That's about one and a half miles north. It's pretty well hidden and that's where we spent the last week hiding from the soldiers."

"I was on the road, and it doesn't look well traveled," I added. "It's just off the beach and well hidden from the ocean. Any patrol on the beach won't be able to see us."

The patrol boat we were watching stayed about a quarter mile off shore. I could see men on the boat using binoculars to scan the shore line. Luckily enough, they headed south instead of north toward us.

"Let's go," Lt. Inman said. "They'll be headed back in our direction before long."

We all followed Nurse Mary as she picked her way inland. Soon we were on the road heading north. No one spoke for fear of being heard by the boat.

"Right this way," Nurse Mary said when we got to a wide spot in the road.

We made our way along a little foot path that was almost completely reclaimed by nature and blended into the surroundings. About a hundred feet from the road on a small rise, we came upon a hut made of logs and palm leaves. The hut was barely noticeable until we were within twenty feet of it. Small pine trees and tall grasses hid it from view.

"How'd ya find this place?" Lt. Inman asked.

One of the Filipino nurses spoke with an accent that sounded like she had a mouth full of marbles. She and the other two nurses had been quiet the entire time letting Mary and Jenny do all the talking. I assumed they didn't speak any English, but they did.

"A Guamanian farmer brought us here to escape the soldiers," she said. "We can get water from the spring out back. The food is all gone, but we can find more if need be."

"Is this where you radioed us from?" I asked.

"Yes," Nurse Mary said. "The radio belonged to the farmer, but he took it as soon as you told us you were coming."

"Andy and Ski," Lt. Inman said. "Go get some sleep. I've got some things to sort out in my mind right now, and it's not working."

Right now, my mind's not working either, I thought. *I really do have to get some sleep, and now.*

There were two rooms of equal size on a dirt floor with some well worn blankets scattered on the ground. Ski grabbed one and I grabbed another. We both took them to the other room, found opposite corners to spread the blankets, lay down on them, and quickly fell asleep to Jimisms emanating from the other room.

"I want to beat around the bush for a minute," he said. "We have several issues right now and need to conglomerate them."

"Don't move, Andy," Little Dickey said in a whisper.

When I opened my eyes, I realized why he had spoken those words to me. I was a light sleeper and almost never moved. I fell asleep on my back and woke up on my back. This may have been what kept me from being bitten by a large snake curled up on my chest. I knew the saying "red touch yellow, kill a fellow, red and black, friend of Jack," but this snake had no coloration. What it did have was the triangular-shaped head of a rattlesnake and must have been a viper of some sort.

Little Dickey was standing in the opening between the rooms. Ski, however was inching his way toward me on his hands and knees. He must have seen the snake before Little Dickey did, because he was within arms reach. I did as was suggested and didn't move. I was not afraid of snakes, having played with a lot of garter snakes as a child, but they were small and not poisonous. I had been bitten by one, but all it did was leave a small horseshoe-shaped red mark.

Ski slowly moved his left hand toward my chest. In his right hand was a large knife. The snake's head was in the center of his coil facing my chin and not moving. Suddenly, the snake's eyes opened and its tongue came out in a darting motion, evidently feeling the heat from Ski's open hand. Just as quickly, Ski lashed out with his hand and grabbed the snake behind the head yanking it upward. Before the snake could curl around his arm, he lashed out in a sweeping motion and cut the snake's head from its body just below where he was holding it.

I was up and out of the way before the snake's body dropped to the blanket I had just been lying on. The carcass was bleeding, but was still wiggling as if it were trying to get away. I stepped on it and it curled around my leg. I looked at the head in Ski's hand. The snake's mouth was fully open as if ready to bite. Ski stuck the dripping knife in the snake's mouth and it immediately shut on the blade.

"These things can still bite after their bodies are cut off," Ski said.

"They can still curl up too," I said, looking down at the snake wrapped around my leg. "Thanks, Ski. I owe ya one."

"Thanks for keeping our meal from getting away," he said.

"What's goin' on?" Mr. Inman said, entering the room. "Holy shit! Where'd that come from?"

"It's a snake, sir," Ski said, holding up the head for him to see. "They're probably all over this island."

"Where'd you get that knife?" Lt. Inman asked.

"I strapped it on before we left the Sam," Ski replied. He lifted up his pant leg exposing the empty sheath. "I figured we might could use it."

"Looks like you figured right," Lt. Inman said. "Is that a souvenir from Seal training?"

"Sumpin' like that," was the reply. Ski tossed the head into the corner where his blanket was bunched up, and then bent down and unwrapped the snake's body from my leg. It immediately curled around his arm as if it still had a head attached.

"Take it out and bury it," Lt. Inman commanded.

"Mind if I skin it and save the meat for later?" Ski asked. "We might need it if we don't get off the island tomorrow."

Mr. Inman just shook his head from side to side but not like he was saying no. Ski took that for consent.

"Come on Andy," Ski said. "Gimme a hand with this thing."

I followed him through the other room past the wide-eyed nurses and outside where he handed me the end of the snake where the head had been. The nurses, Little Dickey and Lt. Inman followed us. He pulled his arm free and stretched the snake out to almost full length between us. It was a good four feet long. I could feel the pull of the snake as it tried to coil in mid air. Ski then took his knife and slit the underbelly of the snake from where I was holding it to a small opening near the tail. We had an audience who were grimacing with every move Ski made.

"That there is the anus," he said. "Now if I didn't cut too deep, we can pull out the guts. Hold the tail too."

I grabbed the tail and held it as far apart as my arms would stretch. Ski reached into the opening left by the severed head and opened the slit with his thumb all the way down to the end. He then grabbed the membrane exposed by the rift and pulled it neatly out all the way down, cutting the last bit free from the body. Through the thin wall of the stomach the outline of a mouse could be seen, obviously the snake's last meal. I looked behind me and the others were watching with disgust.

"Let me grab the top part and pull the skin free," Ski said. With that said he worked the skin free at the top and then neatly stripped the skin all the way down to the tail. The tip of the tail was then cut free and I was holding a skinned and gutted viper. It was white as fish meat with rib muscles twisting slowly in my grasp.

Ski picked up a banana leaf, took the snake from me, and set it down on the leaf.

"Watch this," he said.

When he let go, the snake curled slowly into a coiled position as if it were still alive and ready to take a nap. It was moving in slow motion and gave me, and I assume all but Ski, goose bumps. When it had finished its dance of death, Ski wrapped it in the banana leaf and tied it with a thin strip he ripped from the leaf. He picked up the snake skin and placed it around the package, tucking the ends in the loose leaf folds.

"Dinner," he said, with a smile.

"What time is it?" I asked.

"Time to go find us a Jap," Ski said.

"It's two o'clock," Mr. Inman said. "You slept for six hours. Ski slept for about three hours, got up and then went back to bed just before you got up."

He said this like I shouldn't have slept so long, but he didn't know I had been the one up all night standing watch. If necessary, tonight I would use some of those bennies the Doc had given me.

"I'm ready," I said. "Make sure you have your toad stabber along, Ski."

He patted his leg and said, "I got her. Watch the dinner so nothin' gets at it."

"Will do," Little Dickey said.

The nurses just shook their heads and bade us Godspeed, which I thought was ironic considering we were going off to kill someone. I picked up one of the forty-fives and we left the hut, found our way back to the road, and headed south.

"Where was the lookout?" Ski asked.

"I made a little pile of shells on the road just below the hill. When we get there we need to head right and climb the hill."

"It might be best we don't say much more in case he's listening," Ski warned.

"Okay," I acknowledged.

At the little pile of shells, I gestured toward the right. I then scattered the shells as quietly as I could with my foot. Even though there was still a lot of daylight left, the brush blocked out the sun giving us good cover. When the terrain started to ascend, Ski motioned that we should work our way around to the right and come in behind the lookout. I nodded in agreement and we headed in that direction, Ski in the lead. I held the forty-five in my right hand pointed toward the sky by my ear. Ski had yet to unsheathe his knife.

We angled up, circling around to the back side of the hill. Although the vegetation was dense it was easy to pick our way along. About fifteen minutes later we came upon a well-trodden path. Since it led upward, we took it. It must have been the path used by the Japanese lookout to get to his vantage point. As we inched our way along, the jungle growth subsided. The path was leveling off too. Ski motioned for me to get down low and move off the path to the left. He did the same to the right. We came upon a clearing at the crest of the hill and Ski motioned for me to stay back as he proceeded cautiously.

There was a loud crackle from a radio and someone started speaking Japanese. I couldn't see where the lookout was from my angle on the left because there was a large volcanic rock directly in front of me. Ski looked at me and held up one finger, and then pointing toward the rock indicating there was one person on the other side. He unsheathed his knife and continued his crouched walk up the path. He was directly in front of me and working his way around the rock.

The talking stopped and Ski suddenly sprang forward like a cat springing on its prey. I heard a sickening slashing sound and a garbled noise as if someone was trying to speak with a mouth full of water, only it wasn't water and a mouth making the noise. It was an open throat and the man's blood. Even though I couldn't see the scene, a little wave of nausea came over me and I set down the gun. The sickening feeling quickly vanished when another man rushed into the clearing from the right, naked from the waist down, but holding a dagger in his right hand.

Forgetting the gun I jumped up and startled the man who was headed straight for Ski. I entered the clearing as the man was about to jump Ski who had already sheathed his knife and was staring down at the dead man. He turned to see the man just as I did my best attempt at a side kick with my left foot and caught the man in the gut. He doubled up and Ski noticed the ten-inch dagger just inches from his chest, but aimed now harmlessly toward the ground. Ski reached down and with one motion unsheathed his knife and with an upward motion, sliced the man's throat.

The same gurgling sound came from the second dying man. He fell to the side and I could see excrement smeared down his legs, either from an interrupted session in the weeds, or from the shock of having his throat cut. I dropped to my knees and started to dry heave, sickened at the sight of blood which by now was everywhere. Ski did a quick check of the edges of the clearing and satisfied there were no other surprises, came over to see if I was okay.

"You gonna be all right?" he asked.

"Yeah," I said, as soon as I could clear my throat.

"First time always makes ya a little sick," he said. "Second time ain't so bad. Third time it's routine. This one was beyond routine." I didn't ask him where he got his other kills.

He wiped his knife on the second man's shirt and put it back in the sheath.

"Let's get the fuck outta here," he said.

I stood up and for the first time looked out and saw the view the lookouts had had from their vantage point. It was a beautiful panorama of the South Pacific in the area where the Sam had left us off and where we had landed on the beach. It was amazing or pure luck that they hadn't seen us come ashore. Ski grabbed the transmitter, ripped the mike from it, and tossed both down the hill toward the beach.

"Where'd ya learn that karate shit?" Ski asked as we headed back down the path.

"I picked up a little from Brown," I said, "when we were in the shipyard." I bent down and retrieved the forty-five.

"Brown the steward?" Ski said. "I never woulda thought he knew karate."

"He knew enough to teach me side kicks in between basketball games at the gym."

"I'm thankful for that," Ski said. "It looks like we're even now, for the snake thing that is. Good thinkin' about not using the gun. A shot could probably be heard all over the island from the top of that hill."

I didn't want to tell him I had carelessly set the gun down. We continued on down the path in silence. I noticed the path wound toward the left and hoped it intercepted the road further up from where we cut to the right toward the back side of the hill. I was shaking too badly to fight the underbrush so I followed the path. Ski took my lead and we did end up back on the road.

"Everything go all right?" Lt. Inman asked when he saw us enter the clearing at the hut.

"Real good," Ski said. "They did have a radio, but I think they called in their last report just before we popped 'em. And I do mean their last report."

"Them?" Mr. Inman asked.

"Yeah," Ski said. "There were two of the little nips."

"Don't forget, people are human too," Mr. Inman scolded. Ski let the Jimism slide.

"You two are covered in blood!" Mary said when she saw us. "What happened? Are you all right?"

I knew we had some blood on us, but we were far from covered. Ski had more on him than I, but I guess we did look like we were splattered.

"It's just some snake blood that finally dried," Ski said. "It ain't all that much and we ain't had time to wash up. Where is my snake meat?"

Mary let it go, but I could tell by the look on her face she knew better than to believe his snake blood story.

"Over there," she said, pointing to a corner of the shack.

"It's starting to get dark," Little Dickey said. "We'd better head down to the beach and get ready in case the sub is back."

"Are you okay?" nurse Jenny Ray asked, noticing how badly I was shaken and the blood on my clothes.

"Yeah, I'm fine," I lied wanting to end the discussion of what went on up on the hill. "Let's go look for the Sam."

We gathered what little we had and headed back to the road. Ski made certain to take his snake meat still tied up in the banana-leaf sack and wrapped with the snake skin like a morbid Christmas present.

"Without getting the horse before the cart," Lt. Inman said. "I want a full report of what inspired up on the hill when we get back on the Sam. But first let's get back. Then we can compare apples to oranges."

That would have been almost a triple Jimism if he hadn't stopped to catch his breath. I noticed the nurses had covered their mouths with their hands to stifle their laughs. I'm glad they could find some humor in our situation, Jimisms or not.

It was dark when we got back to the raft. Little Dickey and Mr. Inman stayed with the nurses among the rocks while Ski and I headed down to the edge of the beach where we had landed last night. I propped myself up against a palm tree so I could look straight out to sea. The sky was overcast with some breaks in the clouds. Even without the moon or stars I was still confident I could spot anything breaking the surface in the vicinity of where the Sam had dropped us off. I wasn't worried that they'd leave us again. I had the key to getting back to 1968, even if it was without the Sam. When Ski came up to sit with me for awhile, I had been wondering if we would all have to all hold hands or something to make sure we'd be transported together.

"See anything?" he asked as a conversation starter.

"Not yet," I said.

"I sure hope I can stay up tonight. Sorry about last night, my falling asleep that is. Were you awake the whole time?"

"Yeah. I've got these if you need some," I said, showing him my package of bennies.

"I need one now," he said taking the package, extracting a pill, and popping it into his mouth. He had his own, but must have preferred mine. He swallowed it without anything to drink. "Thanks."

Ski was not one to talk a lot. He was one of the old salts, nearing the end of his hitch in the Navy. The seven hash marks on the sleeve of his uniform indicated he had been in at least twenty eight years. Another two and he would be able to retire with max pay. Somewhere along the way he had seen action in World War II and had served on a lot of pig boats. Whenever I saw him on the sub he was alone, reading a book. I had had to talk to him for the sign off on my quals for the oxygen system, but other than that we were just shipmates. So, when he started talking about himself, I let him. I guessed we were a little closer, having gone through what we did together that afternoon.

"Don't ever get married," he said. I knew from others that he had been married two or three times, but that was his business.

"I'll give ya some advice about women. You'll never figure them out, except here's my two cents worth. First they wanna get married just ta have kids. They look for a man who has good genes, ya know, strong, nice lookin', and a good provider. It's in their makeup from somewhere back in the caveman days. It's Mother Nature's way of preserving the species.

"Then, they lean more and more toward the security part of it. They want you to bust your ass so their kids can survive. Again this is caveman shit. They can't help it. We stay with 'em just ta get a piece. As males, we gotta have pussy every once in awhile. If they don't give it to us, we go lookin'. Hell, even if they give it to us, we go lookin'. It's in our genes. We can't resist some strange now and again. Just like a caveman, some broad bends over down by the stream, we give it to 'em."

I was not going to let Ski stop. The bennies must have wound him up and he was keeping me awake. I started thinking that he was a lot closer to his caveman roots than the rest of us. I'm sure he was treating this as a father-to-son talk, especially since he must have known I was still a virgin and maybe could still be saved.

"If ya don't treat 'em too bad and they don't catch ya cheatin', they'll stick around 'til the kids is growed. Then, shit starts ta change. They want romance. It's part the fault of all the crap in the movies, ya know. Good lookin' guys makin' eyes at good lookin' women, flowers, candy, fancy restaurants, and romantic getaways. Next thing ya know, they're hoppin' in the sack with some young snot on the gold crew while you're out on patrol with the blue crew."

The story was that when one crew was out, the other crew was "taking care" of the left-at-home wives. I never witnessed it, but when we went into the shipyard, a lot of guys transferred to other boats rather than be in the same town with jealous husbands. Some of the men on our crew said they knew which wives were cheating and which weren't. The left-at-home wives had no fear of being caught by husbands who were five thousand miles away and one hundred feet under water. Then when their husbands were home, the wives' lovers were gone for three months and they wouldn't have to face an embarrassing encounter with her husband and her lover at some restaurant or grocery store.

"Then they go through this "menaphase" thing and that's the beginnin' of the end. They wanna run off with a younger man what ain't got scars all over him, a bald head, and half deaf from all the goddamn noise back in the engine room. When they do leave ya, they think they're entitled to half a what ya got, and them goddamn lawyers help 'em.

"It ain't worth it, boy. What's best ta do is wait until your older, like maybe forty or fifty and get one that's already on the outs with her old man, but don't marry the bitch. Just fuck 'em as long as ya kin stand 'em and move on to another one. Maybe when yer sixty ya kin find a keeper, but still, don't get married. That's some good advice."

"What about kids?" I said, regretting the question as soon as I asked it.

"Whada ya need em fer? They sap ya for all yer worth and ain't the least bit grateful. If they don't move on when the time comes they make yer life miserable as adults. And, if ya think they're gonna take care of ya when yer older, think agin. Them days is long gone. They'll just let ya sit in yer rocker and waste away. They got these homes now all over the country where they stick older people and let 'em rot. The kids don't care. They's just sittin' around waitin' fer ya ta die so's they can get what little ya got saved up. So, yer better off checkin' yourself into an old sailor's home when ya get to be seventy or so. Mark my words."

I expected him to end with a "yuk, yuk, yuk, yuk," just like Popeye, but instead he just quit talking. I was busy scanning the sea for signs of a periscope or some other indication that the Sam was out there so I didn't give him any visible feedback to keep him going.

"Hear somethin'?" I asked.

"Nope. Your ears is a lot better than mine, but now that ya mention it, I do hear some crunching sound off to the north."

"Yeah, that's it. Sounds like something up on the road, but a ways off."

We both went dead still. A second later Little Dickey was making his way toward us, bent over and moving fast.

"There's someone coming," Little Dickey said.

"Yeah, we hear it," I said. "Sounds like a car up on the road."

"I bet it's the Japs lookin' for their two men," Ski offered.

"What happened up there?" Little Dickey asked.

"We had to kill some Japs," Ski said. "Andy here saved me from gettin' bad hurt, maybe even killed."

"No shit?" Little Dickey said. Ski then told him the story bit by bit while we listened to the approaching vehicle.

We could see lights heading south on the road in our direction. We hunkered down as low as we could get.

"Oh fuck," I whispered. "There's a periscope out there. Go back and tell the others to get ready, but not to make a move until I signal. Bring them up as close as you can get without being seen from the hill."

"I thought you took care of the lookouts," Little Dickey said.

"We did, but that vehicle might be somebody wondering what happened to their men. There was a radio up there. As soon as they find the dead guys they're gonna get real curious about who did it."

Little Dickey took off back to the others while I scanned the horizon. I thought about zapping us back a day, but wasn't sure we would all make it, or even if I could get us back exactly one day. Besides, there would still be the patrol boats to contend with. I just patted my perpetual calendar to make sure it was there and kept my eyes on the periscope.

The lights coming from the road were a lot closer now and almost parallel with us. We held our breath as they went past and then headed farther south. As soon as the lights went by, Little Dickey came back, not as cautious this time.

"Here," he said, handing me a flashlight. "Lt. Inman thought you might be able to signal them."

"Good," I said and took it from him.

I watched the periscope and when I could see that the glass was facing in our direction I scanned the horizon for patrol boats, and seeing none, aimed the light out to sea. It was one of those grey navy signal lights with the button on the on/off switch. I turned the switch to the middle position and pushed the button. I didn't know what else to flash so I did the dot-dot-dot, dash-dash-dash, dot-dot-dot Morse code for SOS. I was soon rewarded with a dipping of the periscope up and down three times.

"They know we're here," I said. "Ski, go back with Little Dickey and get the others and the life raft."

I turned my attention now to the road. I didn't see the vehicle any more, but could faintly hear it.   I looked back at the sea and saw the periscope in the same place as before. They must be hovering until they see us in the water.

"Let's go," Lt. Inman said when the others got there. Ski and Little Dickey were dragging the boat, with the nurses doing what they could to help.

"Be as quiet as possible," I warned. "That vehicle is still nearby."

The eight of us walked across the open beach. I was scanning up and down the shore line looking for any movement. I saw none. The women were giggling the entire way, obviously glad to be rescued. I was going to ask them to be quiet, but what good would being a "hard-ass" do now? If we made it, we made it and that was what was supposed to happen. If we didn't get back on the Sam so I could take us back to the future, someone else could explain how an entire submarine disappeared without a trace.

"Okay, we got a little problem." I said. "This is an eight-man raft and there are nine of us. Somebody has to volunteer to stay behind and fight the Indians."

No one laughed. I guessed this was not the time to inject some John Wayne humor.

"I think we can all fit in the boat," Lt. Inman said.

"I'll hang off the side," Ski volunteered. "I'm the biggest and take up the most room."

"No, you're too good an oarsman," Lt. Inman said. "We need your strength."

"I can hang off the back and help push with my feet," I volunteered. "With those flippers, I can really get some kick going."

"No, we need your eyes up front to guide us," Little Dickey said. "Let me do that. Just watch out for sharks and pull me in if they get too close."

"Okay," Lt. Inman agreed. "Let's get this thing away from the shore and headed out to sea."

The raft had four extra life jackets in it which were handed out to the nurses. Little Dickey took his and handed it to the remaining nurse. Ski tossed his snake package into the raft.

"We don't have room for that," Lt. Inman said, but seeing the most chilling "fuck you or die" stare from Ski, he backed down.

"I'll hold on to it," Nurse Mary volunteered, averting a potentially deadly situation.

We would be one life jacket short, but with Little Dickey paddling, all in the raft would be wearing one. We pushed the raft out a little way until the water was up to our knees. I patted my pocket holding my perpetual calendar and pen in the plastic wrap. I didn't know if salt water would diminish its power any, but was glad I had protected them. The nurses all crawled up the side and into the raft.

I turned back to look at the hill and saw two headlights pointed out to sea. The Japs must have driven up the path we followed and found their lookouts by now.

"The Japs are on the hill," I said. "We'd better hurry."

"Wait," Ski said. "Don't we have to wait until ebb tide? That's another four hours away."

"We're supposed to," Lt. Inman said. "But I'd rather take our chances out there floating around until the sub picks us up."

Ski followed as I worked my way to the bow and took my position staring out toward where I had last seen the periscope. I had lost sight of the scope when we had gotten into the water. Ski handed a pair of flippers to Little Dickey who put them on with one hand, hanging on to the raft with the other. Ski and Mr. Inman started to paddle; Little Dickey started a slow kick so as not to make a lot of splashing. I stared straight ahead and was able to find the periscope, now that we were up a little higher from the surface of the water.

The two oarsmen followed my hand as I pointed the way keeping it directly on the periscope. The cloud cover was gone and the stars were out. I could see even better now with the light from the stars so bright they were almost casting shadows. I looked back toward the hill and didn't see the car lights this time. They must have left or turned them off.

"How ya doin', Little Dickey?" I said.

"Good," he said. "This is the most exercise I've had in a couple of months."

"You're brave," Mary said. "We're so grateful."

"Yes," the other nurses said almost in unison.

After that discussion, silence fell over us with the realization that we were all alone in a foreign land. We sailors also realized we were in a foreign time. Only the splashing of the oars and Little Dickey's kicking broke the silence, until....

Zip! Splash! A spray of water hit just to the right of the raft, then another in front of us. The bullets had beaten the sound of the rifle fire from on top of the hill. Two more hit, this time on the left followed by the distant pop, pop from the gun.

"Shit," Lt. Inman said. "We're being shot at."

"We're almost there," I said.

"I can see it now," Ski said. He stepped up his paddling effort as did Mr. Inman.

Two more bullets hit the water, this time on either side of Little Dickey, who was kicking as hard as he could.

"I see it now too," Mary said.

I turned on the light and aimed it toward the scope. I could see the scope was looking in the opposite direction, probably searching for any surface craft. I switched off the light, but turned it on again when the scope rotated toward us. We had no pre-arranged signal, so I just moved the light back and forth in the general direction of the bobbing scope.

"I don't see it any more," Mary said.

"That's because the scope just went down," I said. "Either they saw us and are surfacing, or they thought we were the enemy and are moving away."

Just then, the surface of the water started to move upward. I had never seen the Sam surface from outside the hull before and was impressed. First the sail broached the water, then the rudder. As it continued upward, the missile deck and the rest of the sub came up like a fart in a bathtub.

"Wow," Jenny said. "That's the biggest submarine I've ever seen. Is it a secret weapon?"

"No," Ski said. "It's just the Sam." Then remembering that we were from another era, added, "It's a unique sub for this time."

"Whada ya mean?" one of the other nurses asked.

"You'll find out soon enough," Little Dickey said.

Then I realized that no one had bothered to tell the nurses we were from the future. I just assumed Lt. Inman had "conglomerated" it with them while I was bedding down with a snake.

Bweeing! Bweeing! Bullets were now hitting the Sam, but with its almost two-inch thick steel hull, they would just bounce off, especially at the distance the Japs were firing from on the hill.

I didn't have to point the way this time. Mr. Inman and Ski started rowing in toward the turtle back and Little Dickey resumed his kicking. Two men appeared on the bridge and waved.

Pow! Pow! The sound followed from the previous two shots.

"We're being shot at," Lt. Inman yelled to the bridge.

I was happy the sub was now drawing fire instead of us. It certainly was a larger target. The sail hatch opened and men poured out onto the afterdeck. We were headed for the port side, straight toward where our little adventure had begun.

When we were within twenty feet of our destination, a line was tossed from the sub toward us. I grabbed it as it sailed across the raft causing the nurses to duck out of the way.

We were pulled safely to the side of the Sam next to the turtleback where I had slipped in at the Loch. The turtleback wasn't slimy in the warmer tropical climate. The nurses got out first, and I pulled Little Dickey onto the raft. Then the rest of us climbed out and onto the turtleback. Ski took his precious snake package from Nurse Mary and tucked it under his arm.

Everyone but the COB and a couple of deck hands moved up toward the sail and started going through the hatch. Bullets were still hitting the water and the Sam, but were more of a nuisance like a marauding fly on a hot summer night than a real threat. The snipers would have one hell of tale to tell about the huge submarine once we were gone. Their story would probably be dismissed and they would be accused of hitting the sake wine too much. Rather than try to deflate the raft and bring it on board, the COB scuttled it by slicing it with his boson's knife.

Everyone who worked on the seaman gang had one of the black knives with a three-inch locking blade that seemed never to get dull. On the opposite side of the blade was a three-inch locking awl. The storekeeper listed them as "knives, boatswains mate, one each." Bosun was the shortened term used throughout the navy for boatswains mate. The COB was a bosuns mate. The knife was used to cut and splice lines together, but in the modern Navy it was used to make the neat rope-like macramé patterns seen on ships stanchions.

I stayed topside to enjoy the air, which by now smelled pretty good. I took a look around and thought I saw something moving on the horizon. I stared off a little to the right of the suspected movement and confirmed that there was something coming our way.

"Sir," I called up to the OOD on the bridge. "I believe I have a contact bearing one seven five, sir."

All hands turned and looked in that direction. Radar was not on because it could give away our position. After a few moments, the lookout confirmed my sighting using binoculars.

"Contact has changed direction." The lookout announced. "Angle on the bow is zero one zero and turning."

"Clear the deck! Clear the bridge!" the OOD said. The order was repeated and we scrambled into the hatch. The lookouts were right behind us as we made our way down the ladder and into the control room. When the OOD was sure all were inside, he closed the hatch.

"Take 'er down," he said.

Since we were still rigged for modified silent running, there was no ooga, ooga sound of the Klaxon. Ballast tank valves were opened allowing water to flood the ballast tanks and the sub to sink. There is always a moment when the center of gravity passes through the center of buoyancy. At that point the sub could flip over, theoretically. For that reason, we didn't waste any time submerging or surfacing.

A puzzling question that circulated the boat almost every patrol was "what would happen to the buoyancy and center of gravity in a submerged sub if everyone on board jumped up at the same time?" Some of the crew would actually sit around and discuss the question for hours at a time, usually when their eyes had failed open.

I went down the ladder to the passageway to make my way to my bunk. On the way I passed by the doc's office and there was Little Dickey getting a shot of rum.

Sum-a-bitch! I said to myself. *He gets a shot every time he gets wet.* I headed for my rack and a well deserved nap.

episode twelve

"So, what happened with them there women?" Captain Bob asked.

"That's another 'Once upon a time story," I said.

The officers briefed the nurses in the wardroom immediately after they entered the submarine. They had many questions and, when told, were skeptical about the time travel. The items that they saw, magazines, books, electronics, and even dates on food cans, had them convinced; dazed, but convinced. They were assigned to the first six-person cubical in the missile compartment, which was not full. The three previous occupants of that cubicle were moved to the upper level of the missile compartment.

After an all-hands meeting to introduce them, they were provided with extra poopie suits donated by the smallest sailors. To supplement the meager supply of cosmetics they had brought when rescued, a collection of other items was gathered and given to them. They were offered cigarettes, but none of them smoked. They had never seen aerosol deodorant before and were enthralled with the concept. They were given permission to go about the sub as they wished, except for the restricted areas. Their presence on the sub reminded me of the movie "Operation Petticoat" that I had seen at the base movie theater while I was in sub school. I saw the nurses from time to time, walking with an officer through the compartments, as they were being indoctrinated. It wasn't until two days later that I actually got to talk with them, face-to-face.

"Hey." Little Dickey said, when he entered my cubicle. I was lying in bed looking at the WWII book again. "Wanna know what the latest scuttlebutt is?"

"Sure, what?"

"We're headed to Pearl Harbor."

"Shit, does the ol' man wanna stop the day of infamy?"

"Maybe," Little Dickey said. "They don't know what else to do since we jumped from '45 to '41."

"Damn, if we dick around with events of history, we could really screw things up," I said. "We might even do away with our own existence."

"You're right," he said in response. "But we must have interfered with Nagasaki and Hiroshima. We know they happened, yet we saw that at least one of the two bombs didn't detonate."

"Shit!" I said, and then thought, *I'd better get us back so we can observe Nagasaki.*

"Shit what?"

"I gotta go take a shit."

"Oh," he said, and turned to leave.

I took my war book with me to the head to make it look like I really had to go. When I was safely in the privacy of the stall, I sat down and pulled out my perpetual calendar and pen. I rested the calendar on the book, set the 62 back on August, touched the pen to AUG, and then touched the seven. As before, the pen crackled with each touch. The seventh of August would give us two and a half days to get back and launch a missile if we had to. The Sam would have to go better than twenty knots to cover the fourteen hundred miles, but that shouldn't be a problem. The by now familiar rumble indicated to me that we had passed through time again.

We had another all-hands meeting to announce we were changing course and heading back for Nagasaki and were on schedule to be able to launch a missile in case that bomb didn't go off as designed. All the officers were perplexed about our popping in and out of the years, seemingly at random. "If anyone has any suspicions of how this is happening, he better speak up, now," the XO said.

Or else what? I thought. *Take away my toy?* I wondered if someone else could make my perpetual calendar work. Before we re-visited Nagasaki, I wanted to make another test doing something a little different this time.

The next day before my watch started, I went to the crew's mess with the calendar clipped to my belt loop. The days of reduced rations and adventure on Guam had caused me to lose some more weight. I was able to tighten my belt just a smidgeon. When I got to the mess there was a crowd, mostly huddled around the nurses.

"Hey Fatso!" Kozy called.

I ignored his nasty comment because there were women present. Sitting next to Kozy was Nurse Ray, the cute blond, and she was staring at me. It would be a few more weeks and a lot of lost pounds before I would get up the nerve to talk to her on my own. I felt a little uncomfortable under her gaze, but was somewhat elated because she was distracted from the moves Kozy was trying to put on her. I didn't understand the attraction women had for Kozy. He must have been hung like a donkey or he had the best pickup lines in the world. The line I tried in the bar in Charleston with him present didn't work for me.

"Hey Dick," I said to Little Dickey. I dispensed with using his nickname in deference to Mary, the other blond nurse to whom he was talking.

"Hey Andy," he responded. I was glad he didn't call me Fatso. He never used my sub-name, which I appreciated. He also couldn't use Cap'n Gio on the sub which was my shore name, because that would be a breach of etiquette.

"Freshen up our cups and I'll let you sit down with us," he said, half kidding.

"Sure," I said. "Nurse Mary, do you want anything while I'm at it?"

"No, thanks," she said with the cutest smile. "I have a full cup already."

As nurse Ray watched, I took Little Dickey's cup and prepared his "candy bar." From many hours of running coffee on the bridge I knew he took two sugars and two creams.

"Here ya go," I said, handing the cup back to Little Dickey. I slid the end seat out next to Little Dickey and straddled it.

"Mary's from Burlington," Little Dickey said with a broad smile. He had a smile that spread across his face like sunshine peaking through a cloud on a rainy day.

"No kidding," I responded. "I've been there with Dick a couple of times while we were back in New London. It's a beautiful area."

"We went to the same high school and are the same age." Little Dickey continued. "Of course she went years ago."

"I still have a hard time believing we've traveled in time, or at least your sub has," Mary said.

"I know. It's unbelievable to me too," Little Dickey said. "Andy thinks he knows how we did it," he continued in a whisper. I had told Little Dickey only that I had a theory, not what it was.

I felt the hairs on the back of my neck stand up as I felt the softest touch on my shoulder and the brush of someone sliding behind me. When I turned sideways to see who it was, Nurse Ray moved around the table and pulled out the chair next to Mary opposite me. I turned around again and briefly noticed an icy stare from Kozy who had gotten up to freshen his cup. Nurse Ray obviously took that moment to find someone else to sit next to.

"Mary tells me you went to the Naval Academy," Nurse Ray said with a smile so sweet it was dripping honey.

"Yes," I said shyly. "You could say I was an Academy drop out. I decided not to make a career of the Navy so left after plebe summer. Besides, there were a lot of smart guys there with the numbers III, IV, or V after their names. I would have flunked out my first year if I'd have stayed."

"Getting into the Academy is a feat in itself," Mary added. "Were you selected right from high school?"

"No," I added. "It's a long story, which is boring."

"I'd like to hear it," Nurse Ray said, and then noticed Kozy approaching. "Oh no! Here he comes again."

She bent over and whispered so that only we could hear. "He won't leave me alone whenever I come in here."

"Stay in the wardroom," I said. "You're officers. He can't go in there."

"The officers aren't very entertaining, and they encouraged us to mix with the enlisted," Mary said. "They said it would help morale."

"Hey, Cherry!" Kozy exclaimed smacking me on the back as he went by to sit on the bench next to Nurse Ray. I guessed that since he hadn't gotten a rise out of me with Fatso, he would try another degrading nickname. The nurses ignored him, probably out of ignorance of what the nickname meant, which I was grateful for.

"Well, look at the time," Nurse Ray said as she got up. "I would like to hear the rest of the story about the Academy sometime, Cap'n Gio."

She said that with a wink toward me as she left us, walking behind Mary so as to avoid any close encounter with Kozy. She had to have learned my shore name from someone else which meant she must have been asking about me. I blushed a little at the thought.

Kozy lifted his armpits and sniffed as soon as Nurse Ray had left our table. "Well," he said. "It can't be me." Since the object of his attention had left, he also got up and left.

"What's your theory?" Mary asked.

"Oh, it's nothin'" I responded. "I want to try something later on and if it works, I'll know if I'm onto something or not. Then, I'll let you two know first, before I tell the captain."

"How will you be able to tell if it worked?" Little Dickey asked.

"Today is supposed to be August 8," I answered. "If what I do sets us back a day, then I'll know for sure how the time changes are occurring. I've gotta get ready for watch, so I'd better go. Nice talking to you Nurse Mary. See you guys later."

"You can just call me Mary," Nurse Mary said.

"Okay," I answered, "But only in front of Dick. I don't want to breach the enlisted-to-officer protocol."

"Later, Andy," Little Dickey said.

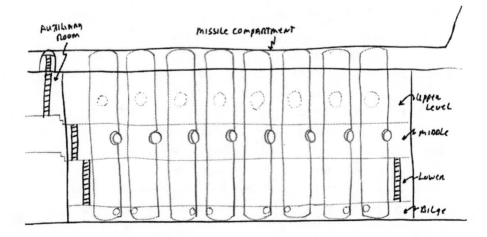

"Yeah, see ya," Nurse Mary added.

"Boy," I heard her whisper to Little Dickey. "He really is Academy material."

I left the chow hall and headed back to the missile compartment. I passed officer country on the port side and the goat locker on the starboard side with the filter rooms aft of that. I passed through the hatch and turned right to go to my bunk. The missile tubes, nicknamed Sherwood Forest, lined the center of the compartment two abreast, six feet in diameter and eight in each row. The tubes rested on the hull of the sub and stretched up through all three levels and through the top of the third level to the superstructure above.

"Ya got any pictures of that?" Captain Bob asked.

"Yeah," I said. "I think I got some in here." I thumbed through my folder containing pictures and diagrams, selected one, and handed it to him. "This is the front half of the sub showing the missile compartment."

Except for the pipes and valves of various sizes and colors running vertically and horizontally up and down the length of the tubes on all three levels, everything was painted white. Fluorescent shop lights were mounted all along the overhead and between the missile tubes, but were usually turned off, except on the starboard side, middle level. The lights must have been selected for their ability to imitate sunlight. More than once I awakened thinking I saw sunlight, but it was the lights on the other side of the missile compartment. A couple of blinks of the eye, and I would remember where I was.

The three levels in the missile compartment were accessed by ladders at each end of the compartment. Bunk beds lined the port side of the upper level, triced up with chain when not in use. The upper level starboard side was open and was used for traversing between the control room forward and the auxiliary room aft.

The lower level was nearly as high as the upper level and was a secure area, accessed through locked hatches. Because of all the piping, missile compensating tanks used to offset the weight of a missile tube full of water, and equipment running along the overhead of the lower level, it was necessary to bend over to get around the lower level. The only times anyone was allowed in the lower level was to access stored supplies, usually five-gallon cans of coffee, flour, and sugar, or to work on the missiles. Since the two-man rule was in effect in the lower level, two crewmembers were required at all times.

In the middle section on the starboard side forward, was the missile tube control panel which was used to open the topside missile hatches and control all the systems for the tubes. It also had the buttons for launching missiles after they were activated by two keys. The passageway in front of the panel was off limits to all but the torpedoman standing watch, or authorized personnel. All other traffic going between the chow hall and the engine spaces went down the port side. There was always a missile technician on duty in the missile compartment, stationed on the starboard side, aft of the missile tube control panel.

Missile compartment berthing was on the port side. It consisted of three cubicles of three bunks each with a curtain to isolate each cubicle entrance from the main traffic between the chow hall and the aft compartments. Personal items were either stored under each bunk or in a two-foot high, two-foot wide, and one-foot deep locker nestled between the missile tubes. The second cubicle was mine. The first cubicle had been taken over by the nurses. They already had decorated the curtains and inside of the cubicle.

Stretching almost one hundred feet the missile compartment was the biggest on the sub, both in volume and length. If it flooded, the sub was lost.

"Andy," someone said as I walked by the nurses' cubicle. I turned around to see Nurse Ray beckoning me with her finger. I walked closer. "Are you busy?"

"No ma'am," I said.

"You can call me Jenny," she said smiling.

"Yes ma'am," I responded, with my head down like a shy little boy in front of an adult he didn't know.

"We'll work on that," she said, the smile gone from her face.

"Yes ma'am," I repeated.

"Where can we go to talk?" she asked. "That is, without the chance of someone like that disgusting torpedoman interfering."

"You mean Kozy?" I said.

"If that's his name, yes."

"We could go down to the lower level. There is a two-man rule, but I guess that could mean a woman and a man."

"Okay, let's go."

I led the way to the after hatch between missile tubes fifteen and sixteen. I was supposed to let the watch know there were men in the lower level, but since she was an officer and practically ordering me, I didn't.

I had a key and unlocked the hatch, opened it, and motioned for her to step on down. There was a ladder stretching down six feet to the round underbelly of the sub. In essence, the lower level of the missile compartment was a huge bilge with the ribs exposed. All of it was insulated to prevent sweating and loss of heat to the ocean.

She carefully stepped down and when she got to the bottom she bent over and moved out of the way. I followed and closed the hatch behind me. There was no way to lock the hatch from the underside. I just hoped no one would notice it was unlocked and then secure it with us down below.

Rather than turn on the lights, I reached over and grabbed one of the flashlights from the bulkhead and turned it on. I motioned for her to move to the starboard side where there was some light trickling down from the two watch stations above. She headed in that direction ducking the overhead items with me close behind. There were some blankets set between the frames for lying on while working in the lower level. Although the steel was insulated it was still cold. Sometimes, a missile technician used the blankets for taking a nap, just to get away from it all.

"This is cozy," she said as she lay down on the blanket stretched out on the curved surface of the sub. I did the same on the next frame over, close enough to talk, but not touch. Directly above us were lockers and equipment. We could hear the footsteps of the watch moving back and forth while reading meters. There was a hum of equipment all around. We each pulled an extra blanket over us which gave me a comfortable, warm and fuzzy feeling as we nestled between the ribs.

"You said you wanted to talk?" I asked omitting "ma'am" for the first time. I thought it would be all right since there was no one else to hear. "Mind if I turn out the light to preserve the batteries?"

"Sure, turn out the light. I want to know more about you, where you come from, why you are here, and about the Academy. First, do you have a girl?"

"Oh no!" I said as if it were a crime to have one.

"Good. Not even one who sends you letters?"

"We don't get letters while on patrol, just Sam grams."

"Sam grams?"

She didn't know about the Sam grams so I had to explain it to her.

"Where's home?" she asked.

"A little town in Ohio called Alliance. It's south of Cleveland about 60 miles. Near the Akron-Canton area."

"Any brothers or sisters?"

"Two older sisters and one six years younger."

"You're the only boy. I guess they spoil you."

I didn't respond to her, but wondered where all this was leading.

"So you went to the Naval Academy?" she continued.

"Yes ma'am," I said. The words "Naval Academy" reminded me that she was an officer and I an enlisted man. She sensed the tension return to my voice.

"That was a great honor. Tell me about it," she said.

"It wasn't all that much," I said looking in her direction. Our eyes were adjusting to the darkness, so what looked like pitch blackness before was now starting to reveal objects and shadows. She said nothing so I continued, almost starting with 'this is no shit,' but didn't.

"I was in missile "A" school in Dam Neck Virginia when someone came in and asked if anyone wanted to go to the Naval Academy. I thought that would be neat, so I raised my hand. They took my name and later that week I was called to take a physical. I had seen on the form I had filled out that one of the reasons for rejection was extreme ugliness. I almost dropped the idea, but filled out the application anyway."

"You're not ugly," she said. "I think you're kinda cute."

It was a good thing the light was dim because I know I turned red. Not so much from the fact that no one ever had told me that before, but from the fact that she was not supposed to fraternize with enlisted personnel. I didn't know what else to say so I continued.

"I knew my eyes were not so good either, and twenty-twenty was required. I had worn glasses since the third grade until I went to boot camp where they said I didn't need glasses unless the Navy gave them to me. When I was fourth in line for the eye chart part of the physical for the Academy, I memorized the perfect vision line by listening to the others. When it was my turn I rattled off 'd-e-f-p-o-t-e-c' so fast the corpsman suspected I had memorized it. He said, 'that was good, now read 'em backwards.' So I said quickly 'c-e-t-o-p-f-e-d.' He said, 'good job of memorizing,' and passed me."

"That's funny," she said. "That was quick thinking on your part."

"No, just lucky the corpsman was too lazy to change the chart and I was fourth in line."

She laughed and I continued. "I was told I would be notified to take a written test in a few weeks. I was home on leave between "A" school and sub school when I got a phone call to report to the Canton reserve center to take the test, which I did."

"I went on to sub school and on the way I heard that the Thresher had gone down."

"The Thresher?"

"That's right. Sorry, I forgot. You don't know about the past. I mean my past, your future. The Thresher was an attack submarine that was on sea trials when she went down, April 10, 1963. More than one hundred twenty men and some shipyard engineers were lost."

"That's sad." she said.

"I know. In peace time it is sad, but during WWII, the war you just saw getting started, a lot more subs were lost. I think we lost 52 and the Germans lost close to 800. I'm reading a book on WWII right now. Submarine duty is a dangerous assignment."

"It sounds like it," she said. "When you picked us up, the war was only a couple of months old and America wasn't at war in the Pacific yet. I know now from our briefing that it went on for four more years. You'll have to let me borrow your book so I can catch up on what happens… I mean happened. What was next after you took the test?"

"I assumed I didn't do well, and forgot about it. I went on to sub school where I almost flunked the pressure test and was operated on for a pilonidal cyst."

"Another side story, huh," she said.

"Oh, I'm sorry," I said. "I'll leave out the details."

"I don't mind the details," she said. "We have time unless you have to be somewhere."

"No," I said. "I have five more hours before I'm on watch. This sure beats reading another Ian Fleming book or the history book. Let's see, oh yes, the pressure test.

"Every sub sailor has to take a pressure test to see if they can equalize the pressure on either side of the eardrum in case an underwater escape is necessary. Our class was put in a chamber and high-pressure air was let in. We pinched our noses and forced air from our lungs up into our eustachian tubes so that the pressure on the inside of the ear drum was the same as that in the chamber. Otherwise the eardrum would rupture. I don't think it's so much a test of our ability to equalize, but whether or not we could sit in close quarters with twenty other guys and be tortured without panicking.

"Anyway, I had a cold and my eustachian tubes were inflamed. I tried, but couldn't equalize. They took me out through a smaller chamber and finished the test on the others. After the test, they lined us up and made us stand for a few minutes where I almost passed out. While we were standing there, a new group was brought in for the test and they saw me being carried out by two others. I was a big guy then from lifting weights in "A" school. I heard someone say 'if that's what happened to him, what's going to happen to me?' A doctor looked at me and determined I was all right except for a bleeding ear drum. A couple of days later when my cold had subsided, I took the test again and passed. After the pressure test, we had to do a blow-and-go test."

"Blow and go?" she asked.

"Yeah, that's a test to prepare us for escaping from a sunken sub. There's a one hundred-foot tower at New London filled with water. At the base of the tower are chambers where the test begins. Twelve sailors, along with two instructors, are placed in a chamber about the size of small closet. It was pretty tight in there with our life jackets on. Water was let in to about chin level. Shorter men had to stand on their toes to be able to breathe. When the water level was above the hatch, high-pressure air was let in with a tremendous roar. I was able to equalize easily for this test. When the air pressure equaled the water pressure, about 45 pounds per square inch, the hatch could be opened.

"To go to the surface, we had to blow all the pressurized air out of our lungs, hence the name 'blow and go.' When the lead instructor tapped me on my life jacket and pointed toward the hatch, it was my turn to exit. I'm a good swimmer, having spent most of my childhood summers swimming. There is a 'T' handle attached by a rope to the bottom of each jacket and after I inflated my life jacket, I went through the hatch and held onto the ladder. A diver already in the tower grabbed the T handle. I then tilted my head back, put my hands above my head as if I were diving and started to blow. The diver let go and I started a rapid ascent.

"As I ascended, I kept blowing air out of my lungs. Just as I thought my lungs were empty, I felt the compressed air expanding and I was able to keep blowing all the way to the top. I felt the divers passing me off to each other using the T handle. I had heard from others that when they quit blowing they got a punch in the stomach. When I broke the surface, I still had enough air in my lungs to keep blowing."

"That's some test," she said. "I wonder how many sub sailors have used that training in real situations?"

"I don't know about during the World War II, but we have escape hatches if we need to use them. However, at the ocean depths we're operating in, 'blow and go' would be useless. If we were at a depth where rescue was possible by lowering a diving bell, we couldn't let them know where we were because the rescue buoy has straps welded across it. In most cases, the sub would break apart before we hit bottom anyway."

"Now you're scaring me," she said with a shiver.

"From what I know about World War II, I think you're better off here than in a Japanese prison camp. We do have what are called Steinke hoods which let you breathe normally in an air pocket around your head as you come up from deeper depths. I went through the tower the second time with one of the hoods, and it's a lot easier. While wearing the hood, your face is surrounded by air that vents out under the hood as you ascend and the air expands. You just breathe as normally as you can under the circumstance. That circumstance being you're escaping from a submerged sub into an ocean of water with little chance of being rescued before you either freeze to death in the North Atlantic or get eaten by sharks in warmer waters."

"Bastard!" she said looking at me with a shadowy scowl on her face.

"Sorry," I said. I was treating her like another sub sailor and I vowed not to do it again.

I changed the subject in a hurry. I thought her training as a nurse would allow me to discuss my pilonidal cyst experience

"The pilonidal cyst I had right after I flunked the pressure test the first time, delayed my sub-school training."

"How did you get a cyst?" she asked.

"It developed after riding many hours on trains and busses from my home to "A" school, then home again, and then on to sub school. I had to sit for hours in a sitz bath on an air-filled doughnut before they would operate. Once they did remove the cyst, I still had to attend sub school, although I couldn't sit down for a week. The trip back from the hospital up the hill to my barracks caused blood to seep through the packing and my uniform. I wore a towel on my butt for three days to absorb the blood. I was on light duty, which was supposed to be for a week, but I forged another two weeks on the light-duty chit. I milked that operation for all it was worth."

"As a nurse, I know pilonidal cysts can be painful."

"Yes, especially when they changed the packing and didn't warn me just before they did it. That hurt like hell. The Navy doctors and corpsman had no sympathy for me and treated me like a piece of meat.

"The same goes for Navy dentists. I had an impacted wisdom tooth removed and I couldn't eat solid food for three days because of the stiffness and pain. I just hope I stay healthy until I get my six years in."

"You're not going to make a career of the Navy?" she asked.

"No way! I have a plan to go to college when I'm discharged. I'm saving up for it now and there is the GI college plan too."

"What happened at the Academy?"

We heard some footsteps directly above us so I pointed to the deck above and stopped talking for a moment until I was sure we couldn't be heard. The distinct deep voice of Little Dickey was audible while he was talking to the torpedoman on duty.

"Seen Andy?" he said.

An indistinguishable answer came from the missile control panel watch.

"You know, Fatso. Cherry," Little Dickey said.

A short answer came back which sounded like 'ain't seen him.'

"If you do, tell him I need to talk to him desperately," Little Dickey said back.

Then I heard a muffled, "Okay."

"I better get out of here and see what he wants, or sooner or later he'll see the unlocked hatch and come down here. There aren't too many places I could be on the submarine. He'll go aft and then come forward again until he finds me."

"Okay," Jenny said. "We can come back later and finish our talk, that is, if you want to. I want to find out more about you."

"Sure," I said. "Next time I'd like to find out more about you too."

We left our little nest. I carefully opened the hatch to make sure there was no one nearby. Jenny climbed out and I followed. I then closed and locked the hatch. Jenny walked back toward her cubicle and I curled up between the tubes and pulled out *Diamonds Are Forever*, the fourth Ian Fleming "Bond" book. I had already read one through three, *Moonraker, Casino Royale,* and *Live and Let Die.* The War in the Pacific book was still under my pillow for going-to-sleep reading. That was a history book and right now I wanted to escape.

episode thirteen

"So, you met this nurse again?" Captain Bob said, leaning forward in his chair.

"Yeah," I said. "And I told her more about the Navy, and the Academy, all of which is no shit."

"So, tell me about the Naval Academy," she said.

Our second meeting happened when she came into our cubical. I was lying in my bunk in my poopie suit reading James Bond. There was no one else in the cube.

"You can't come in here," I warned, startled. "It's against regulations."

"Fuck the regulations," Jenny whispered. "I'm bored and need to talk to someone. Get out of that rack now, Mister."

She said the last sentence with a smile, which was a knockout punch. The jab that set it up was that this was first time I had ever heard a woman, other than a barmaid, say "fuck." That was almost as much of a shock as hearing the priest lecture me and the other new recruits in boot camp.

The recruits were divided by religion on the third day of boot camp. We all were sporting our new burr cuts, which was a shock to some. All I needed was a trim, since I had had a flattop all the way through high school and what we called a "butch" haircut before that. My dad had cut my hair all my life. He had cut hair in the Navy during WW II so my mom let him give me my first haircut when he got home from the war. I was one year old and by then had the cutest locks of curly hair causing most people to think I was a girl. Sixteen years later, he gave me a send-off-to-boot-camp flattop.

Those who had no religion to proclaim were classified as Protestants and marched off to meet the chaplain. I was in with the Catholics. A priest in a captain's uniform spoke to us about morality.

"It is better to cast your seed in the belly of a whore than to spill it on the ground," he quoted from the Bible he was holding.

First of all, I had no idea what the hell he was talking about. The only thing I got was that a priest said "whore," which I thought was a dirty word. Secondly, as Catholics, we had been forbidden to read the Bible. We would be taught all we needed to know about the Bible at Sunday mass or in catechism class. Thirdly, it turns out there is no such quote, as he stated it, in the Bible. He was probably doing his own interpretation of Genesis, Chapter 38 from the King James Version of the Bible.

"This is wrong," he went on. "Fornication is a sin. So is jacking off. It's just a piece of meat. Let it alone."

Now he was getting somewhere. Jacking off, casting seed, spilling it on the ground. It was all starting to fit.

"Swearing is a sin!" he continued, grabbing an empty chair next to him. "This is not a fucking chair! If the Navy wanted a fucking chair, they'd buy a fucking chair."

After he said that, I went numb and was struck deaf. This was not a priest that I could connect with, but he was an officer, so I had had to pretend I was listening.

So, hearing her say "fuck" was completely out of place, but she was an officer who deserved respect. Because of her outburst, I had almost forgotten that she had wanted the WWII book. I hopped out of my bunk, stuck my paperback in my rear pocket, grabbed the WWII book from the storage bin under my mattress and followed her aft toward the last set of missile tubes. She stood by the hatch, arms folded, smiling as I unlocked and opened it. I followed her down and closed the hatch behind us.

"You stopped just before you got to the part about the Naval Academy," she reminded me, when we were nestled between the frames. "You said something about taking a test. How did that turn out?"

"Before I forget, here is the WWII book you wanted to look at."

"Thanks"

"You're welcome, ma'am," I said.

She frowned, and said, "Tell me about the test."

"I took the test before I went to sub school. After sub school, I went to Dam Neck for "C" school."

"What happened to "B" school?" she asked.

"It comes after C school. I don't know why, but the sequence is A, C, and then B. Anyway, it was four months later and I had forgotten about the Academy. I thought I would be notified a lot sooner after I had taken the test and since I hadn't been, I assumed I didn't make the cut.

"Then, one day, an officer interrupted the class and said, 'We have a sailor in here who is going to the Naval Academy.' It still didn't hit me until he mentioned my name. After class I was briefed by the same officer who had almost written me up for AWOL a year before when I was in "A" school."

"You went AWOL?"

"Not deliberately. At least I didn't think so. I was a member of the drill team in "A" school in Dam Neck and because we trained on our own time, we were supposed to have the privilege of not standing watches. I was assigned to a duty section which stood security barracks watches every third day, but, because of the drill team, my name was never on the list of watch standers. I had been on the drill team in boot camp and would be on the one in prep school too."

"And…," she prodded.

"I had planned to go home for Thanksgiving over the long weekend. I had my train tickets and was ready to go, so when I saw my name on the roster for barracks watch, I crossed it out and wrote drill team next to it. I had thought my name on the list was a mistake, but it wasn't.

When I got back to the barracks Sunday night, several people told me I was in trouble for skipping duty. I sweated bricks the entire night."

"But you weren't in trouble?"

"Yes and no. The officer in charge of the school called me into his office during the first class on Monday. He told me that they had been short-handed over the holidays and had had to use all available duty personnel not scheduled for leave. He could have set me up for a court-martial, but because of my profession of innocence and good grades that kept me at the top of my class, he let me go with a mild ass chewing."

"So, was he surprised you were selected to go to the Academy?"

"He acted like he had never seen me before, so he must not have entered my AWOL in my records. He just congratulated me for being selected, told me I would be going to the prep school in the fall, and then dismissed me."

"And then to the prep school?"

"Yes, I received my orders and was sent home on leave until I was to report to the prep school two weeks later in September.

"The prep school lasted nine months and had a comprehensive program. We were given courses which would prepare us for the entrance exam. It was like a first year of college with military training thrown in. There were a lot of smart sailors and marines at the prep school and I didn't think I had a chance. I took the acceptance test for entrance and must have done pretty well."

"Tell me about that there prep school," Captain Bob interrupted reminding me of where I was and to whom I was really telling the story.

"That was before I was assigned to a submarine," I said.

"I'm assumin' this is one of your 'no shit' stories."

"That's right," I said. "Since you ask, here are some old pictures of the place and some you can look at as I tell the story"

"This picture is from the tower of the school building which was also the officers' quarters. The tower was supposed to be off limits."

"The Naval Academy Prep School was located at the Naval Training Center in Bainbridge Maryland. An old school called, 'Tome School for Boys,' located in Port Deposit, had been taken over by the Navy when it opened the Bainbridge Naval Training Center and the Wave boot camp which were part of the same property."

"Here is a blurb from history of Port Deposit, MD."

The buildings of the former Tome School for Boys occupy the southwest quadrant of the Bainbridge Naval Training Center on a 200-foot bluff overlooking the town of Port Deposit and the Susquehanna River. The buildings are now being leased by the U.S. Department of Labor and are used as the Susquehanna Job Corps Center. The historic district is comprised of 16 buildings on approximately 30 acres: the main academic building (Tome Memorial Hall), the three dormitories (Jackson, Harrison, and Madison Halls), the Director's residence, the Tome Inn dormitory and dining hall, the gymnasium (Monroe Hall), six Masters' cottages, a non-contributing modern metal building, and two non-contributing mid-20th century frame garages.

All the buildings except the metal building and the garages date from 1900 to 1905. The rectangular metal building was added by the Job Corps in the 1970s for instructional and storage space. The buildings are arranged around a quadrangle oriented northeast-southwest, except the Masters' cottages, which are located on a down slope to the southeast of the quadrangle. The stone buildings are in an elaborate, Beaux-Arts-influenced, Georgian Revival style. The Masters' cottages are frame and stucco. The addition of exterior fire escapes, minor changes in fenestration and replacement of doors and roofs have not compromised the integrity of the complex.

The Tome School is significant in military history as the location of the Naval Academy Preparatory School (NAPS) from 1943 to 1974, excepting the years 1949 to 1951. The NAPS, the third oldest school in the U.S. Navy

after the Naval Academy and the Naval War College, prepares enlisted candidates in the Navy and Marine Corps for admission to the Naval Academy. The NAPS was located in the Tome School buildings for a total of 29 years covering a period of three major wars, during which the school played a continuing role in providing naval leadership for those conflicts.

It didn't take long for us to nickname NAPS the "Tome Institute of Technology," which was shortened to TIT. A group of single sailors and marines thrown together will find "tit" somewhere. There was also a fight song that went along with the naming of the school that was sung to the tune of most college and university alma mater songs similar to the *Hail to Indiana University.* It went something like this:

High above the Susquehanna lives a bunch of saps.

They are called the admiral strikers 'cause they go to NAPS

You can take your admiral strikers and the Navy brass

You can take the whole damn program shove it up your...

Susquehanna, Susquehanna, sis boom bah

Napsters! Napsters! Rah! Rah! Rah!

It was sung as we marched to and from the chow hall along the road where the officers from the naval base were living. It didn't take long for someone to complain about the tone of our voices when we got to the "shove it" part.

There were three barracks at TIT, one for marines and two for sailors. The rooms were small with heads in the middle of each of the three floors.

The first semester I lived on the first floor with a "rebel" roommate. We didn't get along very well, but tolerated each other. I slept in the upper bunk and controlled the window; he slept in the lower bunk and controlled the radiator valve. In the winter, he would open the radiator valve and heat the room as hot as it would go, which made me very uncomfortable.

Being from the South he couldn't stand the cold winters in the North. I was used to sleeping in a cold room at night, so when I crawled into my bunk, I would crack the window about an inch. One Saturday night a cold front came through and it began to snow. I woke up on a Sunday morning with some ice crystals on the window sill and my roommate was shivering so hard he shook the bed.

I went to church and when I came back, he was sprawled out with nothing but his skivvies on and no blanket. The window was closed and the radiator was wide open, cranking out the heat. The temperature must have been in the nineties. I was thankful when he flunked out the first semester and I was moved to the third floor with a seaman apprentice named Davidson.

Davidson and I had the shiniest floor in the dormitory. I found a paste wax for hardwood floors that had to be applied by hand with a rag, but the results were excellent. I didn't share my secret with anyone else in the barracks, because it got us through many an inspection during field day.

Just like everywhere else in the Navy, one day a week was set aside for general cleanup followed up with an inspection. The inspectors walked in, took one look at the floor, complimented us for a job "well done," and walked out. Inspectors alternated buildings, so there were a lot of first impressions to be made. After the first "well done," we let the rest of the room slide and never got any room demerits.

Davidson was also from the North and, unlike the flunked-out rebel, shared my desire for lower temperatures, but not my taste in pets.

"Andy, wake up!" he said one night in a panic.

Again, I had the upper bunk, so I peered over the side and asked, "What is it?"

"There's a mouse in here," he said with a quaver to his voice. "I can hear it."

I peered around the room. His hearing was better than mine, but my night vision was better.

"Yeah, I see him. He's over by the radiator. He must have come through the same hole as the radiator pipe. He's just hungry and when he doesn't find any food he'll go away." I went back to sleep while Davidson just lay there with his eyes wide open.

We always brought some contraband food back from the chow hall and stored it in our navy-gray metal desk drawers. Having food in the barracks was not allowed, but almost everyone had a stash for snacking while studying late at night. There were no vending machines and we weren't allowed take a break and go to the geedunk (convenience store) to buy pogey bait (sweet treats), or to the club for food. So we took what we could from the chow hall, or had it sent from home.

The next day, I swiped some cubes of cheese from the chow hall and took them back to the barracks for the mouse. That night while Davidson slept, I took out the stash from under the pillow and started tossing it on the floor toward the hole. I waited a little while, and when no mouse appeared, I tossed another piece, and then another.

"God damn it!" exclaimed Davidson. "He's jumping up and down and trying to get to me."

Davidson jumped out of bed, ran over to the door, and flicked on the lights. His fear of rodents turned instantly to wrath aimed at me for trying to feed the critter.

"Son of a bitch!" he said, when he saw the little pieces of cheese scattered across the floor. "You're feeding him!"

He picked up the pieces of cheese, took them to the head, and flushed them. He came back in the room, his face reddened and an angry look in his eyes. He didn't say anything else that night as I snickered in my bed.

The next day, to appease my roommate, I bought a mouse trap from the Navy Exchange and baited it with a piece of cheese. That night there was a muffled snap as the trap shut on the poor little rodent.

"I got him! I got him!" I shouted as I jumped out of bed scaring the hell out of poor Davidson. I bounded over to the door and flicked on the light.

Sure enough, there was the tiny fur ball, neck broken, mouth half full of cheese, caught in the trap. Davidson told everyone I had acted like it was Christmas morning when the trap went off. I was so proud of my little trophy I decided to save the skeleton. I hung the mouse by its hind feet from a piece of twine tied to a nail outside our third story, back window. I figured the carcass would decay and slough off like a snake shedding its skin leaving a neat little mouse skeleton.

"One of the pictures shows the back of the hall," I said to the captain.

After three weeks hanging outside the window, my prize was seen by one of the senior petty officers with a different sense of aesthetics from mine. I was told to "flush it, or else," so I did.

My second pet was a cat that wandered into our barracks one day. Of course pets were forbidden, but what could be wrong with feeding a stray cat and letting it roam around. Davidson was happy since it would keep the mice away. We had a contest to name what the barracks now considered our mascot. The best names were voted on and one name won by a landslide. From then on the little grey pet was referred to as "Fuckstick." We brought him plenty of food from the chow hall and he used the bushes in front of the barracks as a head.

We got quite attached to him and the other barracks' occupants were a little jealous. Then, one day, Fuckstick didn't show up when we returned from dinner. We found him the next day, dead in the bushes, painted green. Scuttlebutt had it that one of the marines painted him green "to camouflage him." The marines wouldn't tell on each other, so we let it go. That was the last of our pets at TIT.

The Marines had their own fun and games, one of which was trying to duplicate the hard-boiled egg eating record set by Paul Newman in the movie "Cool Hand Luke," but the marines' version had a twist to it. They were going to do with sardines. I'm not sure how many cans of sardines were consumed by one marine, but it was close to a hundred. They said that when he blew them all out in a protein spill, frontal eruption, the stench made the rest of the Marines sick too. God knows what else went on in that barracks.

Two news events stand out in my memory more than any others from my days at TIT. One was Kennedy's assassination and the other was the invasion of the Beatles.

We had a football team called, prophetically, NAPS. We were pretty good and played some of the lesser known schools in the area, one of which was Temple. We played Temple on that fateful day, November 22, 1963. I almost didn't go to the game because we were to have a seabag inspection the next morning and I needed to get prepared. All of the uniforms we were supposed to keep in our seabag were to be inspected for cleanliness and condition. I hadn't had a seabag inspection since boot camp, so mine were clean, but a little frayed. The initial uniforms we received in boot camp were provided by the government, but from then on we were to maintain them from the allotment we received each month. I should have gone to the Navy Exchange and bought new uniforms for the inspection, but instead, I went to the game.

It was a Friday and we were excited about getting away from TIT, if just for a few hours. We were not allowed to have contact with the outside world and seldom got time of our own to leave the base. A few of the Napsters risked punishment and carried forbidden transistor radios, which then were the size of a large pack of cigarettes.

On the bus to the game, one of the men who was listening to a radio station with an ear piece, passed the word that he had just heard some breaking news. President Kennedy had been shot in Texas. I couldn't believe it.

When I was in high school, just three short years earlier, I had gotten up very early on Election Day and, with my friend Adrian, plastered his old Plymouth station wagon with Kennedy posters and bumper stickers. We drove through my little town proclaiming our support for Kennedy who, if I could have voted, was my choice for the presidency. I watched all the debates on TV, following his campaign with a passion. Now he had been shot.

During the entire game, we were huddled around the one little radio listening to the news. The game was a sullen affair. We won, but the country lost. The only good thing to come from the assassination was the cancellation of the seabag inspection. Instead we stayed in our barracks and studied with dour expressions on our faces. Because we weren't allowed to have TVs, we missed all the live broadcasts of the funeral.

The Beatles invasion, however, was a celebration of sorts. Some Napsters got to go home for Thanksgiving the week after Kennedy was assassinated. I was not one of them, but those returning brought news of a new singing group from England called the Beatles. They had haircuts like Moe from the Three Stooges and their music was sweeping the country. Of course we couldn't listen to them, not having radios or televisions. Even newspapers were forbidden.

There weren't very many contraband transistor radios to allow widespread listening to music; however, one enterprising electronic technician friend of mine, named Henle, had a tube radio. The radio had no case so it could fit neatly on a shelf, against the wall, on the hidden side of his metal desk. His roommate had flunked out so he had a room all to himself. The only problem was the lack of a good antenna to bring in the better stations.

I had some transformer wire, as thin as a human hair, left over from a high school experiment when a classmate of mine, Frank, and

I had made a Tesla Coil. I brought it back with me from Christmas vacation.

One night we clandestinely strung the wire from his bedroom window across the mall to a pole on the other side. The wire was so thin it couldn't be seen, even though we knew it was there. With this antenna we could now pick up radio stations as far away as Chicago's WGN. We listened to that station and the Beatles as often as we dared.

Because we weren't allowed off base very often, another favorite activity was "going over the wall" to the little town of Port Deposit. Port Deposit is supposed to be the longest, one-street-town in the States. The western end of the base was delineated with a seven-foot high, barbed-wire, chain-link fence with a drop off to the town below. The fence was not to keep towns-people out; it was meant to keep us in. This was obvious from the fact that the barbed wire slanted toward the base. The fence was not an obstacle since we could go under or over it using various means, but the hill was steep. When the school was first built, a wooden stairway, called Jacob's ladder, was constructed and used to get to the town, two-hundred feet below. I handed a picture of the stairway to Captain Bob.

It was in disrepair, but usable. Once the fence was broached and the stairs negotiated, we would be in the town, but there was nothing to do. We always went late at night, so everything was closed. The only activity was to walk around the streets.

I also handed Captain Bob a picture of the town of Port Deposit.

We had what were called "field days," which were days when we were allowed to drink beer and blow off steam. There was a rivalry among the three barracks, and especially between the sailors and marines. There were touch football games, wrestling matches, and other feats of skill and strength which were supposed to get us ready for the Academy. Each barracks had a flag, called a "guide-on," which was carried when we marched in formation. Stealing the guide-on and putting it in various locations to embarrass the other barracks was done regularly. One was taken and placed on the yard arm of the flagpole in front of the main building. The picture for the yearbook was taken the next day with the guide-on tied securely in place. No one but the perpetrators knew how it had been done. I handed Captain Bob another picture of the guide-on next to the flag.

Athletics were big at TIT but, except for intramurals, I veered away from the physical activities. There was lacrosse, football, rugby, basketball, tennis, soccer, wrestling, swimming, track, and cross country.

Almost all of the athletes at TIT had been high school players. I was not, having suffered an incarcerated inguinal hernia playing football in the ninth grade. The operation in the following summer kept me out of sports in high school. Therefore, I took a less physical and lower testosterone approach to extracurricular activities.

As I said earlier, the tower shown in the picture was supposed to be off limits; however, as a rite of passage, every Napster sneaked up inside it at least once. Henle and I did it one night, but because it was dark, we didn't get a very good view of the campus. It was dangerous too, because there was only a plaster ceiling under the rafters. One misstep and there would be a sixty-foot fall to the floor of the auditorium directly below.

There were also antics in the classrooms. Our math teacher, Lieutenant Schnabel, whom we nicknamed "Uncle Schnapsie," was teaching us one of the finer points of differential equations on the chalkboard one day. He stopped writing, turned toward the class and said, "When in doubt, whip it out. If she fucks she won't faint, and if she faints, fuck her." He then went back to solving the equation.

Another time he decided to explain the difference between extra and excess using an analogy to a woman's anatomy. "What you can't get in your mouth is extra, and the other one is excess.

We decided to play a trick on him, but had to keep it respectful. After all, he was supposed to be an officer and a gentleman. Our joke was entirely visual and percussive. We practiced before the class and when he entered, we stood as was required. The desks were open in the front; and, when we sat down, he didn't notice that we all had our left legs crossed over our right knees pointing in the same direction.

When he was facing the blackboard, the signal was given, three taps of a pencil by a man in the back row. Tap, tap, tap. Whomp, whomp! Whomp, whomp! That was the sound as we switched legs in unison from right to left and then back again. We did it once more when he turned to see what the noise was. It was the best we could do and be respectful.

His only comment was "Very good, gentlemen."

Our English teacher was Lieutenant Resweber, not a good occupation or name for a man with a lisp. When we stood as he entered our first class with him we nearly all burst out laughing when he told us to take our seats.

"Theath, pleath. My name is Mithta Wethweba. I will be your Englith teather." We thought it was a joke until he started teaching us "thententh thructhur."

My forte was the drill team. We marched in parades and at football games. On graduation day, we put on a demonstration in front of students, faculty and guests. Mine was the only screw up, but was hardly noticeable. We marched in formation and did some twirls and salutes with our rifles and then passed them to the men behind us. We lowered the rifles, butt first, and tapped the heels on the ground three times, letting go the third time. The rifles would stand straight up as we marched passed them and, without looking down, picked up the weapon left by the man in front. That was how it was supposed to work.

On my third tap, I let go of the rifle and the sleeve of my jumper caught the rifle sight and slammed it to the ground. That was the bad part. The good part was that it hit so hard, it bounced up and was caught by the man behind me without his having to bend over or break step. It was almost as if we had planned it that way. Cheers went up from the crowd. I knew something had gone awry, but didn't find out until it was over.

"What happened?" I said to Neely, the man behind me.

"Your rifle hit the ground and bounced back up right into my hand," he said.

"It got hooked on your sleeve and went over like it was thrown," said another man who had been in the audience."

I guess my guardian angel was watching me that time, I thought.

The only other extra-curricular activity I participated in was the science club where I saw glass conduct electricity. Henle, the man with the contraband radio we hooked the antenna to, told the club that he had read that glass will conduct electricity in its molten stage. Having training in electronics, I wanted to see that.

He set up an experiment in the lab with electrical leads from the wall outlet connected to a rod of glass by alligator clips with the neutral wire on one end and hot on the other. He heated the glass with a propane torch until it started to get red hot and pliable. Within seconds the glass started to turn white hot and he removed the heat. In a few more seconds, the glass spluttered and bubbled as it conducted current, making us believers.

"Those were some of the highlights of my stay at TIT," I told the captain, who nodded and took a long draw on his pipe. I hadn't noticed the smoke before or noticed him lighting it, but this time his pipe was working. The smoke he exhaled smelled like the Borkum Riff Bourbon tobacco that I used to smoke in my pipe before I quit years ago. I looked down at Dedra, who was looking straight at me. I smiled and scratched her behind the ear. She sure looked like Winnie, the cat I had had in Texas.

Since Captain Bob didn't ask any more questions, I resumed my once-upon-a-time story.

"So you got appointed to the Academy?" Jenny asked.

"It was a secretarial appointment, by the Secretary of Defense. Almost all other appointments were congressional. I happened to be the eighteenth out of one hundred and twenty appointments made. There were almost two hundred thirty men at the prep school, so almost half either had flunked out or didn't get to go. By then, I had made up my mind I didn't want to go, but went anyway because of my parents."

"What did they have to do with it?"

"They were so proud of me that I didn't want to disappoint them. But, after a few weeks at the Academy, I decided it was better to quit than to continue. I figured out how much it would cost to pay for my own college education and decided I could save the money. When I called my parents, they were very disappointed, but supported my decision. I could have put in two more years on a four year enlistment, but decided to get back into subs for four more years so I could save enough for college."

"Was the Academy that bad?"

"It would have been like four years of boot camp. We had to memorize three books called Reef Points, Salt and Pepper, and Military Etiquette. We also sang songs about Bill the Goat, the Navy mascot, before going to bed. The discipline was incredible, even when we were eating."

"What happened when you were eating?"

"We had to square our meals by lifting straight up from the plate, making a ninety degree angle into our mouths the entire time while 'keeping our eyes in the boat,' (staring straight ahead without focusing on anything close by). If a question was asked by an upper classman while we were eating, we were given three chews and a swallow to respond. Otherwise we were given a 'come around.'"

"Come around?" she asked.

"Yes. Any infraction of the rules was rewarded with a come around. After the day's activities we "came around" to the upperclassman's room for some torture. At the come around we were given ridiculous things to do like 'clamping on' or 'greyhound races.' Clamping on required the plebe to sit in a chair and then lean forward supporting his weight on the table with his feet off the floor. The chair was then removed and he had to stay in that position, clamping on to the table for what seemed like eternity until the chair was replaced.

"And greyhound races?"

"When a group of men had a come around, all but one would be told to put on their grey sweat suits. They were the greyhounds and made to chase the other one around on all fours howling like dogs. The man without the sweat suit would be told to make noises like a rabbit and run around the campus. Most just squealed like a pig since no one knew what sounds a rabbit made."

"Sounds funny," she said.

"Not if you're playing the game. It gets very tiring. They were always asking us questions from the three books to see if we had them memorized."

"What were some of the questions?"

"At meal time they asked 'How's the cow?' After three chews and a swallow we would heft the milk pitcher and try to determine the amount of milk left. Then we would respond, 'Sir, she walks, she talks, she's full of chalk. The lactate fluid extracted from the bovine species is highly prolific to the nth degree, sir.' The degree of milk was the amount of glasses left in the pitcher.

Other questions I remember were 'Why do we say 'sir'?' The response was, if I remember correctly, 'Sir, sir is a subservient word surviving from the surly day of old Serbia when certain serfs, too ignorant to remember their masters' names, yet too servile to offend them, circumvented the situation by the surrogating of the subservient word 'Sir' by which I now belatedly address a certain senior cirriped who correctly surmised that I was syrupy enough to say 'Sir' after every word I said, Sir.'"

"You had to say all that? And what's a cirriped?"

"Yep. We had to say all that and if we screwed up, we had to start all over again putting the word 'sir' after each word. A cirriped is a parasitic growth on a ship such as a barnacle. I didn't know what it meant either until I looked it up."

"There were some funny responses, like the one given by an ex-Napster standing next to me in formation, when he wasn't sure of the answer to one particular question.

"'How do you bring a full-rigged ship about, Mister?' the upper classman asked. This was a question with a complicated answer. He responded after a few tense seconds with, 'Sir, full rigged ship, attention. Full rigged ship, about face, sir.'"

"I started to snicker, which drew the upper classman's attention. What are you laughing at Mister?' My response was a canned one. If you could get the upper classman to laugh too, you were spared a 'come around.' So I responded 'Sir, to hell on the class of 22, Sir.

"'Why 22, Mister?' he asked. 'Sir, that's the number of vibrating strings in a vagina you big pussy, you, Sir.' 'You and your Napster class-mate have a come around, Mister,' was his response. He had apparently heard that one before and didn't think it was funny.

"For fun, there was also the goody-goody, yummy-yummy, blue-berry-pie-eating contest."

"That doesn't sound very much like the Naval Academy to me," she said.

"It happened every time there was blueberry pie on the menu. One of the upperclassmen who sat at each table with the plebes would an-nounce the contest after the stewards, who were all Filipinos, brought everyone a piece of pie."

"Filipinos?" she asked.

"Oh, I forgot, you don't know. After the war, Filipinos could earn citizenship by spending a hitch in the Navy. They were trained to be stewards until they completed their requirements and became citizens. After that they could change to other billets. We had a Filipino steward on the Sam my first three patrols and Juan on this one.

"So, after the table had all the pie delivered, the contest began. The first one to eat the pie and be able to stand on his chair and whistle Yankee Doodle, won."

"How was that any fun?"

"No hands were allowed. I won the contest at our table, but my face was almost totally covered with a gooey mess. The stewards brought towels for us to wipe our faces clean after the contest was over."

"What was your prize?"

"Nothing, except bragging rights."

"This is why you quit the Academy?"

"No, I had decided not to make a career of the Navy. I already had almost two years in the service before I went to the Academy. The Acad-emy would add four more years and then another two with the required post-grad courses. There was then a nine-year commitment after all the schooling. Counting my enlisted time, it would have been seventeen years before I could get out. Another three and I'd be able to retire, so staying at the Academy would have made me career material.

"Also, Vietnam was starting to build up. I figured my grades wouldn't have been all that great what with all the smart kids attending who were selected from the tops of their graduating high school classes. I knew I would be near the bottom and probably sent to the war on a patrol boat. From the little bit of training I had already had in "A" school, I decided that I wanted to stay in electronics or electrical engineering and there wasn't any career path in the Navy for that. The upper classman who tried to talk me out of quitting, told me he wanted to be a lawyer and that the best thing for me to do was to stay at the Academy, put in my time, and do what I wanted later."

"I enjoy our little talks, Andy," Jenny said.

"But I know nothing about you," I said. "Where are you from? What made you join the Navy as a nurse and a thousand other questions?"

"Mary and I are from the same home town, Burlington, Vermont. We joined the Navy together for the nurse's education. Had I known we would be in a war with Japan, I would have stayed at home. But, that's all for now.

"We've been down here talking a long time. Don't you think we ought to get back upstairs?"

"Up the ladder," I corrected automatically.

episode fourteen

"Did ever ya talk at her again?" Captain Bob asked.

"Yeah, again in the missile compartment, lower level," I said. "It was once upon a time before we got to Nagasaki."

"Nag-a-sackee? Where is this Nag-a-sackee you been talkin' 'bout?"

"It's a town in Japan that we bombed in the Second World War." I said. "I'll get to that in a minute."

"How did you get the name Cherry?" she asked.

"From a barmaid in Kittery Maine, at a bar named 'Karen's,'" I responded. "We were in the shipyard after my third patrol…." I hesitated, maybe a little too long.

"And?" she prodded. "Were you?"

I blushed a little and was again glad for the dim lights of the lower level. I almost started out with 'this is no shit,' but was still respectful of her as an officer.

My third rendezvous with Jenny came about after I had gotten off watch at midnight. I went to the chow hall to grab a bite to eat and maybe have some conversation. She was all alone at a table reading the WWII book I had lent her. When she saw me, she immediately set down the book upside down on the table, open to the page she was reading. I got the impression she had been waiting for me to arrive.

The "come hither" look she gave me made me a bit uncomfortable, but drew me like a magnet. I poured a cup of coffee, went over to her table and put the cup down.

"I need a snack," I said. "Do you want anything?"

"No thanks," she said smiling as if I had just cracked a joke.

"I'll be right back."

I knew she was watching me as I went to the "reefer" to see if anything was already prepared. Finding something satisfying and low in calories was a challenge. I did find some canned fruit in a bowl. It was laden with heavy syrup, but if I poured the liquid off, it wouldn't be too bad. I returned with a small bowl and a spoon.

"Where are we now?" she asked.

"I think we're more than halfway to Nagasaki. We were headed there when we detoured to Guam to pick you up. Nagasaki is in the northwestern part of Kyushu, southwest of Japan. We should be in position tomorrow, on August 9."

"What happens August 9?"

"We drop the second A-bomb on Nagasaki. It ends World War II.

"I haven't gotten that far in the book yet. What's an A-bomb?"

"It's short for atomic bomb, developed near the end of the war. The bomb's strength is measured in kilotons and the one dropped on Nagasaki was equivalent to twenty-two thousand tons of TNT."

I had just finished my bowl of fruit and gulped down a cup of coffee. She was digesting the information I had just given her. I enjoyed bringing her up to date on what had happened nearly twenty years ago. My knowledge base seemed to impress her, but it was just schooling devoured over the years and now regurgitated like a bird feeding her nestlings.

"Can we have another discussion?" she asked, putting her hand on my forearm.

I immediately got goose bumps, which she felt. She smiled and took her hand away brushing her fingertips on the back of my hand. The goose bumps turned into showers of electricity pouring down my spine.

"Okay," I said, a little choked up. "I'll go first and meet you in the lower level. Make sure no one sees you go down the hatch."

I left after depositing my dirty dishes at the scullery entrance. I hurried through the missile compartment, unlocked and opened the after hatch. I left the hatch partly opened and waited at the bottom. She followed shortly thereafter, a little too quickly I thought. I was still worried about getting caught violating the fraternization policy. When she was down the ladder, I reached up and closed the hatch. Without speaking, we both took up our positions, nestled between the insulated steel ribs.

"Yes, I am cherry," I continued.

I couldn't say "virgin." Somehow that word seemed dirty, especially for someone who had spent the last five and a half years in the Navy.

"I had started down the road toward losing my virginity, but I seemed to hit roadblocks and detours along the way and somehow never completed the journey."

"That's hard to believe," she said. "Do you have a girlfriend back home?"

"No, I've written to a couple, but they only wrote a couple of letters in return and that's that. Here's something even worse, I've only been kissed once." I purposefully omitted the hairdresser in Vermont, not knowing why.

I didn't know why I was telling her this. Somehow telling somebody from the past was not the same as giving away any secrets. She may tell the other nurses, which would give them all a good laugh. It didn't matter, because everyone who knew me knew my status as a lover. Besides, I didn't know what would happen to them when and if I could transport us back to 1968. Perhaps they would fade away like those dreams that can't be remembered an hour or two after you wake up.

"She must have been special," she said. "The girl you kissed."

"I don't even know who she was. I was sitting in a booth drinking beer at the enlisted club in Gourock, Scotland, with my back to the aisle. A Colleen walked by with another sailor, grabbed me and put a big lip lock on me. I was stunned and never got a good look at her."

"But you knew her name."

"All the women in Scotland were called Colleen. They didn't like it, but that was what we called them. I was in love all night long. The next day I came down with strep throat."

"Oh no!" laughed Jenny. "I'm sorry, but your first kiss turned out to be from Typhoid Mary. I'm sorry I laughed at you."

"Everyone else thought it was funny too. She must have known she had strep and decided to pass it along to all those bastard Americans who called her Colleen. I decided that if I could get strep from my first kiss, I better watch where I stick my dick."

I immediately regretted saying the 'dick' word, but penis was not in my vocabulary. Other than "crank," the other term I knew other than pee-pee, was "Johnson Rod," the part on a steam engine that is connected to the piston. My dad had called it that, but the word dick was more familiar. I was starting to feel comfortable around her, like she was one of the guys…, maybe too comfortable.

"That's funny too," she said. "No wonder you're still a virgin. I think I would be too if that had happened to me."

She had just told me something about herself without telling me directly. I was starting to feel uneasy with the way this conversation was headed. Luckily she changed the subject.

"How does this submarine jump around in time?" she asked.

Being eager to change the subject, I decided to tell her. I sat up and detached my perpetual calendar from my belt loop. I held it up in the dim light.

"With this," I said. "This and my pen."

She sat up too, and in the dim light could barely make out the object I held in my hand. She reached for it and seeing no harm in letting her hold it, I let her take it.

"What is it?" she said, handing it back to me.

"It's a perpetual calendar I got when I was twelve. It's designed for 1955 to 1982, but is good for other years if you know how to set it."

I took the perpetual calendar back and returned it to my belt loop. Simultaneously, we turned toward each other while propped up on our arms.

"And, you said, your pen?"

"Yes, my pen. The one I always carry in my pocket."

I explained to her that when I touched the date with the pen, the sub went to that day. In the dim light I showed her as best I could the chart I had made in my pocket notebook of the equivalent years that correlated with those on the calendar.

"Please don't tell anyone about this," I pleaded. "I want to make absolutely sure before I mention it to the skipper. I don't even know if he'll talk to me, but I'll try when the time comes. What I'm afraid of most of all, is that the officers will take it away from me and try to change the time themselves. It may not work if someone else does it and if they try it may not work for me again."

"But, Mary and Dick know about the calendar," she said. "I saw their reactions to the announcement about the time change at the meeting."

"They don't know exactly how it works. I told them that I thought I knew how, but gave no details. No one else knows how it works now, but you. Like I said, I'll tell the others when I feel like it's time."

"I can help when you want. We have access to the officers whenever we need to talk to them."

"Okay. I'll keep that in mind. For now, though please don't tell anyone, not even the other nurses."

"I won't."

"We'd better get back," I said. "We're pushing our luck being down here so long."

"Still worried about my being an officer?" she said, getting up into a semi-standing position.

"A little," I said crouching beside her.

We made our way to the hatch. As she was about to climb up, she turned and grabbed my face with both hands and kissed me softly on the lips. I went instantly hard and red faced at the same time.

"I don't have strep," she said and went up and out of the lower level.

I followed a short time after, still excited. When I got to my bunk, my WWII book was setting on my pillow. She must have been as bored with it as I had been or had gotten all she wanted out of it. I left it there in case she wanted to pick it up again.

On August 8, 1945, the night before we were to get to Nagasaki, I verified the year 79 was set on the month of August. Seventy-nine, like sixty-two, was one of the years that also had the same days of the month as 1945 and I was curious if the year made a difference as to where we ended up. I was lying in my bunk with my curtain pulled shut and my head resting beside the WWII book where Jenny had left it. I wasn't sure how we ended up in the South Pacific in 1945, or for that matter 1941. *Why are we just moving around in World War II in the Pacific?*

Touching the probe to Tuesday, the seventh, would put us back one day and get us to our observation point one day early. If that worked, then I might pass on my suspicions to the XO. If it didn't, I would keep my mouth shut.

My shaking left hand held the calendar and I touched the probe first to the AUG above the number 79, and then to the number seven directly under TU which stood for Tuesday. Just like before, the Sam rumbled as if we had hit turbulence. I was sure now, that we had moved in time, but did we move back a day in 1945, or to some other year? I would have to wait until we were told.

"There you are," Little Dickey said as he peered in between the tubes where I was hiding from the world and reading *From Russia with Love*. "We gotta talk. I just came from the con where I heard it was a day earlier than we thought. The radiomen intercepted some broadcasts and determined it was August 7. What you did must have worked. The question is, what did you do and can you do it again?"

"Yes, I think so. I knew we would get there on the seventh, but who's asking?" I said.

"Me," he said. "I told no one about what you said and haven't told Mary about this recent date change. She was the only other one at the table when you said that you had a theory. You know, it was that first time you met Jenny. When she finds out we've changed dates again, she'll be curious as hell about how you did it. Who else have you told about your theory?"

"No one," I lied, not wanting to reveal that I had told Jenny. "I don't trust anyone else with the information. I am very apprehensive about going to the skipper with this yet."

"So, how does it happen?" he asked.

"With this," I said, holding up the perpetual calendar. "I turn this wheel with the dates on it to the month, and the days of the week line up with the calendar."

"But that says 1955 to 1982. We went back to 1945."

"Yes, but the years 1945, 1962, 1973, and 1979 have the same dates. The dates '41, '42, '43, and '44 match up with, among others, '75, '81, '82, and '72 respectively."

"How did you know we'd be there on the seventh instead of the eighth?"

"I touched my pen to the seven this morning. There was a tremble in the boat and that was my indication we had moved in time."

"You're right about keeping this a secret a little longer," Little Dickey said. "You'd better wait until you're damn sure about this before telling anyone else. What if someone else resets the date and uses another pen?"

"I don't know. You can do it next time to verify if it's just me, or any person and pen that works with the calendar."

"I hope the next time is when we go back to where we were when the time travel started. How come you never tried this before this World War II travel shit started?" he asked.

"I've reset it every month since I've had it and used my pen thousands of times to count days for various reasons. It was the first time after I got my dick knocked stiff by the 440 volt panel that we went back to 1945. When I went to bed after getting shocked, I notice that the jolt I had gotten from hitting the missile tube must have reset the year to 1962 on the month of August, but didn't change it back. I don't know how the day got selected and we ended up in 1945 in the South Pacific the first time. I must have done something in my sleep.

"After the meeting with the captain when he told us where and when we were, I looked to see what year matched up with the dates between 1955 and 1982 so I could reset it. I didn't have to because it was already set. That's when I wondered if the calendar had something to do with the time travel. I noticed my pen sparked when I put it near the calendar, so I wanted to do a little experiment. Since we were already in WWII, I decided I wanted to see the bombing of Hiroshima and set the 79 to August and touched the 6.

"When that worked, I then set it to December, 1975 which corresponds to the beginning of the fighting in the Pacific in 1941. I randomly touched the pen to DEC and then to the 9 and that's when we picked up the nurses. I then thought we ought to get back to Nagasaki and use our missiles to end the war. This last test was to set us back a day while enroute to Nagasaki using the year '79 instead of '62, which I used the first time. Now I know for sure I can accurately control the year, month, and day."

"All off-duty personnel report to the chow hall in ten minutes," the 1MC blared out.

"That's probably about the day change," Little Dickey said.

"Yeah, probably," I said. "Let's go."

We headed forward passing by the nurses' cubicle. As we turned to head through the hatch, I heard the cubical curtains pull back and looked to see Jenny and Mary coming our way.

"Let's wait up," I said tugging on Little Dickey's sleeve.

"Hello Mary," Little Dickey said

"Hello Dick," she said back. I let her and Jenny pass, following Little Dickey toward the chow hall. I nodded to Jenny and she winked back at me. I pulled in behind the trio and followed them.

"Sit next to me," Jenny whispered, tilting her head backward slightly and cupping her hand over her mouth so I could hear from my position behind her. I assumed she was trying to prevent Kozy from glomming onto her again.

We entered the chow hall and sat near the front. Kozy entered moments later and scowled at me as he took a seat near the back. Sailors and nurses trickled in until the attention on deck was announced. We all stood.

"Seats," the XO said after the parade of officers stopped.

"Men, and women," the captain started. "We are stationed off the western coast of Japan about 50 miles from Nagasaki. According to our radio intercepts, we are a day early."

Mary put her hand to her mouth and gasped. She then gave me a sideward glance. Jenny looked at her and then knowingly at me.

"I don't know how that happened, but I have asked the navigator to look into it," the captain continued. Our mission is to remain in the area, as close as possible to Nagasaki so we can observe the bombing tomorrow. Should the bombing fail, as did Hiroshima, then we will determine a course of action. Although the Japanese shipping was pretty much reduced close to the end of the war, there is enemy shipping in the area, so I ask all of you to rig the ship for modified silent running. No sanitary tanks will be blown and use of the GDU is suspended. We will run on batteries with minimum screw turns. Trim tank pumping will be minimized. After this meeting, speak in soft tones and remain in your bunks as much as possible. Meals will be limited to hor..." he stopped himself from saying horse cock when he remembered there were women in the audience.

"...cold cuts and bread," he resumed. Some of the men laughed. "The XO will answer any questions."

"Attention on deck," the COB said. The captain left as we stood.

"Seats," the XO said. "Questions?"

"Has anyone yet figured out how we got back in time?" one of the chiefs asked.

I got goose bumps and noticed Mary again glancing in my direction. Jenny looked straight ahead this time.

"No," he said. "As the captain said, we have the navigator looking into it, which is why he isn't here. If anyone has any suggestions, we would like to hear them."

"What time tomorrow is the bombing of Nagasaki?"

"If I remember correctly," the XO said. "It was just after eleven in the morning."

"Will we be able to watch?" Tetro asked.

"We will be at periscope depth and only those necessary will be allowed on the con. We'll keep all informed as soon as we can determine if the bomb worked or not."

"Why can't we be on the surface where we can watch from the missile deck?" a storekeeper said.

"This is not a circus. We don't want to risk being seen and if the bomb does go off, there is the danger of radiation exposure and possible temporary blindness. We intend to leave the area immediately if the bomb works. Then we'll figure out how to go back again to send a warhead into Hiroshima. If the bomb doesn't go off, then we immediately launch a missile of our own. We believe the delay won't make much of a difference."

"Why don't we just launch ours anyway?" the COB asked.

"There's a slight chance we could hit the B29," Lt. Inman chimed in. "There's also a chance the bomb dropped from the plane could go off too, and we don't want to upset the bottle cart with a double explosion."

"Regardless," the XO said, interrupting any further Jimisms, "we will wait before launching our missile. If there are no other questions, you are dismissed." There were none.

At ten o'clock local time on August 9, we were in position to observe the bombing. The captain had approved our trajectory and height of detonation settings for our version of Fat Boy, the name given to the bomb that exploded over Nagasaki. During the simulated countdown the night before, I had taken a grease pencil and penned the name "Fat Boy" on number 16 missile warhead. Missile sixteen was the one selected to use in case the bomb from the B29, nicknamed "Bock's Car" didn't do the job.

The plan was to watch for the explosion and if none occurred around 1100, then we would decide to launch or not. History indicated the bomb had gone off at 1102 local time. Had that been our bomb, or that of the B29? Since we didn't know, we couldn't launch until we were sure there was no mushroom cloud. If we launched assuming the bomb didn't explode, then we would cause two explosions. It was likely our bomb blast, being the larger would consume any others making it look like only one. For sure, we knew from history there was only one atomic weapon used on Nagasaki.

At ten thirty, the sub was at battle stations missile, awaiting the fate of the Japanese port city.

"There you are," Bear said. "The COB wants you up in the con."

"What the fuck for?" I said. "I've got missiles to tend to."

"I don't know, but I was sent back to relieve you so you could go forward."

"Okay," I said, and headed forward toward the control room.

When I got into the control room by climbing the ladder to the third deck of the missile compartment and then through the hatch by electronics, I walked up to the COB who had taken over as the diving officer. The skipper had the con and all the lights were on because it was daylight outside.

"We can't look out through the periscope," I overheard the navigator say. "If the bomb does go off, the flash of light will be blinding."

"I've got a welder's glass," I said, remembering that I had taken one from a welder's mask in the shipyard so I could watch them while on fire-watch duty.

The navigator and XO gave me a dirty look for speaking without being spoken to, but the captain just smiled.

"Go and get it," the skipper said. I left the control room the same way I had come in and retrieved the two-by-four-inch piece of dark green tinted glass designed to slide into a slot in a welder's hood. I handed it to the captain since he was the one who had directed me to retrieve it. I then headed to the COB near the diving station.

"Bear told me you wanted me," I said.

"Yeah, take over the diving planes," he said without looking at me.

"Sure thing, COB. What ya got?" I said to the man already seated at the station.

"Three degree down bubble, one hundred feet, maintaining six knots, and heading zero one zero," he said as I took his position.

"Got it," I said. I fastened my seat belt although that was only done during rough seas. "It could get nasty out here if that thing goes off." The stern planesman seated next to me reached down, grabbed his belt, and fastened his too.

"You ain't my first choice," the COB whispered to me, "But the skipper asked for you personally so's I'm stuck with ya." I just stared at the console and smiled.

"All clear," came the sound from the sonar room. Evidently when I had gone aft to retrieve the welder's glass, the skipper had ordered sonar to sweep the area for contacts.

"Make your depth zero six zero feet and maintain this heading," the Skipper said.

"Zero six zero feet, aye sir," the COB responded.

He didn't have to repeat it to me as I gave a little tug on my joy stick changing the angle of the sail planes. The hissing sound of hydraulic fluid could be heard responding to the servo motor attached to the end of the control stick. The depth gauge started its slow climb toward sixty feet. At about sixty five feet I readjusted the controls to halt the rise and stopped it dead at sixty feet. Since the COB had decided that he was the one who would respond to the Skipper, I let him do the talking.

"The depth is zero six zero feet, sir," the COB said.

"Up scope," the skipper ordered. There was more hissing as another set of hydraulic valves channeled fluid to raise the scope. Right after the navigator did a three-hundred-sixty degree sweep of the area to visually verify the all clear signal from sonar, I could hear the sound of glass on metal as the navigator fitted the welder's glass to the eyepiece on the scope. I supposed he was using some test-depth tape to secure it in place.

I checked my wrist watch and noticed it was ten fifty five, only seven minutes from when the Nagasaki bomb was to be detonated.

"Raise the whip antenna," the skipper said. Another valve was positioned and the antenna, on the outside hull was raised and locked into an upright position.

There was dead silence in the con, not even the skipper, who was glued to the periscope, said a word.

"It worked," the skipper said shortly after eleven. All eyes went to him, and even though there was a piece of welder's glass on the scope, we could see the glow of the bomb that leveled Nagasaki reflecting off the skippers face. He then turned away from the scope and ripped off the glass allowing a bright light to shine into the con from the periscope's unprotected glass.

"Take her down," he said. "Make your depth one five zero feet, heading two seven zero, all ahead full. Get us the hell out of here."

"Down scope," he added.

That's when the sounds came back to the con.

"Aye, aye, sir," the diving officer said. He didn't have to repeat the skipper's orders as I dialed in the speed, turned the rudder and pushed on the diving stick.

The 1MC blared the Skipper's announcement next, telling the crew of the successful detonation of the weapon. A cheer went up that we could hear coming from below in the mess hall. A half hour later I was relieved of my duties as the helmsman/planesman and I went aft to the missile compartment. Little Dickey, Mary, and Jenny were waiting at my bunk for me.

"Let's go," Jenny said and jerked her head aft toward the lower level access hatch. She had the WWII book in her hand, which she must have taken from my pillow. I was escorted by Jenny in the front and Little Dickey and Mary in the rear as if I was marching to the gallows. Bear saw us and turned to make sure no one was approaching from the starboard side as we slipped below decks. I felt that our little rendezvous spot had somehow been violated when all four of us plopped down on the blankets, me and Jenny on one side and Little Dickey and Mary on the other.

"We want to make sure your little toy is working," Little Dickey said. "See if you can get us back to a time before Hiroshima."

"Okay," I said and pulled the perpetual calendar off my belt loop. I grabbed my pen while Mary pointed the flashlight at my hands. The perpetual calendar was still set with 62 on August. All I had to do was touch my pen to the correct day.

"I think I'll touch the three," I announced to my entranced audience. I felt as though I was the main event at a magic show. "That way we'll have plenty of time to get ready to launch a missile."

"How far are we from Hiroshima?" Little Dickey asked. "We need to make sure we can get close enough to launch a missile."

"All we need to do is get within twelve hundred miles," I reminded him. "I think we can do that easily, but I better go back to the third of August just to be safe. We won't need to sneak into the bay this time."

"Okay," he said.

I clicked open my ball point pen. I wasn't sure if it was necessary to have the pen tip out, but I wanted the point to be able to touch the correct date. This was the first time I was to do this with an audience and I was a little nervous. All four of our heads and one flashlight joined together as we hovered over the perpetual calendar and pen. Jenny rested her hand, the one with the book in it, on my back.

Dramatically, I slowly lowered the pen toward the three. None of us flinched as sparks started to emit from the tip of the pen and the surface of the perpetual calendar as the two got close to each other. When they were within a couple of millimeters of each other, the aura became stronger and a slight crackling sound could be heard above the hum of the sub's machinery. The sparks seemed to repel each other bending away momentarily as if they were opposite magnetic poles.

As I touched the number three and then pulled away, a spark connected the pen and perpetual calendar for a split second, and then the sparking ended.

"That's it," I said. "The show is over."

"What happens next?" Mary asked, but she didn't have to wait for a response. The Sam shuddered as before with the rippling rattle moving from fore to aft like dog shaking off water.

Both Mary and Jenny let out a little "eep" of a sound as if they recognized the event from a previous time -- a partially silenced squeal of recognition.

"That shaking is what I heard each time," I said. "I think that's what happens when you pass through time, at least on a submarine,... this submarine. Now we just have to wait to see if radio broadcasts verify where we are in time."

"I can't believe it was that easy," Jenny said.

"That's all I did before," I said. "Unless it's not me that's doing it."

"Oh, it's you alright," Little Dickey said. "You and that calendar thingy."

"Okay. Let's go find out," I said.

Thump! Thump! Someone had hit their shoe down hard on the deck above us. Between the deck and missile tube sixteen, a white sheet of paper protruded and wiggled a little before dropping down right next to Little Dickey. Without saying a word, he picked it up and held it up to the flashlight to read it.

"It's from Bear," Little Dickey whispered, proffering the note to me. "He wrote that the COB is watching the hatch and he has P.O. Foster with him."

"Shit," I said. "The nurses aren't supposed to be down here, especially with us. Let's see if the forward hatch is clear." I took the note and scribbled a short response asking Bear to check the forward hatch. I then handed it to Little Dickey who stuck it back up through the same gap that it dropped down through. It was pulled up, hopefully by Bear.

"The forward hatch is more risky," Little Dickey said. "It's locked too."

"Maybe Bear will unlock it for us," I said back. We waited for a minute or so and a return note dropped back down.

"He wrote that he'll check it out and unlock it if it's clear," Little Dickey said, after reading the note.

"Let's move on up to the hatch just in case," I said. "They may get curious and look down here if we wait too long."

"I'll stay here in case Bear comes back and drops another note," Little Dickey said. "Lock the hatch behind you if you get out that way. I have an idea."

"What are you going to do?" Nurse Mary asked, sounding concerned.

"Just go," Little Dickey said.

I led the way to the forward hatch with Nurse Mary behind me, closely followed by Jenny. When we got to the hatch, I heard a key in the lock and the latch being opened.

"Wait here," I said. "I'll see if it's all clear."

"Here, use this," Jenny said and she pulled a small compact out of her pocket and opened it so I could see the mirror.

"Good idea," I said, and took it from her trembling hand. I carefully pushed up on the hatch enough to be able to put the mirror at the deck level and look around. I saw no one and opened the hatch further.

"Go on up," I whispered to Nurse Mary. She climbed the short ladder and disappeared above. Her hand stuck back down and beckoned us to follow. Jenny needed no urging and climbed up and out. I followed closing the hatch behind me and locking it with my key. There was no one else near the forward end of the missile compartment. I handed Jenny her compact and she and Nurse Mary headed forward toward the mess hall while I headed aft toward the missile compartment head. As I approached the head, I saw the two Fosters around the corner standing against the aft bulkhead watching the hatch.

"Hi COB, hey Don," I said, startling them. I then opened the door to the head and walked in. As I closed the door behind me, I heard Little Dickey loudly open the hatch. I left the door to the head partially open so I could hear.

"What were you doing down there?" asked the COB.

"Taking a nap," Little Dickey said.

"Who's with you?" The other Foster asked in a smart-assed manner.

"Nobody," Little Dickey said. "Look for yourself."

Realizing the forward hatch was unguarded, P.O. Foster started forward at a half run. Bear came around the corner acting nonchalant as he always did.

"That's a restricted area," the COB said. "You can get in trouble for going down there without observing the two-man rule."

"We take naps down there a lot," Bear said. "I knew he was there and checked on him every once in awhile."

"I'll take this up with the weapons officer," the COB said, and stormed away heading forward where P.O. Foster was returning from.

"That hatch is locked up," P.O. Foster reported.

"I don't doubt that," the COB said, as they both faded away forward.

I exited the head and walked back to where Bear and Little Dickey were standing smiling at each other.

"We owe you big time," I said to Bear.

"Just get us back," he answered. I realized then that he must have overheard our conversation from where he was standing above the lower level. "How did you hear us?"

"Conversations travel right up the curve of the hull like a funnel," he said. "I can hear everything from my stool if I lean toward the bulkhead."

"Everything?" I asked. He just nodded his head and smiled. Little Dickey laughed and headed toward the mess hall. I went to my bunk and crawled in to take a nap before I had to relieve Bear in two hours.

There was no all-hands meeting to make the announcement that we were on track to go back to Hiroshima. The word was spread by mouth within moments of the star shoot and confirmation by radio of the date. We had three days to get into position and we were already less than two thousand miles away. At twenty knots, we would be within range with time to spare.

That was plenty of time for Jenny and me to meet again.

"What happened at Hero-sheema?" Captain Bob asked.

"We got into position, and at the precise time, launched number sixteen missile. I was able to change its name to "Little Boy," which was the name given to the bomb by the crew of the Enola Gay. The blast must have been greater than anticipated, but the only ones to see it and live were on the B29 that dropped it. They had no way to measure its explosive force. We were too far away to see it explode, but heard the radio broadcasts soon afterwards."

"Did ya then go to Hawaii like ya started out ta do before?"

"No, since Guam was no longer occupied, the skipper decided to head there to decide what to do next."

episode fifteen

"You're saving for college?" Jenny asked as we were snuggled in be-tween the ribs of the lower level. Since her kiss after the last meeting, I lay down first and she nestled between my legs with her back against my stomach and her head on my chest. I couldn't help but get excited, but she didn't seem to mind the poking in her back. She rubbed against me a few times; on purpose I thought, just to see how I would react.

"Yes," I said. "Ever since I decided to quit the Academy and save up for college. If I had stayed at the Academy, I would be graduating this year, but would've had another several years in the military."

"And, you would never have met me," she said, turning her head a little giving me a sideways glance.

"True, but I don't know if that's good or bad, ma'am." She reached down and pinched my thigh causing me to wince.

"Behave, Mister," she warned. "Remember who your superiors are. So have you saved enough to make it?"

"I think so. With the GI bill I should make it okay. I've worked landscaping jobs, slung burgers, worked in a factory, and made sand-wich runs on my off days while I was stationed at New London awaiting a sub and while on the Sam."

"What a waste of time."

"Tell me about it," I said. While awaiting the Sam assignment, all we did was polish floors and clean toilets. I even had a job setting up the projector for a training class. I hated the waiting, but there was nothing I could do. I took some college history courses from Harvard University on base. The government paid for them and they can be used once I get into college. So it wasn't a complete waste of time."

"Tell me about each of the outside jobs," she demanded. "They may help me prepare for life in the States thirty years from now."

"The landscaping job was only for a couple of weekends. One of the guys in ComSubFlot Two got me the job. That's an acronym for Commander Submarine Flotilla Region Two which is part of the sub base. It's a fancy name for a pool of men awaiting assignment to a submarine.

I was in it for six months before being assigned to the Sam. The sub sailor who recruited me and another sailor for the landscaping job was a Native American. I had never met one before, but he wasn't any different from others. We had been working on a very dry, warm and dusty Saturday spreading dirt around a newly constructed home with nothing to drink. He pulled the branches off a tree and was pretending to use it as a divining rod, searching for water. We heard a door slam shut and an elderly lady from next door came out with a pitcher of ice water and some glasses."

"I thought you boys could use some water," she said. "You've been working all day and I haven't seen you take a drink."

"Thank you very much," all three of us said.

"See, I told you this shit really works," my Native American co-worker said, after she left us.

"The factory job I had was working on an assembly line filling arm and back rests with foam. It was monotonous and I was glad that I didn't have to do that all my life. I felt sorry for the guys that had done it for twenty years or more. I was glad I was on my way to college so I didn't have to work as they did.

"The sandwich run job was my own creation. There was a sandwich shop off base that the guys in the barracks liked to order from. We would take orders and then take turns going to get them. The owner gave us a discount in the form of cash back based on the orders. I started to announce the sandwich runs over the PA and soon had thirty or more orders each time I went. I would call them in before I left and they would be ready when I got there. I was making fifteen to twenty dollars a run doing that. It doesn't sound like much, but when I only made $250 a month in the Navy, it was a nice supplement toward my education.

"The burger joint job was another job that made me glad I wouldn't have to be doing that type of work the rest of my life. I was the "bun man" in a burger joint on weekends. Little Dickey and I worked at the same place. You'll know what I mean by burger joint when we get back. They're everywhere now.

"Speaking of getting back, have you decided to go with us when we go back to 1968? That's assuming we can go back. I know how to travel in time, but don't know how we get to a specific year or place. I guess we could sail the Sam from the Pacific to the North Atlantic assuming we can get back to 1968."

"The other nurses and I have discussed it and we don't want to go back to Guam during the war," she said. "Mary definitely wants to stay with Dick. I think they're in love and will get married. None of us have family that will miss us if we disappear. I like you, Andy, but I don't think we could hit it off like Dick and Mary did."

I felt a little hurt in my heart, but she was right. It was nice she could be so objective about it and besides, I had college to get through before I could start a family.

"We'll have to figure out some way to get you all back and into a new society, one completely alien to what you've experienced so far. There are plenty of places you can get work as a nurse, but you'd have to take some courses to catch up on modern medicine. You and Mary are already Americans, but the Filipinos can't get jobs without a social security number. Marrying an American is the fastest way for them to get citizenship."

"Why don't you let us worry about that," she said. "I think we could all stay with Dick and Mary until we got work."

"I think they're all young enough, that with a fake birth certificate, they could apply for a social security card and then get jobs. No one would check on the fake cards and then once they get married, it wouldn't matter anymore. It'll be funny to see the look on people's faces when you tell them you're forty years old and you look twenty."

"That's not a bad thing, sometimes," she said.

She turned on her side and I did too so that we were facing each other. It felt good to hold a woman like this.

The last time I had been this close to a female, was when a group of us left Karen's bar late at night with some women to go skinny dipping at a lake nearby. It was a warm summer night and when we got to the lake in the woods of Maine, the moon was almost full. I had a sleeping bag I kept in my car. The others had beach blankets that they kept in their cars for trips to the shore. We paired off and I took what was left, a woman who was heavyset, but not too bad looking. We got in the sleeping bag and I thought I would get laid finally, but she kept her back to me, and we never even kissed.

Some of the guys, but none of the women, stripped down and went skinny dipping. They weren't in the water long because even though the air was warm, the water was cold. I asked the woman to turn around so we could be face to face, but she broadcast the request to the others and they laughed. So, I just sat up and drank some beer, which suited her fine. Another chance to lose my virginity had disappeared like a puff of smoke in the wind.

She was not as bad, however, as the dog I woke up with after a wedding in Toledo, Ohio. I had just gotten out of the Navy and was home awaiting the start of the college semester when my childhood friend Duane and I went to his cousin's wedding. His cousin's name was John-John, but we called him Jack-Jack. I slept on a sleeper sofa in Jack-Jack's parents' home. Since Jack-Jack was on his honeymoon Duane slept in his empty bed. I got pretty shitfaced at the reception and crashed when we got back to the house. The next morning, I woke up and when my eyes could focus noticed a body under the covers and a head on the pillow next to mine.

I rose up to get a better look and was rewarded by a lick on the face by the family dachshund. I was relieved that it wasn't some dog of a woman from the party, but wondered what had happened during the night. I was assured that the dog always slept with Jack-Jack the same way she had crawled into bed with me. For the first time in my adult life, I was happy to have retained my virginity.

So when Jenny turned to me face to face we kissed gently, but there was no real passion. It still was a very pleasant experience and the memory lasted me a long time.

"We'd better get back," she said after a few minutes.

"Yeah," I agreed. Another experience with frustration, but I guess that's what life's all about.

After I returned to my rack, I started to research how we could get back to the year 1968. I pulled out my World War II book and turned to the page where I had left off. It didn't occur to me until I started to read about the Japanese occupation of the Philippines and Guam that maybe the book had something to do with where we had been transported.

I had fallen asleep with the book next to me the night of our first time-travel episode. I thought about the other episodes and recalled the book being present during all of them. If this was the link to the location, then to get back to 1968, I would need something about the East Coast or the North Atlantic that happened just before we left on patrol. I searched the material I had brought with me and found nothing. This would require someone else's help. I got up and looked for Little Dickey.

"Little Dickey," I said, locating him in the upper level missile compartment. "I think I found the key to getting us back to where we were in 1968, only I need some help." I told him my theory and he took off on a mission to find something to link us with the future. I didn't dare go to anyone else with this problem, at least not yet.

"Find any literature dated about the time we left on patrol?" I asked a couple of hours later in the mess hall.

"Not yet," Little Dickey said. "I looked everywhere and asked as many people as I could without raising suspicion."

"Not even a magazine, or newspaper article?" I said. "Nuthin', huh?"

"Nope, but I'm still lookin'."

"If we can't find anything, I'm going to have to go to the old man and ask his help." I said. "I hesitate to do that, 'cause I would have to go through the COB and you know how that SOB hates my ass."

"Yeah. That would be a last resort. Somewhere on this sub there is something we can use. Maybe it's just the thought of a place in time that gets us there. You were reading about the Second World War when we were transported the first time. Maybe all you have to do is remember what we were doing just before we got transported. It's worth a try."

"Maybe that's true," I said. "I'd hate to try it and we'd end up someplace else. The sparks between the perpetual calendar and my pen seem to be getting weaker each time I use them. I don't know how many more times it will work.

"Any idea what the nurses are going to do when, and if we get back? I talked to Jenny and she said they all wanna stay with us when we go back to 1968. Or should I say they don't want to go back to Guam during the war."

"That's what Mary said too. I guess you know she and I hit it off pretty well. We're even talkin' about gettin' married."

"Yeah, Jenny told me. I wonder what's going to happen physically to them if we go ahead in time," I said.

"I hope they'll be all right," he said. "We didn't get younger by going back to the 1940's, so I guess that means they won't change either."

"We won't get a chance to find out unless we discover a sure-fire method to transport us." I said.

"I'm headin' back to the engine room to see if I can find some magazine or something about 1968," Little Dickey said. "I sure want to get back and resume my life. Consider my theory of just thinking about it."

"I will," I said.

At thirteen hundred hours, I found all the nurses and Little Dickey sitting in the mess hall. As soon as they saw me they motioned for me to sit down with them.

"The others decided to go back to Guam since the war is over," Nurse Mary said. I looked at Jenny for an answer directly from her.

"Not me," she said. "Mary and I are going with the sub."

"Can you transport us back to Guam?" one of the Filipino nurses asked me. I looked around to see who else might have heard her ask.

"Why do you ask me?" I said, in case someone had overheard. "Ask the skipper. I'm sure he can sail us there in no time and then drop you off the same way we picked you up."

"They know," Jenny whispered to me. She winked at the nurses and they acknowledged by nodding their heads.

"That's okay," I whispered back. "I just don't want anyone else to find out until I'm sure I can trust them."

"So, how do we get Mary off the sub and back to the States once we get back to our own time?" Little Dickey asked. The Filipino nurses got up and headed back toward the missile compartment.

"I don't know," I said. We probably can get her off the Sam if the gold crew doesn't get suspicious. The skipper will have to help for sure."

"Could we get her off the same way we got Rod transported by helicopter to the Bahamas?" Little Dickey asked.

"Boy, that would be tricky. Maybe if you were the one being transported as the sick one, and she was your buddy just like Kozy was when he left on the helicopter with Rod. We have extra uniforms she could wear. Then once you are miraculously cured, you both can head for the States."

"If we're in the States, then it would be easier," Nurse Mary said.

"You're right." Dick said. "If we haven't started the patrol yet, then it would be easy to dock the sub and have Jenny, Mary and I leave at the same time. I think that's our best shot, but we have to go back to a point in time when we were about to start the patrol."

"The correct time might be easier than the correct location," I added.

"Nurse Mary, you have to speak to the Skipper, officer to officer, and convince him," I said.

"He already knows about the other nurses wanting to go back to Guam," Nurse Mary said. "He's going to make an announcement today at fourteen hundred hours."

"Hey!" I interrupted. "If you could ask him if I could bypass the chain of command and come to him directly about my time change theory, we could also discuss the plan to get you three off the sub."

"I'll do that," Nurse Mary said.

"If he wants an explanation, I want you both there for moral support and to verify that you saw that my little device works," I said. "Jenny, you can be there too, to reinforce my theory."

"I would like to be there," she said, and gave me a smile that caused the back of my neck to tingle.

"See ya," Little Dickey said, and he and Nurse Mary left me alone with Jenny.

"I hope you understand our situation, Andy," Jenny said. "I really do like you as a person, but know there is nothing beyond that."

"I'll survive," I said. "I'm not ready for anything as serious as Dick and Mary are getting into. Just keep in touch when you get back." I somehow knew she wouldn't. It was painful, but I managed to keep back the tears as she got up and walked back to the missile compartment.

I pulled out my latest Bond novel and made a half-hearted attempt to read until the announcement was made for the all-hands meeting with the skipper.

"The captain wants to see us in the yeoman's office in half an hour," Little Dickey said. After the all-hands meeting I had stayed in the chow hall and attempted to read my book. Since Jenny had left me alone, I had only turned the page once.

"Okay," I said. The yeoman's office was along the same bulkhead as the missile compartment cubicles. We could meet there without raising any questions from the rest of the crew. Had we all walked into the skipper's stateroom, scuttlebutt would have passed from stem to stern before the meeting was over. I decided to hide my perpetual calendar and pen in my locker in the missile compartment in case he wanted to confiscate it. I could just describe it and hoped the others would go along with me. Just to be sure, I would brief Little Dickey and Nurse Mary about my plan just before the meeting.

"I don't have it with me," I said. Little Dickey, Nurse Mary, Jenny, and I were alone in the yeoman's office waiting for the skipper. "Just play along with me when I say it's a device." They all nodded in agreement.

"You do the talking," Little Dickey said. "When you want our input just ask."

The door opened just as he finished and the skipper walked in.

"Don't get up," he said. With the five of us in the ten- by six-foot room, it was a little crowded. Little Dickey, the skipper, and I were standing and Nurses Mary and Jenny were seated in the two office chairs.

"Lt. Grimes said you think you know the secret to our time travel," he said.

"Yes sir," I said. "I think I found out what causes it." I was making it sound as if I hadn't known the entire time. He could have asked a lot of questions, like how long I had known and why I hadn't brought it up as soon as I had found out, etc, but he didn't. He didn't say anything else, so I continued.

"Sir, I discovered two devices that, when brought together, may have caused the time travel. I don't think it's a coincidence because I tested the theory out a couple of times."

"So, it's just a theory?" he asked. I nodded to the others, who in turn spoke up.

"We all saw it, sir," Little Dickey said.

"Yes we did," Nurse Mary said.

"And so did I," Jenny added.

There, I thought, *two officers and a gentleman have verified my statement. He has to believe me now.* He turned back towards me.

"May I see them?" he said.

"They're not in this room sir," I said, a bit nervously.

"The devices lose power when I move them," I lied. "I don't want to risk not being able to get us back to where we were. One piece of the puzzle is still missing, and if we can't get that I don't think we can leave 1945."

"Any idea what the missing piece is?" He was leading me with his questions, although I felt he knew I didn't need any coaching.

"Yes, sir. I… we think," I said, with a slight sweep of my hand toward the others, "That if I'm able to find some written material from the time we left on patrol, that'll be the catalyst to get us back where we were. I don't want to announce it to the entire crew, because if that doesn't work, then there'll be a lot of unhappy sailors on the Sam, sir."

"Okay, I'll scour the wardroom for material and pass the word discretely to my officers who will help in the search. Is that all you need?"

"Sir, if I may speak for Mary and Jenny," I said, realizing my mistake immediately. "I…, I mean Lieutenants Ray and Grimes. We think we have a way to get them off the submarine." Realizing I was stumbling, Nurse Mary took over.

"Sir, we want to go back to your time and start our lives over. We have no relatives who will miss us and, if we are missed in Guam, our disappearance will be blamed on the Japanese."

"We're heading back to Guam to drop off the other nurses. Will they say anything?" he asked.

"They have promised not to," Nurse Mary continued. Obviously she didn't have to call him sir although he was three grades above her and the captain of the ship. "Who would believe them anyway?"

"You're right there," he said, with a chuckle. The rest of us laughed a little uneasily. "What's your idea about getting you two ashore?"

"Sir, if we can get back to the right date," I said, "we can fake a sickness like we did in the Bahamas."

"That was fake?" he said bolting upright.

"No, sir," I said. "I mean to say that this time the illnesses will be faked, but we'll have to find a port so that Little Dickey, I mean Petty Officer Schweinehun, and the nurses can get off the boat. Then we can go back out on patrol. If the faked illness is done just as we're ready to start across the Atlantic on patrol, then we can easily pull into a port in the States and let them off. Otherwise, we'd have to hide them from the gold crew in Scotland and then get them across the Atlantic with us on the plane, sir." The last sir indicated I was through.

"Okay," he said. "I'll contemplate this and discuss it with the men I know I can trust. I appreciate all you have done for the Sam, and intend to give you letters on your meritorious service. I just can't mention the trip to Guam and saving the nurses, but I'll think of something else." With that said, he turned and exited as quickly as he had entered.

"Well, that went over well," Little Dickey said after a moment of silence.

"Jenny, what'll you do when you get off the Sam?" I asked.

"Stay with Mary and Dick for awhile. Once I get a job, I'll be off on my own."

"Oh," was my only response.

Two days later, we were off the coast of Guam near the same place we had rescued the nurses. The radio room picked up the news that the Japanese had surrendered unconditionally, so our troops were not alert for enemies. The Japanese had been cleared from the South Pacific for months now, so we only had to evade our own warships for fear of being mistaken for a stray enemy sub. The skipper had a little trick up his sleeve for the nurses who were going back to Guam. I had overheard him discussing it with the doc.

"Doc," the skipper said, "What can we do about the nurses' memory, the ones who are going back to Guam?" The skipper had walked into the doc's office by himself. He had been pondering the problem of the crew's memory of the recent incidents and was wondering if there were any drugs that could 'erase' what they had just been through.

"We could try some scopolamine," Doc said. "I have some for emergency surgery."

"That was the drug used by the Germans in World War II as a truth serum?" the skipper asked.

"Yes. It produces amnesia. If not totally, it clouds the memory so that the past events seem like a dream."

"Any other side effects?"

"Some, but in small doses it's not harmful."

"Do you have enough for the entire crew should I want to block their memories also?"

"Yes, but how can I give it to everybody?"

"We can tell them it's to prevent malaria or some other disease brought on board by the nurses. Is it in pill form or liquid?"

"Liquid, and can be given orally. We could put it in a cup with bug juice and tell them it's quinine."

"Let's do that," the skipper said. "We'll give it to the Filipino nurses now, and the rest of the crew the last day of the patrol."

I had been outside the doc's office when I had seen the skipper go in and close the door. I wanted to see the doc about my medical records since I was getting out in two months. I leaned up against the bulkhead and was able to hear everything. There was no way I wanted to forget about the recent events. I headed aft when I had heard enough.

Little Dickey and I were not on the landing party that took the three Filipino nurses back to shore. They left with their meager belongings and some provisions that had no dated information. Nurses Mary and Jenny said a tearful farewell to them and promised to try to get in contact if they arrived in the U.S. sometime in the future. That, to me, would be a reunion to witness. Twenty three years aging three of them and only days aging the other two, only I doubted they would ever meet again. I saw the doc give them each a little swig of "anti-malarial" medicine just before they left to get in the raft

Now it was time to try sending us back.

episode sixteen

"Was ya successful in getting the Sam back," Captain Bob asked.

"I'm here, aren't I? I quickly discovered I had had the key to getting back to 1968 all along."

"The captain said they have nothing," Nurse Mary said. "No one has anything that will remind them of the time we started this odyssey."

"Why don't you try my suggestion?" Little Dickey said. "It can't hurt."

"We won't know that until we do it," I said. "Let's try it now. No use prolonging not knowing. I want you three to be with me and help me concentrate."

"I don't think that's a good idea," Jenny said. "We're from the war period and might distract you from thinking about when you left."

"You know, she's right," Little Dickey said. "I'll go with you and help you concentrate on what happened just before we started the patrol. Mary, go tell the skipper we're going to try something within the hour. Tell him to wait for the rumble and then find out from the radiomen what year we're in."

"Will do," Nurse Mary said and headed back to the wardroom. Little Dickey and I went to the missile compartment to give this idea our best shot.

"Wait a minute," I said. "I think I may have something after all."

"What's that?" Little Dickey asked.

"A book," I said. "I hid it from the crew so no one would borrow it until after I had read it. It's a James Bond book, *Octopussy*, that I bought just before we left for patrol. I locked it my locker between tubes thirteen and fourteen. Let's check the date." We headed to the missile compartment, port side, just beyond the cubicles.

I unlocked the small metal storage box that I kept my personal items in. Most of them were for use during the patrol.

"Here it is," I said, holding up the book. I quickly turned to the publication page. It was the second edition, published in 1968. "Let's try this to get us to the right year anyway."

"Yeah," he said. "And we can just concentrate on the location."

We then headed to the lower level via the hatch. We told Bear we had to check on the integrity of the lower level missile tube hatches and down we went. We went to the port side under the nurses' quarters so no one could hear us.

"Let's concentrate on the time right after we dropped off the visitors and were heading out to sea to cross the Atlantic." Little Dickey said.

"Yeah, that was April Fool's day," I said in recognition. "I remember thinking the captain had played a joke on us by saying we were now in World War II." I reset my perpetual calendar putting the 68 on April and got out my pen. "Ready?"

"Let's go," Little Dickey said, with a raspy voice.

I tucked the book inside my poopie suit against my chest on the left side and carefully aimed the pen at the APR above the 68. Both Little Dickey and I were holding our breaths. There was no crackle as before when I got the two objects near each other. I felt no tingling in my hand. As the two touched, there was a tiny spark that was just visible in the dim light of the lower level. Little Dickey was chanting 'East Coast 1968' over and over. I continued to hold my breath as I touched the 1 in the upper semi-circle. Again, a tiny spark flew. Just to make sure, I touched the pen to the 68 and a third spark flew, even smaller than the other two. I then separated the two objects and we both waited.

"I don't think there'll be enough energy to do it again if this fails," I said.

"We'll just have to get you connected across the four-forty volt line again," Little Dickey said, half heartedly. I gave him a look that said "don't even go there," but the look turned to one of joy as the rumble came. This time the noise came from the stern to the bow causing a shudder similar to the others.

We both scurried for the hatch and climbed out of the lower level. Neither of us had to say anything as we headed forward to the radio room. When we got there, the skipper was already talking to the man on duty and both were smiling. The skipper looked at me and gave a thumb up signal.

I made a tight fist and gave a jerk and a silent "yes." Little Dickey patted me on the back. I wasn't sure it was the James Bond book or Little Dickey's and my wishing that got us to the right location in time, but I didn't care.

"You know," he said. "I'm feeling a mite poorly. It could be my appendicitis flaring up. I'd better go see a nurse."

The skipper said something else to the radioman which I found out later was directing him to send a signal to the shipyard in Kittery. "Two members of the crew have contracted appendicitis. We are dropping them off immediately with another crew member as escort, after which we will be heading out on patrol. Signed Captain Alford, Commander, USN, Sam Houston, SSBN609.

I met Jenny for the last time in the mess hall just before she departed.

"Here," I said, handing her the small Monel ring I had made in the shipyard. "I want you to have this to remember me by.'

"What is it made of?" she asked, putting it on the ring finger of her right hand.

"It's made of an alloy and was a bolt from the Sam before I made it into a ring."

"Thank you," she said, and gave me a peck on the cheek. She turned her head just as I spotted tears forming in her eyes. I also started to well up. She walked over to the doc who had just handed Mary and Little Dickey their anti-malarial medicine. I knew she wouldn't remember me, but maybe the ring would trigger an unconscious fond thought.

"So Little Dickey didn't make that patrol after all, did he?" Captain Bob asked.

"No he didn't, not the second time. The power supply on missile number sixteen didn't act up either, so I never had to get re-shocked. We headed across the ocean to the North Atlantic at full speed, about eighteen knots or twenty miles an hour. About halfway across, we almost went to the bottom."

"Do tell. What happened?"

I was lying in my bunk talking to Felix when it started. My head was toward the bow and Felix was leaning on the forward bulkhead of the cubicle. First it was a down angle greater than just a change in depth.

"Are we having a bailout?" I asked.

We were about half way across the Atlantic heading toward the States, going about eighteen knots, from the sound the sub was making. The angle was getting steep very quickly, but at about thirty degrees down, started to level out.

"I didn't hear any announcement," Felix said.

Instead of leveling off, we started going up. The angle got steeper and steeper. Felix was hanging on for dear life to the edge of the cubicle entrance.

"If this isn't an angles and dangles drill, I don't know what is," I said. It's not even close to meal time."

Then, just as quickly as we had started up, the angle changed to down again, only this time it was steeper than before. Then that dreaded word came blaring over the 1MC.

"Bailout! Bailout! This is not a drill!"

In seconds, the screw went from all ahead full to all back full. Unlike the bailout drills, someone must have hit the "chicken valves" which forced air pressurized to four thousand pounds into the ballast tanks. The Sam started to shudder like I had never heard before. The deceleration combined with the down angle of at least forty five degrees, caused me to feel as if I were standing on my head in my bunk. Felix was lying against the forward bulkhead of the cubicle, the G force keeping him from moving his arms and legs.

"We're gonna die! We're gonna die!" Felix kept shouting.

"Shut the fuck up," I said, but he didn't.

The noise grew worse as air from the ballast tanks popped and banged against the outside hull. The screw, running at all back emergency, was pushing water over the sub increasing the decibel level inside. The steel, floating decks of the missile compartment were moving side to side and fore and aft. Since there was no warning to rig for small angles, loose items were flying down the passageways. Then, abruptly, we experienced a momentary weightless feeling as the Sam broached the ocean surface going backward, and then she came down level on the top of the sea.

"Surface! Surface! Surface," the 1MC blared forth, indicating we were heading to the surface, but it was just a tad late.

"Jesus Christ!" I said, and made the sign of the cross.

Felix got up and I noticed his pants were wet between the legs and this morning's breakfast was all over him and the deck. Normally he would have run to the head to throw up when he got seasick, but this time he had puked all over himself and the cubicle. This was the first and only time I had ever seen him upchuck and I couldn't blame him. He wasn't the only one who thought we were about to die.

Bear told me later that he was in the aft end of the missile compartment when the ordeal started. The angle was so steep he had one foot on the deck and one foot on number sixteen missile tube.

"The angle was so steep, I was almost standing on missile tube number sixteen when the bailout was announced," Bear told me. "I was waiting for a wall of water to come crashing through the forward bulkhead of the missile compartment. All I could think about was my infant son and how he would never know his father." Stories like that one abounded.

After Felix got up and headed aft toward the head, I carefully jumped out of my rack so I wouldn't land in the protein spill and headed for the chow hall.

The scuttlebutt spread quickly about what had happened. An auxiliaryman on his first cruise as a qualified sub sailor had found a leak in one of the hydraulic accumulators in the engine compartment. Hydraulic systems are the life blood of the submarine. That's why there are two parallel systems, main and vital, and emergency pumps on critical components. Without hydraulics, most mechanical systems have to be operated by hand.

A hydraulic leak is not a big problem un-

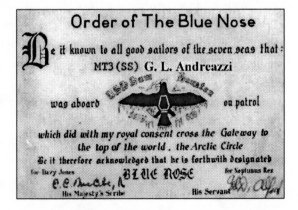

Order of The Blue Nose

Be it known to all good sailors of the seven seas that:

MT3 (SS) G. L. Andreazzi

was aboard   USS Sam Houston   on patrol

which did with my royal consent cross the Gateway to the top of the world, the Arctic Circle

Be it therefore acknowledged that he is forthwith designated BLUE NOSE

for Davy Jones   for Neptunus Rex

His Majesty's Scribe   His Servant

less it's under high pressure and the fluid vaporizes when it escapes. Any leak can be isolated and fixed while the secondary system handles the load.

"What did he do?" I asked Rat, who happened to be on duty in the engine room when the "accident" happened.

"He shut off the fucking valve to the fucking stern plane fucking actuator. The fucking stern planes started to fucking fail in the fucking down position and we fucking dove." The over use of the "f" word told me he was still agitated by our (almost) kiss with the ocean floor.

"But, we started on our way back up," I said.

"Yeah, the sail planes gave us an up angle, but because we were at flank speed when the stern planes reached their full dive position, we headed back down. That's when we bailed out." He had calmed down a bit after the initial tirade.

"How deep did we get?"

"I don't fucking know," Rat said.

"I do," Savage, a torpedoman said. "I was in the torpedo room and our depth gauge said fourteen hundred feet when we started to pull out of it." The torpedo room had its own depth gauge for inputting information into the torpedoes. If I remembered the Sam's specifications correctly; design depth was six hundred feet, test depth was thirteen hundred feet, and crush depth was eighteen hundred feet.

"That's below test depth," I said, shocked.

"We still had a ways to go before crush depth," Savage said. "Because of the steep angle, from the torpedo room back we were at or above test depth, so not to worry."

"I bet that auxiliaryman doesn't make another patrol," I said.

"You'd fucking probably win that fucking one," Rat said.

"It's like the skipper always said, it takes two events to cause a disaster," Savage said. "In this case it was a leaking hydraulic system and an inexperienced man shutting the wrong valve. We're just lucky we got away with it."

The next day, after a severe ass chewing, the auxiliaryman was assigned to the laundry. True to my prediction, he was stripped of his dolphins and sent to the surface ships.

The only other major event I remember occurring was crossing the Arctic Circle and becoming a member of the Royal Order of the Blue-nose. Here's my card.

"What was that about?" Captain Bob asked.

"There is an initiation ceremony for sailors who cross the Arctic Circle. It's a spoof of sorts about King Neptune and his court. The circle is the southern limit of the area where the sun doesn't rise on the winter solstice nor set on the summer. It's approximately 1,650 miles from the North Pole and the water in the winter is very cold."

When it was announced that we had crossed the Arctic Circle, latitude 66° 33' north, there was talk of a Blue Nose initiation. I had been in the area before, but there was no ceremony. For some of the crew, this was their first time and our new skipper permitted the ceremony to take place. It was near the half-way point, so we included the ceremony as part of the halfway party.

Because we had been above the Artic Circle before, Larry and I were given our cards and were recruited to gather the initiates to be presented to King Neptune and his court. King Neptune was selected based on belly size. It was "no contest" and Bear was selected. Not only did he have a large stomach, but it was covered with hair. He was dressed as King Neptune and given a trident, a crown, and a robe, open in the front. He already had a beard, and when seated on a chair in the mess hall, stomach protruding, looked regal.

Black grease was smeared on his belly mixing with the hair and making a very uninviting mess. The inductees got on their knees in front of the King and were to kiss his belly. Naturally, the initiates didn't want to perform this feat and hid throughout the sub. That's when Larry and I did our job. We roamed throughout the sub looking in every hiding place we knew, locating the men and dragging them to the mess hall one by one to be initiated. Through our experience ferreting out stored canned and dry goods while mess cooking, we knew every nook and cranny on the sub and found every man on the list. We even found one man hiding in the battery compartment under crew's berthing, a space only two feet high. His eyes were wide when we jack-lighted him.

"Shit," he said, "I didn't think you'd ever find me here."

"Don't feel pregnant," Larry said, as we hauled him out. "We know all the hiding places."

When we got the men to the mess hall, we held them in the passageway to await their audience with the king and his court. There was a brief ceremony and then the moment everyone was waiting for, the kiss.

The initiate got on his knees and bent forward to kiss the King's belly, only to be whacked in the ass with a paddle. This sent the poor unsuspecting sailor sprawling face first into the matted greasy hair to the amusement of the court and audience. I was glad I was part of the enforcement squad and not one of the inductees.

"Whatever happened to the snake meat?" Captain Bob asked.

"After Ski got the package on board he was able to stick it in the freezer when everyone was distracted by the excitement of women on the sub. We all sorta forgot about it. All but Ski, that is."

"What the fuck is that?" Cooky asked, when the mess cook retrieved the banana leaf package and brought it out to be identified. The mess cook had been after the night's meal in the middle of the patrol, so discovered the snake meat under a box of steaks. The snake skin was missing since Ski had taken it off before putting the package in the freezer. He had the skin curing in the engine room where it was hot and dry.

It wasn't identifiable as snake meat while frozen and wrapped in the banana leaves so Cooky tossed it into a large pan and put it on the deck in the mess hall. When Ski found it, the sparks started to fly.

"What are you doin' with my fuckin' snake meat?" Ski demanded, hands on hips face to face and toe to toe with Cooky.

"Snake meat!" Cooky said. "What the fuck was that doin' in my freezer? I 'm gonna toss it in the compactor right now." A look at Ski's face disclosed that wasn't going to happen, not without bloodshed. The COB happened by and wasn't going to take sides in this dispute, so he summoned the XO.

Most of the crew had heard the story of the snake by now, but the officers had not been briefed. So, when the XO was told the story of the event which led to the snake meat being brought on board, he tried some diplomacy.

"Since it's already here, can't you let Ski cook it up for himself for midrats?" Midrats was short for midnight rations when the watch changed.

"I don't care," Cooky said, giving in to Ski's icy stare. "As long as Skinny doesn't object and he cleans up after himself. Do it tonight before that thing bites someone." Cooky walked away defeated, his head down wiping his hands on his apron.

"Good," the XO said, feeling proud that he was able to broker a deal between two combatants.

That night with all the curious watching, Ski cut the snake into sections that looked like small catfish portions with white meat clinging to "U" shaped ribs. He breaded the pieces and pan fried them in some oil.

The old saying "it tastes just like chicken," held true (I think anything breaded and fried tastes just like chicken) and all who wanted to, sampled the snake meat. There wasn't a lot of meat around the rib bones. Most of what I got was next to the back bone, but it was edible. None of it was thrown out, however.

"That's what happened to the snake meat, Captain."

"That was it on that patrol, were it?" Captain Bob asked.

"Other than the dosage of "quinine" to most of the crew on the last day of the patrol. I almost forgot, there was only one other notable event. It happened the night before we were to board the plane for the flight back to the States and we were tied to the tender during turnover to the gold crew. I was on guard greeting and recording all visitors and making sure no unauthorized personnel came on board. Nearly everyone who came on board were people I knew and were in uniform. I had left my post to read the keel depth, called the "draft." Two readings, fore and aft, were taken every hour and recorded in the log book. I left the guard duties to the other man standing watch with me. Since this was his first patrol, he was not yet qualified. I had returned with the number for the aft draft reading when I saw him delaying a short man in civilian clothes at the brow."

"Sir," he said. "You can't come aboard without identification."

"Sailor, do you know who I am?" the man asked indignantly. I recognized him immediately from my days at the Academy.

"Admiral Rickover, Sir." I said. "Permission to board, sir. Please go right ahead." He then headed to the sail hatch. I picked up the 1MC and turned it on.

"Admiral Rickover arriving," I announced. I didn't know if he had a title, but it didn't matter. To test security, he sometimes tried to get onto submarines without being announced. He may have been a little pleased that he was stopped for a security check, but a little pissed he was not recognized immediately.

"How did you avoid taking the drug to make you forget?" Captain Bob asked.

"That was easy. I just pretended to drink it and then threw the cup in the trash with the scopolamine still in it."

On the last day of the patrol, a memo was posted stating that the SubFlot had sent a message that Little Dickey had had malaria and the entire crew had to take quinine just in case. Pill cups with the drug were placed in the mess hall and the crew came by and took a cup to drink while the doc checked off their names from the roster.

I kept my mouth closed, covered the cup with my fist, raised it to my mouth, and pretended to swallow. I then tossed it into the trashcan sitting on the deck nearby. I washed any liquid off my face before I drank anything else. The drug seemed to work on the rest of the crew since no one mentioned the episodes to the gold crew when we were tied to the tender. I saw some of the officers watching and listening to the crew intently during turnover. They must have been the ones who were not given the drug.

We did have to tell ComSubFlot II that we jettisoned one of their missiles. "We ruffled some eyebrows," as Lt. Inman said. The skipper explained that the interior tube sensors on missile number sixteen had detected a rapid rise of temperature, which was an indication of a fire in the tube. The official report stated we had no choice but to jettison the missile immediately and all indications were that it sank in ten-thousand feet of water in the North Sea, too deep to be recovered by the Rooskies.

HQ was not too thrilled with this "Broken Arrow" incident, which is defined as "...an accidental event involving nuclear weapons or nuclear components but does not create the risk of nuclear war," i.e., " the jettisoning of a nuclear weapon or nuclear component." But what were they going to do? The missile was obviously gone, the report was filed, everyone who could remember told the same story, and there was no unexplained nuclear explosion anywhere in the world. Case closed.

During the turnover to the gold crew, I was getting anxious to get back to the States and out of the Navy. I'd had my fill of six years of a lot of military bullshit and wanted to get on with my life and everyone got on my nerves. I was sleeping in the upper level of the missile compartment above the missile technicians' watch station. Having quit smoking only a couple of months ago, cigarette smoke irritated me, so when Bear smoked and it drifted up to me in my bunk while I was trying to sleep, I got irritated. He also whistled constantly keeping me awake. When he refused to change his habits after I complained to him, I used his real name in the last entry in my little green book and wrote, "Rosenau sux."

I was getting so fed up with all this "happy horseshit" I decided to speed up the patrol with my perpetual calendar and pen. This time, however, it didn't work. There were no sparks when I touched the two together and no rumble from the sub. I was not willing to shock myself again, so I put the two devices away.

During the patrol, I had grown another beard and decided to keep it until I got home after being discharged. Despite all the things I hated about the Navy, I was feeling a little sad on the flight home to the States from Scotland, but I was anxious to put these episodes of my life behind me. When we got back to New London, I had a week to be debriefed and get my final orders sending me home to my place of record. My ID card was confiscated and I was dismissed. That afternoon, my seabag was crated up and shipped to my home of record. The next morning I put on my uniform for the last time and took a cab to the train station for the ride home.

I thought for sure the MP's that I saw in Grand Central Station would give me a hard time about having a beard and no ID card, but they never gave me a second glance. When I got home I had my dad use the same clippers he had given me my first haircut with to remove the beard. It was a symbolic gesture that I was home from the Navy just as when he had come home after World War II to see his son for the first time.

"That's all I have to tell you Captain," I said, but the room was empty. Dedra and Captain Bob must have gotten up silently and left while I was telling them about my father. The tears I had shed for my dad clouded my view. There was the slight scent of Borkum Riff in the room. The clock indicated a shade past one-thirty as I tossed the folder on the floor that I had been pulling photos from, rolled over, and, just before I went to sleep, I felt a cold nose against mine as if Dedra were giving me a farewell cat kiss.

episode seventeen

I woke up before the alarm was set to go off at six thirty as if I had slept the night through. I looked around and there was no captain and no Dedra. I got up and went through my routine deciding to skip my morning jog. By 7:15 I was packed and ready to go so I went down to get my "light fare" breakfast, parking my overnight bag in the hall at the foot of the stairs.

Junior rested his jowls on the top of the Dutch door and wagged his tail as I walked by and patted his head. I went into the open kitchen and saw an orange juice in a hospital pill cup and a store-bought cinnamon roll on a paper plate still warm from being microwaved. She must have heard me using the bathroom and had gotten my "sumptuous" breakfast ready before I came down. There was also a styrofoam cup of hot water beside a jar of Folgers instant coffee crystals. No decaf could be found.

I sat down and sipped the orange juice, being careful not to down it all in one swallow. I was nibbling on the bun when she came in from the other part of the house and greeted me.

"Good mawnin'. Who was that you wah talkin' to last night?" she asked.

"No one," I said, perhaps a bit too quickly.

"No one sounded like someone, and it went on for owahs too. You have a habit of talkin' in yah sleep?"

"I don't know. I'm asleep when that would happen." I regretted the smart-ass comment as soon as I said it, but she just ignored it.

"It wouldn't of been owah captain, now would it?" She was propped up against the refrigerator wearing the same clothes as last night. Her arms were crossed in front of her in a defiant Yankee manner.

"Don't know. What's he look like?" I asked. I crossed my arms right back at her.

"I'll be right back," she said and left the room. When she came back, she was holding an old picture in a gilded frame about twelve inches square. When she turned it toward me, I saw the man I had been talking to sure enough. It looked like one of the paintings so prevalent in New England painted by traveling artists who stayed with families and painted everyone in the household for room and board. As soon as they finished the portraits, they moved on to another family. The paintings were remarkably good for the skill level of the artists who did them.

"So that's the captain?" I said, not really a question. She could tell by the look in my eyes that I had recognized the man and that she was right in her assumption that I had met him last night. In the portrait the captain was seated in a chair, his left hand holding the meerschaum pipe, and seated in his lap was the cat with the red eyes.

"Dedra," I blurted out.

"Who?" she asked.

"The cat," I said. "It looks like a cat I used to have named Dedra."

"Ay-yeah. Funny thing about that cat. Hangin' in the tavahn down the street, theah is an old photo of the living room in this house. In that photo is this heah pictcha on the wall ovah the mantle and I can't see no cat in it. Now someone musta painted that cat in afta the tavahn pictcha was taken."

As I drove away from the B&B, I decided to take a stroll down the street to see if I could find the tavern she had mentioned. The street wound around to the left as I drove in the direction she had gestured toward when mentioning the tavern. About a quarter mile away I saw the sign hanging over the sidewalk touting the Cap'n Bob's Tavern and Restaurant. There was an open space in front, so I parked and walked in.

"Mahnin'" came a greeting from behind the bar. "What can I do ya fo' yah?" The voice belonged to a burly man with dark hair, a dark handlebar moustache, wearing a not-too-clean apron. There were tables with white cloths on them on the left, devoid of any patrons. Directly in front of me was the bar.

"You got any decaf coffee to go?" I asked.

"Shah ya do," he said. "Lahge, medium, owa small?"

"Large, no cream, no sugar."

"Comin' up," he said and went through the double swinging door behind the bar.

I looked around for the photograph and found it on the wall at the end of the bar. I stepped up to it and, though the light was rather dim away from the big window at the front of the tavern, I noticed that the old woman was right. No doubt it was the same portrait in the old photograph, and the captain's lap didn't have a cat on it.

"That'll be one dollah fifty cents," the man said returning through the doors with a large white cup in his hands. I pulled out two one-dollar bills and handed them to him.

"Keep it," I said. I turned and headed for the exit.

"Have a good one and come back again some time." he said.

"I might just do that," I said, and closed the door behind me.

I gave one last glance back toward the B&B. The back of the house could be seen, not the front side where my room was. There was a window in a dormer on the third floor which had curtains pulled back on one side. I took a sip of the decaf, winced a little from its heat, and looked straight at the window. There was a man standing there, a man with a cat on his shoulder, a cat with red eyes. He waved at me and, getting in my car, I waved back. I then drove off for my next destination.

epilogue

the seagypsy and her mate

She invites:
Afternoon lowers her eyes
As dusk steals across the vision
Of two touching,
The Seagypsy and her ocean.
Silk laughter fills the air and
Competes with the lapping of the waves
You are the ocean in my dream
Begin to find me in the dark
Only then, will I take you with me

He responds:
The cold wind blows across the sea.
A squall is seen far out near the horizon as
The old sailor searches for his lost love, but
She is not there.
He squints as the sun sets, his eyes focused "in the boat,"
Terms remembered from his days at the Academy haunting him.
Goose bumps rise on his skin as he feels the wind
Caress him and surround him as a gossamer sheen.
He feels as if he is contained in a dream and
The squall moves inward.
The sea slowly covers his sandaled feet, moving with the
Rhythm of the tides and, like time, "waits for no man."
He remembers only her, only her above the others.
"I need to go, but I can't leave without my Seagypsy,"
He speaks to no one but the ocean, the waves, the wind,
The setting sun.
"Come with me," replies the wind as the rains
From the squall kiss his weathered cheeks.
"Come with us," calls the ocean, the waves, the golden sun.
"Please do not leave me alone," he cries back.
"You are not alone," he hears as the squall is upon him,
Holding him close.
As the last rays of the sun echo through the squall clouds,
The day turns dark, he is the ocean, and they are together.